D0360127

# Italian Stories

Other books by Joseph Papaleo

*All the Comforts*
*Out of Place*
*Picasso at Ninety-One*

# Italian Stories

## JOSEPH PAPALEO

Dalkey Archive Press

Copyright © 2002 by Joseph Papaleo
First edition, 2002
All rights reserved

Library of Congress Cataloging-in-Publication Data:

Papaleo, Joseph.
      Italian stories / Joseph Papaleo.— 1st ed.
             p.  cm.
      ISBN 1-56478-306-5 (alk. paper)
        1. Italian Americans—Fiction. I. Title.

      PS3566.A6 I83 2002
      813'.54—dc21
                                      2001028789

Partially funded by grants from the Lannan Foundation and the Illinois Arts Council, a state agency.

Dalkey Archive Press books are published by the Center for Book Culture, a nonprofit organization with offices in Chicago and Normal, Illinois.

www.dalkeyarchive.com

Some of these stories first appeared in the *New Yorker, Commentary, Harper's, Dial, Epoch, New American Review, Evergreen Review, Paris Review, Swank, Montrealer, Activist, Attenzione, Transatlantic Review, Remington Review,* and *Italian Americana.*

# Dedication

To the good folk who kept me going with their brains and their hearts—and in some cases, even with their furniture: Kathleen, Philip, and Jolie, who came by with goodness and affection and the right cheerful words and ideas to get me out of my depressed chair and go do my writing.

And to the physician-friends who kept me alive, Mahesh Amin and Stephan Scranton and staffs. And of course, Bruce Hall and the whole crew at the Wellness Center, who were and continue to be, cheerful and encouraging me to keep at the exercises—day after day, year after year, instructions for the life-force to grow more collateral blood vessels inside this old corpus.

A special thanks to the editors at *Commentary,* Bob Warshow, Ted Solotaroff and others, who publised a struggling, uncertain new writer.

And leading the entire orchestra, with patience and care—and still more patience: the gutsy Antonetta, beloved mix of Sicilian and Cherokee and continuous caregiver, chef, and boss.

To all, my deepest affection and thanks.

# Contents

## Part Three: Blendings and Losses

# Italian Stories

# Prologue for an Ethnic Life

I think sometimes I have been influenced by everyone, which might mean that there isn't an original part in me. But I do try to rebut this daily when I take up my incredulous Royal Electric, once a marvel of modern typing science but fast becoming as ancient as keeping cash under the mattress, which my wife insists *I* do like an old-fashioned Calabrian landlocked in the USA.

My prospects of success in this writing racket may be, then, as bleak as a teenage vision of the future, fed by films and special effects.

I turn to my big mouth friend, Tony, who claims to be the ultimate reality in his ranting: "I NEVER THINK ONE FUGGIN MINUTE ABOUT THE FUTURE. YOU COULDN'T STOP THEM FUGGERS, CAUSE THEY ALL BURY THEMSELVES INSIDE A FUGGIN MOUNTAIN. AND ONE NIGHT THEY GONNA PRESS THE BUTTONS, AND TEN SECONDS AFTER, *WE* PRESS OUR BUTTONS. THAT'S THE WAY IT IS."

Tony's visions always increase my substance abuse, which in the case of me (and my people) enters in the form of starches, beginning with bread and pasta and ending with anise biscotti wet with *Sambuca*.

I try to avoid the secret terror, the modern eye-chewing-gum, the soothing blue light that makes me long for the happy voices of youth, saying, "WELL, HI FOLKS, AND HERE COMES WHITEY FUKSAK UP TO THE PLATE. WHITEY'S BATTING .286 AND HAS SIXTY-NINE RUNS BATTED IN SO FAR THIS SEASON. WHITEY'S JUST BACK FROM A BAD ELBOW AND A VISIT TO HIS MOTHER, WHO JUST GAVE BIRTH TO ANOTHER ILLEGITIMATE CHILD. THAT'S RIGHT, FOLKS, BRAND NEW, AND IT'S A BOY. AND FROM ALL OF US HERE IN THE BOOTH, FROM

THE NETWORK CREW, FROM OUR DIRECTOR TONY COSTA, CONGRATULATIONS, MRS. FUKSAK, AND MANY MORE WHERE THAT CAME FROM. NOW HERE COMES WHITEY UP TO THE PLATE, STILL LIMPING A LITTLE FROM THAT TOUCH OF SYPHILIS HE HAD — AS YOU FOLKS WILL RECALL — AT THE TAIL END OF LAST SEASON. HERE COMES THE FIRST PITCH FROM RIVERA — "

This genuine language is to prepare you. There will be no deceit or trickery in this volume—and no plot, character, conflict. Just my screaming voice telling you the truth. And don't even believe that. Even the truth is a hype. Words can be a hype. Like the TV news. Ten seconds for pictures. Five seconds for bullshit voice-overs. Tones of voice to suggest that God is speaking. And all the while they're Donald Ducks delivering the news.

THE END.

Epilogue to the book: all writing tries to go somewhere and, unlike life, has no endings. Forgive my stories, dear reader, for not being a new *gumba* book that all you folks like to buy for the joy of watching suffering ditchdiggers and the great myth of killing relatives. I know you buy that in quantity, and I am trying to do what you like.

My only defense is obedience: Momma and Poppa told me to always dress important, walk important, act important, and people would treat me as if I *were* important. And this would make me believe I was important.

*Then,* and only *then,* would I have the power and time to help my fellow human, especially if he or she were an Italo.

While we're at it, I forgive you your Chef Boyardee, your worship of gangsters you think are my brothers, and dark-haired film stars holding big guns like iron peepees that turn you on.

THE LAST CHAPTER.

When I reached the entrance of the funeral parlor, I could hear them through the heavy doors. Tony's mother, Blanche, his wife, Rose, Rita and the sisters, all in the front row, all in black, all screaming in grief. So Tony had dropped dead in the street waiting for his car to be ready.

In this day and age, their screaming was just too much. I was so embarrassed. Not in White Plains, I thought. Are we still going to show them we're *Gavones* who just got off the boat?

I walked inside, and I sat down, and I said to myself, *I hope I never get like that. Look at the sight of him. Powder all over his skin, and perfumed like a cigar-store Indian. I don't care if it's still a mortal sin, me they are definitely going to cremate.*

So Tony's dead, and what can we do, any of us; we can't bring him back, and nobody in Westchester really believes in heaven anymore. So what the hell did he work like a dog for—even on weekends—borrowing money from sharks to pay bills on his second superette? They probably shot him, though they all say the sharks don't kill you, because it means they don't get paid back, which is all they want. The Vig.

If God is up there, then he's a sadist the way he left the women suffering. There's no end to it. They used to say we Sicilians, we always wear black, the men with the black band on their jacket sleeve, the women the whole dress. They say we put the black on as kids and never take it off because somebody's always dying with us.

Aunt Lena saw me and brought me to the body. I kneeled down and said my prayers and looked at Tony's hands, like wood carvings around the rosary beads. The whole sight of it made me sick.

I wanted to scream, but she thought I was crying so she took me back to the seats again to calm me down. I watched the women crying, and I thought of him, live, alive, many years—Friday nights in his gold chains going out to find some young divorced singles-bar drinkers who might be attracted to his chest hairs. What are we, really, I thought—now he's a piece of wood in a blue suit with no blood inside and about three feet smaller than that pig in gold chains which was at least life, no matter how much of a sleazebag he was.

Pretty soon I had to leave, but I was stopped at the door by two big guys holding guns (this is the required ending). They were pushing everybody back as they yelled, "Where is he? Where is that ratfuck who won't pay the Vig?"

"He's dead," I screamed at them, but they only laughed and went straight for the casket as Uncle Tony tried to sit up and get out of it. Shots rang out (I borrowed that sentence from a best-selling novel). We all fell to the floor as the dark brutes finished off Uncle Tony with their semiautomatics blazing, shooting him in the mouth and other orifices. One of them was heard to say, "Death to those who talk and betray the totally Italian Mafia in which every Italian has a cousin."

I am interrupted now by the sound of a Datsun 280Z roaring up the Corniche; it is Frank Santora thinking to himself, oh man, another day, southern France, and who can I lay?

The scene now shifts very abruptly, like a movie, and we see a close-up shot of Frank wiping his sweat just after a tennis match. His head is faced down, he is feeling despair—or acting it, because you never know with people who earn over 150 thou per annum. He is talking about fear and trembling, the new fear and trembling, and now looks up to face the camera, which is also yours truly, *me*.

He says to me, "Oh shit, Mike, I'm living in one room again, and I'm sleeping alone again, always facing the door even though it's got three locks. I even bought a pistol. Took me three days to buy bullets, but I did. I'm living alone again, and it's dropped me back to age six. I can't sleep with the lights off. Plus, I think the light will inform an intruder that a sucker is waiting up there in the room with the light on. And I ask you why are we all like that, why is our vision one of being on the verge of annihilation all the time?"

Frank drinks his post-singles Coke and wipes more sweat. He has already forgotten the joy of his fine volleying this morning. He says, "Now I have three households to support. I'm a machine to make money to give ex-wives for child support. And at night I wait. I wait for the missiles to come in from altitude."

Michael (that's me) is listening but suddenly feels that he is being lifted up, like a man on a camera dolly, pushed up and back in time: at last he sees himself, and he is talking on the telephone with Frank, saying this: "Frank, you must somehow understand it isn't a crime to fall in love more frequently than most. Maybe you're just like everybody else, only *you* admit it and go for it while other guys say not again, I can't handle another one."

"I think I say that but only *after* I get married again," Frank says in a voice without affect, though sufficiently dismal.

"You must think of marriage as some kind of consecration," Michael says. "Your Catholic, guinea mind. I do it a lot, though not in this way—with women. I am not that naive."

6

"I know what you mean. I have thought about all this a lot; all the women I know, they want their space, their privacy—they're not rushing into marriage these days. They can spot a fucked-up guy like me. Nothing tells them they have to marry anymore. They get into a decent relationship and see what it leads to. It's *me*."

Michael is silent in the presence of the epiphany. Then Frank looks up with pain removed from his face, able to think now beyond himself. "Michael," he says with calm, "you too, you better watch the liberation language. Try to plug in to your own emotions more and get some signals. You know what I mean. Don't make your rationalizations too good. Like last night, you told me some great shit about how human beings couldn't remain together for a lifetime because they are physiologically and psychologically made for seven-year relationships. Closeness is brief. It was wonderful shit."

Silence. Thunder and lightning. Background music begins. Michael is sitting at his desk, time present: he is looking at a snapshot of his father taken in the twenties or thirties. The old man has retained—still—the old-fashioned face you were sure was turn of the century, a face that framed the same old questions wearing the same curled mustache. An old guinea face from Ellis Island black-and-whites, with those big immigrant eyes of consternation and confusion, still asking with that silent look, WHY AM I HERE? WHAT AM I DOING? WHAT CAN I GAIN? WHY DO THEY TREAT ME LIKE A PIECE OF SHIT—STILL, TODAY?

And yesterday, at the party to celebrate Michael's Ph.D. from Yale, Michael's father (with that funny curled mustache), a former immigrant, now owner of stock and a large oil delivery business, told Michael that in his life he had given up every dream, had never even had a dream or time to play baseball or be a child. He had given it up for work and its rewards, starting with the main reward (they told him), a house to come back to and rule over every night, with rooms full of kids and women who obeyed his wishes.

But, he reminded Michael, power brought opportunity and each opportunity for each child meant more work for the father, who in America is worse off than an Italian tenant farmer, whose sons and daughters worked for him and did what *he* ordered. In the USA, Father did what the Children said—bought what they needed and wanted, all to become better than Father on the ladder, laughing at his accent (but not his money).

Finally, he confided to his son that the Italian master became the American slave, transformed by the act of immigration into the victim of a demon that drove him away from his ancient home to this strange new land where he did nothing but behave well with strangers for thirty years, to make money. Obeisance was success for the immigrant hustler, he explained. Though he never expected the buckets of hate it produced within.

Late that same night, Michael burned his books and asked his God why Poppa could not expire from a heart attack like so many other good American men.

God's answer was clear. The old man rotted slowly in the green chintz chair for twenty-eight more years, finally becoming impotent and infirm and a burden who peed in his pants and did not know anyone's name anymore. (Old age was also like America—it did the same thing—it made you comfortable with cash and food while it chopped off your balls.)

Still, Momma worshiped the old stalwart image she remembered, and came everyday to tell that old hero that he indeed *was* the good old days, incarnate.

And so forth.


CHAPTER ONE

Once upon a time, there was this tall, blond Italian family from Sicily and Naples, who moved to New York, America.

And they didn't like spaghetti or tomatoes or *scallopini* or eggplant *parmigiano* or even shrimp *fra diavolo*. And even though the year was 1907, they didn't piss in doorways or lobbies or live in the basement. And not one of them went into the ice business or the construction field or go to *worka* on the railroad.

However, they did become—after Smith and Harvard—chemists, paleontologists, numismatists, doctors, and lawyers.

They are sitting in a wide living room that contains well-rubbed parquet floors, a few Danish minimalist couches, a Milanese coffee table in black styrene and glass. The walls contain a large Rivers, a larger de Kooning, and a mighty Rosenquist, with an obscure Matisse in the corner as an accommodation to classicism. Near the front door in the magazine rack, copies of *Interview* cover up five unopened *New Yorkers*.

Father Tony speaks to his wife: Darling, Junior tells me he would like to go out to the Hamptons for a few days with friends before he heads up to Cambridge.

Rosa replies: But Darling, he's due to start classes in two weeks and hasn't shopped for a thing yet.

Tony Junior: I can always pick up a few duds at the Coop when I get on campus. I'd really like to go out to the Island now. Its a toast to Nubby Burnham—his first symphony has just been taken by Mister Mehta.

Rosa: Oh, that must be Muffy Petcock's boy again—she married Carter Burnham the year we both left Smith. I was her bridesmaid. You must go, I suppose. And I can pick up some basics at Brooks Brothers and pack them for you—or mail the rest.

The sun sets as the family sits for a reflective Chivas on the rocks. Shortly after, Twombly announces supper is served, and the three enter for the evening meal. Tonight it's pasta with *fagioli, braciole, broccoli rape* with *fusilli,* salad with conch and squid, finished off with *espresso* and *Sambuca.*

Tony raises his small liqueur glass and waits for his wife and son to join him. "Here's to a good senior year at Cambridge," he says just as a squad of American-Way-of-Life-Protection hitmen bursts through the doors and shoots all three dead in their chairs.

The squad leader says, DEATH TO ALL THOSE WHO BETRAY THE STEREO-TYPE.

Reader, these fragments have I shored against my ruined Royal typewriter. I have introduced you to the trail ahead, most serious stuff in pursuit of actuality.

# Part One:
# Immigrant Epiphanies

# The Kidnap

In those improving years after the Depression, when Mrs. Bonomo next door prepared meals every day for a family of twenty-two, and when all the families in the Bronx neighborhood ate Sunday dinner outside under their grape arbors, it was well-known along Lorin Place that Mr. Mauro's raincoat business was doing well. If anyone coveted his good fortune, it was Gualtieri, whose house was on the corner. Gualtieri was called "Mussolini" because though he ranted, he did little else but break up the stickball games that the boys played when the mornings were warm.

On just such a warm morning, Reni Mauro found a letter in the mail on the porch, addressed to MAURO. She read it in the sunlight and then walked quickly to the kitchen.

"Ma, listen," she said. Her mother tried to release her thoughts from the nostalgia of Naples and the pots which were already bubbling with the evening meal. "This letter that just came, Ma. Maybe it's a joke, but listen: 'Have five hundred dollars in a bag in two weeks. Go to the corner of Arthur Street at eight o'clock at night. Don't call the police. Otherwise we will kidnap your children.'"

"Let me see," Mrs. Mauro said. She picked up the crudely written letter, but she could not read the English. "Your father's sister," she said. "I know it in my blood."

"What are we going to do?"

"Shut the door."

Reni went to obey her mother and returned a little pale, having begun creating a reality.

All day they listened wearily from the kitchen for dangerous sounds down the hall. At three o'clock they both waited on the porch for little Johnny to come home from school. He became very angry when they immediately ordered him to stay in the backyard and play.

"What did *I* do?" he asked with a nasal whine, the common accent of the neighborhood.

"Listen to me!" his mother shouted, touching off a little panic inside her.

"She can't explain," Reni said. "You didn't do anything. But do what she says."

"If I did something, I wouldn't mind," Johnny protested to his sister, an ally of reason in these situations.

"Listen to me!" his mother screamed. "I am your mother. Don't leave the backyard."

"This ain't no Italy," Johnny said, beginning to articulate his ten-year-old rebellion in the fashion of his older brothers.

Reni watched him from a kitchen window as her mother nervously brought the supper preparations to completion.

"A lot we could do if anything happened," she said.

Mrs. Mauro shook her head and held her hair with her hands to keep inner control.

Five minutes after the six o'clock El arrived at the neighborhood station, Mr. Mauro reached the porch.

"It's so good to breathe here," he told his daughter who was waiting on the porch. "What a difference from downtown."

He stood on the stoop and inhaled deeply, soothing his curved mustache with his fingers. The gray and red wooden house fronts of the block absorbed the last rays of spring evening.

"Look, Bonomo has painted his fence. I like to see color. You know, Reni, we need more color to the house."

"Pa, I have something to show you."

As soon as Mr. Mauro finished the letter he came inside. "Wait until Johnny is in bed," he said.

Al came home last, because he worked all the way downtown, near

Wall Street. Mr. Mauro insisted that they eat in the backyard under the grapes, because it was warm. A few of the other families were out to receive the last warmth of the day, and the Neapolitan and Sicilian shouts carried over the fences until it was dark, time for Johnny to go to sleep.

*

When Mrs. Mauro came downstairs to say that Johnny was asleep, Reni put the small glasses and the tangerine liqueur her mother had made on the table, because there would be guests.

As they sat down solemnly, Al said, "I'd like to get them in my bare hands. I'd crush them."

"Oh, stop," his mother said in fear.

"Don't start that," Reni said to her brother. "You'll scare Mama to death."

Mr. Mauro twitched. He rubbed his black mustache like a judge and looked down the long table. "Pasquale and Victor will be coming any minute. I also gave Fonzi a ring."

"Fonzi," his wife repeated, shocked. "Why Fonzi? Maybe even Fonzi did it? I don't trust that hog."

"Nobody trusts him. But he knows everything that goes on. And for a price he tells it."

"Who's Fonzi?" Al asked his sister as he clenched and unclenched his fists.

"Don't you know him? He married Assunta, Aunt Katherine's oldest daughter. He never works. And he's fat as a horse. Some people say he's a crook. You didn't go to Assunta's wedding? Boy, wait and you see him."

As they waited, Reni went to the mirror where she passed on her complexion. What the city had done to fade the olive color even here in the green and tree-filled Bronx, she now covered with rouge.

"You know, I'm getting scared," she said to her image. She stepped to the window that looked out upon the backyard, but from the lighted kitchen it was completely black outside.

"Come away," her mother suddenly called.

Reni turned to look at her mother. The signs connoting an emergency were clear: the strands of usually well-combed hair, now becoming dry and difficult to manage, stuck out uncombed, while the always-moving hands kept rosary beads spinning in endless harmony with her lips.

"This is your sister's work," Mrs. Mauro said to her husband. "I know it in my blood."

Her husband did not contradict her. "If it is, it is that evil eye she married. Marino the devil. *He* would do a thing like this."

"You mean Aunt Katherine?" Al was amused. "She's a toothless nut. But would she send a ransom note?"

"Marino, her husband, is from la Mafia," his father explained. "They all do the blackmail. Down in Manhattan."

"Holy Mackerel," Al said. "Crazy Aunt Katherine." There was a hint of admiration in his surprise.

The doorbell rang and Mrs. Mauro jumped up. "I go, I go."

*

It was Uncle Pasquale and Victor. Mrs. Mauro kissed her eldest son after he had reported on the health of his children. Then, as Victor walked to the kitchen, she turned to her brother: "Oh Pasquale," she whispered hurriedly, "it's terrible. Help us. His cousin's at work. I know. Help us."

Pasquale handed her a paper bag as he nodded. "It's from Concetta. The lace she promised you."

"She made this with her hands! What a saint she is. Such lovely work."

She paused to examine the contents of the bag as her tall brother looked down at her. The joy of the lace, mixed with the fear of the letter, animated her face with an unusual quiver as the mixed emotions expressed themselves in turn.

Mr. Mauro welcomed Victor to the kitchen: "Come in, come in. How's my little grandson?"

"He's fine, he's fine, Pop. We just now put him to bed. Helen sends her best regards."

"Thank you," his father answered gratefully, happy that ritual had not been forgotten.

"Did you hear about it?" Al asked Vic. "Let's you and me get those bastards. Remember how we beat up the Hawks boys? And that was three of them."

"Sure, sure," Vic said, patting Al's blond pompadour. "We'll get them, Al."

Al took a deep breath and smiled victoriously at Reni, who awaited Uncle Pasquale. Vic rested his arm on Al's shoulders, offering the gesture of security that had been Al's since he had first joined Vic in the backyard play place. Al smiled at him.

When Pasquale sat down and accepted a glass of his sister's liqueur, Mr. Mauro began the story. Reni brought the letter from inside, where it had been hidden in the desk.

Vic stared at Uncle Pasquale's large hands as Pasquale studied the note. Mrs. Mauro finally moved Pasquale's homburg to the telephone table so that no drops of liqueur might stain it.

"Well, what do you think?" Mr. Mauro asked. Being a lawyer, Pasquale would speak with the authority they needed.

"This is a joke or a fake. Or maybe the work of somebody who knows very little about blackmail. The date of the payment is not even mentioned. Look."

The letter was reexamined by Mr. Mauro and handed to Vic.

Reni and her mother acted as handmaidens, urging the men to take coffee or cookies, more liqueur, or fresh fruit. Only Al accepted liqueur, and his mother cautioned him about excess.

"I'd just like to meet those guys," Al said after Vic had given him the letter.

"Fonzi will get us the information," Pasquale said. "If it's the real thing, it's somebody who knows you well."

"It could be any of Papa's cousins," Reni said indelicately. "You know how they are."

Her father looked hurt, but he did not answer. His wife stared at him accusingly.

*

17

At nine thirty the bell rang, and it was Fonzi. He slid down the hall as though his soles were thick in syrup. He was short, but enormously fat. When he talked, it was impossible to notice anything but his stomach. He bowed slightly as he entered the kitchen.

"Hello, Uncle Lou, hello, Aunt Rose, hello, Cousin Vic, Al, Reni. Hello, Uncle Pasquale. How's little Johnny, Aunt Rose? Sleeping sound I bet? How are you feeling, Uncle Lou?"

His familiarity annoyed them all. As Mr. Mauro told him about the letter, his lips made a slight smile. His reddened, watery eyes never looked at anyone in the room. They seemed fixed on the crucifix hanging on the opposite wall.

"Yes," he said when his uncle had finished, "it could be Katherine. But who can tell, who can tell?"

"Make a visit to Manhattan," Pasquale said.

"Sure, Uncle, I could do that. That's a good idea." He turned to Mr. Mauro. "But Uncle Lou, you know how I am. Look at my pants. Full of holes. I don't even have money for carfare. You never know what you need in things like this, or where you have to go to get the right news."

"Don't worry about that," Mr. Mauro answered.

"Gee, thanks, Uncle Lou. You have a little to help Fonzi, don't you? Fonzi has a big stomach, don't you think?" He turned to Al, and patted his stomach.

Reni blushed and Al was frightened by Fonzi's vulgar assurance. When no one acknowledged Fonzi's joke, he shut his dripping eyes and continued: "What a big stomach Fonzi has, eh? Nice and round. Got to keep it fed. Aunt Rose, you have a piece of bread for Fonzi?"

Mrs. Mauro went to the back porch where she kept the bread and the wine. When she placed the bottle and the loaf at the end of the table, Fonzi asked for some cheese.

"Here's provolone," she said, handing him a thick slice and stepping back.

"Thank you, Aunt Rose. Got to fill it up, ain't that right? Ain't that right, Al? I can't go far without eating."

After he had finished two glasses of wine, he wiped his mouth with his jacket sleeve. Mrs. Mauro rushed for a napkin.

"It's all right, Aunt Rose. Don't get no napkins for Fonzi," he said, laughing.

As he ate, he saw that he was the center of attention, but he did not know why. "It could be Aunt Katherine," he said to their inquiring faces. He offered the cheese, but no one accepted.

"You don't know Marino, do you, Uncle Lou?"

"I met him at your wedding?"

"You was at my wedding," Fonzi said proudly. "But that's a long time ago. Time flies, they say. Well, Marino is a mean man. You should ask Assunta, his own daughter. She could tell you. And I could tell you, too. How he never gave us a thing, except he paid for the wedding. How he threatened me, to beat me up."

"Is he with la Mafia?" Pasquale asked.

"Some say that, Uncle, some say that. Once, they say, he got in trouble on the docks." Fonzi licked the oil on his fingernails that had oozed from the cheese, to Al's horror. Al turned to his mother, who stood holding her rosary instead of looking severe.

"They say," Fonzi continued, "Marino went away a while. You know, up the river, they say." Fonzi smiled at his secret. "Marino was making extortion."

Mrs. Mauro sat down and looked around quickly, as though someone had entered the house. The sight of her brother puffing his Tuscan cigar relieved her.

"Well, do what you can," Pasquale said. "And come to my office tomorrow morning."

"Yes, Uncle Pasquale," Fonzi said, and stood up obediently. "What time tomorrow?"

"Eleven o'clock."

"Uncle, why don't you see the cops?" Fonzi asked. "You know them good at the precinct." Fonzi started to leave, and Al and Vic pushed their chairs in to let him pass.

"No cops," Pasquale said. "We'll try to settle it quietly. Cops will make trouble."

"Sure, Uncle." Fonzi smiled. "You know what's best. That's the best thing, isn't it, Uncle Lou? Settle it quiet. Nice and quiet. Isn't that right?"

*

Mr. Mauro stared at Fonzi's averted eyes, and then back to his spherical stomach. "Yes, I don't want to make noise. The cops bring your name in the papers. Then the people start talking and everybody thinks you have gold in the cellar."

"You're smart, Uncle Lou. Sure. Well, good night." Fonzi offered his hand. He saw Mr. Mauro wipe his own hand after he had shaken. "Ooh, I'm sorry, Uncle Lou. I got some provolone on you."

"That's all right, that's all right," Mr. Mauro said in an angry tone, holding his right hand behind his back.

"Good night, Uncle Pasquale. Good night, Aunt Rose, Cousin Vic, Al. Good night, Cousin Reni." Fonzi extended the ritual because he knew they wanted him to go.

"Best regards to Assunta and the babies."

"Oh, thank you, Aunt Rose," Fonzi said. "She'll be glad I came over. You don't have any clothes little Johnny doesn't use any more?"

"I'll look," said Mrs. Mauro, and her eyes suddenly filled with tears. Fonzi labored down the hall.

"What's the matter with the feet?" Mrs. Mauro said as she followed him slowly.

"Aunt Rose," he confided, suddenly mild and grateful, "it's my knees. They're all swollen. The doctor thinks it's water on the knee. Sometimes I can't walk, even. I'll be helpless."

He saw her eyes wet again. "Aunt Rose, don't worry," he said in this different tone. "I'll take care nothing happens to the baby. Remember, I have two kids of my own, one Johnny's age."

He left Mrs. Mauro in shock. "I'll send the clothes," she said as he shut the door.

In the kitchen Pasquale was making a summation: "There's no doubt Fonzi knows about it. Tomorrow I'll see O'Brien, the chief of detectives. We'll have to get some marked money. And you, Reni, go to school and tell them not to let Johnny go home with anybody who calls for him. Only members of the family."

"Yes, I'll go tomorrow morning."

"Maybe you'd better walk to school with him for the next two weeks. Until it's over."

"Yes, I will."

"Shouldn't we have a gun?" Al asked.

Vic patted his shoulder. "You're all the protection they need around here." Al expressed his gratitude with a smile, and showed a fist like a club. Vic nodded.

"Uncle," Vic asked, "do you think there's any danger for my family?"

"No, this is small-time work. It's somebody who wants a little money. What could they have dreamed you make, Luigi?"

"As soon as you make a little money," Mr. Mauro answered, "all the faces turn green. And that Katherine, with her two rotten teeth, envies the whole world."

"Well, I'll see you tomorrow."

Pasquale left with Vic, and the house was locked, each door and window checked by Mr. and Mrs. Mauro after Al and Reni had secured them.

Only little Johnny slept with calm that night. After the midnight bells of the parish church rang, Mrs. Mauro left her bed to see if Johnny was still asleep.

"Rosa, what is it?" her husband asked.

"I can't sleep. I look for Johnny. Tonight I feel the house is open. Luigi, call the witch and pay her. Give her the money or something will happen."

"Don't worry. Pasquale will take care of it. He has many important friends."

*

Sunday afternoon they met again. Reni took Johnny to a movie right after lunch, and Al went along to protect them.

Vic and his family had come for dinner. At four his wife had taken the baby back for his nap. Pasquale arrived at five, and they sat around the cleared table in the kitchen.

"Fonzi should be here soon," Pasquale said. "He went to the old neighborhood today when everybody is around."

"Did you see O'Brien?" Mr. Mauro asked.

"Yes. O'Brien will come with us when we go to meet them. We'll take the marked bills."

"I have the money," Mr. Mauro said, taking out an envelope.

"This is the five hundred, Luigi. We are not going to take all the money." Pasquale smiled. "We just take a few bills and some newspaper cut up. But leave the envelope here so that Fonzi can see it. If it's Katherine, he'll report this."

"Good," said Mr. Mauro, warming up to the intrigue.

"Do you want me to come?" Vic asked his uncle.

"Yes, Vic. You will drive the car. We need somebody in the family to be recognized. Does Katherine know you?"

"They know him," said Mr. Mauro. "And they know I bought a Buick."

His wife clutched her hair as she listened to this plan of dark streets. She could not see any figure but Death's, unless all the money were given immediately, and without question, to the larger forces of evil.

"Give them the money," she said, as an antistrophe to their words. "Do you want your life or the money?"

"All right, Rosa, I am ready to get it all over with," her husband said. "I'll give it."

"You don't have to worry," Pasquale said with irritation. "We will handle this thing, Rosa. It's just a bunch of cheap *cafoni*."

"Cheap *cafoni* act without reason."

"Leave it to us," her brother finally said, and Mrs. Mauro was quiet. As the men continued to plan, she labored to bear her possible losses, assisting her spinning rosary, hissing Our Fathers and Hail Marys.

Fonzi arrived from the streets where they had all lived when they first came from Italy, the neighborhood held in mild disdain by the prosperous families who had moved up to the Bronx to buy the mock-Bavarian frame houses that the earlier Germans were leaving for the cleaner air of suburban Mount Vernon.

In front of coffee stores, and in the various apartments he visited during a normal Sunday social excursion, Fonzi had searched for information.

"Oh, how tired I am," he said, and sat down. "Aunt Rose, you got a little water or something?"

She went to the back porch for the wine. "Fonzi, could you eat some macaroni left from lunch?"

"Your macaronis are the best in the Bronx."

*

The others waited while Fonzi ate the macaroni, and then a little extra veal his aunt found, and finally some provolone, with a little wine to wash it down. Fonzi seemed to enjoy performing at eating. He twirled his spaghetti with artful style, but no one laughed.

"How's the old neighborhood?" Vic asked.

"Getting crowded," said Fonzi in a low voice. "A lot of niggers moving in. You know what I mean, a low element."

The men nodded, but watching Fonzi's vein-stained face, they were suspicious even of what was supposed to be a simple sociological fact.

"Did you see Katherine?" Mr. Mauro asked.

"She sends her regards," Fonzi said, licking his fingernails.

"You told her you were coming here, you *ciúccio!*" When Pasquale shouted, it was frightening. His sister jumped up. Fonzi sat back in alarm.

"No, no, Uncle. She sent regards because, you know, we both live up here in the Bronx. She thought, you know, maybe we might run into each other sometime."

"Is it her?" Mr. Mauro asked.

"I can't tell. She ain't innocent, you know what I mean. Something, she knows. But I can't tell nothing definite from what she said."

"Didn't you hear anything up and down Arthur Street?"

"Well, Cousin Vic, it's hard to say, you know what I mean. You hear a little here, a little there. You got to keep buying drinks. Then you got to figure it all out." Fonzi ate the bread and cheese crumbs hungrily, having difficulty catching them in his thick oily fingers.

"Well, what did you hear?" Pasquale asked.

"I heard a lot of things. All things happen down there. A thing like this happens every day. And what do people do? They settle it nice and quiet. Ain't that right, Uncle Lou?"

Mrs. Mauro looked at Fonzi's fat hands on her table as fearfully as when she chose a live lobster from the fish markets on Friday.

"Look," Pasquale said, taking the envelope from Mr. Mauro's lap. "Here's all the money already."

He threw it across the table. Mr. Mauro looked frightened. His wife bit her right index finger.

"Well, look at that," Fonzi said, as though reaching for food. "Twenties, eh? You're really a smart man, Uncle Lou. Nice and quiet you're doing this. Sure, you don't want to get mixed up with those rough people. They're bad people." He smiled at Mr. Mauro, who turned his face away.

"You'll tell Katherine the money's ready," Pasquale said.

"Oh, sure. Wait! What do you mean? How can I tell her anything like that? How do I know she did it? They didn't say nothing."

"You say it just so it can get around," Vic explained. "Somebody might pick it up down there, and they'll know. The letter never said what time or exactly where the payment should be."

"Oh, I see," Fonzi said. "Sure, I get it. Spread it around, eh? Oh Aunt Rose, you got a little fruit?"

Mrs. Mauro placed the cut-glass bowl before him, and he chose a tangerine.

"You can tell the spring is here," Fonzi said after he had tasted the fruit. "The tangerines are no good no more."

"Try an apple?"

"No, Aunt Rose. I got to go. I got to go home."

In the hall, after he had received the clothes Mrs. Mauro had promised, he confided to her that he had been on his feet all day and his legs ached. "I got to put my feet on a chair, to ease the blood."

*

Mrs. Mauro watched him waddle down the street, a rag-picker of evil, holding a paper bag with Johnny's used clothes.

"I feel sorry for him," she said when she returned to the kitchen. "He's a sick man. His legs give him pain."

"That pig has his finger in this," Pasquale said. "I think if I got O'Brien to pull him in, it would all be over."

24

"Oh, *Dio!*" Mrs. Mauro screamed. "No, no, Pasquale. He is sick. Please."

"And he has a family," her husband added. "Two children. Except for him they would not even have rags to wear."

"But Pa, he doesn't even work," Vic protested. "He stands in front of the candy store all day long. How the heck does he support anybody?"

"Assunta does laundry," his father explained sadly. "But he is the father and he is needed."

"But Luigi, this is the man who may have made the whole job."

"I know that, Pasqual', I know. But his wife is my niece. I can't send him to jail."

His wife nodded, clutching her beads again. She stopped as she noticed the dirty table, and went to the sink for a wet cloth.

"And don't forget the revenge if he goes to jail," she added, as she removed the remains of Fonzi's snack with a sour expression on her face. "The Sicilians do the *vendetta* still today."

Vic said: "I understand all that. But if Fonzi is responsible, he must pay before the law. That's not our fault."

"My son," Mr. Mauro said, "this is poor. He is a *disgraziato*. You know what that means? Bad luck and misery all his life. I can't give him to the police. I can't have that on my soul. A member of my own family."

"So he married your sister's daughter. But Papa, he's broken the law."

"I don't care. If you insist, I will pay the money now, all of it, and forget about it." He reached across the table and took the envelope.

"All right," Pasquale said. "I'll handle this the right way. You save your money."

Mr. Mauro looked relieved and turned to his wife. "Thank God," she said to him.

Vic stood up, angry now: "Boy, Pop, you Sicilians do things in funny ways." He walked down the hall.

"Funny," his mother called after him. "Go ahead, funny. Italian is funny. You know. You American wise guy. You know everything. You know what the law is and you fix everything. You should know what law is."

"Don't get excited, Rosa," Mr. Mauro said, taking her wet hand. "Watch the pressure."

A few days later another letter came, with more specific instructions. The house was already in tumult because Reni had reported seeing a man watching her when she met Johnny at three o'clock. Vic and Al had to take a day off from work and follow Johnny and her home in the Buick.

To Al's disappointment, they discovered that the man was the superintendent of a nearby apartment house who always came to watch the children leave school at three. Nobody knew why.

On the night of the payment, Vic met Uncle Pasquale and the detective in front of the house. It was a warm night, almost like summer. Mr. Mauro was there, under the maple, whose new leaves were small but already perfectly formed.

Pasquale introduced Detective O'Brien, who was even taller and stronger than himself. Mr. Mauro meekly gave him the bag of paper and marked bills.

"Don't worry about a thing," O'Brien whispered.

They drove away, leaving Mr. Mauro under the tree in the dark silence. His sense of relief released some tears. Then he went inside to tell his wife and daughter to go to bed. Al came downstairs to wait with him.

It was after eleven when the car finally pulled up. The shade in the front bedroom moved as Mrs. Mauro and Reni looked down anxiously.

Vic was smiling. "They ran away," he said.

"What, what?" his father whispered.

Pasquale showed his pistol. "We gave them a little bit of this." He was still angry.

"Oh boy," Al said, staring at the gun. "Where's the detective?"

"We brought him home," Vic said.

Pasquale explained: "We met them at the place. Two men came. When they reached us O'Brien went to grab one, but he ran away. And the other one, too."

"Uncle fired shots in the air," Vic said. "You should of seen those guys run. They looked so scared they must of let go in their pants."

"But it is all over?" Mr. Mauro asked.

"I'm pretty sure," Pasquale said. He noticed his sister's face in the upstairs window and waved. She waved back and disappeared behind the shade.

"Just one more thing," Pasquale said. "We have to wait for the bird."

"The bird?"

"The bird is Fonzi. I think he'll be here."

*

Because of this prediction, Mr. Mauro and the boys were amazed and frightened when Fonzi appeared less than a half hour later. They watched him struggle down the street, trying to run.

"What happened?" he asked as he reached them, trying to make them all out in the darkness. "Who's here?"

"They ran away," Vic said excitedly.

"Did you give them the money?"

"No, they ran away," Vic said.

"Stupid," Fonzi said, forgetting himself. Then he paused. "Uncle Lou, I thought you was a smart man. I told you they were rough men. Don't you understand?"

He was facing Mr. Mauro, with his stomach almost touching him. Mr. Mauro stepped back.

Suddenly Pasquale grabbed Fonzi by the jacket, and spun him around, slamming him against the trunk of the tree. As he spun his shoes made a high, squeaking sound. The noise of his body striking the tree was very loud on the silent street. Mr. Mauro gasped.

Pasquale pressed his left hand against Fonzi's neck, and with the gun in his right hand, pushed it into the soft stomach.

"*Animale!*" he cursed in Italian. "*Porco, bestia!* If you make more trouble I'll spill the food from that fat *pancia* with a bullet."

Fonzi's eyes were white. Pasquale released his left hand from what little neck Fonzi had, and struck Fonzi across the face with the back of his hand. The sound of the slap echoed all along the block.

Fonzi began to fall, but Vic rushed to hold him up. Still, he sank to his knees because Vic could not support his weight.

Mr. Mauro stepped forward to help, but Fonzi held up his hands.

"I'm sorry, I'm sorry. Uncle Lou, forgive?" He held his hands in a mock attitude of prayer, and his lips and chin shook as he cried. "I'm sorry, Uncle Lou. Don't hurt me. I'm sorry. Don't let them hurt me no more. I'm sick, I'm sick. See. I can't walk. Uncle Lou, I'm a sick man. I'm dying."

"Come on," Mr. Mauro said, "they'll drive you home."

Vic and Al sat in the front seat, while Pasquale helped Fonzi into the rear.

"We'll be right back," Vic said.

"I'll see you tomorrow, Luigi," Pasquale said.

When Vic and Al returned, their father was waiting in the kitchen. "He cried all the way home," Al reported. "He said it was not his idea. He was trying to protect us."

Mrs. Mauro and Reni came down to make coffee. After they had heard the entire story, Mr. Mauro spoke up:

"Tomorrow, I will look to find him some work."

"Maybe now he will listen," his wife agreed.

"How do you like that!" Vic said. "I give up. Now you're going to get this guy a job. What can you do?" he said to Al.

# Mission

"Oh but the articles are *beautiful,*" Reni said, and faced her mother's frown of scorn. "And it's only once a year, you know."

"But not to sell, sell—*inside* the church." Mrs. Mauro answered in Italian.

"It's only near the door where you *enter*." Reni held out her hands, describing a rectangle. "A little table they set up for the Mission days."

John sat listening to their argument. They had called him in for supper as they did each evening long before it was ready; he would sit and listen to their voices, a spectator at a show whose emotions were the same. At least he would become irritated along with sister Reni and begin to play with the knives and forks and glasses on the set table. His mother would barely turn.

"Can I wait on the stoop?" he would ask, thinking that now Galarello's sister had come out and was standing there. "Momma, Momma."

But she did not turn around; she focused on Reni, who went on: "Oh I'll bet they're expensive all right—they've got these glass statues of the Madonna, it's like a thick blue glass. Filled with holy water from Lourdes."

Mrs. Mauro turned to the pots of supper. "Buy, buy, buy," she said over the steam. "The church is a store. America, *Ameri-cane.*" Mrs. Mauro turned away with her joke, and Reni had no face to confront.

John remembered his finger exercise and ran his fingers along the tablecloth. "Look. Momma. Look," but she did not turn; it had always pleased her before. These days she turned from him with sourness, these days he had learned to say *go to hell* to her.

Reni's voice struck a tone like his own feelings. "Oh, Ma," she said, "you don't like anything. Here it's the biggest Mission ever came to the Bronx. People from Saint Mary's are coming up *here*. Six fathers they brought. The Redemptorists, no less. *They* brought the articles themselves, you know."

John looked at the clock. Galarello's sister was on the stoop; she stared back at him when he stared at her, and she had turned one morning while he followed behind her to school and given him a smile that knew he was watching her backside.

"I'm going out on the stoop," he said, and stood up, waiting. His mother did not turn; he stepped away from the table: the late sunlight, which had been on his back, now struck the empty glasses and white plates. The shine was not warm on the table; only tips of light appeared in all the glasses, like a row of cool candle flames. He slowly stepped off, suddenly striking the table with his fist, as his father struck when he came in and asked if supper were ready. "Pronto!" And a bang.

They did not turn as he walked away, hearing Reni's voice driven to a shrill pitch by Mrs. Mauro's dissatisfaction: "And they're perfect gifts, too, a nice thing to get for Mrs. Laudisi or Granma for Mother's Day. Little prayer books in mother-of-pearl. Gold rings. Sacred hearts in felt, like a sachet. You know, for up on the wall. All kinds of saints' medals and painted statuettes. Pictures—hand tinted, like a picture of Jesus and the flesh seems real—the body's made to stick out. And silver rosaries imported from Italy."

Reni pronounced it *Itlee* and gave *It* emphasis.

Mrs. Mauro's associations released some relieving fumes: she had heard of this done for the Missionaries, special dispensations to get them money to go to Africa and China and help the cannibals.

John shut the door on their voices and turned: Galarello's sister was there, the sunlight that cut through the alley touching her legs, red for autumn. "Waiting for your father, Johnny boy?" she called.

"Yes," he said, and came to his side of the fence between the houses.

She stood on the top of her stoop looking down at him, her arms folded in the chill of six o'clock, a blue shawl over her hair because of the October wind.

"You going to Naval Cadets?" she asked. "Isn't this the night?"

"It's tonight," he said. "Except for this week it's tomorrow night. Tonight's the Men's Mission."

"Will they let *you* go?" she asked. "You're too young."

John looked up at her face. "Some *can* go at fifteen," he said.

"Oh," she said, and smiled down. John turned to look up the street. "I'll get you something they sell," he said.

"What, John?"

"I'll bring you something," he said.

"Oh really," she said. "The things they bring."

"Yes. The articles are beautiful. Imported from Italy," John said.

He lifted his head, trying to see her face without meeting her eyes. But his glance reached only as high as her knees, which looked as if they had vague, smiling faces in them. His neck felt hot, as though the sunlight were on it, and he turned away again towards the street where the fathers would come walking home.

She laughed behind him. "Are you walking home tomorrow night after Cadets?"

"Yes," John said.

"Maybe you'll be met." She laughed again, then stopped. "Look. There's your father coming," she said in a different tone.

John saw his father striding up the block, always the first man from the subway station. Mr. Mauro was a man who had kept his mustache, and wore a vest and spats. He knew that the neighborhood men spoke about him because he had not become Americanized and answered this each evening in his own way, by beating all the other men home and arriving first at Lorin Place.

John went to his door. "Poppa's coming," he called in.

"Come in!" his mother's voice answered. "Wash!"

He looked back at Galarello's sister; her arms were still folded, and she was dancing from one foot to the other. The blue shawl shook on her arms. "See you tomorrow night, Johnny," she said, and he went inside.

\*

While John was washing, he heard his father arrive, stamping his foot at the door and calling out his sonorous *BUONA SERA* to everyone within.

In the kitchen Mr. Mauro dropped his newspaper on the linen tablecloth. His wife quickly removed it. "Don't change," she said. "The Mission."

"Oh yes," he said, and sat down at his seat. John came in from the bathroom and sat next to him. Together they watched Mrs. Mauro's preparations: finally, she set the macaroni down. Reni came in from the living room where she listened to Bing Crosby until it was time to serve the meal.

Mr. Mauro stood up and carefully removed his jacket. "Take this inside," he said to John. "Put it neat now. On a *wood* hanger."

John obeyed and came back to supper. He ate silently because his father did not permit conversation until the fruit was served. But while the meat course was being eaten, Al and Vic walked in.

"Come on, Pop," Vic said. "We're gonna be late."

Mr. Mauro looked at his two large sons. "Sit down," he said, and Vic and Al obeyed. They watched as he finished his supper. When his coffee was poured, they urged him again to hurry.

He smiled in his power and stirred his sugar longer than necessary. "I will miss *Paradiso,*" he said, lifting his head towards the ceiling. "What a shame."

His wife looked at him, then away to the crucifix over the clock. John took the silence to speak.

"Can't I come, Pa?"

"I don't think they allow at your age," his father said, and looked at his wife for information.

"I'm fifteen, Pa. I know what it's about."

His father smiled. "Here's a good boy," he said to his wife. "The holy one you wanted."

Mrs. Mauro accepted this too, with sour patience, but without troubling a look to the crucifix. "Johnny," she said softly, "Padre Grasso said at least eighteen for boys. Your school will have the retreat next month. This is like the Mission—for boys."

Al came to John's chair and stood behind him. "You got plenty of time before you got to go," he said, and placed his thick hands on John's shoulders.

"Sure," Vic said. "Why have the pants scared off you before you have to."

John's neck felt hot, and he sat very still, hoping that the inner burning would not rise up and be seen by Al.

"John," his father said, reaching into his vest, "here, take this money." He offered John a half dollar. "Tonight, make Holy Communion with a nice soda."

He stood up and called for his jacket. John went in to get it. He held the jacket behind his father, the shoulder high—the correct way—while his father eased his arms in slowly.

"Can't I come and just *buy* something?" John said from behind.

"They will allow this," his mother said. "Before the start. Luigi, let the boy look in and buy."

"Come on, Johnny, ANDIAMO," Mr. Mauro said, and walked out.

John walked along the street beside his father, taking great steps to keep in stride. They passed under the Elevated tracks and on out to the church, Al and Vic's footsteps close behind. Across the churchyard the footsteps knocked against the slate: it was the sound of marching.

At the bottom of the stairs, they saw that the pews were almost filled. John heard his own heavy breathing, and then the whispering of the men. The sound seemed to come from the wall niches where the saints were, an unusual trick of echoes. The heads of the men turned occasionally towards the altar, in quick, furtive movements. They were like soldiers down in trenches.

John stepped up to the table. An old man was seated on a low stool next to it, his head, on a level with the top, looking like part of the objects on display. He did not look at John, but read studiously from an old black missal, with the care of one who rarely reads. The book was in his left hand; with the thumb and forefinger of his right, he gently stroked the white hairs that protruded from his nostrils.

Mr. Mauro whispered, "We will sit down, Johnny. *Buy* and go home."

Mr. Mauro walked down the aisle flanked by Al and Vic. John watched all three genuflect at the side of the pew, then stand up, waiting to be let in. The row of men looked up at them; then their shoulders swayed as they moved to make room. There were grunts as the seated men pushed in tighter. The wooden bench creaked a response. Mr. Mauro, Al, and

Vic sat down at the same time and the wood echoed another straining cry.

A priest in a plain black soutane came out of the sacristy and walked quickly to the pulpit. His head was very large; it rested on the black collar (no neck could be seen) like a stone carving, and long black hair covered it like a hood. The black locks were tangled across his forehead and over his ears, matted, one upon each other, as thick as clay.

The redemptorist, John thought, and picked up a small silver medallion. "How much is this?" he asked the old man.

The old man took the coin from John's hand and dropped it into a wooden cigar box under his stool. "Any offering within reason," he said without looking up.

The priest's voice suddenly began. "Let us pray. Dear Lord, grant this Mission—" It was a prayer for the success of the Mission.

"I gave you half a dollar," John said.

"That's all right," the old man said. "It's within reason."

"Is this for a girl?" John said.

The old man looked up and sighted the medallion, "Women or men. It's the same," he said.

The congregation behind him rumbled a deep *Amen*. John took the medallion and left.

The noise followed him up the steps. But after the first flight, the staircase turned and rose to a narrow passage. Here the latecomers heard Sunday Mass without being seen. John sat down on a step. The wood was coated with sandy grit.

The priest's voice spoke again. It was deep, like a radio announcer's but filled with anger. It was telling the men that God knew their secrets, knew that they forgot Missions in a week.

"Everyone take out a match," the voice said. It was suddenly jovial. "We'll make a memory. Oh come on, come on. We all smoke here. I like my cigar every night. Don't be bashful."

The benches creaked again and strained; then the sound of coughing rose, and after a short silence, a lighter, rustling sound.

"Now light that match," the voice said. "Hold it—like this—like I'm doing. Here, right here under the finger. Come on. You're men! Do it! Feel it! Do you feel it!"

The voice was screaming and each scream seemed to have an echo, but the echoes were scattered moans among the men. The odor of spent matches blew up the passage.

"I want you to know that pain tonight, you *men,*" the voice said in almost a whisper; then it shouted again: "And remember it. And remember Hell when your burning bodies welcome sin. Remember your little finger of pain and think a million times more and more and more."

The word rang like an echo in a cave, back and forth through the church and, hardly diminished, up the passage. John stood up.

"You could not stand that bit of pain," the voice said. "But there's one you can. There's a burning every night, the bonfire of your souls. Until they're black and charred with sin. But *you* feel no pain. You see no black spot. You don't see Jesus and his Blessed Mother writhing there when you *strong men* take your lust for burning in your hands.*"*

The voice grew loud again. "I have seen the strong men, *strong men,* in asylums, strapped down, with their screams reaching the highest stones, trying to break loose, to destroy themselves."

The voice paused. John went to the edge of the cool wall and looked around. The air still held the grey match smoke, a cloud over the heads of the men. The rows of backs sat hunched tight against the carved wooden backs of the pews. It was like a picture in his Latin book—Roman slave rowers.

Then he saw his father's face among the stiff heads; his skin was dark red, the same color it had been when he became sick from shouting at Al when Al had run away to Pittsburgh.

"Can no man today," the voice began again, "in his black burning mind, ever dream of the one pure woman who was the mold of womanhood? Can your minds never see *that* woman, that mold of purity, that lady of light? *Our* Lady! Oh!" it groaned. "Come down here, come down here on your knees to her. Can you answer her question tonight at her altar in the sight of God? Oh!" It groaned louder, and John turned and ran up the steps to the vestibule. He pushed the big red steel doors open and leapt back as the night air rushed through the crack.

He stepped out and leaned on the doors to shut them, but they were tight and scraped against each other. He let them go and ran across the churchyard and out along the street.

He stopped running when he reached the sight of the frame houses of Lorin Place. Along the entire block the porch lights were lit. The bulbs blazed against the screenings like a row of monstrances. He saw the porch light of his house at the end of the block.

When he reached it, his mother was waiting. She had been saying her rosary and marked her place in the beads with her fingers as he stood at the door; she mumbled the end of her prayer, then looked up and spoke: "It's late. No? Did you stay?"

"No. Ma. They don't permit it."

"Did they let you buy?" she said. "Something nice?"

"I got this medal," he said, and held it by the chain.

"A miraculous medal," she said in Italian.

She took it and read the back of it. "Wear this now," she said. "It will show your love for the Madonna. It brings grace."

The silver oval glistened under the porch bulb, twisting left and right, like a separate light itself. The gleam passed across John's eyes.

"It's for you," John said.

"Oh no. Oh *Caro*. It's too nice. You wear it. The Madonnina will watch you."

"No, you take it Ma," John said.

"My first present from my Johnny," she said, and placed the medal around her neck. "Kiss," she said in Italian, and reached her arms up.

John had the sudden desire to turn away, but she held her arms out. He leaned down to accept a kiss, turning his check slightly aside. Her hair gave off her musty indoor odor.

"Do you want a little drink?" she said, and stood up very energetically. "Some cherry syrup I made?"

"Not now, Ma," he said. "Tomorrow's school."

"Yes," she said. "Good boy."

"Good night," he said.

She watched him go into the dark hallway and up the steps. "Thank you, *Caro*," she called when he was part way up. He stopped for a moment in the darkness, and then went on.

His room was hot; Reni or his mother had shut the windows again.

Damn them. It was an inside room that faced Galarello's house across the alley. It avoided the winds and kept the heat of summer until October.

He undressed in the borrowed light of Galarello's hall bulb, which shone dimly across the alley to the polished sides of his bureau. He folded his clothes slowly and placed them on his desk chair.

Then he stepped away and saw the outline of his body in the mirror; momentarily, it was another person in the room, nude, standing there before him.

He shut his eyes and made his way slowly across the room until his legs struck the bed. He climbed under the sheets and pulled the covers completely over him. He liked to do this until his body became warm; then he could lift his head out to the pillow and face the silent darkness.

# Nonna

Johnny suddenly saw his grandmother; she was hiding in the hall shadows as he came down the steps from his room. She was staring expectantly through the glass of the front door, her nose touching the stiff curtains. Her breathing made little sucking sounds; whether it was the air through her mouth or not he did not know. Outside, the swirling snow swept before the gray wooden housefronts of Lorin Place.

"Nonna," he called to her.

She did not turn as he came up beside her but answered by pointing towards the snow. He watched it with her for a while; she did not speak; then he started for the kitchen.

When he came out of the hall darkness into the kitchen, he found his mother and sister poised against the wooden cupboard. "Nonna's watching the snow fall," he said.

His mother pulled him towards her.

"A half hour she's been there," his sister Reni said. Her dark face was imitating the high rage of her mother. "We're scared," Reni said. "The crazy thing, she's going to run out."

"*Silenzio,*" Mrs. Mauro said. Although Nonna did not know American, she had the power to understand what people were saying about her. Mrs. Mauro was sure of this and other ominous auguries.

Some of the old Calabrians on the block called on Nonna for incantations when they had sore throats. Nonna took them to her room and placed powders and herbs on their skin while Mrs. Mauro muttered in the kitchen about the *strega,* her mother-in-law, and pointed up to the ceiling and emphasized the fear in Reni. "*Strega* they say; *ecco, strega* she is."

Slow, soft footsteps came towards the kitchen: Nonna had heard again. Mrs. Mauro looked at her children, and Johnny said, "But she can't understand."

Mrs. Mauro stood silent as Nonna entered the kitchen and went directly to her chair and sat down; she did not look at them.

Relieved, Mrs. Mauro returned to her Christmas preparations. In the afternoons, after shopping and before supper, there were a few hours to bake the seasonal pastries. The hot, dry kitchen took on that fragrance of honey and orange which Mr. Mauro loved to return to after an hour on the subway from downtown, which, he said, smelled of the remains of dead people.

Nonna munched her gums and watched Mrs. Mauro. The criticism of her silence had begun ten years ago when she had arrived, the last immigrant, brought over by Mr. Mauro because she was alone (and not that she wanted to come) and because there was nothing else Mr. Mauro could do. "Could I leave her there in the Sila alone?" he had asked, and the arguments ceased.

Mrs. Mauro rolled her yellow dough and kneaded in controlled fury while Reni, with the scalloper, cut the strips for the fried butterflies.

Nonna began to speak, using the Calabrian dialect and her beggar tones: "Rosa, would you grant me an old glass you don't need?"

"An old glass?" Mrs. Mauro repeated to get her bearings and prepare for the deceptions. "An empty glass or a full one? You mean an empty glass in which there is caffe latte inside the glass?"

"Only a glass," the old lady said. "I will give it back right away. Luigi will not scream when you tell him."

"I know it, I know it," Mrs. Mauro said, fighting to control herself. "Luigi is your son. Your son does not say anything. No one says anything here."

Reni leaned towards Johnny, who had sat down at the table and was watching: "You see that; she does that to torture us," Reni said.

On a cupboard shelf Mrs. Mauro found a dusty glass that contained some old rosary beads. She held it for the old lady's approval, but Nonna merely stood and waited. Mrs. Mauro went to the sink and rinsed the glass. Nonna took it and started down the hall. Without looking back she opened the front door and stepped outside.

"Mamma!" Mrs. Mauro screamed after her but did not move from the kitchen. "The snow! You will get sick."

Nonna came back inside and stood with her head against the door. Beyond the curtains she looked through, the winter night was descending on the mock-Bavarian homes of Lorin Place. Upon the hill, the lights of the few stores were lit: in the early darkness Johnny often mistook them for stars.

Reni looked at her mother. "What's she going to do?"

"She will go begging with that glass," Mrs. Mauro said aloud in American, for safety. "She will beg in the streets to disgrace us the more. The more."

"She better not go out," Johnny said. "I saw the shoes she's got on. And they have holes in them. In the tops, now."

Everyone in the neighborhood had seen Nonna dressed in her rags from the old country, but few knew that Mrs. Mauro periodically bought clothes for her. Her closet was filled with new black dresses and new black shoes.

"Why should we stand this?" Reni said, but her mother looked at her, and she stopped. Mrs. Martucci of the Altar Society could suggest the old people's home, but not Reni.

"Oh, yes, she will win here," Mrs. Mauro said to her daughter as a way of apology. "More and more the *strega* wins and gets what she wants."

"You always talk like it's a plot," Johnny said.

"Oh yes, she will win," his mother repeated, then turned and saw her mound of dough on the table. "Reni," she said, "quick," and attacked the dough with Reni.

The door opened slowly and Nonna walked out again. Mrs. Mauro and Reni ran down the hall. Johnny smiled.

He saw them returning with Nonna in the lead. She was holding the glass, and it was filled with snow.

"That's the end," Reni was saying. "I swear to God."

"Maybe it's one of her magic medicines," Johnny said, and turned to his mother.

"No. Watch," his mother said. She was smiling as she walked to the ice box and found a jar of her grape jam and placed it before Nonna, then gave her a spoon.

Nonna mixed the jam with the snow as they watched. Her face bore a grin like the look of madness it had when she was hiding some useless object she'd stolen from the house.

Nonna licked her glistening gums. Mrs. Mauro smiled again. Reni offered a hesitant counter-smile. Finally, Nonna held the glass in the air and recited in dialect.

"She's going too fast for me," Johnny said.

"A *poesia* for the *dolce*," his mother said. "She says the snow and the red jelly makes a crushed rose."

"Who wrote that poem?" Johnny said.

"Who wrote? Nonna makes them. She makes them all the time. She does not write them."

Reni said, "Didn't Pop ever tell you? She talks in poems."

"All the time? I didn't know that," Johnny said.

"Well, I mean, what she does, it rhymes when she talks. And she will tell stories that way. About history."

"Get her to say more," Johnny said, then turned to the old lady, who watched him as she ate: "Nonna, *parli pui', parli piu'.* "

Nonna gave Johnny her shrivelled smile and stood up, still holding her glass. She walked around the kitchen, stopping at the icebox, the stove, the sewing machine, and for each object she recited a verse.

"I can get some of it now," Johnny said. "They sound like poems."

Nonna opened the cupboard doors and made verses for the water glasses, the wine glasses, the dishes, cups, knives and forks. She turned and saw a wine glass, half full, on the wooden shopping board, and put her brown index finger on it. "The glass turns red upon the wood, the wine of life is very good."

She moved, now with a slight swirl of her skirts, to the bread box near the door. "Without a knife we can't cut bread; without the bread, the knife is dead."

*

Mr. Mauro came in from work while they were listening. The time had gone by so fast that his wife had fallen behind on the supper. "The water is just on," she said to him.

Mr. Mauro was not impatient with the neglect. Instead, he was pleased they were enjoying his mother, who was his cross. "Tonight I'm not so hungry," he said to his wife. "The broccoli has been repeating all afternoon."

"What did I say this morning? Broccoli is too heavy for lunch. I'll make a bismuth."

"No, go on, go on," he said, trying to turn his wife away from him because he saw that Johnny was excited to tell him something.

Reni took his hat and coat, then held up his grey wool cardigan when she came from the closet. He put it on; he was a short man and had trouble with the sleeves. His wife shook her head at his new paunch.

"Pa, Pa, do you know what Nonna did?" Johnny told his father about the snow and the poems.

Nonna sat in her chair signalling with her gums that she was hungry. Usually, they would ignore her. But tonight they smiled and looked at her. Mr. Mauro said to Johnny, "Did you know she was a *cantastorie?*"

"And that, too," his wife said with a little sarcasm.

"What is that?" Johnny said.

"Like the word *canta* is sing. *Storie* is stories, the history. She goes to the piazza. The people sit and listen. She tells about the great knights, like Orlando. She knows books in her head. And she will make a new poem for a marriage or a baby who is born."

He was remembering the sweet side of nostalgia, the taste that comes first after twenty-five years.

"I remember the people at the door, the farmers holding their caps. And they would ask for her. I was a little boy behind her skirts. She asks them the name of the new baby. Then she looks into the empty air. Then she says the poem. Then she makes the fortuna. The farmers go away with the head down. They fear her, too."

Mrs. Mauro placed a few macaroni in the tasting dish and added a spoonful of sauce. "Tonight Nonna will taste," she said.

The old lady snatched the plate and sucked up the thin strands, testing their softness with her gums. Mrs. Mauro managed a small smile.

The old lady spoke, holding the dish up: "For toothless ones they should be tossed until they are extremely soft."

Mrs. Mauro let the pot continue boiling though her husband liked them *al dente*.

During supper they continued to speak about Nonna, and she watched them with a rare smile, a crack in the wrinkled stone face, the face her son called the stubborn peasant.

After Nonna left for her room, Mr. Mauro drank coffee and continued talking to Reni and Johnny while Mrs. Mauro piled the dishes for washing. "All things return," he said. "What a cruel woman she was. When my father died—still a young man—she took us all out of school and made us go to work. We still had property, but she was *avara,* greedy for more. She never had it, she didn't like my father's family because they were high-class to her. She collected the money in a chest. Just like a witch. But my father *was* high born."

Mr. Mauro held his cup while he remembered. "The worst thing was my older brother Giacinto had only one year to finish the university and become a lawyer like my father. She took him out. But he said *no.*"

"Is that the brother who was lost?" his wife said from the sink.

"Yes. He ran away, and we never heard from him again. We heard he was in Argentina, in Brooklyn. I searched for him. But better now to forget. Live with the *now*. Don't remember hate. In this country the *vendetta* is through."

His wife nodded; many times she wished she could forget Nonna's ways and act as she did tonight with her.

Johnny listened while the talk went on without him. He went upstairs to his room while they kept talking as if he were not there. In his bed he thought of Nonna in the spare room at the end of the hall: behind the dark of her room, which had been the storage place for demijohns, were the unseen objects she had brought from Calabria. He had only seen the carved bunches of grapes and lemons on the posts of her enormous bed.

For the next few days, when he found her in the kitchen waiting for food, he asked her about her village and the people who came for poems. But Nonna's memories, like her possessions, were few.

Still she tried to please him by reciting verses and tilting her head in the storyteller's poses as the words came out. After a few poems she would stop and stare across the table like a machine that went dead. Eventually, Johnny would become embarrassed with the silence and waiting for her brown face to move again, and he would leave the kitchen.

\*

The morning after Christmas, Johnny came downstairs to find his mother setting a breakfast on a tray. "Bring this to your Nonna, and don't talk to her. She's sick."

"Where's Poppa?" Johnny asked as he took the tray.

"Your father is at the club," his mother said, and he went down the hall and up the stairs.

Nonna's head was propped on two pillows when he walked in; the flesh of her face seemed stiffened, and the many wrinkles, which always seemed to move, were still. He called to her but stayed a few feet from the bed.

Her eyes opened slowly and then went light with recognition: Johnny rested the tray on the green table beside her bed. It was a table he had made in shop class and had held plants on the front porch before Nonna came.

Nonna made sounds, and Johnny held her cup of caffe latte and slowly placed the bread in her hand. She tried to take the cup and dip the bread, but her arm would not bend.

Johnny fed her, watching her rigid lips unable to hold back the thin, laced lines of the milk-stained coffee that ran down her chin. He saw his right hand shaking.

Abruptly, she pushed him away; then her neck began to recede until her chin was against her chest, Johnny put the cup on the tray; the chewed, wet bread fell on the coverlet. Nonna's cheeks filled with air; her eyelids closed, and a groan came from deep in her body.

He called to her but her face did not move, the bloated cheeks did not deflate. He ran into the hall and called his mother and sister.

In a few seconds, his mother with Reni behind her rushed into the room. There was so little space that Johnny had to move to the window for them to get near the bed, which took up most of the room.

"She's breathing," Mrs. Mauro said quickly. "It could be bad gas."

"Oh Ma, look at all the milk all over the floor." Reni stepped back. "Johnny, Johnny, Johnny," Mrs. Mauro said.

"He's getting just like her," Reni said.

Johnny turned away. In the mirror with the carved frame, the thick white morning clouds lined in grey seemed as cold as the day outside.

Nonna broke the silence with a great belch, then groped again for her coffee and bread. But as Mrs. Mauro handed both to her, she began to shake violently.

"Reni, call the doctor," Mrs. Mauro said to her daughter and left right after her, leaving Johnny in the room. He watched Nonna slowly stop and then open her eyes and speak.

"What is it?" he asked in Italian. "I can't understand." Her words were crushed by her lips and gums hardly able to move.

She raised her stiff right arm slowly and pointed while she tried more sounds, which came out shrill and high, like orders. He looked at the bureau and touched it, and she nodded. She was excited by her wish, and for some reason he understood it. He raised a statuette of the Madonna in the air. She wanted him to put it and the other articles on her bed. He held up a rosary of black beads. She nodded.

Johnny twined the various rosaries and medallions on chains around the carved wooden bedposts. Nonna motioned for the statuettes and the saint pictures tacked to the mirror frame. He put them on the board between the posts but not everything held. He went to his room and found some transparent tape and came back to paste everything solid.

Nonna stared at the figurines silhouetted against the wall: Jesus, with his pink right hand catching the Bronx sunlight in the middle of a blessing; Saint Francis, his chipped brown arms in the air ready to receive the landing of the birds; Saint Joseph, holding his staff and staring at Nonna. Upon the bed they had some new life and their own silent language.

"Pray?" Johnny said in Italian, and folded his hands together. Nonna pointed to the saints and began to speak. It was a prayer, and it sounded like the rhythm of one of her poems. But he could not make out the words: her mouth hardly opened.

"*Buono, buono,*" he said, and took the tray to hold as she ate.

"Tell *her,*" Nonna said, "to send enough for all the birds next time."

Johnny picked up the tray and went downstairs.

"Why did you leave her?" his mother said as he came into the kitchen.

"She stopped shaking. It's all right. She ate." Johnny sat down to have his own breakfast. "And she said send more food next time."

Mrs. Mauro turned back to her heating milk and looked hurt. She brought Johnny's breakfast in silence. While he ate, Reni came running in: "Johnny, what did you go and do now? Don't you know I have to clean that room? I have to vacuum and make that bed."

As Johnny began to explain, Reni turned to her mother and described the scene on the carved bed.

"Ma, listen," Johnny said. "She only wants them to look at. She wants to pray."

"Very nice you like your Nonna," his mother said.

"But Father Grasso will come now, every Sunday, and give her the sacraments," Reni said.

"What else can she do all week?"

"You hear that," Reni said. "He takes right after her. It's the craziness got right in his blood."

"It's *her* stuff," Johnny said. "She's got the right."

"*Her stuff* we do not touch here." His mother spoke in a loud voice. "Nothing of hers is needed here. It goes to the cousins on your father's side. And your Aunt Clara will be here to collect the minute she goes."

Mrs. Mauro turned to the *Last Supper* on the wall next to the icebox and intoned: "Look, look at the face of your sister. Do you know the dirt she cleans that makes her white. Every day and night touching her sheets, cleaning the entrails—"

"Well, she doesn't have to clean the statues," Johnny said. "The saints stay clean."

Reni was about to answer, but her mother shouted her name and then said to Johnny, "Go for your father at the club. Hurry up."

Johnny ran to the closet for his mackinaw and then went to the top of the hill. The Italo-American Club was on the avenue in a rented store with windows covered with thick green drapes from one member's house. When Johnny knocked, he heard voices call back in Italian, but he did not enter. The club was a sanctuary for the men of the neighborhood, and only Italian was spoken there.

He opened the door a crack and called to his father, who was sitting at a long wooden table under the light of a bare bulb overhead. Across from him was Mr. Marino, the shoemaker, who often left his next-door shop for the pleasure of a game of Three Sevens.

"Nonna's sick" Johnny called, and looked inside at the Italian flag on the wall. "Momma says come."

Johnny and his father reached the house as the breathless Doctor D'Amato was leaving. They met in the foyer. The doctor was confirming to Mrs. Mauro that Nonna was indeed sick, was fading fast, as he put it twice. "But you know these old people," the doctor said. "They're tough stock. None of this soft food we get. They grew up on the real stuff. They can hang on for years."

Mrs. Mauro watched the doctor walk to his black limousine and then drive off before she turned to her husband and told him the whole story of the bed.

"Johnny," Mr. Mauro said. "You don't want to get like that. These ways they will get inside you."

He saw his wife holding her small handkerchief and touching her eyes. "I will go talk to her now. I'll stop her."

He turned to go upstairs, but Mrs. Mauro held Johnny's shoulder. "No, I have to hear what Poppa says," Johnny said, and ran out of her gentle hold.

He stood just behind the door: Nonna's musty odor came through the tiny cracks where the heavily-painted hinges kept the door always a little opened.

"I tell you Reni needs to clean this room," his father was saying, and a grunt replied. "Why don't you listen?" His father said, "Momma. We honor you."

Nonna cleared her throat with little coughs before speaking. "Honor is fresh air," she said.

47

"What?"

"*Your honor—*"

"We do everything for you here." His father stepped to the closet door. "Look, I buy you clothes. You never use them. And food. When do you go hungry?"

"Luigi, you are too fat," Nonna said clearly.

"I know," Mr. Mauro said, and his voice became mild. "What can I do?"

"Push the table away." Nonna laughed and coughed.

Mr. Mauro was silent. "Where is my orange juice?" Nonna said.

"They brought it, you had it."

"Two drops for a bird!"

"Two drops? I will speak with her," Mr. Mauro said. "Do you need anything else?"

"The juice, the juice." It was almost a scream.

Mr. Mauro met Johnny at the staircase but knew he had been listening. Johnny followed his father downstairs, to the curtains of the front door.

"Johnny, I forbid you to go into that room." Mr. Mauro looked up the dark staircase. "I know that woman. You don't realize the hard thing in the heart to have to admit your mother is what they say. I can still see her eyes. She didn't listen to me. Like a piece of stone. Don't ever get like that."

He turned and walked to the kitchen.

*

The winter turned to spring and Nonna was still in bed. Johnny saw her on Saturdays when the door was open and Reni cleaned, the vacuum spreading Nonna's smell down the hall.

Doctor D'Amato came often. For a while he had a nurse come all day and night, but Mrs. Mauro could not sleep knowing there was a stranger in the house.

One Saturday, as Johnny was leaving his room for the game, he heard a call. He stopped in the hallway: the odor of Nonna's musty smell seeped through the slightly opened door.

He went to her room. She was still against the pillows. The pillows seemed much larger, as though they had grown around her. She was like a wooden statue. Her face had a cast of green over the many wrinkles; her mouth was stuck open. She raised her right hand again, on the coverlet, reminding him. He was frightened and stayed back, watching her hand. "I can't do it," he said.

She began her shrill sounds, like whining, like crying muffled by pillows. Johnny turned to the bureau and took up the beads and the medallions. As he fastened them to the posts, her cries subsided. Johnny looked at her face only once; then he kept his head down and worked.

The statuettes did not balance on the board. He went for the tape and did a better job securing the pictures and statuettes.

He saw Reni at the door. "I'm telling Momma about this right now," she said, and ran.

Nonna called. Johnny watched her hand and fingers. She was signalling the drawers of the bureau. He found thick tablecloths, violet colored skirts, a lace blouse, a black bolero jacket in felt—costumes. In the second drawer was the peasant dress his father had told him about.

Johnny placed it beside the linens and skirts. He found speckled red combs, curved combs of bone, necklaces, copper bracelets—he placed everything of the drawers on the bed.

The last was a photograph, a young woman with a man in a square-cut beard. Johnny brought it to Nonna: she said nothing. She sat motionless, the squares and colors piled around her. She was cradled.

His father stepped into the room. Johnny stopped. Mr. Mauro turned to the bed and stopped, then quickly leaned close. He placed his fingers on her eyelids and raised them carefully.

Johnny was afraid to step closer. The silence was something new to him. His father stood erect and held his shoulders, then kissed him and led him down the steps to make the arrangements.

# Wedding Day for Ingebordo

What I did not know about the Pirro family was this: they were midgets or the size we call midget. They lived on our Italo-American block, Lorin Place, when it existed during the thirties. That stable world was under the command of our fathers, who led us with the modes of living based on their memories of nineteenth-century Italy.

My Pirro playmate was Julie, three years older but four inches shorter than myself. His eighteen-year-old sister Ingebordo, called Gina, was no taller than he. Still, I did not comprehend. When you are ten, abnormality is merely ambiguity, and ambiguities are enjoyable—in fact, the better part of living.

Surely, the Pirros were joked about in a manner I *could* understand. They were the *Piccolini*—the little ones, or the *Pirrolini*—the little Pirros. And I even thought I knew why the men at the *boccie* alley laughed when they spoke of how tiny certain parts of Mrs. Pirro must be, and how they would miss the keyhole in the dark.

The Pirros were also the cause of a ridicule I now know was envy. They took American life very seriously, kept in touch with all the quick changes that the other Italian families were reluctant to admit.

They were the first to buy a player piano. (An invention for donkeys, my mother said.) While Julie and I rode daily on a sawhorse we called *The Stagecoach,* the strains of Gina's pumping from above reminded me of the piano anyone could play. The melodies, even the rhythms that slowed down or speeded up as Gina became tired or shifted in her seat, were more appealing to me than the relentless arias my mother and sister sang and played on frequent shame-filled Sundays when I was forced to sit with cousins for culture.

The piano was in the attic where Gina and her mother spent most of their time. Only Pirros gained entrance to that sanctuary, a Pirro response to the neighborhood mocking, though they recognized nothing. They went blithely ahead with the first Con Edison three-way lamp, the first push-button radio, the first Japanese lacquer box, the first rumble seat roadster.

One day, in the middle of our afternoon trek, it began to rain, a March rain that drove us in. We hunted in the cellar until the odor of Queenie, the giant Pirro dog, sent us to the first floor for air. All the doors were shut, and the piano was silent. Julie motioned: we were going to the attic!

We entered on a scene that will always keep the Pirros magical for me, visual, like tableaux. (Many years later, on just such a rainy day, while I was caught in Piazza Santissima Anunziata in Florence, my eye saw the terra-cotta reliefs of Della Robbia on the façade of the foundling home. I watched them in the rain, wondering why they kept me there, until my mind recalled the memory of Gina.)

Gina was being fitted for her wedding dress that day. She was standing on a red leather hassock (the new, revolving type) being fitted by her mother and Signora Succhina, who owned what was called The Bridal Millinery Shop.

The white lace of her gown was still uncut. It was folded loosely about her, fell below her feet in such a way that she seemed to be rising out of the hassock. Her little face, so finely cut, with cheek circles of rouge that was then the style, stood like a tinted cameo on the white neck that filtered up from the lace.

Gina called to me. "Hello, Johnny. Momma, here's Johnny boy."

Her mother looked up and took the pins from her mouth. "Johnny, you like the bride?" she said.

"Yes, Mrs. Pirro," I said.

Julie led me to the other room; we stood before the player piano.

"Play the 'Wedding March'," Mrs. Pirro said to me. I looked at her and Julie and Gina: they were smiling in the Pirro way, but Signora

Succhina was glaring, a stare that said I should not be here.

"Julie, get the roll," Gina said from up high. "Make Johnny play."

Julie looked through the boxed piano rolls on the upright top, found the right one, and put in on the spindle. Still, I stood back.

"Go ahead, Johnny," Gina said. I sat down.

The music whined out woefully until I felt my strength and began to pump hard.

I raced Mendelsohn through the attic air with my wet shoes, staring at the roll, unable to look at anyone.

I was allowed to play it four times; comfortable at last, I leaned back and looked across the room to Gina. Though she had to stand on the hassock, she was acting out her march down the aisle with the upper part of her, suddenly very solemn, very believable.

When Signora Succhina left, Gina joined us dressed in her red Chinese kimono. She showed me the latest rolls and sat down to teach one. After six playings, I sang a solo of "The Boulevard of Broken Dreams," a song I remember perhaps because Gina said that the Broken Dream Boulevard was Bronx Boulevard, a few blocks away. (It was a very dark street that ran along Bronx Park and was also called Lover's Lane. Young children were warned to avoid it.) Gina was about to say more, but she left her lost loves in silence.

That evening I went home to tell my family about the wedding to come. We were at supper.

"That's right," my mother said, and went inside for the mail, which was always kept on the piano in the parlour. "Luigi," she said to my father when she had given him the invitation, "what will we do?"

"Go," he said.

"The reception, too? Go there?"

"Yes, yes," he said. "The Continental Hall is right here on the avenue. It's no Brooklyn."

He was referring to Dominic Pirro's wedding, when we had been lost in Brooklyn for two hours.

My own pleasure lingered on Continental Hall, called simply The Hall. Every Saturday night the orchestra music for the dances reached Lorin Place as I was going to sleep. On Sundays the band played more tarantellas because they played for wedding parties. Loud or harsh, interrupted and joined by the passing Elevated trains, it was my lullaby, and I waited to get closer.

Two nights before the wedding, I stayed very late in the attic and was there when Mr. Pirro came home from work. Mrs. Pirro had joined us, singing her own accented version of the songs. Her performances excited me; moments as incongruous as, say, one of my frigid public school teachers suddenly dancing the cancan in class.

Mr. Pirro shook my hand earnestly. "Having fun, Johnny?"

"Yes, Mr. Pirro," I said. "We're all playing the piano."

"Very nice," he said. "Play. Play. You coming to the wedding?"

"We're all coming," I said. "To The Hall, too."

"And what do they say down your house?"

"They're coming," I said. "We're all coming. The whole family. Even my brother who moved away." I sensed that I was not giving the correct answer. "Poppa bought the gift yesterday," I said.

"All right, all right," he said, and patted my head and quickly left the room.

When I left, a few minutes later, Julie walked downstairs with me. "Didn't you hear about the fight?" he said.

"No," I said.

"The Di Pressos want to get my father." Julie looked upstairs. "They hate Queenie," he said. "She eats up their garden, they say. They sent the warning."

The Di Pressos were the beasts of Lorin Place—Calabrians. They spoke to no one, not even to each other, it seemed. Mr. and Mrs. Di Presso sat on their front porch each evening facing the street like massive sculptures, clothed. Both looked large and thick enough to swallow Queenie whole.

"Why don't you call the cops," I said. "For protection."

"We can't. They're getting up a petition to send *to* the cops. They're asking the whole block to sign. To kill Queenie."

"My father never said anything," I said.

"And now they'll come to the wedding and raid The Hall," Julie said. "Maybe."

I was not sure how this would happen, but breaches of honor had caused beatings in the neighborhood. Julie and I had found blood one day; it was thick as paint drying on the almost white concrete near Filippo's house. Filippo was a widower with four blonde daughters; an Irishman had been keeping company with the youngest and had done something to her. Filippo had stabbed him.

*

The wedding morning was too perfect for raids. The sky was deep and distant and dark against the red bricks of the Pirro house. You can picture Italy in it, I had heard my mother say at breakfast.

On the street after Mass I saw the neighborhood overdressed and expectant. My father talked with Di Presso under the sun. Both wore white carnations. We stood at our front gate until the last bells of the twelve o'clock Mass, the Sunday signal for dinner.

At three, we were on the front porch when Victor came from Mount Vernon, the home of success, driving his Chevy. My father ordered him and his wife to park, and we all walked to Saint Mary's.

The church, which was so solemn in the morning, now was like a hall itself. The saints and the altar had a new lassitude; Saint Michael had none of his morning wrath, though he still pointed to the gash in his thigh and held his spear.

Father Grasso came out in his black soutane, the top snaps unhooked, and circulated among us telling jokes to the men. When his sextons came, he supervised the unrolling of the red carpet. "Five dollars extra," my mother whispered to my father.

Signora Succhina arrived with eight girls and an organist; Father Grasso took them to the choir loft and set them in place.

At four, the noises died away; the bells were rung through the silence of the afternoon, echoing into the stillness of Sunday. I shut my eyes and saw the whole neighborhood in my head, as far as the bridge in the park where the bell sounds came like the cries of hollow birds.

When I looked again, an altar boy was lighting the banks of candles behind the altar rail. The men were nodding at the arrangements. My

54

father told my mother that the Pirros had spared no expense, and she reminded him that each candle cost ten cents to light.

I began to count, but someone behind me said, "The cars are here." Father Grasso walked out of the sacristy with two altar boys behind him and went to the top step to wait. He adjusted his chasuble with his thick hands that seemed barely able to lift thin communion wafers from the goblet.

The organ began, followed by the choir with the melody I knew so well; my feet reacted.

We looked back at the staircase. Julie appeared first, dressed in a cutaway. Behind him, and the most miniature of all, was Dominic Pirro's daughter holding a blue silk pillow upon which the ring reposed.

Then, four flower girls, more daughters of the Pirros, dropping petals of flowers from blue baskets. Last, Gina and her father, slowly marching, around them the assistants of Signora Succhina straightening the train at each turn.

Our eyes followed Gina. By the time she reached the altar rail, we had turned to realize that there was a groom. He was much taller, yet nothing was wrong. Husbands and fathers were protectors, and brides were born to accept the strong arm beside them.

We followed Gina out along the red carpet after the ceremony, and walked to The Hall while she went to be photographed. I ran upstairs with the other children and slid across the floor until the adults arrived. At the end of the room I saw a platform and on it two thronelike chairs, painted, trimmed with paper flowers. A man's voice called me away.

The bridal party had come, and the guests were to stand at their tables. The band (I had not noticed it yet) struck up the "Wedding March." Gina and her husband, her father, brothers, the flower girls, the ushers and bridesmaids made a very fast entrance. They walked straight through the room to the platform as we cheered.

Mr. Monachino, the owner of The Hall, appeared at the center of it and called in Italian for the Grand March. It was a kind of ritual in the neighborhood; I have never known another name for it; following Monachino's calls we marched, two abreast, guests of all ages, down the center, around either side in a large circle, then dividing into two smaller circles, then joining again. The music was very fast.

When it was over and everyone calmed by its exuberance and formality, my mother sent me for sandwiches. At a counter near the door, Dominic Pirro, wearing a white apron over his tuxedo, stood before a wall of large rolls filled with ham, sweating and filling trays handed him.

My mother took my hand after I deposited the tray at our table. My father held a large box wrapped in white paper; we walked towards Gina's throne.

Di Presso stopped us on the way; he whispered to my father. My mother squeezed my hand and drew me away, calling my father. He told Di Presso that he had to see the new little king and kiss the queen of small female figs.

But when we reached the throne, my father changed. He spoke very formally, and presented our family gift with ages of good fortune and blessings and bowed before he stepped up to kiss Gina's cheeks. Gina then leaned down to kiss my mother and introduce her husband, who took my mother's hand and kissed her cheeks.

She caught my eye. "My Johnny," she said, and held out her hands. I walked up the steps to her. She embraced me and suddenly began to cry.

"You are my baritone," she said, and began to wipe her tears. I saw her husband smiling at me. "Maybe we'll play together again some day," she said, and began to cry again; her body shook.

"Yes, we will," I said. She turned her face away.

"Now go and have fun," her husband said to me, and I stepped down, leaving her alone.

*

Many sandwich trays later, my father and Di Presso found themselves alone at our table. I had crept behind them to spy on Di Presso and to watch him drink from the wine pitcher. He had not used a glass.

My father tried to restrain him, but not with any will. From time to time, Di Presso stood up to make a speech and as he started was pulled down into his own laughter.

"Let's ask Johnny," he suddenly said, turning on me. "He goes upstairs."

"No, no, no," my father said. "Not the baby."

"Come on. Johnny's a big boy, now," Di Presso said. "He goes out to visit. Hey Johnny, you go upstairs and see the *Pirrolini*. You ever see the peepee of anybody?"

I walked away, knowing it was a rudeness not permitted children.

Suddenly, he was out in the middle of the floor. But Monachino stopped him with a shout for everyone to sit down.

When there was a trace of silence, Monachino clapped his hands twice, and the sons of D'Alessio the pastry maker marched in carrying large silver trays, the first five piled high with small white boxes of sugar-covered almonds called *confetti*. The rest were cream puffs entwined in strands of silver foil.

Gina and her husband came down to lead them from table to table for the Presentation.

We were far down the line; Di Presso got up again and came to my father. My mother heard them. "No!" she said. "For the love of God. Don't say to their face."

"*Cherubini*," Di Presso said. "It's very nice. Why not say?"

The Procession came closer and closer, and Di Presso looked determined. Gina at last came up.

Di Presso bowed. "I wish, I wish you—" He held the table to push himself erect, then waved towards the table that held his family. "A large family for you. Your children will be—"

My father began to shake his hands for Gina, but she held her innocent smile.

"Your children will be *cherubini*," Di Presso said, holding his hands to show the size.

Gina's husband did not like the word. His smile fell away as he stepped towards Di Presso.

Mr. and Mrs. Pirro looked about for their other children. Dominic began to trot towards us. Two other sons, Danny and Vito, came down the line.

"What's that?" Gina's husband said.

Gina raised her right hand. "Angels," she said. "He means the chubby angels with wings you see over the altar. Like my Johnny here." She suddenly kissed me.

The kiss had the scent of flowers from her bosom. She stepped past Di Presso, her head at the level of his belt, and her delightful train followed her quickly into memory.

# The Weeks of Charity

Every Christmas Eve afternoon of my childhood I returned from Confession to the kitchen of my home and found my father and mother at their usual preparations.

While he boiled rock candy, prunes, orange, lemon rind, and raisins for rock and rye, and my mother shaped yellow dough for a *torta* of *ricotta*, the windows became steamy against the oncoming early darkness. As the neighborhood lights came on in the houses across the way, they appeared to me as monstrances; the kitchen was floating alone, like a dream.

That afternoon of essences brought me into the family mysteries and away from the thoughts I had had standing at the *presepio* in a niche behind the confessionals; saying my penance I used to gaze at the creatures standing in the strawy pen, awaiting some movement from their painted plaster bodies.

My father and mother spoke as they worked; there were new stories every year, of neighbors and relatives, and at that time, of a Mussolini.

But the winter subject invariably returned to the lost: first, my father's oldest brother, who had left Calabria, landed in New York, and never been heard from again. He was, to me, a ghost with a mustache; he lurked behind every dark man I saw leave the poolroom on the avenue.

Then my mother's brother was recalled: an officer in the Ethiopian war of '96, he wore a monocle, ruled the family, and disappeared into Argentina. The detectives my father had hired to search for his brother had once made inquiries in Buenos Aires for my mother. An Episcopal bishop with my uncle's name had been found, but he denied any connection. We had no photograph of him, but we had that bishop's image before our suspicious eyes whenever the story was retold.

After the lost came the cold, the downtown cousins who could not afford the Bronx. Every family on Lorin Place, our four block street of wood frame houses, had relatives that comprised the underside of their rising, new American character.

On one such afternoon, I returned to an argument. My mother's voice was attempting calm over the moving dough. "Luigi," she said, but did not look up. "*She* does not want it. *We* don't want it. Tell her to stay there."

"What could I say? What can you say to a *disgraziata?*" He used the word that meant degraded, crushed, belittled by the world, a prideless thing beyond pity.

But my mother understood with pity. She nodded and did not reply.

My sister Reni walked in, and my father told her: "Your Aunt Lena is coming tomorrow. For dinner."

"On Christmas day? We have *her?*"

"She wants to see us. It is the holiday. The time you go and visit your cousins."

But my father was uncomfortable: downtown relations came only for packages of old things, but never on holidays. Their presence on the days of celebration was bad luck. They were *pezzenti,* those fated to rags, unwelcome in the Bronx of private homes and trees and ownership.

That night my married sisters and brothers came and were told. "What a subject for Christmas Eve," my brother, Al, said. "You know about her kid, Joey?"

"Wait a minute," my father said. "He ran away from the home. He's disowned. Lena never sees him."

"Pa, but all people say is he's *our* cousin." Al spoke with my father's terseness. "And he was caught robbing a Woolworth. Right in our face."

"I see it now!" My father permitted himself some indignation. He struck the table. "She wants more money. Lena comes to visit her bank on Christmas."

"*Meno male!* The light goes on." My mother turned from the stove pans. "And you *give*. She lives on your blood. Pretty soon she can't walk without your blood."

"Yes, yes," my father said. "And what's the use of talking?"

"Give. Give. Give to make them weak." My mother turned back to her concern.

We ate the vigil meal of spaghetti and fried eels in silence. After, when the table was cleared of plates and we had walnuts and tangerines before us, my father began again. "Well, tomorrow she comes." He looked at us all; the others turned away respectfully. He smiled at me. "Johnny, you remember your Aunt Lena?"

"Yes," I said.

"You remember you played with her Arthur and Funzio at Uncle Dominic's wedding?"

"Their bodies stink," I said.

My brothers rose and moved away from the table. My sisters went to the sink to wash the dishes, and my mother went out of the room, returning in a moment with her rosary beads. Alone, my father poured himself some rock and rye.

My mother was standing above him. "Why? Why this pig?" She looked at me and stopped, but my brothers moved closer and my sisters stopped rattling the plates. "Who spent her life under half the men in Manhattan," my mother said.

My father stood up, still holding his glass. "I will drive her out," he said, and went to the telephone in the living room. He called back into the silence. "Where is her number?"

"Number? She has no number!" My mother's tone was desperate, and I absorbed the fear of an invasion that could not be stopped.

My father came back. "No phone?" he said, but my mother disregarded him now.

"Gangster. *Cafone*. Racketeer. Wife of the Mafia."

"All right." My father raised his arms. "The bad husband is gone. Some things, remember."

"She has more horns than all the bulls in the world," my mother said. "She is the queen—"

My father turned and left the kitchen.

\*

Next morning came with the parish bells that woke me at six. I had heard the bells of midnight Mass through sleep and then time had stopped until the bells of morning.

The sun shone through the lace curtains of the front windows when I walked down to look at Christmas Day. It was clear and sunny after a night of wind that had swept the usual mists of the city away, and the neighborhood houses appeared like a painted village.

I had my breakfast in the hot, dry kitchen: milk and pastry cookies of leftover dough from the *torta*. I went to the children's Mass at nine and returned to set up the electric trains that had been Al's before me.

My father came home just before noon, and I went to the kitchen. He had been downtown trying to stop Lena but had not found her. Instead, he was speaking of the old neighborhood, still making the best salami, cheeses, bread and pastry. My mother looked at the white box he held. "What did I bake for?" she said, but she was not angry because of the pastries.

We sat down for the meal as though no guests were coming, but they came as we were having fruit. If my parents were displeased, it could not be seen in their welcome of Lena, who was not dressed in rags.

Lena sat down, and I was given her coat to place in the closet. As I carried it inside, I detected its odor: it was like the aroma of church pews, the musty stench you caught kneeling at overcrowded early Masses where the old women predominated.

When I returned I sat and stared at Lena; her dress was a grey-black covering, like a smock over her small, heavy body. She smoothed a lace collar with her hands as she spoke; the color of the lace, its shine, reminded me of the doily on my father's armchair, yellowed by his hair.

"Show your cousins the toys." My father's voice broke my staring.

I took Arthur and Funzio inside; they sat down on the rug while I operated the trains.

I offered the transformer to Arthur; his hands shook as he kneeled to turn the dial. In the kitchen the voices were rising. Suddenly, there were tears.

"What's that?" I said.

"It's Momma," Funzio said. "She's crying again."

"Does she cry a lot?" I asked.

"Yes," he said. "I guess so."

"Who's your father?" I asked.

Arthur looked up. "He works in Florida. He's building the buildings there."

"Momma says you're our Uncle John," Funzio said.

"Uncle? I can't be an uncle."

"Yes," Arthur said. "You are an uncle to us."

"Wait here," I said. "I'll see what's going on inside."

I walked quietly to the kitchen door. My father's face was puzzled or frightened; I could not tell.

Lena was rubbing the fingers of each hand against the opposing palm. Her voice was calm again.

"We die or we live," she was saying, and rubbed. "For me, living is dying. I am dead every day." She studied her hands and rubbed. "I have nothing. The babies eat my flesh. Momma, eat. They look at my hands for the food. Where is food? Arturo is in Florida. He sends no more money."

"Wait," my father said, and pointed at me. "Johnny, what do you want? Something to eat? Here. Take some *torroni* to your cousins."

I took the candy as far as the living room entranceway and stopped again.

"I must get him," Lena said. "He must take his family again."

"How does he come back?" my father said. "You know *him*."

"On the train," Lena said. "I get him back."

"How can you find him?" my father said.

There was a long silence; the *torroni* began to melt against my fingers.

"Don't look at me," my father said. "There's plenty of money in this. And the boys."

"They stay here," Lena said.

"Here?" My mother's shout startled me.

"Just a little time. A week or two."

"Beds, clothes, school," my mother said. "We are not ready. We have no space."

"This big house?" Lena said, and I looked in because her tone had changed. She was staring at the walls and the ceiling of the kitchen. "You have rooms here. Many rooms it must be."

"Not enough," my mother said.

"Just the attic," my father said. "But it's a floor, and that's all. It's unfinished."

Lena laughed at him. "For them, it's better than home. It's riches."

There was another silence; from the parlor I heard Funzio's voice. He had touched a wire and received a slight shock. He was seated in the armchair with his knees up under his chin, sucking his sounds from a heaving diaphragm. The lines of tears from his eyes were uninterrupted, like water pouring; I tried to catch them at his chin, to stop the stains on his white shirt. I touched him to quiet him, certain that my father would blame so much crying on me.

"Leave him go," Arthur said. "He'll finish."

"Does he cry a lot?" I asked.

"Yes, *he* cries a lot," Arthur said.

"I'll get him toys," I said, and went to my room.

I went again and again. Funzio took the toys with a meekness that made me feel benevolent; yet I filled his arms to avoid his streaked eyes, and I turned away with another emotion—of wanting to hit him. I saw that he would have accepted the toys and the blow with the same hungering gratitude.

The parlor rug was filled, and we played on our knees and forgot the kitchen until my father turned a light on in the early evening darkness. "Come in to eat, boys," he said, and then to me, "Johnny, you like your little cousins?"

"Yes, I like them," I said.

"How would you like a visit? If they stay?"

I said yes, and he leaned down, smiling, and patted Arthur and Funzio; he touched them as I had touched Funzio, with a kindness that has no love.

After supper we all walked Lena to the door.

She did not smile as she kissed her boys but told them to *listen* to what everyone told them.

Then she was gone, down the darkness of the Christmas street. Over her head the windows along the way gave hazy outlines of parlor trees in the small light of pointed red and green bulbs.

We left the dank porch, with its odors of rubber shoes, and went to the kitchen. Arthur and Funzio sat still and upright and watched my father as he transferred the remaining wine to smaller bottles. While he explained how air hurt wine, my mother and Reni went upstairs.

A short time later they called the boys. I went along with them to look. They would sleep on mattresses placed against the chimney wall of the attic floor; and each had a flashlight in case they had need to use the bathroom during the night. I went back to my room, which was still called Al's room by the family, hearing the slavish words of their gratitude. They were like campers, I thought, and I resented them.

For the next week they went to the attic as often as they could and would not come out to play. I found that the Christmas cookies, which usually lasted a few weeks, disappeared; not satisfied with this, my mother served them bread and her own jam twice an afternoon.

When I was becoming resigned to their hunger and consumption, I had to go back to school, leaving them at home all day. I hated the house each morning as I left but ran back to it every afternoon to see where the boys were, to check all the rooms, particularly my own. But they took nothing.

One evening—it was the middle of January—the tablecloth was left on the table after supper. Reni did not go to her room for Bing Crosby but remained to make coffee in the large pot. My father stayed seated at his place, and my mother brought him his new portable radio so that he would not miss Gabriel Heatter.

At nine my brothers and sisters came for a family council. I was sent up after being reminded that Arthur and Funzio were already asleep. I went and changed to my pajamas, then came down to the head of the staircase.

"How do you like that?" Al's voice rose as I reached the last darkened step. "I figured, can she comb the whole state?"

"But now she comes *here*," my mother said. "With this crazy thing that runs."

"He worked for Di Napoli," Al said. "In construction? That's all we know. Right, Pa?"

"I know a little more, a little more," my father said, and waited in the silence. "I could give a book on this man. But I don't know him. This man is—what can you call him—peculiar. He gave to Lena the paycheck. They lived. I know that. I never had to pay the rent for years. But what can I say—he's not a man."

Silence again. Then Al spoke. "A queer, Pa? He's a queer?"

"No, no, no. He's a big man. He's a strong man. But with no man inside. You sit with him. He talks in a dream. One time I heard Lena played around. I went downtown there to stop *him* from using the knife. He tells me, don't harm Lena. She's a good mother. He thought I came to do the revenge. I don't know. I lived in two worlds for my life and have known men of all kind. This I never knew."

"Still sounds like nothing under the pants," Al said.

"I think more high up. The heart," my father said. "Nothing there. Nothing that feels. A blind man. If he stepped out of the block, he forgot. Wife. Kids. Where his house is. That's him."

"Well, thank God it ends tomorrow," my mother said. "Let them come. Let me clean my house."

I had heard enough and went quietly to my room, knowing that I would see him the next day.

They came at noon while we were awaiting lunch. Arthur and Funzio called to me from the porch. I ran out to see Lena leading a man up the slate walk, a man not fitted for the season: he was wearing a blue, double-breasted blazer jacket over white flannel trousers.

He came up the steps and smiled as he saw us. Lena opened the door for him, and he stepped in.

"Hello, boys," he said, and leaned down to pat our heads; he patted all three of us with equal affection but did not call us by name. I looked up at his white bow tie and then down at his black and white shoes.

The boys greeted him timorously, reaching their hands to him, pulling back. They smiled as they would smile at a stranger they had heard good about, some hidden saint passing by.

He looked around the porch, either to admire the potted plants or

66

avoid the boys. His glance came to Lena again.

"Where's Uncle Lou?" he said. "Let's say hello."

We followed him and watched as he greeted my mother and father. He did not ask about brothers, sisters, or cousins, but walked to the kitchen walls. "Just painted?" he said. "Very nice. Just like cream."

"No," my father said. "It's not new paint."

Uncle Arturo lapsed into silent smiles that came and fell in little spasms. My mother told us to sit down to lunch, and while we ate, Uncle Arturo told us about Miami, where a new world was rising.

"Just like *Itlee*," he said. "Working in bare sleeves. Kissed by the sun."

While we were eating apples, Lena signalled to her boys, and they left. My father told me to go, but I went as far as my station on the staircase.

"Well, let's talk straight," I heard my father say with his heavy Calabrian tone. "What is going on now, Arturo? I must know for myself, and my sister here."

I looked over the banister and saw Lena's dishevelled head behind my father's tightly-brushed black hair.

Across from them, with two empty chairs beside him, Uncle Arturo smiled. He looked at the walls, then took his wallet out. It was light tan and new, with gold pieces, initials, glued to the leather.

He hummed a song as he removed money from the wallet and placed it on the tablecloth. The green bills made a mound thicker than the wallet.

Lena stared at it. My father tried to avoid looking directly at it. Arturo pushed it gently towards them. "Here," he said. "It's for Lena. I don't want this."

"Arturo!" My father looked at him now. "Don't show me a payoff. I need no proof. What is it you will do now?"

"Do? Do what I do. I do what I do, Uncle Lou. That's me. I help out."

"Help out yourself," my father said. "That's what I ask you."

"Look, here's an empty wallet," Arturo said. "It's all right, now."

A small, white envelope fell to the floor from a pocket in the wallet. As Arturo picked it up, Lena began to moan.

"It's only hair," he said. "See." He took a lock of silky infant's hair from the envelope. "That was *me*. I was a blondie. That's *my* hair."

"Were you born here?" My father asked this as Arturo fingered the curled lock of hair.

"On the other side, Uncle Lou. *Mare chiare.* That's me. The sunny boy from Naples." Suddenly, he slipped the envelope into his wallet and the wallet sat folded on the table. My father and Lena stared at it as he tapped it with his fingers.

"A blondie boy," he said. "I came over with my mother when I was four. She was only a girl."

The words made silence. My father looked with a hard stare that was often confused as anger; by now I knew it was embarrassment.

"She's in heaven with the saints," Arturo said. "She left me alone. I was fourteen. I had no relations. I got a room on 103$^{rd}$, right down the block. The only thing I had, I had her wool shawl. Years I had it."

"Don't you want a nice family now?" my father said in a soft voice.

"Uncle Lou, I'm like every man. I want peace."

"I advise you, the best peace," my father said. "Take your family for good."

"Yea, thanks a lot, Uncle Lou." I thought Arturo was angry now, ready to start a fight. "But lookey here," he said, and took out the envelope again. "You once was this clean blondie and then you go to dried straw, to a bald head. That's the truth, Uncle Lou."

"We all grow old," my father said impatiently. "You're a nice young man. With a good presence. You're strong."

"Sure I am," he said. "Tell Lena."

My father turned to her, but she did not speak. He reached for the bottle of vermouth. "All right," he said. "Now you can go home and be good children."

Arturo stood up. I backed behind the banister. "What is it?" my father said.

"I'm going like you told me," Arturo said.

"I mean when you go. That was joking." My father shook the bottle. "Sit down. Take a drink."

"Thanks, Uncle Lou. Thanks very much."

After the silence of the drink, I heard my father again, speaking quietly. "You want my best advice, Arturo. Stay where people love you. You're wanted."

"Don't worry," Arturo said. "No more Florida. That's a dream ended."

As my father began to answer, Arturo stood up again and walked quickly along the hall. Lena began to moan. "Where do you go?" my father called, then came after him. They stopped just below me.

"Oh, that's all right, Uncle Lou," he said. "Lena can come later. I'll just go back a little early."

"Brother!" Lena shouted from the kitchen.

I saw Arturo's face below me. He had stopped in a smile, but it was not one that made you smile; instead, it helped you to notice his eyes— light, green, flat, with a stare of glass.

My father looked up at him, then back at Lena, whose head was on the table.

"Uncle Lou, it is all right," Arturo said. "I'll just stretch the legs a little. Get some cigars for us, digest."

My father was still speechless. He turned away from Lena to stare at Arturo's strange face. He stared hard, until his stony Calabrian domination rose to conquer the joyless smile and invisible eyes. Arturo's smile broadened; my father grasped his belt. "Have your cigars here," he said. "Go in the kitchen."

Arturo did not move. My father's thick face turned red. "You get in! You go home tonight! And you stay from now on. Or answer to my strap. Can you hear? *Cretino!* Can you hear?"

Arturo walked to the kitchen and sat down next to Lena. She looked angrily at my father, who followed. "Make some coffee," he said to my mother, then turned to Lena, ignoring her expression. "Monday, you get him down in my office for work. *Capito?*"

Lena nodded and looked at Arturo. "Thanks, Uncle Lou," he said. "I knew you would help out."

They called the boys; my mother packed their clothes, with fruits and candies in the bundle. After they left, I stood on the porch alone. My father listened to some radio music, but the house was quiet; it had forgotten them.

I stared along Lorin Place; there were walkers, but no strangers to help my dreams of afternoon, only neighbors, bundled up and hurrying to their homes. Many of them waved to me as they passed the house.

# Winds

The bell rang and Uncle Vinnie appeared at the door, opening it for himself. But then he hesitated, like a windblown object that suddenly stops in its blowing along the street as it is caught by some invisible confluence of winds.

Mr. Mauro's *come, come* brought him down the long hall to the kitchen. Vinnie placed a gallon of homemade wine on the table; it shook the table.

As Mr. and Mrs. Mauro protested the kindness, John recalled, in the still-shaking table, his childhood fear of Uncle Vinnie.

Vinnie was the tallest man John had ever seen, unusually tall among the Neapolitans. All his movements were thick and powerful, and his high-held head contained a glass eye. Whether it was glass or damaged in some way, John never knew. His parents did not like to talk about it because Ida, fanatic and crazy though she was, did say that it could give the evil eye, which the older Mauros believed in enough to avoid the subject.

"We will be inside," Mr. Mauro said to his wife, daughter, and son. "John, when do you leave?"

"I don't know. After a while."

"Stay, John. Wait for my Frankie," Vinnie said. "He is coming to pick me up." John agreed.

Reni filled the silver guest tray with bottles of liqueur. "Johnny, take it in, will you," she said.

John knocked at the parlor door, set the tray down on the coffee table as his father stared impatiently, and went silently to the door.

"Johnny!" Uncle Vinnie called anxiously. John turned to him. "How many years have you now?" Vinnie asked.

"Twenty-seven." Mr. Mauro answered for his son.

"I thought so. Fine *giovanotto.* Same age as my Tony. Tony is in Italy twenty-five years."

"Too long to know what goes on here," Mr. Mauro said.

John saw his father's face again, and excused himself. He had been staring, the moments before, at Vinnie's eye, the color of iron, the unclosing lid jutting above it. Once noticed, it drew the attention that facial imperfections do.

In the kitchen, Reni was sniffing at the wine Vinnie had brought. "Yes, it is, I'm sure," she told her mother.

"Tell me what's going on," John said.

"This here's Liborio's wine," his sister said. "You remember him? He eats cherries, pits and all. From Arthur Avenue. This here proves the uncle came from Arthur, not Westchester."

"John, you don't know anymore. You never come around." Mrs. Mauro was accusing her son of local sin: he was not current with the aural history of the family, and it meant that he did not care. By forgetting the fate of sisters and uncles and cousins, he was showing his preference for the world beyond Lorin Place.

"Look, it's like this," Reni said to him, and spread her hands on the tablecloth. "The uncle wants to get married again. He found a wife in Calabria, through some service, a nice woman, they say. Well, the son in Italy, Tony, he wrote a terrible letter. All about the disgrace to Aunt Maria's memory and how could the uncle live with another woman in the same bed, and all that."

"And what about son Frankie, the big executive?" John smiled, but Reni and his mother were caught in seriousness; it was real.

"Frankie yelled all over the place. He wants to go to Italy and shoot Tony with a gun. But he's mad because the uncle won't live now in the big house in New Rochelle." Reni lowered her voice. "We kept hearing the uncle's living down the old neighborhood. This wine proves it."

The bell rang. Reni stood up and ran to the door. Mrs. Mauro came to John's chair. "*Now,*" she said, "they say your father must decide. Then watch the trouble come to *him*."

Frank swept into the kitchen, bowing and greeting. He went first to Mrs. Mauro and kissed her cheek. "Aunt Rose, we still giving you bother. Uncle Lou's a saint."

Mrs. Mauro nodded, and Frank brushed his hands against his silk suit that was woven to look like tweed. Then he leaned back against the sink and tilted his bright grey fedora to the back of his head. He kept his hat on in the house: it was a clothing industry habit, and he had been dubbed The Rabbi by Aunt Ida many years before.

John looked at the gallon of wine. "Frank, *do* you keep the old apartment on Arthur?"

"Sure, sure, it's Pop." Frank's hands pressed the sink. "He lives with his dreams. And I made a whole wing on the house for him and Mom, may she rest in peace."

Mrs. Mauro crossed herself, and Frank looked towards the parlor.

"Aunt Rose, I had a hope. I bought that house. I said, some day they retire here. Take trips. Their own car. Florida, anyplace. You *know* what I mean, Aunt Rose?"

"You're a good son, Frankie." Mrs. Mauro pointed a hand towards the parlor. "Now help your father with this."

Frank pressed his hands against his chest. "What did I say? *What?* I said, Poppa, my father, do what you want. And use this house. Go to Florida. Go to *Itlee!*"

Frank watched Mrs. Mauro nod and imitated her. "Yes, yes," he said slowly, "I don't even want him to work. But every day he comes to the place. All right, he's got to keep busy. But Aunt *Rose,* he sits down and he goes to work on a *machine.* Like an *operator!* He likes to do *buttonholes!*"

Frank's hands were shaking before his eyes. "The boss's *father!*" His shouts were high, uncontrolled, an unmasculine tenor. "I got three floors, I got a volume in thousands. Poppa, Poppa, I says to him, come with me in the office, at least. Or even, he could stay home. I'll keep him on the payroll."

Frank was suddenly aware of the silence he had caused, and he stopped. His indiscretion made him bite his underlip. He brought his fedora back into place. "Tell my father I'm going over Lou Branca's, and I'll pick him up in an hour."

John escorted him to the door. Frank patted John's shoulder when they were at the stoop. "*You* know what I mean, don't you, Johnny. The old people, they can't help feeling small time; it's right in their bones. They like the *smell* of the Bronx."

"Perhaps it's change," John said. "The first one, the big change, was too much. And a part of them is in Italy, still."

"And they don't like whatever we do, anything with a little class. Everything we do, it's dirty diapers. Right? And don't tell me *Itlee*. I don't want to hear that fucking word. *Itlee*."

He shut the door abruptly, and John walked back. The table had been cleared, and the crumbs brushed from the linen tablecloth, but because a guest was in the house, the cloth was not removed.

Mrs. Mauro began to wash the dishes; Reni cleaned the large coffee pot and boiled water. Slowly she dropped spoonfuls of ground coffee into the center of the pot. The Elevated train sounds were still muffled in the enclosed house, but the winds along the alley grew louder, a sign of spring. The winds shouted against the walls of the Bronx, shouting against the warmth inside, the noisy whistling of unforgetting seasons.

John read the evening paper while the women worked. His mother finished, sat down and took out her rosary. Reni watched the pot as it dripped; when the pot began to ooze about its center, she placed a flat dish under it.

"Well, what do *you* think, John?" Reni asked, and Mrs. Mauro stopped praying.

"It sounds like everybody's right," John said. "They all have a point."

His mother shook her hands with disgust for those who weigh morality like butter. "Ask the Virgin Mary," John said to her, and pointed to her beads.

She shook her head and spoke the word *sin* in Italian, as though marking a score. "*Peccato, peccato, peccato.*"

The doorbell rang and the outer door opened wide. Frank's voice called, and he walked in.

"*You* need coffee," Reni said as she watched Frank wavering.

"Maybe I better," he said, and sat down. "Lou Branca's a guy, he makes you *drink*."

"We know *him*." Reni placed the cup before him and filled it. "Nice and hot, nice and hot," Frank said. He held the cup with both hands to keep it steady. "Poppa should see this."

"Frank, they're still in there," John said.

"Yeah, yeah, the big boys. The kings, the two kings. And that other king on the other side. Tony. Oh, he's very mad on us. He's disgraced by us. We get no respect from him no more. That's the way they all are, all them big kings. They send orders and they're miserable all the time. Tony writes the old man he lost his honor, and me he writes I forgot Momma's memory, and I don't respect Poppa if I let him do it. If *I* let him do it. I got four hundred people working for me and my father's got to run a machine to make him happy. But Tony, he don't forget the P. S., please send a little money order. He respects that."

He looked at the three of them; his lips were wet, and he kept the cup near his lips as he spoke.

"Here we forget. We too far from *Itlee*. We need their lectures on how to live right. But they're saints. In rags! In rags! What do they think I did, build the place from a little attic on Houston Street with three machines—now with a gross over a million—and I don't know nothing about life. Aunt Rose, I laugh."

Frank drank the remaining coffee and settled the cup on the saucer. "What'd I do," he said suddenly. "Yes. Now I left the lights on in my car. I'll be right back." He stood up, swayed for a moment, then walked down the hall.

Reni began to speak, but Mr. Mauro and Uncle Vinnie came into the kitchen. "In three months, Vinnie goes to Italy," Mr. Mauro said, and the others stood up to shake his hand.

Uncle Vinnie was rocking on his heels, but smiling. He shook hands; then he passed his hands across his eyes and sat down. Mr. Mauro poured a glass of wine for him. He held it in his right hand, then drank it down quickly.

"Where's my Frankie?" he said.

"He went to his car a minute." Reni said.

"Now he will say I must build a new house."

Vinnie smiled again.

The doorbell rang once, and Frank came in. "Frankie," his father called. "*Finalmente!* I made up my mind."

"Whatever Uncle Lou says," Frank said.

"He will get married," Mr. Mauro said.

"You know what I said, Pa. I'm ready to buy the tickets. Both ways. I'll get you a wardrobe. I'll ship a car; see all the places; take Tony for a ride. Let him be a big shot. But you know what I think for this marriage?"

"What is it, Frankie?" His father understood something the others did not.

"It's a mistake, that's what it is." Frank pressed his hands against the sink. "An old man doesn't get married! Start the wedding bells? What you going to do, open up a new place on Houston Street? Start a whole life again? Have some more kids to take over the new business? What do you *want?*"

"To have a good woman," Mr. Mauro said. "Company your own age. A man, he wants to be remembered at home. Somebody is home for *him.*"

"I'll give him everything, everything!" Frank covered his mouth: the shout had startled him, too. "Look, let him marry who the hell he wants, Uncle Lou. But *you* ask him to stay out of the place. I'll send him payroll every week. I'll take care of everything."

"Frankie, I like the place," his father said.

"But you got to get packed. You got to buy tickets, clothes; you got to find *wedding* presents."

"I can take care after work," Uncle Vinnie said.

"You see that, Uncle Lou. I did that just to show you. He's coming *in.* The workers, now they'll say, what does he do, make his father work 'til the last day, the slave owner. Is that sense, Uncle Lou?"

Mr. Mauro shrugged; he was caught between.

"Come on, Frankie. Let's go home. We talk again. Now, let's go home."

Frank's rage went out of focus; he let his head go down, allowing Lou Branca's wine to loosen him again.

Mr. Mauro escorted the two men to the door. Mrs. Mauro, Reni, and John listened from the kitchen. Frank's voice rose and fell; his body leaned against Mr. Mauro's. "Uncle Lou, *make* him stay home," he said again

*75*

and again. "Make him *rest, rest.*"

Uncle Vinnie called to the others, and they came to the door to say a correct goodnight, as though in their good-byes none of this had ever happened. The ceremony ended, and Frank led his father out to dimly lit Lorin Place. The winds were still blowing.

Mr. Mauro shut the porch door and stood beside his family. Frank started the engine; the black hood shook; in its shining it reflected red and blue points of light from the Elevated track signals.

Uncle Vinnie took his large linen handkerchief from his pocket. It puffed out in the darkness like a white flower. He dabbed at his eyes as the car carried him away.

# Graduation

Something had happened to the river, perhaps when the city had taken it for sewage. The green banks had worn down and been washed away to wherever it was the river went, away like the nineteenth century Miss Rafferty told them about. No boats with striped umbrellas went by carrying the Dutch: only the waste of the people in the new apartment houses floated on the slow tide.

John looked back once at the school on the hill. The building seemed to be moving while the moving clouds stood still. He was dizzy again and his face and ears felt hot. It was like the feeling in class when Miss Rafferty announced his name with Ferdinand's, and the class clapped.

He ran for home, to leave his books and tell his mother about the library.

"What is it?" she said as he ran into the kitchen. "No kiss?"

"Me and Ferdinand have to go to the library."

"Oh no," his mother said, and ran to block the kitchen doorway. "No *viaggiando!*"

The library was beyond the two blocks of Lorin Place, and Mrs. Mauro could not see it from her vantage at the front porch.

"It's important!" John shouted. "It's for graduation. We were picked to do the tapestries. It's honor!"

Mrs. Mauro came back to the table and looked down at her son's hair. "What is it? *Che cosa fai?*" She said softly.

"Me and Ferdinand were voted the best drawers. The 8B's are doing

77

history of the North Bronx. We get to copy the tapestries. Did you know the Dutch people on Gun Hill Road?"

Mrs. Mauro touched John's hair. "Then eat something," she said. "Take my jelly. I got your American bread."

She shook her head as she handled the soft bread, but still she smiled. John's distinction had cancelled her hatred of the absorbent cotton, as she called the bread.

He ate his jelly and bread and left.

That was all Mrs. Mauro heard until graduation morning when her oldest son, Victor, drove her and her husband to the auditorium in the Buick.

She smiled during the entertainment although she understood few of the words. Most of the Italian parents did not understand, but the sixth and seventh grades performed skits (Tom Sawyer painting the fence, Huck and Jim on the raft, Grace Drew at the state fair).

When the eighth-grade pageant on the North Bronx settlers ended, Miss Rafferty announced John and Ferdinand, who walked up the aisle holding their pictures.

Vic waited at the gate after the ceremony. "Come on, artist," he said, and led John to the Buick.

"You kept this secret from me," Mr. Mauro said to John from the back seat. "Two can play with this."

Mrs. Mauro laughed to show John that the words were a joke. Vic drove them back to Lorin Place, to the kitchen where Reni and Edith were preparing lunch, trying to act as nervous and busy as Mrs. Mauro. She had given her daughters charge of the preparations for this day, one day.

"How do you like this kid," Victor said as he walked in. He was leading, holding the tapestry aloft. He smiled at Aunt Ida, who had come from Astoria, and was seated between her two daughters, Grace and Stella.

"This kid did this," Victor continued, slapping the picture. "What do you say, Uncle?" (Uncle Paul, the lawyer, was Mrs. Mauro's brother.)

"That's a nice picture," Uncle Paul said. "Is that some of your art work, Johnny?"

John stood at the end of the long table, facing everyone. "It's a copy of a Dutch tapestry. That was here in the Bronx. Our class—"

But Mr. and Mrs. Mauro were too anxious to speak, to recreate the scene of honor. Mrs. Mauro began abruptly—only two boys, the other an American boy, she explained, out of the whole class—that was the crux of the honor. And John the best.

"*La storia,*" Mrs. Mauro concluded, "*la storia del* Bronx."

"In the nineteenth century," John began, "the Dutch settlers had a tapestry plant down near Gun Hill Road. There were Dutch and French—"

Mr. Mauro placed his hands on John's shoulders. John stopped. He knew it was time for the gift because his father could never wait until the meal was over.

He took the small package. By the size of it, he knew it would be a pen. *To the graduate,* the card read, *auguri e bacioni.* John knew that the card had been written by his father because of the word *bacioni,* which his mother once said was a dialect word of Calabrians, who were all mountain farmers. She was from Naples.

"Write with it," Mr. Mauro said. "It has ink."

"Not now, Pa," Edith said, "I'm setting the table."

But her father persisted and got a sheet of his office stationery from the living room desk. John drew a few lines.

"Press. Press as hard as you wish," his father said.

"Go ahead," Victor said, smiling with the secret.

John pressed harder and drew thicker lines. The pen cut into the paper resting on the linen tablecloth.

"Press, press anyway," his father said.

Aunt Ida, who had been slicing provolone and was eating a good deal of it, began to giggle. She enjoyed watching uncomfortable moments. The older members of the family enjoyed her uncontrollable laughter and her crooked front teeth, which seemed to shake in her mouth as she laughed, but Grace and Stella never reacted. They were very silent girls, who went along on all the visits, but never laughed.

"It's a special point," Victor explained, turning to the table-sitters. "It never separates, no matter how hard you press."

Aunt Ida nodded, but her teeth still showed.

79

*

Mrs. Mauro grasped the tapestry and held it aloft once more. She showed it to Aunt Ida. When Aunt Ida reached a cheese-stained hand for it, Mrs. Mauro drew it away.

"A toast!" Uncle Paul shouted, and laughed. Mr. Mauro rushed inside for the vermouth and the special glasses.

"Sit down," Uncle Paul said quietly to John. He put his hand over John's and whispered to him, "Say to yourself, they all love me, they love me. Five hundred times."

"What is this?" Mrs. Mauro caught her brother. John was smiling.

"Corruption! *Filosofia!*" Paul shouted and laughed at her. *Filosofia* was the modern sin, and Mrs. Mauro knew this. Everyone knew that handsome Paul read the anarchist paper that was sent from Sicily, and never went to church.

Her husband rushed in with the yellow vermouth and began filling the shining triangular glasses. Reni helped him serve. "To the artist, to the artist," he said, and clicked his glass with John's. "Everyone touch for *buona fortuna,*" he said.

His wife still stared at Paul. Mr. Mauro sat at his seat, giving the signal for the meal to begin.

When the coffee came, John asked if he might go, but his mother looked at him sadly. The bell rang before she could speak. It was Mr. and Mrs. Mimmo, from next door.

"*Ben venuto!*" Mr. Mimmo shouted and stamped his foot, "Aha!" Mr. Mauro answered, and motioned entrance. Mr. Mimmo used the phrase "*benvenuto*"—"welcome" or "happy that you have arrived"—for all high occasions. It was an echo of himself, of his own good coming to the Bronx and a house of his own after ten years in the downtown tenements.

His wife, just behind him, was a waddling record of his growing success. Each year Mrs. Mimmo was pinned or braceleted or ringed with another decoration. Her silk print dresses held ruby and diamond pins, her fingers groups of rings, her bulging wrists bracelets bought when the wrists were lighter.

Mr. Mauro stood up as they walked toward him. He exclaimed in surprise and delight at Mr. Mimmo's gift.

"This wine," he said to John, "is for your day. Kiss Signor Mimmo."

John obeyed and then, without being told, went to Mrs. Mimmo. "*Carino,*" she said, and rubbed his cheeks with her hands.

"Look," Mrs. Mauro said, holding up the tapestry. "This was made by Johnny. Chosen *specialmente* to do this."

Mrs. Mimmo rubbed John's cheeks some more, giving them occasional pinches. "Nice work," her husband said for her. "We have an *artista.*"

"*Carino, carino,*" Mrs. Mimmo cooed again, and stroked John. Then she remembered something. "Now maybe the Irish will not talk so much of wop and guinea."

Her hands stopped on John's cheeks. All the adults turned toward the window. Beyond the garden stood the gray wall of Foley's house. Foley was the last Irishman in the neighborhood; he had not sold his house and moved to Mount Vernon as the others had on the swollen sums they charged the advancing Italians. Foley had been left to mock.

Mrs. Mimmo held the tapestry before the window. "*Bella, bella,*" she said. Then to the window facing Foley, in Italian, "Blind yourself on this. Blind yourself."

The table grumbled in accord, all except Paul. Mrs. Mimmo turned back and began to praise the tapestry for all to hear. Aunt Ida became uncomfortable—not sure now that all this praise did not deprecate the position of her daughters, who tap-danced very well.

"You tell us something about the picture, Johnny," Paul said. "Go ahead."

Everyone smiled. "The picture?" John said. "It represents a tapestry of the early Dutch settlers who lived near Gun Hill Road on the Bronx River. They had—"

"Ah, you know your history," Mr. Mimmo said. "Remember, Giovanni, the history is the most important. The study of great men. What is the story here in this picture? Is this a great battle?"

"It represents the French knight Roland, defeating the infidels. It was executed in 1840."

"Here I must stop you," Mr. Mimmo said, and smiled to Mr. Mauro, who nodded respectfully. Aunt Ida looked up hopefully, and Victor clenched his fists.

"This is Orlando," Mr. Mimmo said to all. "A great *Italian* knight. Orlando. Orlando Furioso, Orlando who captured the *Morgante*. One thing I know. Orlando is Italian knight."

"But this is Roland," John said. "The book says that. My friend and me studied it at the library."

"Tell your friend and tell your teachers," Mr. Mimmo said, looking at Uncle Paul, "this is Orlando, who fought with his back to the cliff the army of the Saracen. In Calabria. The home of your father and me."

Mr. Mauro nodded.

John looked toward his mother. "Maybe this is American word," she said pleasantly. "The story is changed for American words."

"Then the story is wrong. The teacher is wrong. America is wrong," Mr. Mimmo said. "Orlando is Orlando. The true name does not change."

He nodded to Mr. Mauro, who joined him in an angry stare. They were thinking of Dr. Russo, who was now legally Dr. Rust.

\*

John had edged his way to the kitchen door and was making faces at the adults. Uncle Paul caught him and smiled. "Five hundred times, John. Remember. I love their hard Calabrian heads."

*"Paolo,"* Mrs. Mauro said, and Paul was quiet. She was sure that Calabrians were unable to tolerate levity at such moments, though she understood her brother.

Mr. Mimmo continued, turning back to John. "Tell your teachers that the names of great men you cannot change. Italian names you can say more simple than American. Orlando. Or-lan-do. Say that."

John did not speak. Mr. Mimmo went on. He doubted that there were ever tapestry-makers in the Bronx. Where had they gone? Where were the excavations? Being in the construction business, he could identify even the oldest ruins.

"Is Jenny coming?" John asked suddenly, and Mr. Mimmo stopped.

"In the backyard," Mrs. Mimmo anwered, and her face seemed struck by some harsh force. She looked at her husband, but he had turned his face to the floor, his lips touched by some sourness.

"Maybe she comes later," Mrs. Mimmo said. Her husband's lips, twisting but unsuccessful, were trying to expel the taste.

John left the silence of the room. At the end of the hall, his mother's voice called out, "Don't take off the suit. Padre Grasso is coming."

He continued up the steps. In the darkness of the upper landing he looked down and made his faces, with his tongue out. Then he backed into his room.

A sketch pad lay open on his desk catching some afternoon light allowed through the alley between the walls of the Mauro and Mimmo houses.

He drew a knight, but had trouble doing the feet. On the tapestry he had covered the feet with the big stirrups of the knight's horse.

A voice called in the alley. "Johnnay, Johnnay!" John opened the window and looked down at Jenny Mimmo. "My mother, father there?" she said.

"What do you think? They're downstairs," he said.

"Don't you get no cake? You locked in for graduation?"

"No. I just came up a minute. To rest."

"I heard you made a masterpiss," Jenny said. "Where's your masterpiss?"

"Shut it," John said, "they'll hear you."

Jenny leaned against the sandy red shingles of her house. "My neck hurts looking up. Go make another masterpiss. I'll see you later."

John took a gum eraser from the desk top and broke off pieces, which he dropped on Jenny. She did not move as the chips struck her curly black hair. She stood smiling, her eyes squinting at the opposite wall.

"Master Piss!" she shouted, "Master Piss!"

John shut the window; his mother's voice was calling. He went out to the landing. The quiet voices in the silence meant that Father Grasso had come.

He saw Mrs. Mimmo first as he entered the parlor. She was holding her hands carefully on her lap and sitting erect in her chair. Next to her, Mr. Mimmo looked a little worn, his dry complexion dusty, as though plaster had been falling on him from somewhere. Uncle Paul and Aunt Ida were not there.

"Get the picture," his mother said after he had greeted Father Grasso. "In the kitchen."

John brought it in, holding the tips of the upper edges as Miss Rafferty had shown him.

"Ver' nice," Padre Grasso said. "Such good colors." He smiled toward Mrs. Mauro, then Mr. Mauro.

"*La storia del* Bronx," Mrs. Mauro told the father, and took the picture from John.

"It shows Orlando Furioso," Mr. Mimmo said quietly.

"*Una tapestria,*" Mrs. Mauro said, passing the picture to Padre Grasso.

"Aha!" Padre Grasso was pleased, and showed his hands in a mimicry of a blessing.

"Nice. Defender of the faith. I did not think they allow in public school, which is *Protestante.*"

"My friend Ferdinand is Lutheran," John said in the strange silence. "He goes to Redeemer Lutheran, on Barnes Avenue."

Padre Grasso gave him a smile for children, unreal. If they were going to inherit the earth here, it would be without a knowledge of Italian but with an excellent memory of the addresses of Protestant churches.

" 'Ave you seen inside this church?" Padre Grasso asked.

"No, Father," John said, and lowered his head.

"Come, come," Padre Grasso said, "tell me of this picture. What is the tapestry?"

Mrs. Mauro reached for John, to restrain him. But her girdle held her down in the soft armchair. "It is the *epoca* of Orlando Furioso," she said to Padre Grasso. "He was chosen, the only one to make this."

"Ver' nice," Padre Grasso said. "You must get a nice frame. Put it up." He pointed to the bare blue wall.

"It's not that good," John said. "It's just a crayon sketch. I did an oil painting of the old men playing *boccie.*"

"What old men!" Mrs. Mauro said. She reached out her arms again. "Yes. A *gold* frame."

"You must hang the picture, Giovanni," Padre Grasso said, looking into John's face. "Your mother and father are proud."

"Father, do you know about the early Dutch settlers—"

Protestants again. Padre Grasso covered his pain with a smile. Mrs. Mauro thrust her head up. "What Dutch, Dutch? This is Orlando. Orlando!" Mr. Mimmo laughed to his wife.

*

Padre Grasso watched John back his way to the hassock at the end of the room. John sat down and lowered his head again.

"Ah, *bambini, bambini d'America,*" the Father said. "How they drink this America. How they forget the voice. Mother. Father." He held up his right hand, three fingers up, two down, as in the Mass. "The voice of the mother, the blessed mother."

Edith came in with the silver tray. Padre Grasso stopped to watch the row of demitasse cups surrounding the bottles of liqueur and dishes of pine nut macaroons.

"*Bella,*" he said.

"And this," Mrs. Mauro said, taking up the bottle of her own tangerine cordial.

"*La vera qualitá,*" he said.

Everyone smiled. Reni served Padre Grasso first, then the others. He ate and drank rapidly, then stood up.

"Pleasure must sit while duty rides," he said with a sigh, and everyone nodded, knowing of the many calls he had to make. His visits were now briefer than Dr. Russo's.

He was escorted to the gate by John. Everyone watched and waved as the black limousine drove away. Mrs. Mauro permitted John a few minutes outside, but only in the backyard while he had his suit on. John went back to look for Jenny.

He found her at the rain-stained picnic table, which was partly covered with shingles and cement sacks.

"Hey, come here, Master," Jenny said. A checkerboard was before her on the table speckled by the light through the grape leaves above.

"Who you playing with?" John asked.

"I'm not playing yet. I just got it here in case they call me. I tell them I'm playing. What'd Father Grasso say?"

"He said hello and good-bye. What could he say?"

"Did he say prayers? Did he have the robe on?"

"No, no. He drank vermouth and talked to my mother and father," John said. "And your mother and father. They all said my tapestry was Italian."

"He drank *vermouth!* That's a sin, isn't it? A priest can't drink vermouth. He has to confess now." Jenny moved the palms of her hands over the checkers, sliding them back and forth on the board. She looked up at her kitchen windows, but they were closed.

"Did he eat?" Jenny asked.

"He ate. Sure. He ate pastries."

Jenny looked back at the windows again. In turning around her long black curls swept across her face; some of the eraser chips were still stuck there.

"Do you stay in your room a lot?" Jenny asked.

"Not so much," John said.

"My mother and father's room's next to mine." She began to whisper. "But you know what I do. I say spaghetti gives me upset stomach. And when I talk Italian I say it hurts my tongue."

John looked at Jenny. Jenny put her tongue out, between her teeth, and made childish sounds. John began to laugh.

"Shut it," she said. "They'll hear. They'll hear."

But no one heard.

# On the Mountain

Our main street, which we called The Avenue, was lined with two-story red-brick buildings containing rows of stores on the street floor. Upstairs were offices, hidden if you did not know they were there. You started from a small door on the ground floor by ringing a bell, opening the door at the buzzer, climbing the dark staircase. Downstairs was all the energy, people out front buying foods at the outdoor stands.

When you were on the second floor you could look from the office windows and feel very close to the Elevated trains (Third Avenue El and Lexington Avenue subway) rushing by on their way to downtown Manhattan. All of us in the neighborhood grew up with that noise, proud of its power and frequency, thinking of it as our time's engineering marvel.

And that it existed in our neighborhood, where we lived, was a sign of our superiority to the Old World (as well as other neighborhoods). The Old World had Kings and Dukes, we were told, who still used carriages and horses and made people bow down and owned all the land and paid the workers in vegetables. Some of my friends resented kneeling down in church, during Mass, saying *mea culpa* when it was somebody else who did the bad stuff.

But we had our great city train that zipped you to Times Square, our unique pride until we started straggling back from our war to discover an infernal grinding noise that never stopped and brought back my war allergy—machines grinding, crashing, blowing up.

And it was a kind of noise to move away from now. It no longer denoted classy progress. It made the neighborhood embarrassing as more and more of us went to silent suburbs and the sounds of birds. In a few years the neighborhood was a place where the unlucky had to live. Escape from starvation was also getting away from big industrial, lower-class noise.

And while we were dozing before my war; my favorite uncle, Paul, had one of those upstairs offices along The Avenue. His door sign read Law Office in American and Italian. Paul worked with everyone, but specialized in what he called "my own people," and built up a solid practice. He was known as honest, generous, more like a special kind of priest, and he never charged people who couldn't pay.

The morning it started I was awakened by the kind of raucous, scratchy voices that signaled one of the fixers or local *padrones* of the neighborhood world. It was rare for us to get such a visit because my father made what was called good money and didn't need such consultation.

I thought we Italians had a monopoly on the silent loathing of those fixers who made politics work by trying to manipulate the bigger power people (none from our neighborhood yet). My father and my mother's two brothers, Paul and Pasquale, were becoming part of the edges of local politics, feasting on the democracy that permitted them participation.

My father enjoyed leaning on the oilcloth tablecloth at the kitchen table counting and examining votes for petitions for new candidates (us) collected by volunteers like my brothers and sisters, whose reluctance made me question their volunteerism. My sisters never were turned on, but my oldest brother, Vic, gained his first sense of joining the ruling class by doing it each year, knowing more people, winning at last.

Once my father looked up at me watching him count the names and said simply, "In Italy you can't do this."

And there also was my father many years later on a Westchester front porch, sipping his homemade wine, talking with Pasquale and saying to me about New York politics: "We had to leave it because the crooks began to give the orders. Some of that you can't help, but when it becomes everything, City Hall is just another store."

Poppa got his peace in Mount Vernon in his house off Grammatan Avenue three doors from Pasquale and a new Italian deli down the hill run by a *paisano* from Calabria, who managed to import even the packages of small fish in red sauce so peppered that after one burning taste you doubted that swallowing would return to you and which others told me only Calabrians could digest because they had inner tubes of steel and many of their specialties were of the flaming variety.

And too soon after that, my father took a place in Valhalla—that is, the Westchester cemetery town rather than the Norwegian heaven.

It was during my months of teary loss of the old explorers—Pop, the uncles—I kept remembering the night with Uncle Paul, when he said he could not take the air from the top of the mountain and sat in his bed in shock and recognition.

Paul was a volatile Neapolitan and had fewer mechanisms for sloughing off flatterers—not that he couldn't recognize them as fast as my father. He just had no defense against their pretty melodies; he needed steady praise and thanks more than money to feel worthy enough to believe flattery. That night he said he saved a million sinking ships but not his own.

Paul's story started that day of the raucous voices on the front porch. As I came down the steps I saw Tasca smiling over my mother and saying, "*Onore,* Aunt Rose. We need to see Paul right away. The party wants to get him a big honor."

"*Onore.*" My mother repeated the Italian word with a tone that I knew included her suspicion: how much would it cost him for this honor?

Tasca's face composed some stories with the help of his arms and hands: he was talking about OUR rise and where we were headed—the mayor's office, if THEY ever let one of us get the nomination.

That face was a choice example of our political leader type: it should have been saved, mummified, placed in a museum. It was much more important than another second rate Roman copy dug up in places like Calabria because Tasca's face was the story of the thin, olive-skinned, bright, hardworking, hustling immigrant who climbed the ladders on brains, well-focussed anger, and a sense of the exquisite differences of America and Italy and grew comfortable and bulging. Not exactly fat, not quite rich, but bulging, a big, brown statue-face of locked-in rage, sense of power, fear of losing control and finally certainty about his own power within his neighborhood borders.

"We got a chance, Aunt Rose." He used the aunt appellation out of what he called respect but which may have also been a parallel to the famed Aunt Jemima, she who cooks and cleans and cares for and forgives with laughter all the boys and girls.

"For a judgeship. Understand? A judge from our people. Our Paul. This man who helped so many in their need and never took a penny if they had too little, who lives like *Gesu'* and *San Francesco*—he's a saint himself—what better man to judge people with fairness?"

"Very nice," my mother said, who often used the phrase as a diplomatic non sequitur with assorted meanings.

I stayed back in the hallway at the bottom of the steps while Tasca described the plan. Paul would get an appointment for sure, but he needed exposure so more people could see him and hear about him and talk about him. He would join the election campaign and make speeches in the Bronx and other boroughs for the candidates of the party. They would be better described by Paul while he would get the chance to be seen in high moments that would prepare for his own appointment.

Tasca saw me and called. "Johnny. Is that you, Johnny? Johnny? Come out here. Maybe you would come along with Uncle Paul and be his right-hand man?"

"And why had they come here?" I asked him. Well, Paul had not been at his office or his apartment for over a week. It was June. Yes. This was his meditation season. I said to Tasca, "I think I know where he must be. Up in the Catskills. A town called Amenia. He goes up to think about things and walk."

"And *think*. You see that," Tasca said. "What a man. Is this not the mind of a judge?"

It was also nice for me to be filled with illusions of strength and approval. Paul was my favorite person. And Tasca was a man who could make you feel your increased sense of power had permanence. He was a natural big shot—or he was *our* big shot. And he did go to Washington for meetings with the senators. He would get elected to something big any day.

Now I am in the office with Uncle Paul. All has been divulged to him. Paul sits at his desk. His full head of gray hair and warm brown eyes do give him the saintly look Tasca seeks.

"I don't know, Johnny," Paul says to me. He has pushed his chair back, and his legs, raised, touch the desk. "Do I want to go with them? I mean, they're all right. I mean, they could be worse. They did start out as good local men fighting for their community, fighting for a voice, *their* voice, to be heard and help wipe out the dirty dumb guinea pictures and lies."

A new word for me: *community.* I still knew only *neighborhood.* It was my innocent teens. "What's wrong with being a judge?" I asked.

"I don't know if I believe them. So I say 'Yes. I'll go to work for them, and we get some people elected.' But then they tell me, good job, but not enough majority to make the power to get the appointment for us. *Us* they'll say."

"But don't you always take a chance in politics?" I said. "One side wins or the other side wins? Right?"

"Yes, I know. But I am also thinking what I was and what I thought I was and what I have become by now. What ideas did I have? Good old Socialism: at least it made my dreams; it had Heart, you know what I mean? Or we thought so. Now they use it like a curse word. The Democrats have the private code—they say come over here, we got the good stuff saved from the Socialist idea and none of the bad stuff they have over there, with Russia top of the list. But I saw a little history myself, Johnny. I saw the Anarchists turned into devils and shipped out on boats and also killed right here. Especially the Italian ones—they were all pacifists— you know what that means: they preached some cloudy revolution and refused to join the army in the First World War—at the same time. So they wouldn't touch violence: then violence destroyed them. The good guys are using the violence as much as the bad a long time now. The violence is the power we will grow more over Europe. To be a little stronger than all the rest of them put together. Understand? *Gabeesh?* Then we can kill any *stronzo* with a European idea. Is this the time to join?"

Paul could not decide what to say, though two months later the cool weather announced it was campaign speech time. Paul went out with Tasca to what they called "functions" and shook many hands. I would go to his office frequently to hear the latest and some of the time join him at a social hall for a meeting. I did this more and more as I saw many neighborhood people along, many who came to be near him, touch his arm, shake his hand, the way we Catholics touch saints.

Paul finally told me he would do a few talks. He scheduled the first for Columbus Day—very ethnically correct, though a new ethnic gang in the University was announcing that Columbus was a Spaniard, and the story of a Genoese navigator was wrong.

A week before the big event, Paul came one night to supper with Tasca and Di Russo, a powerful man of consequence, someone always there, like a supporting actor you've seen in a hundred movies without remembering his name.

They talked on (to my weariness) all night about the "in" things for effectively working the voters. My father was the voice of pure discouragement: nothing makes a political winner but good luck and a warm election night where our people had time to stand and talk and laugh and also vote.

"But what is the opposition these days," Tasca said a little later in the night. "Isn't it the ones who stay away and say that everybody on the ticket is a crooked politician?"

"You mean you're telling me you don't run robots?" Paul said with a joke in his tone.

But Tasca was almost grim, like a father defending his daughters. "Please listen to me. The party is good. With better people today. Better. Consider. Think what's going on. You got more and more of our people going to live in Westchester and making themselves Republicans. No more robots we can have. Is also why I call on you. You are the face of the best in this neighborhood, in this county. And all I am asking you—be Paul. Be just what you are. Don't give big promises. Speak what it is—in your own voice."

Paul rose slowly: he had been sitting a long time. There was a deep curvature in his lower back, something that had happened recently but was permanent in its stiffness and its pain.

Tasca turned away to give a cigar cough. Then he embraced Paul and walked with him to the porch and the view of our night sky. Tasca shook my father's hand, gave my mother a hug, me a pat on the back, looked inside where my sisters had begun doing the dishes. "Give the girls a kiss. We'll take Paul home."

Columbus night. I am the designated guide or translator for Paul. Tasca liked the idea (looks like family: good).

I am waiting on the front porch. At seven thirty, a black Cadillac, with American flags attached to the front fenders, arrives. The driver is Petey Loscalzo of the neighborhood, whose limo-driver expression stays the same for rallies, weddings, funerals.

We pick up Paul at his place and drive through the neighborhood, the once-crowded streets. Paul and Petey are bantering. "Petey, you drive here every day. Tell me, where are all the people?"

"All the people? Ain't you heard, Mr. Di Martino? They all go inside and watch the blue light. Only the blue light excites them now."

"Ah, yes." Paul was in his mocking tone. "To hear and see the great American philosopher."

His silence eventually made Petey ask, "Who is that, again?"

"The great American thinker, Mickey Mouse."

"And it keeps the streets clean," Petey said. "Even the garbage men can stay home and the cops can work fast—anybody they see on the streets got to be a crook, and gets arrested."

We had reached a line of limos and moved very slowly towards the big Parkway Inn full of lights, a wooden elevated speaker's stand built out front in the parking lot. Tasca was there working the crowd already. And it was lines of faces we knew, like a catalogue of our lives.

I got out and saw the platform with flags and bunting. There was a small band at the rear of the platform, and they began to play when someone noticed Paul's car.

Di Russo opened the door and leaned in. "Paul. Listen. Pretty soon he's gonna introduce you. You go up, you say a few words, you thank the people for coming out, you tell them we are here to serve them but we got to get elected first, so go vote. Any way you want to cover these points is just fine."

Di Russo smiled and pulled back just as another band came up the street, this one mostly trumpets and base drums. They played and boomed, then ceased abruptly, and a man—it was Di Russo with a big campaign hat on—stepped up and began talking. His voice went loud and soft, echoed and then became shrill through the P.A. speakers.

But he was getting ready to introduce somebody. It was a congressman who then introduced a senator—both of whom said a few words that included Paul. It worked on this crowd: they were screaming and cheering and jumping up and down.

I was sitting next to Paul, who held the hand support high up near the door and stared at the platform and kept his face averted from me. "Is something the matter?" I finally asked.

Paul rubbed his forehead, then covered his eyes. "I have felt this way before," he said. "More and more. Like very shaky. Like something is coming. Going to happen. Explode."

"Which way do you feel now?" I said.

"Now?" he said. "Hard to breathe. Little dizziness that isn't dizziness. Afraid to move my arms." He stopped and seemed to catch his breath, then spoke again: "Long ago. In Bronx County Courthouse. I met a man just before my case started. I forget the client. The man, though, he was the Tasca of those days. Now he's gone. He laughed at me and called me the Legal Aid for the World and Heaven. And asked me why did I give so much time to the *disgraziati*. Bad enough there're too many of them on the streets already and moving into the rattiest apartments in the neighborhood. And when he went upstairs he said to me, *Good-bye, Saint Francis of Jesus,* and I went right into court. I sat down and broke into a sweat. I couldn't get up, I couldn't turn around. I couldn't move. Even talk."

"Sit back," I said. "Breathe easy. Don't talk just now."

"The judge, God bless him, he caught on," Paul said. "He called a recess. They all went home. I sat there a long time. I couldn't stand up."

"Later, Paul, later."

"If I got up, the roof was coming down. My chest would explode. Then this man who called me Saint Francis, he was passing by again—his office was upstairs—he saw me and took me home."

Another speaker stepped up and began very loud. It was Tasca, shouting and smiling and waving. I watched him move the crowd, get it responding stronger and stronger and stronger with his words that included Paul's

94

name over and over. The crowds were at last ready: Tasca paused and looked around for us. Di Russo pointed down to the limo, and Tasca jumped steps as he came down to the door and pulled it open. "Paul. Come on! Its your time. They are ready. Now do your speech if you want or do a piece of it here and the rest inside later. Or the whole thing here? What you like. I'll introduce you now."

He leaned in to take Paul's arm. "No," Paul said, and drew back against the car seat. I remember the stiff leather making a crinkly noise. I stepped out the other back door and came to Tasca's side. "Something's wrong with him," I said. I waited: I saw the anger: "He's sick in some way," I said.

"He's, what do you mean, sick? Did you say something to him?"

"I told you, something's got him." I was watching Tasca's face as though I could find the words about Paul there. I only knew that Tasca's was a paranoid stare at Paul, which now transferred to me.

Then his face went pensive. He spoke more slowly, enunciating care-fully: "All right, then, we just get him up there. I will introduce. And let him just wave his goddamn arms to the people while he stands up there."

"He can't get out. He can't move." I heard my voice getting loud and stopped.

"Can't get out?" Tasca leaned again into the rear compartment. "Paul!" He started to scream with his own fear now. "Come on, I'll help you. It's only a few feet. Johnny and me. We'll hold you." He touched Paul's hands.

Paul drew back. He stopped talking and pulled his head out of the car turning to me. "Johnny, I will carry him. I will carry him in my arms. Myself."

The bands stopped. Di Russo looked down to ask what was wrong. Tasca looked in at Paul, whose hands now covered his face. Then Tasca slammed the door shut. "I don't know what's been done here." He was holding his rage. "If he wasn't, if he wasn't a poor old f——." Tasca turned and pushed his way up to the platform and climbed the steps fast. I got back into the car next to Paul.

"Friends!" Tasca's voice had some inspiration in it. "Tonight, the best friend our people ever had for voters of the Bronx is here with us. A man who got up out of a sick bed to be here with us. Too sick to walk yet. But his heart is pure courage—as it has been all these years. You know who this is. You have heard of all the people he has helped and protected. You know who this is—the real friend of all the people—Paul Di Martino!"

It caught the crowd. The cheering began, and Tasca smiled. He had learned how to use everything. Last minute adversity like this moment. I saw his glowing smile. Yes! He had learned everything: how to turn bullshit into gold and pave a road to the White House.

In his strange triumph he went to the platform edging fence and pointed down to the limo that contained Paul and Petey Loscalzo. Then he set up a chant: "Paul! Paul! Paul!" Until the crowd took it up and rolled it like drums down the streets.

Waves of watchers began pressing against the car. I watched faces that looked like visitors to a miracle shrine. Paul was the miracle touch tonight—even while he was shaking, a bit sunken, in his panic attack.

People began to shout their names aloud for Paul. I turned to look at him: his right hand methodically rubbed his forehead, and now, at moments, he would pause, raise his head, and wave to the faces.

It was unplanned, but it worked, too. The crowd could not explain the little gray man curled up like a guru. It therefore meant something unknown, which meant holy in some way—they could be helped by it.

But I watched the fear, felt its strength, thought he needed doctors but did not know what kind.

Petey backed the car slowly out against the crowd. We drove out of the lot and along neighborhood streets to my house, where my mother came out and saw me helping Paul move out of the back seat. Petey came round and helped me get him upstairs to the spare room and down on the bed. I looked at Paul turn away, once he was down on the bed, and slowly draw his knees up. My mother was behind me, and I turned to her: "Mom, call the doctor," I said.

The doctor she was able to find was Lou Del Vecchio, a new young internist in the neighborhood and one of the last of the house-call doctors. He saw Paul for a long time and then came downstairs from the bedroom. "His pressure is up. A lot of fear, some tacchicardia. But I think he's OK. Nothing very serious. I'll stop by and see him tomorrow. Let him stay in bed the night and tomorrow till I come."

I went upstairs after the doctor left. Paul was sitting up in bed. "Don't worry," he said. "I feel better."

"The doctor said nothing serious. You're not sick."

"Sick? Am I sick? Maybe sick of me, the man of rags I have to be again. Johnny, you understand? There's some who choose it from inside."

"Don't do that," I said, sensing what he was doing to himself, against himself. And for no reason I could see.

"My soul is old rags. Only old rags for sale inside here," he said. "I made it this way. Myself. You believe that?"

His eyes closed. I looked at the small, strong face, with thin, fine lips and a narrow chin, almost like a woman's delicacy. He resembled my mother. Why did I only just notice it? I was somehow hovering between ages myself and did not know it, did not understand that growth was awareness.

Like the word "community." I had not known and never used: an awareness that didn't exist.

"Was it wrong what I did?" Paul asked into my thoughts, and I was startled, unable to understand if he was talking about the way he felt rather than what he had done or thought he had done.

I said, "Paul, how can a good life be wrong?" I was learning the message we must know for friends and relatives.

"I never hurt no man," Paul said to the air, then looked at the room for the ghost he was apologizing to and then finally me. "Maybe, Johnny, this is my trouble. I saved it all for myself."

"Don't think about it," I said and knew I had reached the fool's level of advice. I had wanted to say something like this: "Don't think and feel what no longer exists except for dreams in your mind."

"I don't think about it now. It is right here. It's whenever I won a case big. It's when they want to push me up. Like being the judge. A judge. No matter what he is, Tasca was serious about that. He wanted me to have it. So I must get sick. I tell you—one breeze from the top of the mountain, and I am shaken down."

He turned his face away, shut his eyes, then reached back with his hands and squeezed mine, keeping his head averted.

I hugged him and then, about to cry, went downstairs to the porch where I saw moving lights flashing through the night sky: the cars of the parade were still moving somewhere under the spots.

I sat and watched until they disappeared, thinking of Paul and slowly of myself. It was the first time I had thought about myself like this. Was there something inside me that could keep controls working but could be preparing itself—so that when the top of the mountain was in sight, I would shut down?

I sat in that darkness until my mother's hand touched the back of my neck. She told me she had brought Paul soup and tea and coffee and suggested it would be best for me to sleep now, rest, prepare for morning, perhaps some cinnamon buns (an American invention we applauded loudly), and creamy cappuccino and the same present as the past had been, and the comfort of the kitchen to make me blind a little longer to my knowing.

# Resting Place

The old priest was asleep in the front seat of the undertaker's limousine, which was parked in front of the church. I was sitting on the jump seat. I turned toward my mother, who was in the back seat beside my sister Reni, to see whether or not she had noticed. Her eyes were looking out beyond the street of shops to where the dim outlines of Long Island Sound could be seen behind some fig trees still covered with rain-crusted winter blankets. Through the front windshield I saw the hearse, containing my father, alone on his last journey. The sleeping old priest wheezed. Leaning forward, I tried to make out his face, hidden by the brim of a broad black fedora. His head sank forward, bit by bit, until his chin touched his chest. Sounds, like the muffled squealings of a pig, came from his throat.

"He has just finished two funeral Masses. He is ninety-one," my mother said, sensing my irritation. "See how he sleeps. To be ninety-one. . . ." She turned toward the window again.

Across the street, Signor Di Miele had come out of his bakery and was standing with his white hat in his hand. Lining the street and looking into our car were neighbors who had come to the Mass. They stared at us with that look of embarrassed curiosity given to those whose emotions have been exposed. The old priest had conducted the funeral service, stepped into the limousine, and fallen asleep immediately.

The cortege began to move. The black fedora jumped. "It's all right Fodder. *Buono, buono, dorma, dorma,*" the driver, who was young and seemed to know him, said, but the old man looked frightened.

"We are going to the cemetery now," my mother said in very correct Italian.

"Yes. Oh, yes," the old man said, and sat back against the black leather seat, and the squeal of sleep began again.

"It is Father Matteo," my mother told me in English. "He is a new priest. He says the weekday Masses and the Sunday seven o'clock in Italian. You do not know him. Your father did not." Because of where we were, her face suppressed the look of accusation reserved for those who have fallen away from their holy obligations.

"The parish is so big lately that Father Grasso asked him to help out," my sister Reni said. "His sister is Signora Gronchi—maybe you know her. He's from Naples. He retired there. Last year, he came here to his sister and her family. They live near the pastry store on Two Hundred Street."

Slowly the cortege wound around the block, under the Elevated, where the striped shadows sped past the circling cars, and then along our block of small frame houses. This was the last look, or last good-bye, for the deceased. On the stoop of the old gray house across the way, my father's *boccie* companion Onofrio sat holding his cigar. He shook his head. The young children suddenly stopped in their stickball game and stared from the edge of the street.

Father Matteo woke up again. I saw his hands for the first time as he raised his black book to whisper prayers. His head rocked back and forth. I heard my mother behind me. She was whispering "Amen" to his strophes. Father Matteo seemed lost in his words; at least, he spoke in a voice unmoved by the crying in the back seat.

When we were finally on the highway, he shut his book. I could see that his right hand, clasped over the closed missal, was bent with arthritis. The hair on the back of his hands was light and, like the close-shaven hair on his neck, silver hued and shining. When he turned to ask us which cemetery we were going to, I saw his face again. It was a sad southern Italian face.

"Not St. Peter?" he asked. "There is another place?"

"Good Shepherd, Father," my sister Reni said. "In Westchester."

"Good Shep-erd." He tried to pronounce the name of the cemetery we were headed toward.

My mother explained it to him in Italian.

"Oh, yes," he answered. "I think I have heard of it. But I have never been there."

He turned around again as the cars continued along the highway, waved through traffic lights by police. His face seemed many years younger than his age, but his voice was worn down to the kind of whisper that accompanies an early-morning rosary.

When the cars reached the cemetery, the hearse pulled away down a slight macadam lane between evenly spaced trees. The cars stopped on a slight hill. Below us, a broad field of gravestones lay planted in the grass of a tree-encircled lawn. The hearse stopped near a canopy at the foot of the hill. I saw a few workmen come from behind the trees and speak to Mr. Marteri, the undertaker. I did not hear a sound from the back seat. I felt like turning to see if they were there. The driver had become as anonymous as the limousine itself. Everything seemed suspended. Then Father Matteo coughed. It seemed to be the signal for the cars to move down the hill toward the canopy. The undertaker's men removed the casket from the hearse. At the bottom of the hill, we stepped out and were lined up neatly at the foot of the casket by Mr. Marteri and his wife, who moved us into place as though we were blind.

Underneath us, on a false floor of green carpeting, rushes were strewn about. Father Matteo was helped from the car, and as we watched he walked slowly to the head of the casket. My brother Victor suddenly began to weep. Father Matteo made the sign of the cross with his right hand, and his coat fell open. The white surplice, incongruous with so much black around it, drew all eyes. The lone weeping stopped. Father Matteo began to read his whispered prayers. We were led past the casket. My mother stepped forward. Someone clutched at her arm, fearful that she might throw herself upon the bier. She stopped and turned. It was Mr. Marteri; he released his hold.

"Good-bye, Luigi," my mother said, in Italian. "I will see you soon."

I do not remember how we got back into the car, but we were on the highway again. Father Matteo was staring out the window. He turned toward me.

"That cemetery," he said, in Italian, "is a beautiful cemetery. Better than St. Peter. Do you know St. Peter, near the bay?"

"Yes," I said.

"They don't take care of St. Peter. The grass is full of weeds; the graves are untended."

We rode on silently.

"What was the name of the good soul?" he asked suddenly.

"Luigi Mauro," I answered. "My father."

"I will pray for him," he said. "I will mention him in all my Masses."

My sister Reni tapped me on the shoulder. I leaned back. "Mama wants you to give him this," she said, and put a five dollar bill in my right hand.

I gave it to him and thanked him.

"I will say a Mass for him with this. I will mention him in all my Masses," Father Matteo said again. "I will pray for the good soul."

I turned to repeat this to my mother, but she had heard, and she was smiling. She motioned for me to move closer. "He is a real old country priest," she said softly. "A little saint of a small parish in the mountains. Sometimes he is so funny. You know Signora Mennino? She was complaining to him about how sick she is all the time. Always eating. He told her she spends too much time feeding her stomach and not enough feeding her soul." My mother smiled, and then, seeing that I did not, she turned toward the window again.

"Giovanotto," Father Matteo whispered from the front seat.

"Yes, Father," I said.

"This is a lovely cemetery. Is it consecrated ground?"

I asked my mother. "Yes," I repeated, "it's consecrated. It's the newest cemetery of the Church."

"I think I have heard of it," he said. "It is very clean, very well-kept. Is that not true?"

"Yes, I think so. Very nice."

There was a pause. "A plot here must be expensive?" he asked.

"No, not as much as St. Peter," I said.

"Are you sure?" He turned almost completely around, and his black eyes looked directly at me. "Do you know how much?"

"No," I said. "But my brother Victor called St. Peter. We have a family plot there. We were going to take my father there. But they wouldn't allow us to use the family plot again, so we were going to buy a new one there. But then we called Good Shepherd. The mortician told us about it."

"Good Shepherd," Father Matteo repeated. "Good Shepherd was less in price?"

"Yes, and I think the plot is even a little larger."

He turned to look at the highway again. "Excuse me," he said. "My neck becomes stiff."

When we stopped at the next red light, he turned around. "What was the good soul's name?" he asked.

"Luigi Mauro," I answered.

"Luigi Mauro," he repeated. "Yes." He turned and leaned back over the seat close to me. "Giovanotto," he said, "will you ask your brother for me? Ask your brother how much the plot costs. Ask him if he is sure it is less than St. Peter."

"I will," I said.

"Do you know that St. Peter is in the swamps?"

"No, Father."

"Yes, there are swamps all around it. The odor of the palude is everywhere. It is cold and damp. I know it from services. I do not like to go there. I always get a cold."

He sniffed, as though the suggestion were bringing back an old cold. Then he turned around to get the handkerchief in his coat sleeve.

"Close the window," my mother said.

The driver heard her and pressed the button next to his seat that raised the rear window.

When the car reached the edge of the city, our limousine made a left turn. The others continued straight ahead.

"We are taking the Fodder home," the driver said to me. "He lives on Two Hundred Street. It'll only take just a few minutes."

Father Matteo turned around again. "I live with my sister," he said. His voice was louder, with a new energy. "I have been looking for a plot for myself and her family. It is one thing I can do. I have the money, too. So do not forget, Giovanotto, to ask your brother."

"How shall I let you know?"

"When we arrive, you come inside with me and take the telephone number. Call me."

As soon as the car stopped, my mother said, "Help him."

He was stiff from the ride. I eased him from the seat and helped him to the curb, lifting him by taking his elbows. We reached the stoop and started up the stairs one at a time, slowly.

"This is my sister's house," he said, lifting his head. "She had a hat store."

It was a gray, asbestos-shingled house, like most of the other houses on the block.

"The skeleton inside me wonders what I am waiting for," he said, and smiled.

We finally reached the door, and his sister let us in. She was short and hunched, dressed in a grey smock and grey slippers.

"This Giovanotto needs our telephone number," he said to her. "Give him the number."

His sister hobbled away. We stayed on the glass-enclosed front porch.

"Did he have a large family?" Father Matteo asked.

"My father? Two daughters, three sons, and my mother."

"I will pray for him in every Mass," he said. "I do all the Masses for the dead. Do you know that?"

"No, Father," I said.

He smiled. "Today is the first time you have seen the inside of the church in years. Am I right?"

"Yes, Father. That's right."

His sister returned with a square of paper and handed it to me. I read the number aloud as she watched me.

"Thank you," I said. "Thank you, Father. I'll take care of this. Good-bye. Good-bye, Signora."

He grasped my right arm and walked to the door with me. "Do not forget, " he said. "Some things cannot wait." He smiled at me and put his hand on my shoulder. "Look at this Giovanotto," he said to his sister. "Isn't this a handsome Giovanotto?"

His sister nodded slowly.

"Go, go, they are waiting," he said suddenly. "Take care of your mother. Watch the steps. Do not forget to call me. God bless you." He raised his right hand, to make the sign of the cross.

"Is he all right?" my mother asked when I reached the car.

"Yes, he's all right," I said.

I got in the front seat, where Father Matteo had sat. As we drove away, I looked back at the house, with all its windows shut and most of the shades drawn.

# Part Two:
# Losing the Bronx

# Agon

Regan drove towards the Salvini Villa. He had been in the bakery ten minutes; some Florentine kids had walked around his Borgward, looking at the trophies and cups on the back seat while the girl was wrapping the *panettone* in stiff red paper.

He smiled at them; Italian kids took themselves so seriously: they were amusing to watch—innocence. They touched the windows of his car and stepped back on their heels, like old men in the piazza. When he came out he heard one say, "It is the American ace, the Regan."

But his mind was like a sieve. He had driven to the store for reasons he could not explain; yet someone had asked him to bring a *panettone*, and specifically from *Robiglio's* in Florence—had said, *don't forget; the shop in Via Rucellai.* Someone he was going to meet in Bologna. And the demand had been pressing on him; though, like a fool he could not remember who would be waiting in Bologna.

Driving into Piazza Cavour he had remembered and stopped the car near the large café on the steps. It was Von Sneidern; he had asked down in Sicily. But then he had crashed: only his request was alive.

He started the car again, over the canal, and turned left, on Via Vittorio Emanuele, to the Salvini house. He was going to skip them, but now he had to give someone the *panettone*—he could not take it or throw it away.

Elena came to the door after the portiere had let him in at the gate. When Elena seemed touched by the gift, he felt the chest pressure momentarily. He watched her finger the paper until he had to turn away.

He waited on the terrace while she went to call Renato, who had television now, and like an adolescent American boy, lived by the set when he was home.

Renato had embarrassed him last time, too obsequious, asking him about Khrushchev, the Asian war. Eight years ago it would have been a great joke to say Salvini would come to this state. Does a bad leg make you this way? Was it Italian? When they fell, from position or wealth—felt the decline, they became servile and smiling, like old peasants.

But in Renato it was sickening. Salvini, who used to slap his cars during races; then he was the next Nuvolari and knew how to walk like a Lord. The rage. Where could the rage go? Does it fall out, like a tooth gone rotten?

Regan saw him with his cane, smiling as he approached.

"I'm on the way to Bologna. And I remembered this time," Regan said.

"Good," Renato said. "*Finalmente* you give us an hour. Now stay for *pranzo.*"

Renato went to a straw chair near the edge of the terrace and sat down. Regan watched the left leg snap out stiffly, with no control of its own, like a stiff tube of metal suddenly reeling. "I can't stay. We are looking at new machines tomorrow. I have to meet them in Bologna in the morning."

"Bologna is better in the dark," Renato said. "Start later." He raised his cane and pointed it at Regan, then smiled. "Next year you will not have time for the Salvini house."

Regan had no answer; he was tired. The statement was like the questions of reporters: you answered in a controlled voice, holding most of the feelings in.

Renato shouted for Elena, but she was already on the way in with a tray of drinks; she remembered that Regan loved San Pellegrino *aranciata*.

They sat in silence while they drank. "Now you use a glass," Renato said, and Regan smiled. When they had met in forty-eight, Renato had called him the Coca-Cola man.

"I remember the bottle man," Renato said. "Who spoke no Italian. I said to Moretti that day, let me see, I said, Clemente, does this boy play a game with wheels? We never thought Americans had to make money."

"Did you know how lonely and afraid I was?" Regan said. "That I was only at home while I was driving."

"In that we were all friends down there," Renato said.

Regan turned to look at the roofs of the houses. "I always forget how much I like Florence," he said. It was early afternoon, the sky too bright to have deep color, but the red clay roofs bright.

He had not been watching Renato and Elena smiling at each other. "How long do you pass things, and say, *Well next time I'll enjoy this.*"

"Next year!" Renato said, and tried to stand. It would take too long, so he sat down again. "This year you will be on the top. No one can catch you now with the points. You will be champion."

"He knows that," Elena said. "Notice how happy he is." She came to refill his glass; then she placed her hands on his shoulders and he looked up at her.

"You always catch me," Regan said. "I never can decide if I wished I had married you or not."

"Yes, Yes," Renato said. "And every liver pain that turned down your mouth, she would tell you it's the work. You hate it, she would say. A real *strega,* this one."

"She would have me out of racing now," Regan said.

"Our Lady of Sense." Renato smiled at his wife.

Regan looked at Elena's face taking their jokes without effect. "I must go," he said, and stood up.

"No!" Renato seemed hurt.

Elena took Regan's arm and walked with him to the front door. Renato limped behind. The three met at the door.

Renato embraced Regan. "I feel it," he said. "You did it really *bella* this year. Everything." He stepped back and shook his head. "The little Coca-Cola from Florida. I see your green face. And I said, *Paura molto?* And you said, *Sí, sí.*"

"Yes," Regan said. "I was very fluent."

"What you did in Belgium this year. It was perfection, they say." Renato stamped the cane. "Everything is right."

"Except for Von Sneidern," Regan said.

"But what was it?" Renato's lips pursed and twitched.

"They say he hit Monti, coming in to take his position. I don't know. It made a turn impossible. He ran up in the hay. You know it; it's a corner that's soft. But the car went over. And somehow reached the concrete—as if it flew. No one understands it."

"He pushed and pushed," Renato said.

"He always drove that way." Regan felt angry, a wish to insult Renato.

"He had to run ahead, if you understand," Renato said. "I mean the character of the man. He could not be a chaser."

"Yes, I imagine," Regan said. They shook hands. Elena walked down the steps to the gate with Regan.

"How is he now?" Regan said.

"The garage makes millions. He is a capitalist."

"And his leg?"

"No trouble," Elena said, and stepped back. "But how are your legs?"

"I thought Von Sneidern was alive today." Regan looked at the laurel hedges in the garden. "I went out to get something for him—"

"There is always one bad occurrence." Elena took his right hand. "Worse than the others." Her face turned to Renato in the doorway. "Time keeps it from shaking inside."

"What do you want me to say? I don't have a business." Regan pulled his hands back. "I can't go up to a monastery. I don't know how to read or write. And I am monk enough these days."

"Carla is gone?"

"She married Folena."

"The cheese man?" Elena smiled.

"The largest *parmigiano* in the world. And Regan sleeps alone."

"But that is not what makes you this way."

Regan would not look at her. "Oh, really," he said. "Thank you."

"You must think what it is."

"Thank you. Maybe I will find it up in the mountains to Bologna."

"Yes. A cow will tell you," Elena said, and kissed Regan's face, and ran back. She did not wave.

*She's crying,* Regan thought. He could see it in her back, hunched and moving. The position, the sound, the shaking always made him feel bad: it was old, stale disappointment in him, from far back.

Carla might have been like that; yet she loved the life of the circuits. They had not met in love like Renato and Elena. Carla loved to go with him: the restaurants, the parties, the track, the bed.

In Modena, last year, she had cried after making love. He had rushed her as he always did a week before a race. It was an awful sound, and it ended four months later with the news of her marriage to Folena.

But he always felt his desire for her; while they sat at breakfast or when they were walking; if he saw a bit of thigh under her skirt while she sat, he became excited: her legs and arms in his mind were as vivid as her self.

He shut the gate and went to the car. *Stop for a loaf of bread on the way home.* He mimicked the woman's voice in his mind.

He drove the Borgward to the Bologna road and up the hill out of Florence. The edge of his eye ran along the view of the city below: the mist was green. Then abruptly the road began to pass through mountain villages.

The sun was moving lower, casting still, long shadows through the hills. The villas were quiet and closed; he liked the green Italian shutters, the *persiane*. When he saw them, he felt the cool darkness held inside Italian stone rooms on hot days, women's legs in that shade.

He went on. Coming over a small hill, he recognized the place; it was a noisy spot in the Mille Miglia. There were always crowds here, flag-wavers, right down at the road's edge, and attempts at passing. Adolph Brandon had run off the road here and hit a cow barn. Farther on, along a straight road near the *Futa* Pass, he thought he remembered the place of telephone poles: where De Portago had hit.

He had the chest feeling again, and it made him think of respiratory disease and of Jimmie Clerkwell, the Irishman, who had TB. He had been drinking with Clerkwell in Naples and tried to remember if they had exchanged glasses at any time.

He drove another hour; the sun was beginning to slide, back behind the highest mountains already, sending upward rays to a sky of orange, almost golden.

His eyes caught the whitewashed wall of a building and painted letters that announced an inn and service station. He turned off the highway onto gravel and rode to the pumps near the door. A boy of about sixteen came out and filled the tank while Regan walked to the entrance. "I will park the car," the boy called, and Regan waved at him.

It was a big room. A counter had been placed about ten feet from the entrance. On the long marble top were cheeses, a gateau, some *zuppa inglese,* and at the end two espresso machines.

A woman came out and greeted him. "May I get a meal now?" Regan asked in perfect Italian. He saw her eyes go up in surprise; she pointed to the main room behind the counter.

He followed her around the counter and sat down at a large wood table. A young girl, about eighteen, came up and told him the list. He ordered their soup, pappardelle with wild hare sauce and pecorino. And lambrusco to drink.

When the girl brought the wine, he was looking about the room. Near the center of the room was a long table full of men. A few of them, in suits, were probably salesmen from the cities. Most were dressed in corduroy jackets and trousers, with leather boots, the uniform of farm managers—*fattori*. They were talking over their coffee and drinks and looking back at Regan. Finally, one man stood up and came to his table. He was smiling, with his chin down, a big man trying to act soft. "You are Regan?" he asked.

"Yes."

"How strange. We were just talking about you. And that you should then walk in. The owner asks to meet you."

"Tell him to come."

The man raised his right arm, and a short man in a blue shirt with brown corduroy trousers came to the table. He introduced himself and held Regan's hand in a long shake, wishing him the best for the remaining races. Then he was stuck for words, dropped his hand and ordered the girl to bring a wine. "This is special," he said. "Diners don't see this," he said, and laughed.

They went back, to allow Regan to eat his meal. The girl came with the soup, but as she was placing it down let it go too soon. The plate fell on Regan's trousers. He jumped up with a little sound of pain.

"*Cretina!*" The owner shouted and came back with a towel, but since the wet had struck Regan's crotch, he stood holding the towel. Regan finally took it.

While he wiped himself, the old man shook his head. He looked at the girl and spoke a curse to her and she ran from the room. A short time later, the older woman came from the back with a pair of corduroy trousers, bowed and began to ask Regan's pardon.

"Put these on," the owner said, and stopped her. "And we will take yours to be cleaned."

Regan took the trousers and followed the older woman to the bathroom. He had to walk out back behind the building and along a concrete walk under a grape arbor.

The trousers were too large, but they were all right. When he came inside again, the men began to laugh, and they all stood up and came to him.

"Sit with us for a while," one of the city men said. "We will protect you from the girl."

Regan had his soup with the men. They had eaten and were drinking coffee and grappa. They spoke to Regan about having seen him at this race and that.

"You will surely finish first with the Ferrari," the owner said.

"This year," said one of the city men, "—even in a *seicento.*"

The owner noticed Regan still uncomfortable with the large trousers, and he leaned over. "Let me take you to a table outside," he said, pointing to the back. "Then, later, when yours are ready, come back."

Regan nodded, and the owner spoke to the men. "Regan will eat in peace. And return when he has younger trousers."

The owner walked before Regan, bowing as he led him out the door. A clean table sat under the grape arbor. He had his meal there, finished the Lambrusco and most of the special wine, to gratify the host.

The young girl had served him, setting the food down and walking away immediately. She had been so humilated her cheeks remained red. When she brought his coffee, she told him his trousers were ready; they were in the *gabinetto.*

He left the coffee and went to change. They had cleaned them perfectly and pressed the creases. It was amazing.

He came out, the trousers neat and tight against his body. As he was walking back, he saw the girl at the end of the long concrete walk, sitting on a wooden bench. Her legs were tucked under the bench, making her wool skirt pull tight against her hips and thighs. The top line of her leg curved up from the knee, showing a bulge of strength; then the line dipped in to where the leg meets the pelvic area.

The skirt was also tight against her stomach, which bulged but was hard. She was a thick, heavy mountain girl, with lucent white flesh.

He went back to his table and drank his coffee, looking down at her. Finally, he called her, and she came to his table.

"Have a drink with me," he said.

"Oh no, signore, I cannot sit down. I can *not.*" She looked towards the building. "I am not allowed."

Regan poured two glasses of wine as she spoke. He held a glass out to her. She looked at his hand, then took the glass and drank it down quickly, like a peasant, with her head thrown back.

"Thank you, signore," she said. Her white face was flushed.

"Then stay," Regan said.

"Thank you," she said, and stepped back.

"Do you know who I am?" he said.

"I heard them talking," she said. "You are the champion."

Regan stood up. "You're very pretty," he said, and placed his hand on her skirt, along her thigh. She looked down for a moment, with no shock, then touched her stomach. "They said I am going to have a baby," she said.

Regan watched her run down the concrete walk and around behind the stone wall. He turned and walked quickly to the main room. He was trying to smile. The men looked up.

"I see it is later than I realized," Regan said. "I must be in Bologna very soon."

The owner stood up. "We gave you so much trouble. But in the end I hope you liked it."

"Yes, very fine. It was all very good. We don't eat like this in the city."

The owner smiled and placed an arm gently on Regan's shoulders. "May I have the check?" Regan said.

The owner turned to the men. "There is no check."

"Then thank you again," Regan said. The men got up and came in a line to shake hands and wish him *buona fortuna.*

The owner walked with him to the door. They waited while the young man brought the car. "I personally have been honored." the owner said.

"I will have to come back again." Regan said. He gave the owner a thousand lira note. "Will you give this to the girl?"

"All this? For that girl? No."

"She was very nice," Regan said. "A nice child."

"All right," the owner said, and averted his head.

Regan stepped into the car and the boy slammed the door. He drove along the cinder road that led to the highway. The darkness had come, and he switched on his lights. The dash clock said 7:45. At least he had passed the *Futa.*

In a short while, the road began to go downhill, the beginning of the descent into Bologna. He was very anxious to see the lights. When he did, he sensed the chest pressure again. It was the city coming up to meet him. Bologna. Bologna had good doctors. He would see a doctor tomorrow.

# The Golden Fleece Returns via Le Havre

One afternoon, after Marion and I had stuffed ourselves on the eight course meal, with a final bit of baked Alaska brought to us from the First-Class dining room, we fought our way to the lounge on the upper deck.

The lounge was like a movie lobby, chrome where there should have been wood and those modern, diffused neon lamps that make it a trifle nauseating to look at people's faces.

The returning Foreign Service man, who had caught us on the first day, was telling a new capture of honeymooners about the comparative merits of D.P.'s. He had become fixed upon the difference between German and Balkan Jews and to show his worldliness was explaining why German Jews were cleaner.

"But you take a Russian Jew," he said very loud, and Marion and I turned away towards the windows and the sea.

"Isn't he disgusting," Marion said.

"Don't mention him," I said.

We had been in Italy for two years, and I had spent many nights over yellow vermouth telling my cousins that Americans weren't like that. And to meet him on the way home. I asked Marion if she would like to change tables.

We moved to a table near the windows. At the next table was a young couple, the woman obviously pregnant. The man looked at me and then at the State Department man and then back at me.

"There's more of them than there are of you," he said. His voice was loud and harsh, and I felt sure that the State Department man would overhear. But when I looked back he was pointing his finger at the honeymooners and bringing one of his insights to its conclusion.

"Dirty and filthy," was all I could hear.

I turned back to the young man at the next table.

"How can you tell?" I asked.

"Your face," he said. "Come on over."

He stood up and waited. On a ship in the middle of the Atlantic, there are no excuses at these times.

When we sat down, he said, "I'm Joe Ryan. This is my wife, Deirdre."

I introduced Marion and myself.

"Mauro," he repeated. "That's an Italian name."

"Yes," I said.

"Seems to me I knew one of the guys from the Frisco fleet with that name."

Ryan did not give you a chance to ask questions.

"I used to run a fishing boat with my old man out of Puget Sound," he said. "Deedy and I were in Paris on a fellowship. I spent the dough on booze and knocked up the kid."

His wife's face was imperturbable. Perhaps she ignored what he said or was too used to his words, but she was always calm, even when he became very excited.

"What do you pick up in Paris?" he said. "A headache and a rotten gut. And if you go down far enough, maybe you come up with a drop of what's good. What were *you* doing, Mauro?"

"We were in Italy," I said. "No fellowship. We had saved up, and I took courses at the University of Naples."

"The academic sludge," he said. "Critics of critics of critics of critics. Three-two beer. Do you know Morelli's stuff?"

"No," I said.

"Morelli and Juan Marinet," he said. "The rest of Europe you can drop in a sewer. I have the one Marinet that's getting through U.S. Customs. They can read, now."

"The sun is setting," his wife said.

"Let's have one more drink," he said loudly. A waiter saw his arm go up. He asked for a double scotch and when we were hesitant about having another, he seemed insulted. We finally asked for vermouth, which he ordered from the waiter.

"Let's go out on deck," he said a few minutes after the drinks had come, before we were finished with ours.

He started for the promenade deck, and we followed him up the staircase to the wide deck where the shuffleboard was.

His wife walked slowly. At first I thought it was her pregnancy, for she was very large. But I saw that she was detaining Marion at the rail to talk.

I followed Ryan to the center of the deck. Above us, between our heads and the sky, a roof of black smoke from the stacks rolled by, flattened by the wind.

Ryan was tall and thick—his hands, his wrists, his neck, even his features were of blunt and broad proportion. But his skin was tan and thin, unscarred and unmarked by calluses or other signs of hard physical labor.

"Look at these faces," he said. "Clean and handsome. Bright as the wheat fields. You'd never think they live in the stone tombs of New York and Chicago. Has one of them ever seen the sun rise?"

He took a book from his pocket and tapped it with his right forefinger. "He's been in prison. He's . . . everything that walks."

"Who?" I asked.

"Marinet," he answered, and held up the book. "I haven't absorbed it yet. I've read a hundred pages four times. But you don't read this. You've got to breathe it. We had a fight the night before we left. Two French queers in Montmartre. We wanted their table, and Marinet went at them right away. The other one got my head before I could get him. That's a good way, you know. Smash the head against the wall. Sure concussion. Then run.

"The place was a mess for an hour. Then Juan yells let's go. Running through Paris. Making the cops think we did something, but they're not sure. It's the way we do it.

"Four o'clock we were near the Gare de L'Est, and I suddenly dropped. Right in the curb muck. I had gone in there with a concussion. From a week before. That's the bloody thing."

120

Ryan did not look at me. He kept his eyes on the water, and he stopped speaking only when his breath gave out momentarily.

"They all know Marinet," he said. "Gide knew him. But vanity gets them when they're old. But Gide said he was the future—Marinet. This is violence—the modern blood—in art."

"What's the name of the book?" I asked.

"In English it would be—roughly—'The World Ends At Night.' But you can't translate this. How're you going to translate the *patois*? The gutter sounds that blow the breath of the bars in your face."

His hands squeezed the book.

"I'll have a tough time with Ted," he said. "The old academician. But he's a real poet. You've got to love him. America spits on him. He's American. When the visiting English poets come, he introduces them. And you can hear the homos sigh for miles. But who cares for a good poet if he's American? He won't give up. But still, don't you see? Ted's in the grove. He's closed the gates. He's let the acanthus grow high. He's never gone beyond the Colonial brick walls. How's he going to see this?"

Ryan tried to crush the book between his hands.

"It's not what they know on Madison Avenue. The guy doesn't take a hundred pages to crawl two inches on the beachhead. Marinet's only the essence of art. They'll never take it. But Ted won't fight this in the end."

"I'd like to take a look at it, sometime," I said.

"After two years in the Renaissance Garden? Well, at least you're young enough."

I thought Ryan was younger than I.

"You grew up in New York, on the streets?" he asked.

"Yes. In a very tough neighborhood," I said.

"If you haven't lost it all," he said, "you'll feel this book. And if you don't, the professors will tell you about it in ten years."

He needed a rest and walked to the rail. He looked down at the water, then turned to me.

"You were in Italy," he said softly. "Don't tell me. You were writing a novel. Thirty pages on the girlfriend and the college you left behind, fifty sensitive pages in boot camp under the sadistic sergeant, a hundred pages of the first battle, and a little open-your-eye philosophy on the Fascist officer and the democratic natives."

"Well, to tell the truth," I said, "I did try to do a little—"

"They wanted mine," he said. "Bob Lurlov liked the arguments with the whores. But I took it back and cut out the rot. Down to the single essence. That big."

He made a figure with his right thumb and forefinger to indicate narrowness.

"They wouldn't have it without the rot," he said, and laughed. In his laugh, like his speech, there was a tension, as though he were fighting to control a scream.

"What branch were you in?" I asked.

"The paratroopers, boy. Nobody comes back alive. Even I died. They patched my bones until the glue ran out. My first wife couldn't stand the smell. But the kid has a soul."

He looked towards his wife and Marion at the rail near the bow.

"She's a beast," he said. "But she's got magic. Look at her bulging like the mother of the earth. She can learn," he said calmly. "We can form her."

He suddenly stopped speaking. The rush of shuffleboard laughter and the sound of the ship striking the water seemed very loud. Ryan looked down at the smooth deck wood, and all the animation, all the lines left his face. It became soft and fleshy. It looked older now. It was a face that needed to be animated, always in violent movement.

"She had hard times," he said. "Three days she had no food. You should have seen her eyes. You would have seen the animal. She sensed the kid inside her. It was the kid she was desperate for. You should have seen her. She broke a bottle of booze over my head. Going down the stairs bleeding like Christ with my shoulders drenched in brandy. I got bread, too, and there was cheese in my jacket pocket, a whole Camembert wrapped in *Paris Soir*. While she ate, I tried to read last week's news through the spots of cheese stuck on the paper, looking over calmly to the corner of the room where she's on her knees devouring the bread and cheese.

"And you know, I smiled. Christ, I smiled. I thought it was the most dramatic scene in the world. Did you ever sit smiling over a hungry dog you've just thrown the meat to? Watch the mutt's fangs sometime. Watch the spittle drop off those jaws. It's the jungle right in Mom's kitchen."

He looked towards the women again. Marion and his wife began to walk in our direction.

"But she's read Marinet, and her guts receive it. That's worth all the fat years on the farm, all the rotten comfort. She's still a beast, but she'll *never* be a pig."

"Has Joe given you a chance to say a word?" his wife said as they reached us.

Marion's face was completely without expression, with that New England mask it assumed when she heard something disturbing.

"I've enjoyed listening to your husband," I said. "I'm interested in his book."

"The academician," Ryan said. "He smells the formal bone."

"You'll love Marinet," his wife said.

Ryan tapped her on the head with the book. "Come on," he said. "Let's make early chow." He turned to me. "Our waiter stands and watches. We're the only ones who eat the thirty courses."

His wife laughed. "We've six months to make up."

They left us on deck. As they walked away I noticed that she was taller than Ryan. She had a lovely figure, but her long hair was matted, still dirty from Paris. It hung in thick curls to her shoulders.

Ryan walked with his feet wide apart, like a sailor. He had almost no neck, just a bull-like roll of flesh between his hairline and the collar of his tweed jacket.

"Did he tell you about their life in Paris?" Marion said.

"A little," I said. "I think she told *you* more."

"It was unbelievable," Marion said. "I can't understand how they're still alive. Do you know he beat her?"

"No," I said.

"When she was pregnant. And he once ripped all her clothes to shreds, even the clothes she was wearing."

"I'd like to see that great book," I said.

"His book? They're publishing it in the fall."

"No. I meant the French book, the Marinet. He told me they turned *his* book down when he changed it."

"That's probably the war book. There's another book—the one that's being published. She said it was like Joyce, only about real things, about his life."

"Didn't she mention the French book?" I asked.

"Why, yes. Just to say it was the greatest novel ever written. He's going to get a professorship on it."

"In fishing boats?" I said.

"He's an instructor at a small college in California."

"I thought he was a fisherman," I said.

"Not since the war. The French book is the new discovery he's made. Marinet is a friend of theirs. He sounds like a terrible pervert. But he's the future. That's what she said."

"I'd like to see that book," I said.

"I'd like to go to supper," Marion said. "And drink a lot of wine and forget what I heard this afternoon."

*

After supper we went to the lounge to wait until it was time for the movie. The honeymooners were watching each other, looking for friendly faces. The State Department man came in and began to examine the room. Then Ryan came in and found us immediately.

His wife followed slowly behind, and Marion and I helped her sit down. She was having a difficult time keeping her balance.

"It's kicking a lot tonight," she said. "It makes me dizzy."

Marion, like many women who want a baby but have not yet had one, sat in awe as Deedy discussed the actions of the foetus inside her.

Ryan leaned back in his chair and smiled. He looked at his wife.

"Have kids, Mauro," he said. "It's the only pure experience left."

"When am I going to have the experience of the Marinet book?" I asked.

"You *have* it. Everyone has it. The book is only a jewel through which we see what it means to have done what we have done."

I nodded, but Ryan smiled at me and moved his chair closer to mine. He took the book from his pocket and slid it into my jacket pocket. "Later," he said softly. "Read it when you're alone, with no domestic reminders knitting in the corner, with nobody to suggest this idiotic world around us."

He spent the rest of the evening buying drinks, becoming insulted, almost enraged when we tried to stop or pass up a round. We missed the movie.

Finally, Marion said that she felt ill and went below to our cabin. An hour or so later, his wife became very pale and asked Ryan if she might leave. He didn't answer, and she left.

It was late. There were many empty tables around us, and the floors were damp. A fog had descended just after nightfall. The windows before us pitched continually, and I could no longer taste my cigarettes. I stood up.

"I think I'll go," I said.

Ryan didn't answer. He was in thought. He had covered literature, politics, religion, and publishing, the last to inform me that complete decadence was at hand.

"All right," he said. I moved away. "Just a little nightcap at the bar."

The bar was silent. The few people there were posing: it was like a background in a bad film.

I was content to stand and hold the wooden railing. Every so often, when the ship took pitches deeply, I belched. Ryan looked at me with pity.

He ordered a double scotch. At his right was a tall man wearing a light gray suit. Before I knew what had happened, they were exchanging angry words, and the tall man had pushed Ryan.

I remember quickly wondering whether or not this expensive ship had a jail.

When Ryan hit him the first time, the tall man fell back over a table, and with a pitch of the ship, rolled to the rail separating the bar from the lounge. The tall man got up and came towards Ryan. There was blood on his chin.

Ryan hit him again, and he rolled back again—this time not as far. He came back and lunged at Ryan, grasping him to smother his punches. They rocked back and forth, punching and clinching towards the door that led to the deck.

It happened very fast, before sailors could come. The big man threw a chair and two other men went for him. The chair hit Ryan squarely, and he fell back through the door into the passageway.

"On deck," he said. "Need some air."

We stepped out on deck, and Ryan sat down and leaned back against the metal bulkhead. His right hand touched his mouth and came away stained.

"Look," he said, and I leaned down.

It was a clot of blood.

"Isn't it lovely," he said. "Touch it."

He held it close to me, and I turned my head away. But his left hand suddenly touched my leg.

"Ryan," I said. "Cut it out."

He said something in French, which I didn't understand, and tried to touch my face with his bloody hand.

"What's the matter with you?" I said.

"Hit me," he said.

I looked down at his lip. It was bleeding heavily. Then I stood up and backed away. He was smiling at his hand that touched his lips and then held the sight before his eyes. His smile was tight but broad, the blood suddenly like clown makeup.

I turned and walked towards the dispensary, intending to get help for Ryan, but stopped on my way and went outside again, to the deck on the other side of the ship.

I could not involve myself with him anymore. I did not want to be known as having been with him.

Looking for my cigarettes, I found the Marinet book in my pocket and took it out and placed it on the rail. As I lit my cigarette, I saw the book sliding from the ship motion; I lit match after match as it slid—and it finally went overboard.

I looked around, suddenly embarrassed. Then I stared at the water that came clear only in black patches through the fog. But I was relieved and I was rid of it. It was like spitting out Ryan, whom I now knew was too much for me, his book, his world. . . .

I hated Ryan: his ugliness was at least action, commitment, an outside fight against the rottenness I had seen on the ship and had simply moved away from. But I could meet Ryan's self-destruction only with pity—and then revulsion. And my revulsion would not be strong enough to condemn him. I threw my unlighted cigarette to the fog and rushed down the dimly-lit staircase to the darkness of my windowless cabin.

# Homes and Rooms

Lucky got off the Rome plane at 7:55 and made the mid-Manhattan terminal in an hour and a half. He called Jack's number and Elaine answered. When Lucky asked for Jack, Elaine's voice said with a sound that came tired and without timbre: "Jack's dead, Lucky. I'm sorry to tell you—"

Lucky hardly heard the rest; his head went rolling into confusing sounds, bits of thoughts, a wandering off of attention mixed with intense reception of certain words as Elaine kept on: something about a hospital, feeling perfect in the morning, going up for golf, feeling a little ill at night, the doctor coming, going to the hospital overnight; then suddenly dead there.

"Yes, yes, yes, yes." Lucky heard his voice trying to convey more to Elaine than his own fear—his wish to show sympathy, to be helpful, to understand. He felt sweat all over, a need to talk about himself. "I was in Rome four weeks with a bad cold. So I stayed on. If I knew! If I knew!"

"No one foresees a thing like this." Elaine caught his fear.

"Did he cut down the smoking?" Lucky said.

"Not really."

"I haven't had a puff for two months." He was hurt to have it greeted with a murmur from Elaine. "But I'm still overweight, you know."

"You're not really bad," she said. "Unless you put on a lot over there this trip."

"I'm coming up there," Lucky said. "Are you OK? Not too tired?"

"No, it's still early." The voice had drifted away, leaning most likely towards a clock.

Lucky shut the phone and left the booth wet and cold in his own sweat. Jack, his—what would you call him—brother, best friend. Surely best friend. Both of them had begun selling careers at Bloomingdales. The good young years, out to lunches together, all the restaurants, dates, Manhattan together. Apartments together, and some of the dreams coming out. Then Jack getting married and going on his own to make more, domestic selling along the Eastern seaboard, having a family, unable to try anything else while Lucky got the international job and got away to Europe.

Waiting for a cab on the bottom steps of the terminal, he caught the hot air of the streets for the first time: he was back. A porter waved him to a cab.

He was glad he did not have to drive. He did not want to drive again. His head was spinning; the heart attack fears were rolling in like storm clouds—with the winds of excess: liquor, food, cigarettes. Each leisure moment was excess, and the whole country on diets, diet foods and diet books and everyone getting fatter all the time. Each time he came back people looked fatter: the driver in front of him was an enormous bulk, so fat that he was forced to ride with his head way back, a man jammed back by his stomach.

And the radio warning about smoking; all of it, all of it. On the plane he had picked up a magazine that described the air over New York full of poisonous leads, monoxides: breathing in the city was like smoking all day long; even the lungs of babies. Two packs a day.

And the man next to him talked about the Dead Sea outside New York Harbor, the fish with broken fins, full of cancer.

It was hammer blows on the head, like something waiting to go for him while he tried to think about Jack. His face was burning; he was losing his thoughts again. If they all went away he would die.

He did not want to go into Jack's house and began to sweat again when the taxi stopped. But he had to talk to Elaine, see what she needed, give her money. It was hateful the way he felt trapped at the door and yet ignored by something he could not identify, the speaker in his mind.

Elaine greeted him with a dry hug, her tears finished but her emotions flabby, like someone abandoned. Then she served him coffee and pound cake, and her shoulders leaned over the pouring pot in pain: *that* was a widow. He tried to talk about her, but she was unfocused. Then he turned to himself, to ask her.

"God bless you, you look OK. Now take care of yourself, please."

"I do, I do. We all do." Lucky's hands were nervous. "But what do we do now? What are we supposed to *do?*"

"I couldn't tell you, Lucky. I couldn't tell anybody now. I just sit here. The kids go to school. I see some TV at night, May's starting a job in March."

"How can a person stop what he's doing. I guess we just got to go on—"

Elaine was simply drinking her coffee and staring; she wasn't going to talk to him; either she couldn't find words or was going to look past him until the grief ended.

"I think I have to call my boss." Lucky was up. "I'll call you tomorrow. I have a few things I picked up over there for you. They should be coming in soon." Elaine had few reactions, so he went to the door quickly and left, walking along Riverdale Avenue until a cab came by and took him home.

Manhattan was at least something that freed you; up there in Riverdale it had been oppressive; the silence of the streets made it seem that families sat on couches all around, millions of them, all watching TV, drinking coffee and waiting to die.

But after an hour getting settled, getting comfortable again, he had his own TV going and was watching occasionally between getting up for snacks, looking into the cupboards and making a list. Finally, he called for a steak from Stampflers and when it came and was put down, realized that he was sitting alone in the dining nook.

As he ate, he heard his fork and knife hitting together, a terrible sound. He got up suddenly and went back to the window, to get the classy view of the park, then came back because he felt foolish looking with the fork and knife in his hand.

He watched TV until he finished eating, then opened his mail, sat down with *Life* and *Look,* did them page by page.

He wanted a girl; looking at an open page of *Look* had made the thought conscious. He called one of his numbers, and they promised to send one of the girls he knew well. She came in an hour and sat down and had a drink with him, but when he wanted to go on talking, she said, *oh, what's in that nice bedroom* and went in to get ready. He was left alone, knowing he had to get started or feel like a fool. He went in and it was wonderful, like a washing away of all the damned silence of Riverdale. The girl was in her twenties, with a bust only showgirls had, skin color that was tan and smooth, like face makeup, with a white skin line of panty. It was damn good.

But after she was gone, he could not fall asleep, though he was ready to. It was getting late, but he was still desperate, and he knew it was the fact of Jack's going that he could not handle. All right, then. But at least he had the right to sleep.

He went to the bathroom for a sleeping pill and found nothing, not even an aspirin. He went out to the hall and pressed for the elevator, knowing Hugo the nightman had everything. But Hugo had no sleeping pills. Instead he suggested some pot. "You ever try it? Just a little and you'll relax. It's not bad."

Lucky bought one cigarette and went back to the room with instructions on how to smoke it. He sat in the living room and smoked, and finally a light feeling came into his head, then a heaviness filled his body. Now the lights of the park were very lovely, even though he could see very little of them from the low couch.

He was on the couch a long time, thinking on and off about getting into bed, going to the bedroom. But instead he only unbuttoned his robe and lay back on the couch. The TV had been going all the time, even when the hooker had been around, and this made him laugh a good deal. It was quite funny.

When he awoke from a short nap, he knew he was hungry and thirsty, but there was hardly a thing on the shelves. He went to the table and ate the rest of the cold steak, and the fat along the edges, and it was very tasty.

He went to the kitchen and started opening shelves until he found a bottle of wine, which he opened and drank. But it was warm white wine, not too good.

He returned to the bedroom at last and saw the bed and the sheets, the indentation where the hooker's body had been. He leaned down to the sheets and smelled her perfume, just a trace of her. But he did not want to lie down on it yet.

He went to the living room again, for the view and stood still until he saw the rose line coming up over the East Side. The sight of dawn shook him back to himself, made him gather his feelings again, as if they were articulated in him by the sight of the buildings. The city was red, the sky spreading out and its width remarkable, like Rome at early morning, leaving to catch a plane.

He sat down again and dimly, words of prayers he had inside him came out, the *Confiteor,* parts of a *Hail Mary.* But it was hard to recall it; he tried from the beginning again, hoping that the rhythm would bring back all the words.

The alarm clock went off, and he went into the bedroom to shut it off, trying to remember when he had set it. He had wanted to get up and read reports, some figures and orders, and then call Detroit. But it was too early for a call. He went to the phone and realized he really wanted to get some food, and his wish was for Italian food, a fresh mozzarella, some warm bread from La Scala on White Plains Road. He was remembering the Bronx like a set of pictures.

He dialed a car rental place, but there was no answer. He *had* to get up to the Bronx now, so he washed up, shaved, put on clean clothes and went down for a cab. A driver was parked at a stand on Central Park West but did not want to go to the Bronx. Lucky bargained with him and they agreed on an extra three fifty for the empty trip back.

They drove up in silence, across empty Manhattan to the East River Drive, then the Bronx River Parkway to Gun Hill Road, where Lucky got out.

He stood on the corner of White Plains Road, about to walk north, but it was too early for shops, he thought. He walked east along Gun Hill Road and turned up Bronxwood Avenue, passing people going the other way, towards the Elevated trains and buses on White Plains Road.

When he reached 226th Street, he was surprised by the dark brown square that was the rebuilt church of Our Lady of Grace. It had been his parish, and the former church had had a bright look, in orange brick, with large bells in a cupola, the whole structure Italian before he knew what looking Italian meant.

The main church had been downstairs, dark and grottolike, damp and cool, like churches south of Naples. The present thing was like a new bowling alley; it hurt him, like a betrayal; the new thing was unknown. He would have liked to have had some pictures or a piece of the old church.

He walked to the entrance, but the doors were locked, and he strained to see inside. He heard a woman's voice behind him and turned to see an old black woman. "They's an early Mass at Gun Hill. Immaculate Conception. You want a Mass, don't you?"

He nodded and came down the steps, embarrassed, and began to walk towards Gun Hill Road again. The black woman was behind him, walking slowly, her reason for being out unclear to him: she couldn't be on the way to Mass with the shopping cart.

Somehow he went all the way back to Gun Hill Road, as if to satisfy the old woman, who had turned along another street many blocks back. He found a service going on inside the church, not a Mass as he remembered the patterns. A priest alone on his knees, facing the altar, without altar boys, but a few rows of old women, the familiar felt hats and kerchiefs, black and grey and colors that made their own darkness.

Lucky sat down in a back pew, quite far from them and kneeled for a while, again working to bring up one of his prayers in its entirety. Soon he was certain that only pieces would ever come to him, but at least these fragments on his lips in the old church made him feel welcome; he was part of it; he had been to a novena and missions, had said prayers here.

But this was not what he had been trying to do this morning. It was not prayer for Jack, not praying.

Perhaps he had come because he had missed the funeral where he could have done something respectful in him for Jack. But he had been looking for a Mass, yes, hypocrite bastards we all are. A Mass after twenty-four years; he lowered his head, looking away from the altar, the statues and candles: he was like everybody else, a bastard waiting for magic, ready to pay for the magic to work on him.

But the church ignored him, the service went on. The church went right to the old women, into them with its lights and sound—they, who could hardly talk or walk anymore. When he had stopped at the altar rail of Our Lady of Grace the week of his First Communion and stared up at Saint Michael pointing to the gash in his thigh, then he might have let it all enter him. *Then. Then.*

The service was ending. A few women were shuffling up the aisle, stopping to kneel again at the holy water fount. The priest was gone. An elderly monk came from the parish door bearing a large vacuum cleaner, which he set down in preparation.

Lucky left quickly and went out to the steps. The day had begun; there was noise along Gun Hill Road, cars crowding up and high school kids walking towards Evander Childs a block away.

He walked up White Plains Road slowly, stopping at the first pastry shop to buy a *sfogliatella,* which was still warm. He began to eat it while the man behind the counter made change. The man turned and smiled at him and said, "You like Italian pastry?"

"Just like Rome," Lucky said, and saw the blank face. "You get them warm in the mornings down by the markets."

"Oh, did you visit Rome?" The man kept smiling.

"Every two weeks. I work there."

"Oh, you work there. That's nice." The man seemed unhappy.

"I'm Italian." Lucky was pissed at the eyes which did not accept him. "I grew up right around here. Up near 226th."

The man did not answer, the son of a bitch, and Lucky ordered a box of six pastries. "You want assortment?" the man said, and Lucky said, "No. Just *sfogliatelle.*"

With the white box he continued up the avenue, towards La Scala, as he had intended, for morning bread. On the way he passed fruit stores with their bushels out on stands. He stopped at one to look, and a man came out. "You want some fruit? Nice fruit?"

"Is it time for pears already?" Lucky said.

"Here." The man took a small brown pear and gave it to Lucky. "Just taste it. It's sugar inside."

Lucky ate it and nodded. "A couple of pounds," he said.

"Two pounds," the man said, and began to fill a bag. "Look. Just exact. Two pounds." They both looked at the hanging scale. "Bosc pears these are," the man said. "Leave them stay a day or two in the bag. Then they perfect."

Lucky took the bag but did not move on. "How about some grapes? That's Ribier grapes. And I got a special on cantaloupe. Five for a dollar. Where you going to beat that?"

"That's a lot. I don't have a car."

"That's all right. You're a strong boy." The man weighed the grapes, and apples, which Lucky accepted with a nod, and then bagged the melons. Lucky paid and went along the street, a bit annoyed, slowed down. Still he could not resist the fresh bread in La Scala or the cheese store nearby where the daily mozzarella had been brought out to the front counter.

He thought he remembered the cheese man, but again Lucky was a stranger—he could see it in the man's eyes. Then the man remembered: "Sure. You're Johnny. From the Mauro family on Lorin Place. Right? You had an elder brother. I think about my age. I played with him. Which one—was it him that was called Lucky?"

"That's me. So you remember."

"Don't you want to put those bags down?" The man could see strain in Lucky's face. "Here, I'll give you a couple shopping bags. So you can put it all together." He came out from behind the counter and fixed the packages into shopping bags with his store's name on the side. Then he looked up. "Are you down in the neighborhood shopping? Many come from Westchester."

Lucky brought out cigarettes and the cheese man accepted, and they lit up. "Well. I came all the way for some fresh cheese and bread." Lucky smiled at the reddish face. "I was downtown at sunrise. And I just got back from a trip. I got the desire early. It's funny. I suppose in a way it's because of a good friend's death."

"Well, we make it all by hand here. That's why people keep coming.

You want to eat some right now, don't you?" The cheese man went back for a fresh cheese and cut it up.

"Here. Cut some of my bread, too." Lucky took a loaf from the shopping bag. He watched the cutting and took the first pieces and began to eat; then, seeing the cheese man watching, he offered him some.

The cheese man was silent. "I better take something. I turn down my own stuff you'll think it's bad." He was uncomfortable being guest in his own store, but he forgot as he ate.

He began to ask Lucky the common questions, finding out what he did. He was surprised that Lucky was not married. "At your age," he said. "What's it like?"

"What's *what* like?"

"I mean, you can pick up and go anywhere. Just take off when you get the mood. That's what I'd like a little bit of."

"Well, I can't just take off any time. Most of my time, it's the job. Your job takes you."

"Don't I know that." The man smiled and looked into his back room, seen through a doorway. "I'm in there six o'clock in the morning."

"One thing I miss going around. There's nothing like the old neighborhood."

The cheese man smiled. "Yes. But truthful now. Would you come back here to live?"

"I don't know. If I married and got a little house."

"And maybe you wouldn't." The cheese man knew the road out, and Lucky's clothes showed he knew it too and in fact had taken it.

"Well, when you're in Detroit staying in a hotel, you'll wish you had this mozzarella."

The cheese man nodded, with no appreciation.

"Well, this neighborhood," Lucky said as he turned to look at the shoppers and walkers outside. "It's still so nice. The way it is. The people."

"Let's hope." the man said.

Lucky saw a yellow cab double-park outside and went out suddenly to ask the driver if he were going into Manhattan. He came back to tell the cheese man. "I better take this chance or I'll be on the subway two hours."

"Don't forget all your packages. This is what you like."

Lucky picked up his bags and looked at the small square face, heavy and silent. "And there's a good thing about this neighborhood still left," Lucky said. "That's you."

The man smiled, opening up a bit, and walked to the door and then a few steps out on the sidewalk, paused, then went the rest of the way to the cab to help Lucky. He took the bags and set them in the back seat, then stepped back to let Lucky in.

"Where do you go?" the cheese man said.

"Near Eighty-sixth Street." Lucky saw the little man nod with the same face again, trying to show no expression.

As he rode off, Lucky watched the cheese man with his hands against his white apron; he remembered his name: Jimmy. In the daylight some of the features of the boy came out.

The food smells were filling the compartment, mixing together, the sharpness of cheese, the grassy odor of the fruit. He watched the neighborhood as the cab went towards the Parkway: it was all recognizable, and he was smiling, the first time in two days.

He could come back here, stop and see Jimmy, get some of his sausage: they hung red and white in the butchers' windows, like inflated necklaces.

Crowds of women passed the outdoor stands, young mothers in tight slacks and big blue plastic curlers on their heads, as if they were still at home. And enough of the old ladies left, the Mass ladies walking slowly, with capelike black coats regardless of the season. And delicatessens, pizza stands, fried chicken stores, fish stores with painted windows, a white storefront advertising freshly made macaroni. Rows of it, the buying of a pear like an event.

The car was pulsating at the last street signal; at the green they would turn left, down onto the parkway. Lucky began to think about tonight and who he might invite up to his place to share the stuff with him.

# The End

When Angelo had his second heart attack, it was so serious that they were discussing whether he should lie in state with or without his hairpiece. But he recovered and for a long while was at home.

The worst part of it was the change in him, the eyes never focused on anything anymore, as if he were being called by an invisible child somewhere in the room: you'd see his head slowly turn to look away while people were talking to him, then look down and begin to stare.

Arthur Mosconi of the Knights came to visit him a few times, but Angie didn't seem to be interested anymore. "You had promised a contribution to the anti-smut campaign," Arthur said.

Angie stared at him for almost a minute. "I don't care anymore," he said. "I don't want to think about it."

And Phil Di Maris came over to tell him that the Community Action Club wanted to give him an award for his years of help. "I don't want anything," he said. "Don't give me no watches, medals, scrolls. I only gave money."

They were shaking their heads after a few weeks. Angelo's wife, Connie, suggested a visit to the place they had bought in Vermont, but Angelo did not want to go. "I don't know that place," he said. "I never had it long enough to feel at home. When I go there I think I'm staying at somebody else's place. I feel stiff."

"But it's so peaceful up there, Angie."

"Peaceful? Did you ever see the streets of this neighborhood in the daytime? I never knew what it was in the years I worked. It's like a cemetery on these streets. I know. I walk it now. And yesterday I said to myself, what did we do, work our ass off to get out of the Bronx so we could live in a cemetery?"

So Angelo stayed in Scarsdale, day after day, while his office moved ahead and sales increased. He had started a food chain twenty years before, and his stores grew all over Westchester, from town to town, like banks. While he was home, gross sales went up disturbingly; his managers had to call for advice. "Keep increasing your orders," he said from his couch. "Get as much merchandise as they'll send you, put the nightly receipts in the bank, and don't call me anymore."

His accountants took care of the rest, and Angelo was able to sit on his green glassed-in porch and think of death and where its entrance might come, and then why. His mind would ask in silence, *What have I done?* But it wasn't like a trial or a row of judges facing him; only his voices inside shouted at something unseen, screamed like a man on a rack. Angelo on the rack turned to fibre as thin as a spider's web, from now on vulnerable to almost any blow, shock, scream, even rage from another.

One night he dreamed of a volcano erupting and awoke sweating. There was enough light in the room to see Connie's face, and first he became angry that someone had left a lamp on all night and moved his head to look for it. It was moonlight, coming from outside, touching Connie's hair, long and swirling on her pillow and over her shoulders. He loved this secret she slept with, that no one saw but himself, her long, flowing hair, like a woman of an older time. It was a little grey now, but still pretty, and he wanted to lean down and kiss her hair and pull the sheets slowly from her body. But he was not allowed: the doctors said it was not permitted yet.

He placed his head on the pillow and heard his heart, like an incessant door-knocker, like his own front door brass knocker. Fearful of it, he was yet unable to remove his ear from the pillow, thinking that if he stopped listening he would allow the heart to stop.

*What have I done?* came back into his head. Now in the darkness and moonlight he thought he remembered someone actually having said those words.

*Oh my God in heaven.* That little man in Ossining, who had the small grocery; he was old, just him and his wife, and he had nothing else when another of Angelo's markets was going up. He came over and begged them to stop building. He was from Europe, Germany or Russia. Angelo had a big office by that time, and the old man looked out of place and dressed like the poor. Angelo offered him a job; he didn't want a job. He ran out and then came back, about a year later, as he was going bankrupt, and yelled those words.

He would send that man a check. Find him. He could have a manager's job. Angelo looked for a pad to write on, but the moonlight was not strong enough to allow him the sight of the contents of his night-table drawer.

In the morning there was a visit from his daughter Annette, with his grandchild. Connie and Annette and the maid hovered around, ready to intercept the child if it rushed Angelo or jumped on him. Little Bobbie was confused as the women urged him to go to Grandpa, then grabbed his arm or called "watch out" if he moved too close.

Angelo caught the game quickly, and he hated their concern, as if he were a tender egg that might break. He felt awful only when the women hung over him as if he were about to crack, making him worry about himself and hold his chest if he leaned over.

"All right, take him outside," he said.

Annette picked up the baby and carried him into the kitchen, followed by Connie and the maid. Some days he wanted nobody and hated their eyes on him; other times he wanted them all around him so bad he cried inside just from the longing.

He rose from the pillows of the chair and went to the windows. He was going out of here to the office. Connie caught him on the lawn and asked if he were going for a walk. "I'm taking my car to the office."

"No."

"It's no strain. I got to see my office. I'll be right back."

When he got there, the handshakes of welcome came out, and the kind words, but he ended up sad again, like a dead man come back to life, meeting good friends who had buried him. He left right away and drove slowly along streets that did not lead home, the radio playing. The movement of the car was like an energy that filled him up. It was the first thing—of people, objects—of anything that had happened since the attack—that made him feel good, built him up inside.

He drove through the towns along the Sound, especially the roads of Portchester which he liked so much; they seemed old and stable roads, built for homes that had been there forever.

Soon he passed a beach; it must have been attached to a club because he had never seen it before. It was full of kids, high school or college—he could not tell their ages—they could have been eighteen or twenty-five. They were swimming, a few trying surfboards, but there were no big waves.

Two blonde girls were throwing a ball and suddenly dropped the game, ran for the water and swam out, then quickly back. That was it, the way to live, the way he never lived—suddenly jumping into something because the feeling came over you.

Coming out of the water they began to shine, tan skin wet against the sun, bodies that seemed baked, with all the flabby water driven out of them. Their beauty was something special, and it made him smile, though not as if he were watching nude women. They seemed to be doing things together, like twins. He had always hoped his kids, his women, would be like that, but they had settled for cars and the family way, the beauty parlor and the girdle. Once, in Vermont, he found that none of them had ever learned to swim. That night he had told Connie. "We were too poor," she said. "When did you go to the water when you were a kid?"

"But the kids. Didn't they have time to learn?"

"I don't know," Connie said. "Maybe it was something in their minds."

The two girls had come closer and were sitting on a fence. Both were tall, with long legs, but one had very large breasts, covered with a yellow halter; her stomach was brown, her hips thick but not wide, and she straddled the fence like a child. The other, thinner, pulled herself up on the fence post and did some exercises, lifting her body in the air as she held the rail with her hands.

One of the boys came crashing into the sand, his surfboard wobbling, and ran up the beach shouting. He was wearing cutoff light blue pants. He, like the girls, had no hair on his body and was tan already, and his hair seemed to have been dyed with peroxide. The girls ran as he came close to them, and he began to chase them.

Angelo watched them in one game after another until the sun had moved to the right, partially blocked by a castlelike brown stone building, probably the clubhouse. He set the car in motion and drove back.

Connie was at the door, a police car in the driveway, other people on the porch. They had dreamed him dead again, and they all came towards him, letting Connie ask the questions: "Where were you? We were scared to death. The office said you left long ago. We went into panic so we had to call the cops."

Angelo stared at her. "What did you do?" she said, but Angelo only stared. "I'm telling the doctor."

He walked past them and up to his room and slammed the door. Later that night, Connie asked him again: what had he done; where had he gone.

"I went to a place that I'm going to again."

"You can't go out again. Don't you hear your doctor?"

He looked at her standing at the foot of the bed, worried yet a little too fat to be listened to. Connie had not been through it, the end, the casket caked in the head, the gravestone, the fear that made you float like a person locked in a tank of water.

Day after day he went to his beach and watched the kids. He had recognized them and perhaps they had become aware of him; he was not sure. It went on for two weeks, then a third. Then June was almost over. The beach was beginning to get older people, mothers with children.

One Friday he left the beach and stopped for flowers before going home. When he handed them to Connie, she let them drop to the floor.

He looked at her; it was the first time he had been hurt this way since he became ill; she had not done a bitchy thing in months.

"I don't want these payoffs," she said.

"Payoffs? Flowers I brought you."

Connie was circling the living room, partially locked in her words. "I don't care—I don't care what you do. Of course I care. But I meant I don't care if you need some fresh blood. Whatever you want to do right now, no matter how crazy. I don't care. But just think what the doctor said. And what strains the heart."

"*What* strains the heart?" Angelo said. "What are you telling me?"

"The activity you're doing. It's bad for you."

"What am I doing, Connie, what am I doing?"

"You know what you're doing."

"*I* know. Yes. You *don't* know. So tell me what am I doing in your head. Did you follow me?"

"Never. I'm no witch that chases her husband with a knife. I don't care who you go out with."

"It's pussy isn't it. Pussy on your mind."

Connie began to smile. "Are you going to the Musuem of Art every day? Is that why you come back so cheerful, and today it's even flowers? When did you ever bring me flowers?"

"After I died once. And goddamn you, I ain't telling you where I go every day. Let your brain rot before you ever know."

Angelo walked past her, stepping on the flowers, and up to his room. His only wish was to be well enough to get back to work as soon as possible. He picked up a cigarette, then threw it down. He would stick to the line and get out of here faster. The bedroom was hers; the bedroom was the wife's concentration camp. He did not think about it until scenes like this one came up; there had been others, but they were lost in the sadness of the years, Connie's aching words, which were really commands.

Later, he had the maid bring him supper; he did not want to see Connie again. But at ten she came in to get ready for bed, silent, wanting to talk but not certain of her ground anymore.

The next morning she offered to drive him to the doctor, but he refused. "Something might happen to you driving alone," she said, but this time he would not even make the answers she wanted, start the combat.

"Angie, what's wrong? What's wrong with us? Why are you doing this now?"

Angelo watched her cry, her head falling into her hands, her long uncombed hair falling over her face. The tears were uncontrolled, left over from his illness and multiplied by her belief in his betrayal.

"All right, all right." He heard his voice cracking. "All I did was go to the beach every day and watch young kids swimming and playing. And that's the truth."

He left the bedroom as she was beginning to look up. Downstairs he drank an orange juice standing up and walked out to the car. He backed out to the street, adjusted the radio to a pleasant music station, switched on the air conditioning. The car moved along quickly, the engine smooth and quiet. It was a lovely sunny morning, cool inside the car and full of shade and sun outside; and yet he wished he were dead.

# You See What You Did

Henry Giordano came back from the agency at noon; usually he would eat with the salesmen, at the Lido, Hawaiian Acres, or the new Manero's where you could get a nice little steak, just right for a lunch appetite. Before, when he had first opened the agency in Westchester, he went for lunch alone: the salesmen were all young kids from Westchester, but he was from the Bronx. And you didn't just walk over and eat with the guys. Then, he was coming off a stool one day, moving out to pay his check when he heard them and looked back to see four or five of his own salesmen having a great time over their lunch. He had to little by little talk his way in, got himself invited, by one day not being busy. He had said to Marty Davis, who he thought was Jewish: "You like Italian food, Marty? Maybe you'd like to come to have a little lunch with me in Mount Vernon. I can tell you what the different things are." And Marty started laughing. "My mother already did that," he said. "She's Italian. I'm a half and half."

So he had started going out with the salesmen, a different place every day—maybe they didn't all get out every time—one would have a customer and run late and then send out for a quick sandwich or he'd be in with the accountants or somebody from headquarters—nowadays they had a campaign for the introduction of anything—a windshield wiper that you couldn't see, a new doorlock, any kind of piece of crap, and they had to send some schmuck from the main office to talk about it.

But they had a nice lunch crowd. And Henry liked the position: they always gave him a little extra respect—as the boss. They'd save him a seat—always the head of the table. Telling jokes they would often ask him first if he'd heard it. Questions from the waiters, they'd say *Ask our boss* and make it clear it was him, and even with the check, though they always grabbed for it, there were always a few cracks to the waiter about sending it down to the boss, but then one of the boys would always grab it before he could get it. Finally, Henry made a deal with the Lido and Manero to send the bills over to him at the office; and the guys, he could see, were pleased; they came up and shook his hand the day he announced it: it was like a club. And he had said after a few weeks, once, right after lunch, "OK, now that I fed you good, let's go back and sell some cars." It made him blush after it was said, but Mike Bongiorno got up and stamped his fist on the table, shaking the glasses, and he yelled, "Hey, hey, let's go!" This caught on; the other guys got in the habit of doing it, usually on Mondays. First Mike with the "hey, hey" and then all of them.

But now he was home again; he was in an easy chair, the *Herald-Statesman* in his lap, the TV picture going but no sound. Marge had made him a couple of eggs, and he had sat uncomfortably in the kitchen eating them while she dragged herself across the kitchen, putting dishes away, taking things out of the machines. "Why don't you lay down if you're sick," he had said to her.

"I feel better," she said.

"But you call me up to come home because you're sick again, and soon as I come in you're making me eggs. That's not sick."

"You don't believe I'm sick." Marge stopped with her hands aloft, where they had been touching the shelves full of canned goods.

"If you're sick, you're sick. Stay in bed. Call me home. OK, OK. But then let *me* make the eggs. That's sick."

"*You* make the eggs? When could you ever make a lunch?"

Henry had often cooked meals—not big meals—but TV dinners, frozen cannelloni and lasagna, chicken, fish sticks and fried clams and even some prepared lobsters from the Finast. Plenty of times she had called him up in the afternoon to bring home a few things and he was walking through the Finast at 5:30, his eyes staring open from the day and the lights, rolling around the store, barely remembering anything. And getting home, she was in bed or in the bathroom, so he would make the meal. And she would always say: *oh how nice for a change. To have a break like this. It's such a treat for a change.*

It was more than just a change. He was buying things on his own now, stopping off at stores without any special calls, delicatessens he got to know, some people who had moved up from the Bronx and still made homemade stuff every day and had good provolone and imported prosciutto and olives they put in oil and fixed up themselves, and chocolate from Tobler. And he was getting a kick from it.

He didn't answer her about all this, yet he began to think that her moods, her words, were real for a day in the past that hadn't changed inside her. That crack about the eggs was him ten years ago, maybe, when he was a salesman and first learning the ropes. She still talked to *that* man (as her family still did). That's what he was finding in the eggs remark.

What was he doing in the chair? No! How did he get here, waiting for what? After his fucking eggs, where did she go? He sat like this for the whole lunch hour; even when she went someplace, to her room, to the bathroom, he sat like a visitor. He sat. But when he got up to go, she was always around, always got down. "Have to go now?" After explaining why a few times, he stopped answering her questions and just said he'd be back at night.

He would go back to the office, forgetting Marge by the time he got into work there, looking at the windows for a new display idea, and the boys would come around after lunch and ask about Marge, and he would hear himself fall into the worried voice, out of respect to their tone because he had never told them what she had, yet they were sure, most of them, that she was on her deathbed.

So he was home again; the New Rochelle School siren went off: he heard it every day now, and he was puttering around the kitchen waiting for Marge to come down. He came because she was ill; he came in to go up and see her, but she always wanted to come down. All right, so he wasn't that stupid: the poor woman wanted company.

"Marge," he said to her. "I can't come all these lunch hours. I'm losing business."

He heard her voice. "Turn off the oven!" He did it and she came in, dressed in her quilted robe, with her hair brushed right, like Patti Page.

"I had them send up some nice things for that friend of yours."

"Scaturchio. You called them?"

"Yes. I told them who I was. He was very nice, too. He sent the stuff. They have a little blue Volkswagen. Why don't you sell him one of our models?"

Henry did not like this; she should not have called Scaturchio and told him she was his wife. He had an arrangement with them, a friendship, something he had that demanded he at least introduce Marge before she ordered anything. Now they were like any shopkeepers; Marge had called them up and put them in a servant's position.

"Listen, Marge. I can't come here for all these lunches. I'm losing business, I told you."

Margie made one of her statue poses, and turned to look at him. "Yes, yes, business. Customers come at lunch. Buyers. There's a whole world of business happens between twelve and three and I'm sitting here in a kitchen. You understand."

"You want me to call my sister?"

"OK, call your sister."

"I didn't think you'd want her around so much."

"What is so much?"

"Helping. In the kitchen. She'd be here for meals. Giving me my medication. She can give shots. We would save on a nurse."

"I don't know what to say. Your sister's a nice person. Though what else she does, she has to do for herself, I'm thinking. How long can she be here? But that's not my point, I can't run a business from this kitchen, understand? Larchville Motors doesn't grow by itself."

"Aren't you even going to eat what I have in the oven?"

Something inside Henry knew that the question was permission for him to leave, but as yet he was not conscious of any consequences. "I just can't stay for long today. I've got appointments piling up there."

He went for his coat, his hat; he was out the door without touching her; he had not harmed her, bruised her. She could sleep and rest; a little disappointment makes at worst a couple of tears: she looked very good, as a matter of fact, getting chubby and her hair a nice reddish blonde—or was that the wig she had bought? Whichever way, it was very good, very healthy.

Coming into the office, Marge still in his head like a picture book of flapping pages, he heard the voice as if it came out of the air. "Your wife must be better," it said.

It was Rose. Rose. Rose Di Stefano, an Irish girl who had married one of the salesmen and came to work a few months ago. A topnotch secretary. He stopped to absorb, reactivate her words. "Oh yes, Rose. She's getting better. Where are the boys today?"

Rose looked at the sheet on her desk. "Tuesday. It's the Lido. Spaghetti day. Don't you know spaghetti day is always Tuesday?"

Henry was always uncomfortable when non-Italians made this kind of remark; it was worse coming from the lips of lovely young girls like this, who grow up in Westchester, who never learned the street stuff, the wop-toasting of the old Bronx, and Manhattan before that. And since his family had all died, he couldn't take Italian remarks, of any kind. Spaghetti Day. And this kid knew he knew it, as if she was trying to say, "Don't forget you're a wop, Mister Giordano. With a nice dark beard that looks like you need another shave by 2:00." (She had gotten him to bring an electric razor to the place: Rose herself; how she had managed it, he forgot now. But somehow she got it into his head that he could look refreshed by shaving again in the afternoon. And he started doing it everyday after lunch.)

He walked away from Rose, slammed his own office door, trapped inside because he had nothing to do there yet, could not come right out again or Rose would see he had walked in because of his anger. He went to his toilet and quickly shaved, slapped some lotion on his face and went out again. "Rose. I'm going to the Lido. If anything comes up, call me. I'm expecting an out-of-town call."

Rose stood up and leaned over her desk. She was holding a flower, had slipped it into his lapel hole. "You owe me," she said, leaning over him. "I owe you?" he said. "Yes," Rose said. "You owe me for a real poppy. Instead of a fake one." She picked up a can on her desk, for the vets campaign. Henry put a five dollar bill in it. Rose suddenly kissed him on the face; he felt the oil of her lipstick against his skin. "You're so nice, Mister Giordano. I was only expecting change."

"Well, now you got more." Henry felt like an asshole; he had not expected to say such a stupid, obvious thing; his mind was feeling a joke, something a little erotic. He had time. "And kisses like that, I could fill ten cans."

"I've got more expensive ones for you. You should try the ten dollar ones."

"That's a date," he said. He was looking at the doors, part of the all-glass front. He could see the whole lot clearly, yet he was looking, nervous about Bob Di Stefano.

"Nobody's there," Rose said, and he turned to look into her face, see her expression, what she was really saying. She was smiling; her red lips were shining; the silk blouse went around her big, high tits where he had seen the freckles between while he was dictating letters. And she had hard thighs, like drills—

"I like my men dark," her voice was saying. "I like my men Italian."

Now where did it go? Henry looked at her. His pants felt good; he felt stretched. "Rose," he said. "You said *men*. You'd like to try some men."

"Sure." she said. "If the price is right. And if they're cute."

"OK, we'll talk about it."

"Don't wait too long," she said. "I go home for the day at 2:30."

He left her and walked to his car. He had a stiff leg; he was stiff and rough. In the bar he worked it out: she was part-time, left at 2:30; her husband was back for the afternoon about that time.

At the meal, because he arrived late, because he had cut out on Marge, because Rose had hit him with an idea to load his mind, he was not with it, but nobody caught on: they were sure he was feeling good, pleased he had come, heard his voice say the wife was on the way to recovery— (from what?).

And the next two weeks he acted happy, full of chatter. Rose had been setting up a day for them, making a fake appointment on his calendar: she was too good. When he got to her apartment, in a sweat, she answered the door in a black silk robe, brought him right in to sit down, gave him a cigarette, very calmly said it was lots of fun for her, that her mouth always stayed shut, that she wanted fifty bucks each time, an expense account for her, for things she needed. In a minute he got the idea of making it part of her salary and said, "I'll pay it to you through salary." She said, "But do it in cash. I don't want it listed on my paycheck," and just as the deal was set, finished, she had the robe off, and she was on him, the tits in his mouth, her hands in his pants; she was like a storm—he couldn't think. When he had finished and was thinking again of time and Bob Di Stefano coming in, lying on her bed, Rose came in again and was on him, getting him going. He had never had it like this. When they had finished it was almost six; she had gotten him going a second time, with her lips, like a ringmaster, leading him through everything, leaving him after he came, then appearing again as he was waking up, walking in, whipping off the robe, working him up, and wham.

He had driven around to get the smell off him. In the office most of the guys were gone. He sat chuckling, his asshole aching, his groin sore. But it was a funny pain and made him laugh; any quick movement would catch him, a sharp pain, forcing him down in his seat. Finally, he put a pillow under his chair and sat there working until he had cleared his desk of papers to be initialed, return phone calls, reviews of deals the salesman had made during the day.

He made all kinds of reasons to stay late, beginning to check himself for smells. When he got home and took off his pants, he caught the strange perfume again—it was Rose—and took a shower after throwing his shorts and T-shirt into the hamper.

When he came out wiping himself, Marge was standing on his white rug, looking at him. "Well, where are *we* going?"

"What do you mean?"

"What do I mean. You're all freshened up. You look like a man ready to go out on the town. Who's your date?"

"How do you feel, Marge?" He turned away, feeling his face hot: he had almost said Rose instead of Marge; it was his habit to switch names all the time, and he even did it with the salesmen. Like Bob Di Stefano was always with Frank Fortini, so he'd say, "Hey Frank," when he was calling Bob and vice versa. He let the towel fall on the bed and reached up for new shorts in his drawer. After they were on, he stopped. He would get dressed up, instead of settling down in easy clothes for another night at the TV. "Do you feel like a movie?" he asked Marge.

"I think so. If you don't mind taking an old lady along."

"Would you find what's on in Scarsdale and White Plains?" He started to select pants and a sports jacket, forgetting Marge, assuming she had gone until her still-present voice startled him. "What are you whistling about?" it said. He saw her at the hall door, looking at him, makeup all over her face, her hair shining and sprayed, as if she might be wearing an evening gown under her robe. "What's the matter with you, Marge?"

"It's not me. It's you! What'd you do, join a health club? You did some exercise this afternoon."

Henry turned to dress, slowly and carefully. His fingers, his neck, his stomach vaguely—felt her guesses. His eyes felt vulnerable, like clear windows that Marge could see through and catch the scene of his mouth on Rose's big white pink body, so cheap and so rare.

He went back to the bathroom to rub in his greaseless hair cream, then brushed his hair back again. Back in the room, he was alone again and finished, with shirt, tie, clean jacket and trousers waiting in the cleaner's plastic bag.

He walked through the door to Marge's room: she was standing in the center of the room, still dressed in her robe, but her face and hair were perfect, only a little too stiff. She had been getting stiff-looking ever since her illness, the weakness, dizziness, the pains. "Did you get to see the doctor?" he said.

She turned to him, making the frozen pose, her hands stopped in the air. "He came."

"So? So? What did he say?"

"He said the pictures show I have scar tissue in my stomach."

"What is that? What's that mean?"

"That just means if I have a fall, if I have, let's say a shock, a hit, a little accident, I could nice and easy bleed to death."

"I never heard such a thing, Marge." Henry walked around her room, with his boss's nervousness, picking things up, touching everything and talking as he stopped. "Now what does scar tissue come from? Are you born with it? Did you get it in some kind of trouble as a kid? When did it happen?"

"Who knows when it happened? They don't tell you that. They tell you what they see. It's now."

Henry had not looked at her. "Marge, I smell it again. Have you been doing a little drinking?"

"Yes, yes. This thing scared me plenty. I'm feeling myself getting weaker every day. My legs with no strength. And swelling up all of a sudden. It scares me to death. I started drinking again."

Henry went to her. "Now don't get mad. But it's worse when you're in the house. It's no good for you locked in here. You need to meet other people, get out, do something. Start with anything."

"Do you know what sick means? That yesterday after I listened to the 12:00 news, I couldn't get up. I could not get up off a chair. Would you like to see *your* legs like iron pipes thrown down under you."

"Why don't you tell me these things! Tell me exactly what you have. If it's this bad, we need a hospital. We need checkups. Tests." He went to touch her, but instinctively she turned her face aside and her shoulders hunched, as if a kiss or an embrace would hurt her. "You are in bad shape, Marge. Worse than you ever said. Why the hell didn't you tell me!"

"Don't, don't, don't. Yelling after I told you how scared I am. I feel awful about it. You think I don't see myself walking like an invalid— with no legs."

They did not go out. Henry called the doctor with his boss voice, and arranged hospital, specialists, the tests, then removed his jacket, put his robe on and went downstairs to the study for TV. Marge came in smiling, after an hour or so, with a tray, some tea and corn huskies, potato chips, bacon rinds, assorted nuts. "Marge. I made the arrangements. Tomorrow, bright and early."

"I *know.*"

She was like a girl who had just been proposed to, shy, pleased. Henry thought she was grateful that he had called. "We'll get to the bottom of it and get you fixed up. You've got to get back to normal again."

His worry was like a blow; he had never before asked himself what Marge had, had been sure she was in some rotten woman's state (his mother had been sick continuously before dying). The pains, the dizziness Marge complained about seemed like women's periodic troubles which had somehow increased in time. Touching her was out of the question: he had twice in the past few weeks rolled half way on her in an affectionate way, and her hollow voice had come out of the stiff body, "I'll die."

He had not been facing that either, expecting it to go away or happy for a while that Marge was out of order. In five years he had come to treat Marge like something to take care of, protect, surround with stuff of the house, good colors, shining woods, rooms full of large lamps. Marge was the tender thing inside it, like a plant.

But now for her to get stuck inside, shaking at the presence of guests, sweating if anyone stayed for a couple of hours, falling exhausted for a day after a night visit was over. Occasionally, she had hit the bottle and been drunk in the evening when he came in, just dazed and smiling in a chair, her big eyes making Henry pity her; then she shrank away, discovered—cried, caught in lies she told each time before walking across the room and pushing herself against the wall, sometimes sliding to the floor. Henry was sure she had been damaged somewhere in her life. He had asked her about it, the days of her jobs: she had finally been an assistant manager of a small branch savings bank, but there was nothing that happened in those years, nothing bad. She had told him that much, but had not however mentioned that she had once worked very hard on Aaron Berger, one of the bank's attorneys, trying to get married. (But that was only flirtation, and Aaron was a pig, like all men; he had torn her stocking one night, after a movie, the one time he did anything, his long pinky nail getting stuck in her nylons. She could always feel where the nail had scratched along her thigh and always remembered his angry remark (instead of an apology), "Why did you move?" he had said. "Why did you move?")

After Marge left for the hospital in the morning, he was sure he was going to visit Rose, but he waited at his phone in the office, all morning, then went home and called the hospital: there were no results yet. He waited two more days while Rose made calls to the hospital from the office.

He was allowed to see her on the third day and went over for the visiting hours, as Rose took care of his calendar, keeping this time open. Marge lay back in white, pillows at her back, like a lady in a play, speaking very little, asking an occasional question, detached from the house, from outside. She was stuffed with the white room, the smells of medicines.

Her sister appeared in the room, then her father and mother (for one visit), and her brother, a telephone man. But Eileen came daily, and Henry was able to stop his afternoon visits because Eileen was on duty. He put fifty dollars in her hand and said, "Use this to get her any little things she needs. Any expenses you have."

He left the splattered face; he had clobbered them back, thinking of the fifty bucks. Fifty bucks to all.

He came back into the office, ready to go to see Rose, who had left the office, was home in her robe, saw Bob Di Stefano on the showroom floor staring at the light in the lot, and went to close himself in his office, finally phoning Rose, who asked right away about Marge. "No, nothing's happened. She's getting tests. Looks pretty bushed and pale. I was calling about something else."

"It's too late today. Can you make it tomorrow, with the visiting hours?"

"Her sister is keeping watch in the afternoons. I really appreciate this, Rose."

When he arrived the next day, some emotion had changed. Rose was concerned with helping him, his beaten emotions. Everyone felt the loss of Marge was bad: they kept repeating it, as if a wife out of the nest was like a necessary front tooth, ruthlessly extracted. "I'm all right," he told Rose and began to walk around her apartment (as she offered her help), his boss walk, picking up items, inspecting them. "I'm even a little better than all right. The house is quiet; there's peace in it. I go and do what I want. Like a vacation."

"With no woman to keep up the place."

"There's a maid who comes."

"That's for dust and throwing out the garbage. A house needs a woman in it. You know that. We all know that."

His anger prevented his answering. What was in his head he did not know, but he saw Rose's face smeared with an idea. What kind of woman did she mean? All kinds? Whatever the woman was. "Any kind?" he said; he had been moving among Bob's golf mugs on a shelf.

"What?"

"Any kind of a woman?"

"The one you marry. That's the way it is. You made your choice."

"Whatever it is, huh? Whatever is there."

"I don't know what you mean, Mister Giordano. Each of us has his own luck. You don't dump people in the garbage can like kids you don't like, that never turned out good. You don't junk them."

"I never had kids. *She* never had kids."

He saw Rose clasp her hands like a girl at Mass and sit down; he came towards the couch, drawn by the sight of her thighs as her legs crossed. "You don't have such a bad life," she said. "You've got a lot to be thankful for. Don't you admit that?"

"Rose, I thank my god. But don't think I didn't work my ass off for it. I don't have no golf mugs like Bob. My cups are all in the business."

"I know, I know. It's something to be proud of. Bob'll never have anything like that. He's just a different type. He's never going to make real money. But that's my life—see what I mean."

"Rose, you make sense, but that's what you think. What about me, now? Do I have a right to complain?"

"We all get illness," Rose said. "We're lucky when it's the other one, as they say."

Henry was moving towards the door, his hat in his hand. "Thanks a lot," he said. "I'll see you at the place tomorrow."

"OK, see you tomorrow. Thanks for stopping by. Say hello to Marge."

"We didn't do nothing," Henry realized he was leaving, an automatic good-bye after a visit to a relative, an old friend, "We didn't do *nothing*."

Rose was staring, too. She had been caught, trapped by the conversation; she walked around for thoughts to explain what she had done. "Maybe you shouldn't do anything now."

"What do you mean?"

She opened the front door, held it ajar. "You just shouldn't, *now*."

Henry went out into the hall, the afternoon smells trapped in the windowless corridors, a hundred, a thousand suppers starting up, and how many Roses in robes.

On the way home, he started remembering the rudeness of Marge's family; they said hello to him as if he were an inferior. No matter what, he was Italian. Neither her brother nor her father was bad. After all this time, they gave him a fifteen-year-old hello, to the mechanic, as if his dealership never existed, did not take out full-page ads in the papers, wasn't more than they would ever have.

He stopped at the Lido for a drink, and Tony wanted to talk, about car buying, about any good deals Henry happened to have now. The dream used car everyone asks about all the time, the undriven Caddy owned by the rich lady who goes out twice a year and gets a new model every year. Henry heard his lies: "I always have you in mind, Tony. Like a Caddy, an Imperial, something big that might come along. Even a Riviera that could come along. Right?"

"At's right, at's right." Tony spoke like a wop; the Irish would treat him worse; but maybe not: Tony owned a restaurant and took bets on the horses. That would make him better to them, right? Tony in fact had been one who told him—how many years ago—that he was making a mistake marrying out of his own kind, not taking an Italian wife. But Marge had been from the same neighborhood; his mother liked her and knew her from church, from the Altar Society. What was wrong? Some aunts stuck up their nose in disgust, as if he had performed some insult to a bearded Giordano in Avellino. And there were cracks—that Marge had no body, no force, and from the women: that she needed big tits and big hips and not having them was the empty white things you saw in America. That was the damn old ladies.

He found himself invited for supper with Tony at his back table. And it was cars again while they had some homemade lasagna and little fillet steaks that were so juicy. "How come I can't even get these in a store," Henry said. "Why don't you sell me some for the freezer."

"At's right, at's right. You just tell us how many you want. I'll have them deliver."

Then Tony wanted to talk cars again, as if the whole point of working was getting a machine. They went through button windows, disappearing wipers, air conditioners, speakers in the back seat, tables that pop out like in a Jag, stereo players. Then women: Tony liked to guess what prominent women did, assuming that fame created new, wild sexual habits, new departures not permitted to the middle class, never to the poor. To Tony the poor ate and slept, and once a month, drunk on beer, knocked off a

157

piece that made the next dirty kid. By the time they were drinking black coffee, Tony had gone through the movie colony, wives of presidents and prominent governors and was touching on the foreign stars. Henry was sleepy and started to go as Tony was finishing up on Sophia Loren, the Italian boff. "What do you think, Henry? With those lips, with a mouth like that? With that old guy. You think she takes maybe four at a time in it? Isn't that possible? No?"

Henry placed his hand on Tony's shoulder, looked down carefully and saw that Tony sweated while he ate. After an affectionate good-bye—he used the excuse of Marge and the hospital visiting hours—he rode off in the car thinking of Tony, how he was able to stand it, sitting in his own sweat while he ate, a whole meal with the sweat pouring down his face. If he could do it for so long without wiping himself, he must have lost the feeling.

Getting home, he did not welcome the silence; not that he missed Marge very much, knowing she was there where they were helping her. He walked through the rooms thinking of Rose, then of thighs and breasts and flesh. If he could only call a service, have them send up a girl for a few nights. He had not taken his jacket off, waiting instead for something, some intrusion by doctors or a message that was coming. He wanted to go and walked out to the car and drove until he found a new movie. As he walked in, an usher saw him and shone a flashlight at his feet, then led him down the aisle. As soon as he sat he was uncomfortable; he placed his hands on the back of his head, his bald spot, but he couldn't keep his hands there all through the movie. He got up slowly and went to the back rows, which he liked, found a seat on the side (but it was the last row) and relaxed. It always made him nervous to be seen from behind, the damn thing had happened as soon as his spot showed all his head skin: and he always thought that he would be recognized and called by name now that he was getting bald. Marge had gotten used to the last rows. But even then, if there were wind from the lobby and it hit his head, he would go wild with nerves, call the usher, get Marge annoyed.

He tried to see the picture; maybe he was going crazy, too, imagining more than living. What had happened to Marge: you call that real. He left the movie and walked down the street before getting into the car, trying to find a gift shop. He saw a Dennison lighted up, with some statues of JFK and Pope John with barometers in their bases. Marge could predict the weather: it was a nice idea.

When he saw her, she was changed; he did not like the whiteness; what were they doing? Her voice was hollow, an if she'd been emptied. "What are they doing?" he said. "Tests." "What kind of tests?" "They take out blood, they do X rays." Her face to the side. "Internal examinations."

"When can I talk to the doctor?"

"He's coming on late rounds. About nine, ten."

The doctor came and ignored Henry, checking Marge and her card, pulse, pressure, even her feet. Henry followed him to the door. "I'd like to ask you."

"Yes, Mr. Giordano. You must be wondering."

"How long will she be here?"

"She's being discharged tomorrow. In the morning. I'll see you in my office tomorrow night—or the next day. If she's too tired tomorrow."

"Well, can you tell me—what is it?"

"She's probably had some kind of infection, maybe complicating a herniated area from the past. It's hard to say. It could be the vessels themselves. A kind of premature sclerotic process. It's hard to say unless you go in and look around. And we don't want that yet—"

Henry shook his head along with the doctor.

"But we know she's got to be careful. She *could* hemorage. That's the trouble. Now the swelling ankles are nothing serious. We've checked her out completely. Nothing."

Henry was left alone with the *nothing,* the white walls of the hallways, Marge in the white bed. He went back and spoke to her until he was almost asleep. "You got to work tomorrow," she said. "Don't you think you better start home?"

At the door he heard something and turned around. It was Marge, crying; he had never heard that sound in her before, a whimper so light that it frightened him—as if she would break into pieces, as if a dying child cried inside her, part of her, yet another person.

He reached the house by 10:30, but it seemed like four in the morning. He got undressed and lay on the bed to watch the TV, holding the remote box on his chest and switching all around to get something good. The silence finally came completely to him and he spread more of his body across the bed; it had been their first bed, a small double, moved into the study because she got up three or four times in the middle of the night and walked. He had never really inquired into it, and now he would only touch it briefly, only remember that she mumbled and talked sometimes, that she held her arms close by her body, holding herself, not in pain necessarily but knotted in some frightening way, threatened—threatened by her dreams, maybe. Marge was always a nervous type; her lips shook the night JFK announced he was going into Cuba for the Russian missiles.

The shows were changing after the news and he went clicking for a good movie; after a segment he was impatient: he had had an erection, had become angry that Rose turned off, had a dream of late TV shows that were porneys and got excited just thinking about them, like the ones he had seen with the bowling club boys. Then he fell asleep and woke up with gas pains, his stomach going rotten on bad hours and crazy eating.

Next day he had an appointment—people from Detroit—and had to send Rose to get Marge. While talking to the officials he saw Rose spin out of the lot in a big demonstration model, looking as if it were hers already and maybe it would be if she threatened to have a heart-to-heart talk with Marge.

But when he got home in the late morning, Rose was in the kitchen fixing things and Marge was upstairs—watching TV in her bedroom. "Well, how is it, Marge?"

"Oh, pretty good, I guess. Rose was very nice. But she's doing too much. Tell her we'll get the girl to clean up your mess. You know you forgot to call the girl."

"I thought she came in automatic, twice a week."

"She probably came when you were in the office and nobody answered the door."

"Doesn't she know who I am? She could have called the office."

"They don't think like that, I'm sorry to say."

"I'll go down and stop Rose."

"And give her something, will you?"

"Give her what?"

"I don't know. A gift. Something to say thanks."

"I'll send her flowers."

"I mean something *now*. Couldn't you give her something?"

Henry went down the steps and found Rose in the kitchen. "Marge says you helped her more than enough. She wants you to stop. She says the girl will finish up."

"I don't mind. I'm getting paid. And I like to do it. You have such a lovely house. I just love this place. It's gorgeous."

Henry put five tens on the kitchen counter where she could see. "I appreciate what you did, Rose. You're a wonderful girl."

She was out too soon, leaving with a smile but no words, no appointments. Maybe it was the way he had talked that made her think he was not anxious to come see her. His voice had a weakness in it when he talked to her; he shouldn't be thanking her like that.

Upstairs, Marge was wearing glasses. "Did they give you eyeglasses to wear there?"

"Yes. They found my eyes weak."

"What are they, reading glasses?"

"No. Regular. For all the time."

He went to the office and came back with supper to eat in the bedroom. He sat with her, in the silk-covered chair with no arms, like a visitor because something inside him made him quiet. "I got to go to bed," he said after an hour or so. "Watch Johnny Carson with me," she said.

"I'm tired, Marge."

"Get your pajamas on. Then come and watch a while." He went out and got undressed and came back, sat down and remembered he was supposed to go out. "I was supposed to see my niece Jennie."

"Where is she?"

"What do you mean, where is she? She's right in Tuckahoe."

"I mean, she never came to see me."

"She's got six kids."

"They never came."

"They don't know you were really sick."

"What time is it?"

"It's late."

"It's time for the red medicine. Will you get me a glass of water?"

He stood over her with the water and watched her face while she swallowed the medicine; the new circles behind her glasses made her face look big and flat, expanded by the lenses and shining, with blue in it.

At ten she took a pill, and Henry felt he would vomit watching her tongue gagging. "It's only a small pill," he said, trying to relax her.

"I can't swallow pills. You know that. I gag."

"You want me to crush it up in some applesauce?"

"Yes."

He carried the pill to the kitchen and the large spoon back upstairs, with applesauce sticking in it, speckled with tiny white bits of the pill, like desk chalk.

In his bed he could hear her and sat up. He was not sure what she was doing, whether she wanted help. He fell asleep waiting for her to call out.

In the morning he forgot to go to her room and was leaving the house when she called for water, which he brought up. "Get the jar of applesauce," she said. "I'll need it today, for the pills."

He had a cigar while he drove, a large Panatella; he always liked one after breakfast and lately started another in the office. The taste was so good; they had a special aroma, like a get-together.

Marge called four times during the day and at night they had a talk about her sister again, but her sister could only come for a few hours in the day. "How about a nurse for a while," Henry said. "Until you get feeling better."

"No." Marge looked at the ceiling. "I don't want anything like that in here. A strange person all the time."

"Well, don't you need help, Marge? You need those shots."

"Maybe I can go to the doctor for shots. You know how horrible a nurse makes you feel in a house."

Marge's skin had changed, had gotten a hospital color; there were little spots of blue in it. "Today, I was thinking, how about a sunlamp for you. If you can't go out, it could give your skin some tone."

"I can go out on the porch."

"On the porch?" Henry remembered a night meeting of the Dealer's Association, "I've got a meeting. The Association."

"You going there, again?"

"It's important if you're going to keep up."

"Is something wrong with the business?"

"Wrong? We can't keep cars in stock they're running so fast." Henry moved around the room like a dance. "I don't know where all the money's coming from."

"My sister says it's the war. People making more money."

"The war?"

"I don't know. That's what people say. Korea."

"Vietnam."

"All those wars. I don't know."

Henry went for a clean shirt, a new shade of blue he had bought at Wallach's. Years ago if you wore a blue shirt with a suit you were a ditchdigger on his night out. He smiled into the mirror. Now you see a white shirt you think it's a bookie or some kind of greenhorn.

The boys were all at the meeting, the same boys, the jokes, the cigars, and pictures—lately everybody had some Danish pictures. Henry was elected secretary. It was a surprise and he had no speech. "That's all I need." He was standing, making his acceptance, smiling. "Business is so slow these days I got plenty of time to keep records." A big laugh helped him on a little more. "Those of you who know me know where you can expect the next meeting. For the rest of you. I hope you like spaghetti and pizza." Another laugh. "So thank you for the trust. I'm not planning any long trips." A nice ending laugh as he sat down.

After the meeting he stopped to talk with Ernest Shimaky of Ford and a few other guys came up and they all drove over to the Lido for drinks and music. He hadn't done it in a long time, and they talked about trends, things people were doing he hadn't heard about, new selling techniques. *Here* you picked up the secret you needed; people would let them out over drinks, and you had to be here: they never mailed them to you.

Marge was asleep when he got in, so he got ready for bed quietly. When he came back from the bathroom, she called to him and he went to her door. "Henry, are you smoking cigars this late?"

"I was only finishing one in the john. It's out now."

"That smell makes me throw up."

"Well, open a window and throw up. It's smelly in here. It smells like your medicine and your feet."

He went to the window and let in the air. "OK?" he yelled.

Marge did not answer: her head looked up at the ceiling, the eyes behind the glasses like false glass eyes. "You cold yet? Can you feel the difference?" He shut the window. "Marge. I was elected secretary of the organization."

Her head turned towards him, her smile broad, stiff, wrinkled, like a mother's. "Nice, nice." Henry looked at the floor. "You're really making it," her voice said. "Like we dreamed. Remember I was the one who kept telling you. There was a time you didn't want to try to open the agency. You worked for other guys."

"And we had a couple of drinks at Tony's. And the hints I picked up. Oh man. They've developed selling tricks, service tricks. I felt I was living in the Stone Ages. You know, I got to keep in touch."

"Why don't you have some of them out here?"

Henry stopped and looked at her. "Here? After you're better, maybe." He said goodnight and went to his room. Her suggestion had stunned him. It was as if she did not know how she was. He shook his head and got in bed, his head feeling thick as it moved sideways on the pillow. Drinks filled his head up. He could not sleep quickly. He thought of going in to Marge but she was too sick for anything. How the hell! How the hell was she going to entertain if he asked them over! In her robe, holding pills? Fuck!

The word shook him, and he turned over, trying to get up for an aspirin. But sleep was coming, and Rose, too, the color of her skin, white or maybe orange, the legs darker than the top of her, hair he had noticed on her thighs, where she had not been shaved clean.

The next day he stayed late for a phone call while the boys went out for lunch, then left when the office was empty except for Rose. He stopped in front of her desk. "How is the Mrs.?" she said.

No answer came out. He started for the doors. "If you want to see her, take the demonstrator and drive over. Use it any time you want."

"Thanks, Mister Giordano."

He was a little late, but they had ordered for him. He had some potatoes with his steak, some garlic bread they had ordered: he ordered more all around, and then two Nesselrodes, saying to himself that this was his meal of the day. But all afternoon his stomach pushed out against his pants and he was gassy. He looked at Frank O'Hara, who was always tan and went over to talk to him. "Do you have a health club you go to? I've been thinking of getting some exercise. And take off some of the beef."

"No, I don't know any health club." O'Hara looked down at his boss, who was obviously not joking. "I play ball on weekends."

"Like teams?"

"It's a league. I used to play Class A ball a few years. But this is semipro."

"You look like a ballplayer."

"Yeah. I try to keep in shape. Keep off the butts and the booze. My only fault is pussy. Can't leave that alone."

"Where do you go?"

"Go?"

"Where do you get it?"

"Oh. The stuff? You just meet it. Around. Bars. Clubs. Friends. Friends of the friends. There's a waitress at the Waffle Inn; maybe you know her. A redhead named Terry. I'm taking her out now. I just met her over there, having a snack."

Henry could see the building through the window, set in the middle of its black parking lot, the blue Swiss roof shining across the street.

"I think I saw her." Henry spoke after the silence of looking.

"Yeah," O'Hara said after his silence, hands in pockets, looking out the windows.

Henry looked at him, his shining suit. "Where'd you get that suit?"

"This suit? Cye of London. It's a new place in White Plains."

Henry nodded and walked back to his office. It was the slow part of the afternoon; they could just as well be closed. Everyone slept up here, it seemed. And Rose, too. Rose was in her robe.

He went out to the service garage and walked down the line looking at the mechanics at work. He stopped at the desk and Tony, his chief, came out of his glass office. "How's it going?"

"Oh, fine, boss, fine."

"Did you finish the callbacks?"

"All done. And it's been very busy again."

"I got some new tips on prices. I want to talk to you."

"Any time, any time."

"Do you think we could raise some prices? They're all going up on a few things. Like standard clutch jobs. What do you think?"

"Sure, sure. People don't care."

Henry walked back, stopping at the accounting office near parts, where the girls worked. "Is it cool enough in here?"

"Yes, Mister Giordano." Mary Capella had looked up to be the spokeswoman.

"It seems stuffy sometimes," Henry said. "Are you getting stink from the shop?"

"Only when the window opens. When somebody comes to pay a bill. Just a few seconds."

He saw all the girls smiling and smiled back. "Well, you let me know what you need."

Back in the office he felt tired, but he had never had the cot put in. He walked out and told the operator he was going home for a few hours. "If I'm not back by seven, have Tommy Esposito close it up."

"Isn't tonight a nine thirty?"

"That's right. Well, Tommy's on till late. If I'm delayed, have him close it up."

When he came in, Marge was calling. He went up to her and met her sister, who had come a short time before. "Eileen gave me a shot," Marge said. "That's five bucks saved."

"Sure. It's easy." Eileen held up the hypodermic. "I was telling Marge I could teach anybody. Where did I learn it but the Red Cross. Anybody can give intramuscular, though the veins are another thing."

"She can't come all the time," Marge said. "So she'll teach you."

Henry did not understand Marge's smile. "It's gonna make Margie a pincushion for a while." Eileen said.

"Go ahead," Marge said, and turned on her side. "Wash your hands," Eileen said.

Henry removed his jacket and went in to wash his hands. Eileen came in to get the sterilizing can. "I boil my needle and my vial. You stick all the stuff in this little tin, put in about a half inch of water, and boil it ten minutes, but if you're lazy, they sell these plastic sets you use once and then dump. I'll get them for you wholesale, a whole pack."

"Why don't we get a nurse to come in just for the shots. How much can it cost?"

"Try to find one today. Try to get one to come when *you* need her instead of at midnight when you're trying to sleep. Look Henry, just try to do this. It's easy, I swear."

He looked at Eileen, whose big thick body he had increasingly enjoyed looking at the more he went to pick up Marge in the early days when they were keeping company. He had even wished he had met Eileen before Marge.

They went inside with the equipment and standing beside the bed Henry learned how to stick the needle into the rubber top of the medicine bottle, then take out the fluid.

Marge was quiet; she had remained on her side while they were in the bathroom. Eileen threw the sheets back over Marge, then pulled up her nightgown. Henry was nervous, embarrassed to be leaning over Marge's uncovered body in Eileen's presence, but Marge called out. "Hurry up. Do it."

Eileen kneeled on the rug, with the hypodermic in her right hand, held back near her shoulder. She placed her left hand flat on Marge's behind and Henry saw the soft, falling flesh, which shocked him. Marge had had a big, tight behind; it gave him pleasure. Now the flesh fell, like two slabs of pizza dough, one upon the other. "You just bring your hand forward firmly." Eileen's voice was blowing against Marge's skin. "And get the point in quickly. Then you can release the fluid slowly. That way there's less pain."

Henry got on one knee and watched Eileen do it. Marge's skin jumped but she made no sound. Then Henry took the needle, and tried it. Zock!

"Good. You got it right away." Henry paid more attention to Marge's silent body turned away from him while Eileen's enthusiasm resounded around him. "Most people shake; they hold back and never get the thing in."

"How do you feel, Marge?" Henry spoke to her back, and she turned her face and gave him a sexy smile.

"Come in, Henry." Eileen was taking him by the arm. "Let me show you the medicines."

He followed her into the bedroom and heard all the instructions, which dispelled the thoughts he was having about Marge. Then he walked Eileen to the downstairs door, helped her with her overcoat. "You'd better do your smoking down here," she said. "I think the medicine makes her stomach more sensitive."

He went to the kitchen after the door was shut and found some Swiss cheese in the refrigerator. He took it to the table, but then left it. He wasn't hungry, and he could sense the annoying dryness of the cheese on the roof of his mouth even before he tasted the cheese.

He went upstairs to ask Marge if she had ordered any food from the store, and she gave him a list while he sat in the silk chair next to her and wrote.

In the Finast the lights made his eyes stick open and he wandered the aisles a few times before he got it all, then found other new items, frozen food, cookie specials, a Finast canned soda sale. He had to get a boy to help fill the car, and when he got back it took three trips to get all the bags into the house. It was dark when he finished putting it all away, and he made a cake from the mix and brought it up for Marge.

"When did you do that?"

"Just now. After shopping. I started reading the box in the store and it looked easy."

"And the icing too?"

"That's already made. In a can. You just spread it on."

"Very good. But shouldn't we eat it after supper?"

"I got some dinners. Do you like the chicken or the sliced beef?"

"Don't ever get the chicken. They fry it in such rotten oil. Don't you remember, you said it tastes like shellac."

"That's right, that's right. I forgot. You look at the picture of it on the box and it looks so good."

"I *know*. Now you understand."

Henry went down and brought the cake and set the table while the trays were heating in the oven. He called upstairs. "Marge, I just realized. You can't come down."

"No, no. Come and help. I want to come down."

When he reached her she was already sitting up and had her robe on. "You're sweet, Henry."

Her steps were without any strength; she could not move her feet more than a few inches at a time. "Marge? What is it? Is it your ankles? Or your stomach?"

She stopped, and he looked at her face, which had become red. "There's just no strength left. I put a foot down and I think it's falling."

"Maybe in the hospital you got weaker."

"I started to feel this before. That I wasn't going to walk someday."

While they ate, Marge was silent, but she had an enormous hunger. "Maybe you should take it easy," he said. "Save something for the cake."

She smiled and stopped, as if his reminder made her conscious again. "I'm glad to be home again, I'll tell you. The hospital food was like boiled garbage."

"I'll bet."

They had the cake in the TV room, starting early with the news, then reruns until the new night shows. Marge fell asleep in her chair at nine thirty and Henry helped her upstairs again, feeling the great heaviness now as her legs tried to make the steps. They were helpless. Henry saw a little of them between her robe and far slipper: white as paper. He put her into bed and went right back down again, turned off the set and took the dishes to the kitchen.

In bed he thought of the white legs. Was Marge dying without the doctor telling him; what was the matter with that man?

The next day in the office, when Rose finally located him by phone, the doctor said, "I told you we're not sure. We can't make a final diagnosis, but we are eliminating organic diseases one by one. Now I say let's build her up first. Get her blood strong and right. Nutritional supplements, some antibiotics. I gave those shots instead of pills to hasten it."

Through the summer there was no change and then into the fall, Marge got out of bed for a few days, started to make artificial flowers; then he'd come home and she'd be in bed again, white again, her face looking up at the ceiling as if she were trying to remember something.

It was September and he booked rooms at a hotel in the mountains and insisted she try to make it. The first two days were good; after she slowly made it to the dinner table or the entertainment, she enjoyed herself. The second night she had some drinks and later in the room, when she was lying down, she grabbed him. He was so hot he was on her quickly. "I'll bleed," she said. "I can start *bleeding*."

He jumped up and walked around the bed. "You can try. If it's doing something, then we'll stop."

"No, no."

"I don't like you!" Henry had not even heard himself say it.

"Let me ask the doctor. When we get back."

"Shit!" Henry walked in anger. "I've got to get satisfied. I'll have to go somewhere and get it."

"I want to go home, I'm shaking. Help me up."

"Where the hell can *you* go?"

"I'm sick."

"Then stay in bed."

He heard the sound of her vomiting in the darkness before he could do anything. He ran for towels and began to wipe it up, first the rug, embarrassed that the hotel people would see it; he let Marge continue alone in the bathroom.

They drove back the next morning; he had given the maid two tens and was silent in anger for doing it. Marge held both hands on the door rests, as if the car were going to crash any minute and even when he slowed way down, she did not change position. Still, she refused the seat belt around her stomach.

Two hours after they got back, the doctor was in Marge's room. "It was too much for her. What can you say besides that. She's weaker. I think she'd better leave out any trips until she's much stronger."

"Well, what is it?"

"It's only her body's not responding fast enough. So she's getting run down too fast. And I don't want to strain that stomach anymore. Keep her in bed for at least a week."

"Not even downstairs?"

"Better not."

"Should I get a nurse?"

The doctor was running downstairs. "That's up to you."

Instead of going back upstairs, Henry went right to the office to look around. They were putting up a streamer in the showroom, and Bob Di Stefano came over to tell him they had broken the East Coast sales record. Henry went to his office and shut the door. But the boys were in after a few minutes to go for a victory meal, and they all went out to the Lido, where they had prepared a special spread and a big cake. They stayed a couple of hours, and when they were in the parking lot again, Henry felt wonderful. He drove off, north, and kept going up the parkway until he was in Connecticut. He turned off at a roadside stand as it was getting dark, bought a bushel of apples and drove back, enjoying the aroma of the fruit inside the car.

The house was closed up, but he did not mind it. He lit a cigar and sat at the TV set; he was smiling at the afternoon; his mind was getting able to shut out Marge upstairs, but only after a good event. He had joined Bob's club and went there once or twice a week for cards and bowling and an occasional stag.

The cold weather drove him outside more often; he started bowling at the Friday nights and agreed to finance a club: LARCHVILLE MOTORS, EAST COAST CHAMPS. Marge was home all the time, and he shopped, gave her her shots, talked to her while she ate. She was getting pissed about his going out more and more, but she had no reason to condemn it. One night he had the bowling guys pick him up, bringing them up to see her, having a drink with her before they went off.

Just before Christmas there was a big snowstorm, and Henry started out for a club meeting while it was coming down.

"You can't go out in this," Marge said. "You'll get stuck."

"I got chains." Henry had put on thermal underwear. "It's lovely air."

"If you get stuck, I'm all alone here. Suppose something happens to me."

"Just call me at the club."

"And if you get stuck in the snow?"

"Then everybody's stuck in the snow."

"And what happens to me? I just sit here and wait."

"You'll be all right. Just stay in your bed."

At midnight the phone rang in the club for Henry. "Come home. Something's happening."

"What is it?"

"My stomach. It feels awful. I spit blood."

Henry found her faint but not unconscious. "Did you call the doctor?"

"No answer."

"How many times you call?" He went to the phone, found no answer at the office number, no message from the answering service, and called the hospital.

The ambulance came in about an hour, with a young doctor. "Does she have an ulcer?"

"No," Henry said.

"Well, let's get her there anyway. Your doctor is on the way to the hospital."

Henry helped carry the stretcher through the snow; they pushed the truck almost a block before they got it going, and he was dripping wet. "You better come with us now," the young doctor said.

"The lights are on. My house is open."

"Nobody's moving tonight. Come on."

He sat in the hospital corridor, waiting. The doctor had come by and shook his hand, then had a towel sent out for his wet face and neck. A long time passed before the doctor came out again, with the surgeon. "Mr. Giordano, this is Doctor Kelley, the surgeon."

"She's going to be fine. She lost a little blood, not much, but we're giving transfusions. But I looked around, and I can tell you she's all right. No ulcer. Just a herniated area, must have been there a long time. And I think she has weak vessels. It's just a thing she has to live with."

"See," the doctor said, "we checked her everywhere. She's free of disease."

The doctor offered him a ride home and came back to get him dressed in his blue suit again. "Let her sleep here tonight. And get looked over. Let's let her sleep. I've got a twenty-four hour nurse there. We'll get the blood in her."

On the way home the car skidded while the doctor drove as if on clear streets in daylight. When they stopped at Henry's house, the doctor had a last word. "I'm going to try some new medication. With the new coagulants in it. And I think she should be off animal fats of all kinds."

"Will it happen again?"

"We don't think so. Kelley says the herniated area was the cause of it. But we want to build up the vessels and get that weight down. You can't be heavy now, with this weakness. No extra strain, you know that."

Henry went in to wash, first walking through the house to see if it was the same. In his room he took off his clothes and poured a hot bath, but when it was over, he dressed again, waiting for some call from the hospital. He fell asleep soon in the heat of the house, with the silence that he knew having become wider and broader because of the snow, which covered everything and stopped all the cars.

He awoke to the light and went downstairs after washing, shaving, brushing his hair. He went out to the front steps and breathed the clear air. The garage was blocked, but he found a shovel in the cellar and began to dig out the driveway as the sun came up high over the houses across the way. It was warm and cheerful; all he could think was *Christmas*.

He made himself cocoa, then drove out to the local service station and had the chains put on. The owner asked about his reason for being up so early, and he told him about Marge. "I heard people talking about an ambulance that got stuck last night. Was that you?"

"We finally made it. It was close. It was close."

Marge did not look too bad; she was white but at least she moved better. The nurse said she could come back in a few days, in time for Christmas. Henry left and drove to the showroom: the streets were melting fast, but the wet snow covered the trees. After the morning, he had a snack at the Waffle Inn, was served by the girl O'Hara had mentioned, then went down to the Cross County Center and bought gifts until his eyes were aching.

Marge was home in time for the tree. Eileen came over to help them put it up and decorate the house, and Henry realized he had not gotten her more than one little gift, so he gave her the gloves he had gotten for Rose (and ordered a set of silver goblets for Rose the next day). Eileen slept over for the whole week of getting ready, until Christmas. The snow stayed on the grass. On Christmas Day, Marge's parents came to the dinner he and Eileen had cooked, and all afternoon they told him Marge had been the healthiest child in the world; by evening they were all drunk enough to enjoy themselves, tell jokes, even make some cracks about Marge. Her father said, "Don't worry about Marge. She'll get her fat ass back again." And this stuck with Henry, came back later as he was getting ready for bed. Eileen had come down the hall as he was walking in his robe from Marge's room. She stopped him and kissed him. "Merry Christmas, Henry."

Henry reached over to grasp her passionately and struck her tooth with his lips. She was either about to laugh or grimace; he had also stepped on her toes with his bare foot. "Be a nice boy," Eileen had said nicely, and Henry's arms had fallen to his side. "I love you too," Eileen had added, and walked back to the guest room.

Henry went to his room and thought of breaking into Eileen's room, tearing her clothes off; she wanted it, too. He heard the tone of her *I love you, too,* more and more false as the memories made the echoes. False pig and Irish bitch. White asses. Dead cunt, I'll kill you. He shut the door and went to the little desk near the window; on it were the boxes he had started collecting: extra buttons from a promotional contest, pens that had been given to him as gifts, each one with the name of a business on it; near the wall a large brown box was full of calendars. He began to count them, then put them away in the closet, where he had stacked a long narrow red rug used in the fall promotional display for new models. His room was filling up; he had been bringing more home each week.

When he finished, he went to lock his door before getting into bed. He brought out a corn cob pipe he had received and sucked on it while he watched the late news. As the sounds grew louder and louder, the commercials, then the music for *The Tonight Show,* the screaming announcements, he forgot the people here-and-gone and lay back smiling, working on himself, helping himself to sleep with his hands, erupting on himself and lying there, still listening to the music, the voices moving back and forth. A thought began to rise up again—he wished it would snow again, snow and snow and snow.

# The Shylock's Wedding

When Marie Anne Moretti and her boyfriend John Russo decided to get married, they drove over to the Moretti house in North Yonkers to tell the family.

Anna Moretti was home alone watching TV and when she heard the kids already planning the wedding, she asked them to wait for her husband, Al, who would want a say.

Al got home late from a union meeting at AGFK where he was floor manager; the kids had gone out again because they were too excited to wait. It was better for Anna, who wanted to talk about Mrs. Russo's club, which rented out its ballroom in the off-season for affairs.

Al Moretti knew that the Russos expected a big affair, but he was uncomfortable about using their club because he was not a member; nor did he have any club of his own.

"*Now* how I wish I had joined that place in New Rochelle," he said.

"They were all Jews, they told us."

"Who cares what they are. The facilities are there, and the price was right."

"I only meant we wouldn't *know* anybody."

"Sometimes I think Jews are the last Italians left. But who gives a damn. I need a club right now."

"What's wrong then with the Russo's?"

Al went to the kitchen for his night milk and cookies. Anna sat watching him. "Oh those meetings," he said. "It's a lot of fucking talk that don't mean anything anymore. Who needs a union at AGFK? There's more benefits coming out of management than *we* can think up. Only it didn't do nothing yet to clear my headaches."

"I been meaning to ask you, you in that profit-sharing plan?"

"Yes, I'm in that. But I got to have some money left from the paycheck to buy shares, Anna, the money is flying like feathers, I put myself in hock to do the patio because we *had* to have one right now."

"Don't talk to me like that. You're the one who said I *live* for those Saturday night barbecues. That *was* you."

"All right, all right. So I'm overextended. I bought some more insurance, then Bobbie needed a new jalopy to get to college, and I still didn't finish paying off that stupid power motor. Why the hell I went and bought such a fucky thing—"

"I told you he was taking you for a sucker, just because it was a small down payment. Look how long you been paying for that monster."

"If I had a buck for every guy that borrowed it I wouldn't owe."

"You're the jerk who lets it out." Anna shook her head like an old lady. "Don't look at me," she said.

"I will look at you. We got a wedding reception to make and pay for."

"I'll call Mrs. Russo. She really said it's cheap off-season. The club does it to make a few dollars."

Al was up, carrying his plate to rinse in the sink, then the milk bottle to the refrigerator. "Let's go up," he said, and Anna followed him upstairs to the bedroom.

"What's in savings?" she said.

"Dust." Al walked to the bureau and took out his plastic file. "We haven't paid off two loans, in case you forgot. There's the home improvement and the other one, almost finished. They won't lend anymore right now, though."

"Didn't you say you were due for a bonus this year? That was in the wind, wasn't it?"

"What bonus? Mastercharge *owns* me. That's what's in the wind. Now it means, *now,* I got to borrow."

"From who?"

"From privates. Ralph has a friend who lends money six for five. A

shylock, but clean cut. We can get it just before the reception, and I'll
have it paid back with the Vig in two months."

"You're sure? You know those people are no good."

"I wouldn't do it if I wasn't sure. Anna, please have a little faith in me
for once, just *once* in your life."

"I am only *asking* you. I'm only thinking of you. Last year you had to
take that night work."

"I know it, I know it. I had numbers coming out my head."

Al was taking off his clothes like some form of his skin that disgusted
him now after a day of use. First he threw the clothes on the silk chair, the
walnut clothes rack, and Anna's tubular cosmetic table. But quickly his
habits made his neck blush, and he collected all the pieces and hung them
behind the sliding doors. Anna didn't speak, knowing that the movements
were his nerves coming out: he threw to get it out of his system, and in the
morning she was often wakened by his moving around, picking up,
straightening the room until she had to tell him to stop and go down for
some juice.

She watched him go into the bathroom to wash and brush his teeth
and come back in his pajamas. He caught her face. "Don't worry, kid,
we'll get it all. Because I want to give Marie a nice affair. She's our first
one." He sat on the bed with his back to her. "The first one is always
special." He was quiet for a minute or so, then turned around to face his
wife. "You agree with that?"

"Yes I do," Anna said, and started getting ready for bed. Then she
went downstairs to lock the doors and windows because Al had fallen
asleep suddenly.

When she was back upstairs, she remembered they had not agreed on
Mrs. Russo's club. Next morning, as he was ending his breakfast, she
turned from the stove and asked him slowly, "You want me to ask the
Russo's if their club rents?"

"Sure. Go ahead and ask." Al was up. "I'll be seeing Ralph tonight
and see about the shylock."

That night Al was back early, "No supper for me. I'm picking up
Ralph and we talk to the shylock at the Adventurer's. What do they call it
now? Nathan's? I can pick up a bite there."

Al backed the Electra out and drove to the Minute Wash before starting up Central Avenue to get Ralph. The showroom was just closing, and Ralph had his hat on and came out and got into the car. "Oh how those damn lights get me by night." He was rubbing his eyes. "It's the neon, you know what I mean. It tightens up your pupils. After an hour, you squint and you have to look down at the floor the rest of the night."

"How's business?"

"The volume remains tremendous, I swear." Ralph turned to look out his window as the car rolled out of the parking lot. "I don't know what they're doing with these cars. Storing them in cellars? Dumping them in rivers? And all of them bitching a little bit about the price of bread. They got it good."

"Maybe I ought to sell cars?"

"Not sell for others," Ralph said. "But get a dealership."

"That's a good one."

"Listen, you got a steady thing. Pensions, vacations, the profit-sharing. I wouldn't leave it for a job that goes up and down, with no benefits like what you know is benefits."

Al was quiet and pleased. When he saw the lights of the Inn, he began again. "Is this guy we're seeing a broken nose type? Some *cafon?*"

"No! Where you been? Al, this is 1969. This man has clean money. This man is a bank. I don't think he even ever seen a gun in his life. I bet you can't pick him out."

"Well, where's his supply, then?"

"They say some doctor is backing him."

"Then he's safe."

"Well, if you don't pay, I'm sure he knows some telephone numbers, too. He'll get some leg-breakers like anybody else if he gets welched. The man's in business, after all."

"But he's no Mafia guy?"

"Come on with that Mafia crap. Not you, too. What paper do you read in that place of yours? Rosey is a nice person."

They were in the parking lot and parked. "What's his name?" Al said.

"I'm not sure, but he's not Italian. Could be Jewish."

"He's Jewish?"

"You thought it was only the *paisans?*"

Al laughed as he got out. "Jewish sounds better to me, 'cause then most likely he won't be no nut."

"That's what I thought once myself. He's an honest guy. But they're all the same, I assure you."

"Yeah," Al's voice hit the sound with the old heaviness of the Bronx. He heard his own tone and went on with it: "Because they all got the same sucker."

The tone had allowed him to expose to himself what they all felt inside and knew to be true. It was a kind of truth like a pain in the private parts; it was embarrassing, yet it was something you as the sucker wanted to brag about and make jokes about. You were caught like a fish on the hook and still it was a badge of honor: borrowing showed you had made something of yourself but also that you would never come up for air, never get off that hook, never find anything good for the depressions except a new model of next year's car.

"You want to change your mind?" Ralph had been looking at Al, who had stopped like a statue. "Al? You hear me? You want to pull out, it's OK. I know how it is when you get to this point. I'll just meet him myself and tell him we'll call him later, you're not ready right now. He's used to things like this."

Al walked to the door and went right in to the cafeteria line where he took a tray. He ordered sandwiches for himself and Ralph, more than they could eat, and they carried the stuff to the glass porch. When they were finished, a good-looking, tall man wearing a blue single-breasted came along the tables and stopped. Ralph stood up. "Rosey, this here is my friend Al Moretti."

The man shook hands, then sat down. "Ralph says you need a little money."

"About five thousand." Al looked at him, reluctant to mention his reason, the wedding, in front of this man. But the face was not hard, only curious, like a person met at a party. "It's for my daughter's wedding," Al said. "She's my firstborn." The phrase stopped him.

But the shylock had lowered his head, looking down at the trays on the table, "That's very nice," he said, and began to eat from the plate of pickles. "I'm only thinking this. You sure you have some way to pay back? You don't want to get yourself hung up."

"My idea is this." Al cleared his throat automatically; it was like any business deal. He was setting himself to talk right, make a proper presentation. "In about two months I'll have to pay the caterer, the hall, all that. Then I'll start to pay the Vig for a little while; then by that time a piece of property I have will be free to sell, and then I'll have the money."

"You sure about the property? Nothing that will get hung up in the courts?"

"It's over on White Plains Road. Very desirable land. Right next to a Safeway."

"All right." The shylock looked up and turned his face to the side, to look out through the glass; he had a hooked nose that did not show when he looked at you. Al was startled by it. He looked stronger with it, maybe a little ugly, surely something that frightened Al inside.

"I'm giving you a number to call." The shylock was talking to him, writing on a slip of paper torn from a little five and ten cent pad. "Give me two days before you call. Then I'll need a list of your assets, unless Ralph is backing."

"No, he's not. I'll make you the list."

The shylock was up. "Invite me to the wedding," he said, and shook Al's hand.

"Sure, you're invited. I mean it." Al was relieved, and he thought that the shylock had done it, had brought something of himself to the departure. Maybe it was his good suit, the hair so well done.

"OK, then." The shylock was looking at Ralph. "See you around, Ralphie. Tell your friend about too much hock."

Al watched him walk along the tables and push himself out the sliding doors to the lot.

"He doesn't like it too much," Ralph said.

"What?"

"I could hear it in his voice. He doesn't like the deal too much. See, usually, he likes to see a clear line for the return. Like business men. They'll borrow to meet a payroll, but then they'll sell the season's line and pay right off. Yours is a little fishy. Not fishy, maybe. Just not tight. Once he told me he was getting sick of these guys going into hock to buy a patio."

"What do you mean, *patio?*"

"I am only repeating what he said. Examples. Like guys up here in Westchester, always improving their homes. They don't know what to put on next."

Ralph stood up. "Al, I really had a long day under those lights. Are you driving me to the subway?"

"What subway? I am takin' you to the door."

"No. Just to the Lexington, I'll take it down to Gun Hill Road. It's only four or five stops."

They left and drove slowly to the city line, then over to the Elevated tracks that marked the start of the Bronx. The streets were thinning out, but there were knots of boys at the corner stores. "Why don't you move like everybody else?" Al said. "It stinks over here now. Everything closing down. Come to Yonkers and get some grass under your feet. Look at this shit. The same guys rotting on the same corners and now so many black ones mixed in you know they're going to be here for life."

Ralph patted Al's shoulder. "I just like the neighborhood, still. It's comfortable to me, you know what I mean. The kids still play stickball. So now you even hear the Spanish. I think it's better than what happens there in Westchester."

"You mean *my* kids, for instance? What's wrong with them?"

"You dumb *strunz*. There's nothing wrong with your kids. I just don't like the way kids act up there. They all split up and they go around in circles. And drugs, just as much. I don't know what to tell you. I just don't like Westchester kids. Little empty things, they don't do things. You get these kids come in to pick up their family cars. Nice looking, they got money. They know how to drive. I like the way they dress. But I want to tell you, they're like people with heads three feet off their bodies. They're made of air."

The car had stopped at the station steps. "I know what you mean," Al said. "They're like they are not your own kids."

Ralph was out of the car and moving up the train steps. Al waved and made a slow U-turn and drove back slowly through Mount Vernon before cutting across to Yonkers.

Ralph could not catch his thought until he began to laugh aloud, the noise of his voice bringing it to him. He had been talking inside himself, saying sit down and make a deal. Life was a deal a day. You sat, you made the deal, all for the good that came later. To him success came sitting in a chair, in his office, in the cafeteria, on planes.

Deals were riding his clocks; back and forth he was in the car, out; his week was a sweat to reach Saturday, then to meet with the guys, have steaks on the grill and talk and laughter. Which was getting harder, somebody backing out each week, Charlie Baker telling him he had depressions and didn't go out some weekends at all. Angelo's first son was being sent overseas. Danny, head of the Knights, was going crazy over his drug addict kid. Bill Conroy was on special duty in Harlem and slept in the city at the precinct and told them he had to go to the riots, but the order was to not touch them. He was ready to resign. Anna's brother Bob, who had never been right after serving in Korea, was in the Vets' hospital again. They had been told to get him to a psychiatrist, but the family had all been afraid.

When Al got home, the rooms were quiet, and he sat in the darkness on the couch. After a while he heard Anna call from upstairs. He went up and said, "Get some sleep. I'm coming right in." He went for his pills and water. She saw him from the bedroom door. "You getting the pains again?"

"I didn't eat much today, so it's not strong. Tomorrow, we have to start the planning."

The next day they made the phone calls and for two weeks the ordering went on—cards, cars, church, food, visiting and setting up the club's big room. Al was anxious to have a good-looking affair, and by now he owed so many cousins, business friends, he decided to put it all together; he even sent an invitation to the shylock in Ralph's envelope and asked Ralph to pass it on.

When the wedding day came, they were ready for almost anything. Al drove over to the club in the early afternoon, and went through the timing with the caterer: three tiers were set up with desserts, two foot round lime pies with lights behind them making the green shine, ricotta cheesecakes for the old folks, and rows of cherry and apple pies interspersed with pastries, petits fours and chocolate layers. On the top was a disc that revolved and would turn the wedding cake when it was brought in. On the sides of the table, two large butcher block tables had been set up, from where men in gay nineties waiter dress would carve the roasts, roast beef to all.

The room had been built around these tables, and people would be able to walk along the boards in front of them and look at everything.

Al drove back and took Marie Anne to church with Anna and the other kids. The wedding was very soft, somehow. The music in church seemed so light, the crowd later on the steps smiling and airy, all of them laughing at the back of the church and then walking out into the sun, all of them around the bride and groom, talking about memories, years ago. The dead ones who would have loved to see this day, how these kids turned out, how pretty she was. Johnny's nephews, babies, stood on the lower steps and threw rice.

Al forgot everything unpleasant until he reached the reception and found Ralph and the others ready to shake his hand. And behind Ralph the shylock was half-smiling.

Al was sweating; he had been shaking hands for an hour, was flushed from the laughs, the running to the cars, carrying things, ushering people in. He shook the shylock's hand and led him inside. "You're table twenty-one," he told Ralph. "Where's your people?"

"They're inside going around already." Ralph was looking at people entering, faces from ten years ago, seen only at ceremonies.

The band had begun when Al raised his right arm and now, from behind them the bride and groom, in white and black, came pushing through the brown swinging doors, followed by the three ushers and the three bridesmaids in pink satin. Al and Ralph and the shylock moved to one side and the parade went to the dance floor and stood while the people clapped. The band switched to "Let Me Call You Sweetheart," and the bride and groom danced, Marie Anne lifting her long gown and holding it in her left hand, as if she wore gowns every day.

"How much'd the dress cost?"

Al heard the shylock's voice through the noise but had to ask him to repeat the word in order to understand. "You mean the bridal gown?" The shylock was nodding with a small gesture of the face, as if only his chin could move. "About six hundred," Al said.

"I'll get you a C and a half for it, maybe two."

Al was about to answer, but he kept his words. Marie Anne might want to keep it, in which case there could be no sale. He began to move forward as the music stopped, his head still circled by his thoughts, and the shylock was at his side. "Let's sit down with my people," Al said.

"I'll look around first," the shylock said. He seemed worried. Al went to the family; there were cousins, aunts, people from the office who were not Italian and who were beginning to look at the antipasto squid with question. Al went from table to table explaining what the antipasto was and what was in the minestrone and the lasagna to come.

He met the shylock again near the door to the kitchen; the shylock had been talking with one of the headwaiters of the caterer's staff. "I know these people," the shylock said. "What'd they set you back for?" Al told him, and he placed a hand on his shoulder. "Let me talk to them," the shylock said. "We'll get a rake off."

"Don't you want to sit down now?" Al said. "And meet my people?"

"Come on," the shylock said, and walked with Al to the table.

It was clear that everybody thought the shylock was an executive from Al's firm. He had what Al had called, years before, the blue-suit look, his shoulders square, the shirt always white or white on white, his tie silvery in the light, the black leather shoes that never suggested feet inside, his hands soft and long, the finger rings big and brasslike, but really gold worn for a long time, his suit just-pressed, with trouser creases pointing out, like something stiffer than fabric.

Marie Anne began to talk with him, then Anna started him tasting everything while Al stood behind them because there were no more chairs.

Since he couldn't get into the conversation, Al walked the tables again, ending up near the band where Lou Di Santo, the leader and Al's old friend from Laconia Avenue, was smoking a cigarette.

"What is it?" Al said. He knew Lou was pissed off about something.

Lou said, "Didn't we talk about how much the band was costing?"

"Sure we did. I'll give you a check right now if you need it."

"Not that. Why did you send that guy to bug me?"

Al knew he meant the shylock. "What did he say?"

"He asked me what I was getting, so I told him; so he counts the band and he says ten bucks a head. Now you know that comes to less than we agreed on. Guys can't work for that. I never even mentioned 802 scale. It was for friends."

"He's only trying to help me," Al said. "He didn't know we were friends. But our deal is our deal."

"That's what I told him."

"So?"

"Well, not that he threatened me or anything. He only kept saying I better not *putz* around with the price, if you know what I mean."

"Just forget it. He was trying to help out."

Lou did not answer right away. "As long as it's not you that's saying this."

"What I'm saying to you, Lou, is we agreed on a price, and I still agree on that price, and that guy doesn't enter here."

Lou took Al's shoulder and squeezed it. "We better go play a while or I'll start getting drunk with the rest of them."

Al went back to the table and sat down in somebody's chair. "They're all out there dancing," his Aunt Tessie said. "Anna's dancing with your friend."

Al followed her hand and saw the dance floor, with dancers under the revolving lights, finally making out Anna with the shylock when the band changed rhythm to a tango. Anna and the shylock began to do it, movements he hadn't seen since the thirties, and the shylock, he realized, looked like George Raft.

Al turned to the front again because of his stiff tux collar and looked at Tessie. "Is he your boss at the place?" she said. "He's such a *nice* man. He's gonna get me one of those new Italian leather bags. He knows a man."

"He knows a man," Al said.

"What'd you say?"

"I said what you said. He knows a man."

"Do you know those people, too? You never told me."

"No, that's not what I'm saying. What else did he say?"

"What else? He told us a lot of jokes. He goes to Las Vegas all the time. Did you hear the one about the first Italian astronaut?"

"No, what is it?"

"Let him tell you. He's a scream."

"Where's Anna?" Al turned around again.

"She just went outside with him."

"Out? Where'd they go?"

"How should I know. To look at the club rooms? To look around."

Al got up and went to the door, but there were a crowd of guys standing there, his old buddies, all having left their women at the table they were standing, smiling, at the entranceway as they used to do at the candy store.

"Even here you hang out," Al said. "Even here you come to shoot the shit on the outside. Why don't you go dance?"

They all laughed, and Johnny Pacetta came up and said very loud, "We danced, we ate, we smoked, we drank. Now there's only one thing we didn't do yet." And the guys started laughing.

Al went past them shaking his hand at them, finding the outside corridor that led up to white stone steps. A new light covered the gardens ahead as he stepped out. He opened the glass door which was silent: the night was full of cool blue air and empty of people.

He walked between the cut shrubbery and found himself getting closer to a white stone fence ahead: he could see it was the end of the land and that there was water below. He quickened his steps at the excitement of the water.

But as he reached the stone railing and saw the water, his mind was shaken by the cool freshness. He remembered this coast, the Glen Island casino, when portable radios were a new thing and Orchard Beach was liveable and City Island was a place for sailboats: he used to help Joe Paterno in the boatyard each spring. The days left you alone to follow the freshness.

He turned from the water as if it were not permitted: he should also go back and see if people were having the right time.

Down below the moonlight struck something white, a dress with jewels like pins of light. There, below, less than ten feet away, against some bushes, his wife was hugging and kissing the shylock.

He felt the blood rush up and thought he had already lowered his head to charge them. His arms went up, his hands getting ready to grab and kill.

But he did not move. The thoughts went faster and faster. The shylock would have to be killed; if only wounded, he would call hoods.

And Anna. He was surprised she had this jazz in her and shocked that he was surprised by her. He saw her too often in housecoats, in curlers, looking grey and greasy, competing with him for the post of chief family slave. The more Al worked, the more Anna was dressed in a draggy house-dress when he came home, pale and exhausted, as if she had been chopping rocks in Sing Sing.

Well, she was out of the housedress now. She was forty-one; her legs were getting puffy and blue. Couldn't she have one sneaky night?

Al backed away from the railing and started back to the glass door. This would surely affect the Vig, he thought, and bring it down. So say Anna was doing her bit for the family budget. Protecting the family treasury in her own way. It was good to have some help for a change.

# Security: Passing the Torch

What he had told Emma in the morning at breakfast made him drive up to the Bronx. He could not stop the train of his thoughts going up: he wanted to cut out on Sonny: he couldn't go anyplace anyway: he couldn't leave Sonny with all the shit because even though Sonny was always going for too much, Nick had never stopped him or tried to.

He was off the Bronx River Parkway and driving slowly up White Plains Road. The butcher signs had double features now: next to the veal *scallopini* ads came ham hocks and chitterlings available here.

He jiggled around the double-parked cars on the avenue until he found a spot near the precinct. The store looked empty, the sign was falling apart, the big plastic letters coming loose and hanging like dead men, the dirt of the street floating up to them and covering them like lead.

But Francine was inside, at her desk of papers. She never left the desk, always living the life of the product, as if something were still working there.

They had had an item that couldn't miss, and a neighborhood full of Italian kitchen ladies who would be plenty of ladies to demonstrate the stuff at free parties. It moved for maybe six months. Then the houses closed up: everybody had plastic bowls up to their assholes.

"You know, Sonny's been trying to get you." She always spoke like his public defender, as if he were the white knight. "Will you please stick around now so Sonny can see you, Nicky. Please. Don't disappear."

She saw him smile but did not know the reason. "Please, Nicky. Sonny's so scared."

Nicky walked to the back of the store and then downstairs to the rooms of boxes in dust, so much more than they should have ordered, more than they knew existed, the story of plenty three months ago: all three of them hopped up on it, Sonny and Francine making him see it: plastic in shapes women needed all the time, but now cheaper because it was plastic. There were days Francine held the items up like a model hugging a perfumed guy, making the stuff erotic.

She had been the one neighborhood girl who had been untouchable, who was something better than the guineas, something out of California in color and smile. She would drop all of the guys.

Nicky had forgotten she lived in Manhattan but came back to see Sonny, who had won by following her around like a dog: a dog that gave gold chains. She worked downtown, and he picked her up at Amtrak every night in the blue Jaguar. Then they went out to eat and the movies and a club.

No one had ever told Sonny his chances were impossible, that he was too ugly. But then she joined him in his businesses and took over the store office, and here they were seven, eight years down the line, she wider, he selling stuff off the trucks from La Guardia, she defending him like a guinea wife.

Nicky walked upstairs after putting the storeroom in his head again, how much they had, cardboard boxes to the ceiling. He walked up and down the narrow aisles between the merchandise and saw that the up-stairs room was filled, too.

He looked at the piles, and through the boxes he saw Francine up front at the desk, not knowing anyone watched her: her face had lost the color, the California, and the hair was dried out, though it echoed platinum by having no color at all. She was pretty, but the juices had been extracted from her, and the chair and her back were melding together: she was getting flat. He walked up front.

"I can't wait all day," Nicky said to her. "I got work downtown." Nicky moved to the window that looked out. "Why don't you tell him to phone me?"

"I know he's coming back, Nicky. He's doing a favor for the baker. Nicky, what are we going to do?"

It made him look at her again: "The orders pick up at all?"

"Like maybe two a week. I told you."

"Why couldn't we make some signs and sell right off the street here. Factory outlet. No middleman. Buy from the producer at factory prices. Everybody's doing it."

"That's an idea. We did do a sale."

"When?"

"April, when you did not come up from downtown. I figured, spring— they all have to buy new stuff. But what it is, this stuff is not in style right now. Now they go for ceramic and stainless steel. For plastic you got to come up with new shapes, new items. Not what *we* got."

"Why didn't we know that four months ago when we made the order? At least, I told Sonny to not overstock. I said, check what the traffic will bear first. That, I told him. That much. And I blame myself for not checking prices more because we could have got a better deal from the maker. He took us."

"So what do you want? None of us had ever bought a pot before."

Nicky was nodding and smiling and went to the front door, covered with a sheet of plywood. "Listen," he said. "I'm going out a minute."

He stepped out and saw Sonny's car double-parking in front, a tall man walking over and leaning into the car to talk to Sonny inside.

The man left, and Nicky went off the curb to the car. Sonny saw him and motioned him into the seats. Nicky sat down and shook hands, looking very fast at the face, Sonny's black eyes, the holes in his skin from the scarlet fever, when they took him to Fordham Hospital, and his brothers and sisters cried aloud in the night standing in front of his house until Mrs. Milano upstairs took them in.

"I been calling you," Nicky said, and turned when he saw Sonny's eyes picking up the lie. Nicky said, "Look, I have this line on this bar in Manhattan. My boss and a pro ballplayer are in it already. Now is the time to buy a piece."

"Yeah. Nice: with what?" Sonny held the wheel. "They're closing in, Nicky boy. I wouldn't care, alone. I could take off and go west, Vegas or Phoenix. But she pukes every time she wakes up on White Plains Road. Why do we stay here then? Burn the place down, she tells me. But you signed some notes, too, I tell her. I can't leave you for the vultures."

"Did you two get married?"

"She doesn't want marriage."

"Son, we should have had insurance. 'Cause we could of dropped the match by now. This shit will go up like paper."

"I never told you. I tried it. But they said, this close to the precinct, no, that's crazy. They won't do it. How long you think we could stall it off?"

"You mean you stopped paying the Vig?"

"I'm paying the Vig steady," Sonny said, and looked out his side window. "You think I wanted them to come down for you after they made *pasta al fagiolo* out of me?"

"I'll try to get some money this weekend," Nicky said.

Sonny nodded and swallowed a few things. Nicky understood the silence. Then Sonny hit the steering wheel. "One day it's right in your hands. Right?"

"Sonny, if we could get some money into this bar. Invest. If my boss is going into it, it makes money. Guaranteed." Sonny did not respond. Nicky started again. "Listen, I still think there's a chance to move this stuff if we did it the right way. Like move it to Connecticut, Massachusetts, the outlets."

Sonny turned. "Nicky, what do you think I'm doing? I'm running my ass off here just in the Bronx, baby."

"What do people say?"

"Say? They push it back in my face. What's that for, the old *gummara?* Is this Salvation Army stuff? One guy said, where'd you find this old shit: I didn't think they still made it. I swear, I almost hit the fuck."

"All right, I'll be calling you." Nicky opened the door.

"Nicky. Just a minute. Listen. Listen to me. I'm driving around already these days, I can hear the click behind me. Right near my ear, you know what I'm saying. Don't walk away again."

"If you need something this week, I could help. A hundred."

Sonny shook his head. "Know what I mean. Nothing's coming through no more. Not one fucking thing bangs for me."

"Something's coming through. I asked you to come to Pelham with me and see those guys with the new tapes. They want us in. Almost nothing to pay right now."

"Nicky, almost nothing. But with what. We got nothing until we unload this here shit. We got to unload this shit. Remember we got another storehouse, full. Down on Bruckner. Listen, you remember I talked to you about the judge, Judge Greco."

"The one who got jailed?"

"A thousand dollar payoff to speed up some city work. I know guys who squeeze the city, who make Greco look like peanuts."

"All right, so we go sell him. I'm ready."

"Not him. I got a customer for later to meet. It looks good. But first you got to hear Greco's idea. It's a perfect."

"Could we go *now?*"

"Listen, you go in and tell her we're going to see Greco. Tell her I'll be back by four. I don't want to talk to her."

Nicky went in and told Francine.

"He's going a little nuts," she said.

"How come?"

"Doing too much. I don't know. Sleeps like a squirrel. He's too tired for a man his age. Nicky, he's falling apart."

"Just a little bad luck for a while."

"That's all there is on White Plains Road, I'm trying to tell him. Let's move to New Rochelle. Even Yonkers. His family's here. That's why. We invest in bad luck all the time."

Nicky looked at the blond face out of place here. "We'll get out soon."

"Well, I'll be waiting. So tell him. You all know my telephone. I'm always available, too. Just call me and tell me."

"This bar of mine is on the way. I'm just waiting for the news we start."

"Just call. Night or day. I'm waiting for your news."

Nicky heard her anger under the pass: she blamed him, too. He said good-bye and went out to the car. As he got in, Sonny said, "Did you say where's the check?"

Nicky didn't answer, and Sonny smiled as he moved the white Caddy through the street and past the one family brick and stucco houses between them. "I still like it here," Nicky said. "It don't change."

"Tell *her.*" Sonny said, and stopped while he speeded up. Then he said, "You remember we used to pass these empty lots. That was when we should have got some money. Now they sell it by the square foot."

"And where there isn't a house, there's a hamburger or a fried chicken." Sonny was silent. "And that's it," he said after a pause. "This is Greco's idea. He wants to do it, big. Eatland."

"What's Eatland?"

"You remember they used to have Freedomland on Gun Hill Road, like maybe the Disney people owned it. Now they have Coop City there, the biggest apartment house city in the world, like maybe a hundred thousand families. That's a lot of mouths."

Nicky was smiling: every deal with Sonny touched insanity someplace along the way. But it relieved Nicky the way a visit from the neighborhood did—where the dreams turned to deals that became stories to tell almost before they were over, the ends in fact almost always left out because the story was the truth so fast. Nobody asked the end. Nobody wanted an end.

In a few minutes they were in Greco's backyard hearing the hum of thruway behind trees nearby. Grape leaves were beginning to make their green clear, and the wind had begun to pick up the smell of the water again: they were near the Sound. "You noticed?" Greco said to Nicky. "That's how I know it's the Spring. Long Island Sound, the Atlantic waters. Comes right into my house. I can't wait to get back on the water." Greco was handsome, his face pale, with waved hair that was touched with white the way a beautician does it. The white did not fit his face: he could not have been forty.

"Is it swimming or a boat?" Nicky said.

"A nice thirty-six footer, my pride and joy. I keep it on City Island. I go down the whole coast."

Nicky followed him to his white table behind the brick house. There were chairs for four. The grape arbor had been hand-built by some old Italian gardener: Nicky recognized it right away.

"You make wine?" Nicky asked.

"Who's got time for that the way they bust your ass these days?" Greco said and sat down half facing the house, a staircase of white-painted wood that led up to a back door.

"So what about Eatland?" Nicky said.

"Sonny mentioned you were interested. Look, here's a nice property near the Post Road I want to get fast. On the Bronx Westchester line, a few minutes from all the mouths of Coop City. And let us not forget the beach traffic, and you got the Sunday families driving this way and Westchester people and then people off the Hutchinson. We build on this parcel which is in the center—we build, first we put trees and gardens and tables and benches for everybody. They could stop and sit down. And then. And then we have a Dairy Queen, a McDonald's, and a Pizza this and that, so many, and fried chickens, we have all of them, every single one that existed, we have. We advertise all in one place, we have them all in one place. In one stop. Eatland. We franchise it all, you know."

"Do you have figures yet?" Nicky leaned forward. "Like what a concession would go for? Is it better to sell or lease? Stuff like that."

"That's the beauty here," Greco said. "We got all possibilities. Don't you see it? All in one place."

"I see it, but with money today, I would need to see some costs and try to figure out how you break up a deal like this into packages. Today, you try to think first where are the customers, what can they afford, can we make that?"

Greco paused and said, "Sonny tells me you're a CPA and you work for some big banana?"

"He's an investor."

Greco smiled. He called upstairs for coffee, and a woman came down with a bottle of wine and a coffeepot on a tray with glasses and cups. She was not introduced: she was a flashy blonde, but the flatness of her behind in the slacks gave away her age. She showed the truth more than Greco.

Greco poured and held his glass up. "So let's have a little glass for good luck before we break up."

Greco looked at Sonny, who listened intently by biting his nails. Nicky also turned to Sonny's Moorish face, with the Arab sweetness and suspicion mixed together. Nicky had been taught that all Sicilians had that admixture of Africa and the invaders inside them and were half-insane as a result.

Sonny held his glass as the other two drank, then downed his own and tapped it on the table as an expression of pleasure. "Maybe we should go into large scale wine," he said. "You make the good stuff."

Greco was standing now, ignoring Sonny as he held Nicky's shoulder. "We better meet this week. Think you could get us a credit line?"

"I could try for it. But I need to get this bar deal going first. I'll need a month. And that would get us some quick money to put into any other deal."

"I hate to wait," Greco said as he walked them to the gate. "We need the smell of green."

Nicky had not heard it clearly. "The smell of green," Greco repeated. He looked at the front of his house now. "I want my hands to smell of cash again. So I can forget those fucking days in hell."

Nicky shook his hand as Sonny walked to the car without saying good-bye. Greco said, "He's getting too nervous. Something at home?"

"I don't know," Nicky said.

Nicky got in, and they drove off, Sonny hunching over the wheel in a return of anger. "Fuck, *he* needs the smell of green. I wish I had just one of his bags he salted away from payoffs in the good days. It's nice when you can sit down all day under your own grapes."

They were driving along Laconia Avenue: all the faces were black. Nicky said, "What is this, a tour of North Harlem? I got to get down-town."

"Just one minute more: I got a sweetheart right near here you got to meet."

Sonny was timing the lights right from years of memory and finally pulled up at a private taxi stand and parked. "Come on," he said, and got out.

They walked along the street to the one new store, a beauty parlor with the sign in neon saying Rachel's.

"You weren't kidding," Nicky said as he looked into a store full of Black women. "Your girlfriend is from the eggplants."

"That's right, she's an eggplant." Sonny was smiling as he rang a bell in the front.

A young tan woman with copper wire curls came to the door. She was pretty, but her colors made her look like plastic. "Sonny," she said, "come in here. What's happening?"

She kissed his cheek and he said, "Judy, I came to have you meet my partner, Nicky Calico."

"That's a nice name," Judy said. "You want to talk to her? Come on in."

They followed Judy to an office in the back. The parlor was long, with couches in front and long rows for chairs under dryers and set before mirrors. Some of the beauticians were white men and looked Italian.

The office was very red, rugs, lights, desk wood. Mrs. Jackson was tall, heavy, had a round, loving face. "Now what did you bring me?" she said to Sonny.

"This is my partner I wanted you to meet before the deal." She came and embraced Nicky and stepped back. "Now don't tell me you pulling away. Don't go being a white man on me."

"No," Sonny said. "I just wanted to tell you it is all set. I'll have papers drawn up when you say. The stuff can be here in a day. We'll bring it ourselves."

"That's nice. You see, I knew it was my time." Mrs. Jackson traced a hand along Sonny's shoulder. "I got the advertising done. I'm going to sell every little piece. Right here out of the shop."

"You get any interest in the samples I brought you?" Sonny said.

"You see any around? Sold them in two days and got six orders. I told you, I am selling every one of them right here. Many as you got. This is my time. I knew you come along when I needed. That's just the way it is, sometimes."

She turned to the open door, held her arm out to the bustling shop. It was her world, always in action, always with energy, bright and pretty. Nicky and Sonny smiled at her world.

# Prison Notes of the Sixties

I am reading my notebooks, though I confess that this intimate diary I tell you about (as if it were still precious) is lost in time, yet I am condemned to read and reread it, just enough to love it and hate it.

I always find my notes surprising: here is an entry: "Each generation must establish a new vision out of its use of existing values, its own style made from picking up some things and dropping others. This is an important dynamic process which a generation needs in order to maintain its vitality. We are trying to establish a post-liberal tradition, and the Liberals attack us the most. This may be necessary, since they must see most clearly whatever distortions we are making. The Rightists are happy that we are giving a bad name to the Liberal tradition, transforming democratic casualness into sloppy togetherness (their words). If we fail, the people in power will crush us and make a media image of us as junkies with no ideas, no principles except what is flushed out by hallucinogens, and who sleep together in groups on floors and dorm rooms. We are like Socialists, Anarchists, and other fools who assumed that the desire for justice in ourselves existed in everybody. We have but to do the right thing to bring it out."

Carol was sullen, I thought. It was the way she showed her concern for rightness—very Lutheran—which meant everybody getting along in soft tones and discussing until all agree. I watched her eat the scrambled eggs I had bought. I wanted to put my finger in her butter pat. She held an English muffin in her right hand. She was silent. "Want some jam?" I said.

"I'm uncomfortable," Carol said, looking like a sexy blonde after a night of sex.

"What are you thinking?" I said.

"Gerry, have you thought of your position? You've just gotten an academic appointment people would kill for. And you will kill it if you make this speech; you will, Gerry."

I hated those little tie-ons, like a minister shaking the finger at me, like a wife, perhaps, after living with me seven months. Lutherans always become wives (only the women, though). The men are not to be confused as wives, even after sophomoric behaviour. But Carol was a wife down to her toes, right into her bed.

"I thought we agreed on the speech," I said to piss her off by reminding her.

"The idea we agreed on was a good one. But not to do it in a big hall with the whole university watching. And the press. You do know that Sanstaad lost his job by organizing a faculty club against the war? Finished. He's got one more semester; they insist they will not renew. He is finished on this campus."

"Sure I'm scared," I say. "I remember my dear old Poppa telling me, remember, if you're Italian, you will be fired first."

"That's ridiculous, Gerry, and you know it. Things do not work that way in a state university. And you know academic politics—but it isn't that. It's what I am trying to tell you—at this time, in this place, you don't make a big speech to the world if you are an assistant prof who just got appointed. You have one job—you keep your face washed every day."

"I know it. And that I'm still the darkie in the hierarchy."

Carol smiled. I had begun to sweat out those smiles. "Then don't do it," she said. "Let the others like Professor Bernstein do it. He's got tenure."

"The state police are coming," I said. "You want them to club an old professor when they break up the rally?"

"Just let them dare hit an old professor. It would even be better for us if they did."

"Us?" I said. "Do you consider yourself part of the protest?"

"Why not? We all are."

I looked at her face, still calm, her gorgeous Lutheran blond hair. She would be placid at a hanging. Was placid in the sack; no noise, no yelps. Why did growing up in the Bronx make me so nervous about every fucking thing?

She lit her cigarette and looked down at the table, examining her plates for remains. Her breakfast was gone. I said, "You want something else?"

"Tell me, is there a reason why you should expose yourself today?" she said with calm.

"Because we're good people, but we're making war and burning children in their own country and killing their mothers—"

She took my hand, my liberal-fogged hand, and placed both her hands over it, looking about at the other tables. I could see the light of thought in her eyes: she was going to suggest we go back and get in the sack before the meeting. That would make me more pliant and able to listen to her Lutheran words.

But some clouds from Martin Luther stopped her. She could not remember the words for a quickie. A smile deepened.

I smiled back, and we walked out of the Student Union to the stadium and looked down at Professors Flood and Bernstein, who waved hello from the stage. The visiting speaker was a priest who had taken care of burned children out there. He sat down next to Flood and Bernstein.

People started coming in. As soon as the place was half filled, I stood up, but Carol had grasped my pants pocket. "Don't go," she said. "I tell you, don't go."

"Come on," I said. "I have to do it now."

"If you go up there," her measured voice said, "I am not staying—and I am not coming home."

I looked down at her; she let go of the pocket, but the beauty of the blond hair and face was also its power. It remained the same, with little expression; it did not have to put up with anything.

I turned and walked to the platform where I shook hands with the others. The priest said, "Those hills behind us. What are they called?"

"The Naftha Hills," I said, and he shook his head and said, "Just like out there. I come home to speak in Indiana, and the place looks exactly like out there. That's amazing."

He turned away, and I thought, why would he be rude suddenly? But

I saw he was crying. I moved back to give him some privacy.

The music started—Dylan, Grateful Dead, Joan. The students began dancing and chanting. I stood up to speak, seeing troopers already, a semicircle of them starting down from the back; and behind them men with guns and trucks, in brown clothes—army.

I spoke to them as I spoke my words, asking them to stand back for freedom of speech, but they speeded up, reached us and started busting heads. The students were screaming at them, mocking them. I thought: you cannot mock men in obsessively neat and clean pressed uniforms.

I saw a student of mine, Jenny Goetke, with the best shape on campus, suddenly upended, on her back, hands behind her being tied or cuffed, getting some army and cop whacks on her head.

Then they reached me.

*

Carol is outside the cell. She is wearing a black silk kerchief of shawl length to cover her face. It makes what little blonde hair you can see seem to be glowing with lights. She is like a gorgeous young widow, and the cops will let her enter anywhere because she is a major turn-on as widow. They would also love to help me along to my appointed fate.

Carol has been speaking to me; pay attention. "Gerry, I think what you did was disgusting. You just taunted them for no reason—*they* didn't start the war. Your friend Kennedy did. And you asked for it, you *wanted* them to get mad and hit you. And beat you and then the Dean has to fire you after those pictures in the paper. Some people say you look just like a crazy anarchist."

"That's right," I said. "Listen, they could have used their voices instead of clubs."

"Oh sure, and have a little philosophical discussion with you—while there's a war on."

"We're way back in Indiana," I said. "I thought we had a few minutes to talk." I was silent, feeling my head again. Then I said, "I thought you were going to ask me how I felt, how the pain is."

"I am so angry with you, Gerry."

"I am so beaten. I have a concussion, I think, because I'm seeing double. My face is broken here—and you think I deserved it for what I said aloud."

"I moved out. My stuff is with Lisa Drake, who has a big place. I'm renting a room from her."

"That's all right, Carol," I said. "You always were a lousy fuck."

"What did you say, Gerry? Gerry? Gerry? What did I hear you just say?"

\*

"Gerry, come in. Won't you sit down?"

"I am sorry, sir. But I can't quite sit yet. The beating stiffened an area in my lower back."

"See." He moved to help me and stopped as I tried to ease into a soft leather chair. "Good. Good," he said. "Oh, Gerry. Listen. There isn't anything personal here today. Except that I, personally, liked you very very much. You were a little dynamo; you turned the students on; you're a most popular teacher. I'm sorry about all this."

"About all what, sir? The demonstration in which the cops disobeyed all laws? And order?"

"Gerry, please, don't start that. You know what you did. You know I have superiors. I must answer to them and can you imagine how I might justify your attacking state police and fighting them and getting arrested? Don't tell me you're a naif like these flower children I hear about? Frankly, I thought you were much more mature—I mean, in the sense of diplomacy. I'm not sure if that's the word—what do you call it—living by your position? Respecting it? You do certain things certain ways. I thought you knew that. In your position you're an example—even if you do nothing, you're an example. And what you do grows way out of proportion. That's why you cannot lead the troops. You're too dangerous. Too many people will follow. And what if you *are* wrong? Can't have that, Gerry. Do you *comprende?*"

It was Spanish, but I got the insinuation. "Yes, sir, *mucho comprende.*" I said.

He smiled, "You know, some are saying you are subversive; how will I write a letter for you if that gets around? The future, Gerry. The future is governed by the present."

"Who said that?" I said.

"What? What did I say?"

"The future is governed by the present?"

"I can't recall any reference. I must have said it."

I stood up. It was impossible to sit or stand without pain, like a broomstick up my ass and up the spine. He asked me to sit back down. "Sorry, sir, too much pain," I said. "Got to get back to bed. But just let me tell you, sir, that what you have just said to me is all shit. Bullshit. You are about to—you have fired me because your veins flow with piss rather than blood."

"Gerry, you still have time to take that back. I will mark it down to extreme stress-induced paranoia."

"I said, sir, that you are a fucking wimp who stands for nothing but the handouts that come in here—and right now the biggest hand is the Feds, and their Fed money coming to this university will make you sacrifice its mother to get the bucks. And your job is to keep everybody mesmerized. As for me, I am no more controversial than a TV debate."

"Need we say more? You've just acted in a way that fits what they tell me you are becoming. Perhaps your brand of talking goes much better back East where there are more people like you?"

"Unlike the plantation niggers you cultivate out here?"

"Yes, you should definitely be with your own kind—and I wish you would pack Bernstein in your bag when you go. In a way, you do come from another world. I visited New York, and to me, honestly, that isn't America. That is the garbage dump of humans. A way station where we collect the detritus of the world and hope to salvage a few, sift out the good ones. But it is not what this country is. I think it's very wise for you to go back. And I'll tell you what I will do if you go back: I will forget what you said here today, and when called to write letters of recommendation I will stress your excellence in teaching and as a mentor to students, as I told you."

*

On the way home I wrote in my precious notebook of boredom. A small extract here: "The academy in our country not only monopolizes intellectual life, but it also isolates it, leaving the human community outside the walls of its deliberations and processes so that elites come about and then dominate in the name of intelligence, at home only with the life within the walls. And once more a miniature minority rules the gigantic majority, each in ignorance of the other."

Another: "Property is our first love and guiding principle as President Johnson reaffirmed to a jealous world in his speech to the troops at Cam Rahn Bay, telling the boys and a few girls, 'These people want what we got, but they're not gonna git it. So go out, boys, and get your coonskin.'"

"Brilliant! In one imperial swoop the prez served the world our great Empire. We are the world. But oh, if we just stopped copying the British and instead read the Romans, who planted crops and used the prisoners as nursery school teachers. We devastate too much, finally have to send food until the scorched, conquered lands can plant seeds. And we try to make a world of weak, bitter, welfare depressives who can't lift a gun anymore. What a price to pay for easing our fears: moral bankruptcy."

My father was sitting in the white living room when I entered the old manse at the shabby end of Scarsdale where we lived, much closer to construction equipment than the grassy older owners of more beatific Tudor Scarsdale near the park.

"We going to court for you," Poppa said first thing.

That night his friend De Carlo, one of the founders of the local Conservative Party, with his colleague, Doctor Di Lorenzo, also a close friend of Poppa, owner of raincoat-making establishments in lower Manhattan and Pennsylvania, and the theorist Carol Semprucci, well-connected in Albany—sat mulling over their anisette-laced espressos, each in a couchy chair. They had come for me. De Carlo was spokesperson.

A man of some girth, he was nobody's fool except for the fact that he had no idea what people do in Indiana—and these days what so many people were doing on so many campuses that came to him on nightly TV and *The Daily News*. He said, a number of times, "But what is really going on in these places?" referring to extraterrestrial behaviours.

And when I began to explain, he interrupted by saying, "You don't have to explain nothing to us. We are all together here, and nobody hurts one of us without us banding together and defending ourselves. Your father knows this, and we all do."

I was surrounded by the nodding heads that some of you might liken to a Mafia meet, though besides our black curly hair and black eyes (with dark patches underneath them) we thought like real Americans, full of dispatch and efficiency.

De Carlo went on: "Could you answer maybe one or two things so we know what we're dealing with in this situation? Like, did you become connected with any party?"

I smiled: "Like a deep-red color party? And am I now or have I ever been connected?"

"This is no *auto-da-fé*, Gerry. We just need to know facts. Young people, they all do crazy things."

"And old people do nice things by making war all the time on shrimpy Asian peoples with smaller guns."

"Please, tonight, no propaganda tonight," my father said with the weariness that came from discouragement. He had been telling me to keep a low profile, keep the old trap shut, smile for the Americans, don't talk up, make your bucks and stash them away—you can't afford to help the starving millions yet because we're not there yet, we're not established yet, so don't participate in anything for anybody else, let them take care of their business, and we'll take care of ours.

"Gentlemen," I said. "I value your devotion. I am moved by the time you have taken for me, someone you barely know. I am ever grateful for your defense of me. But please don't help me if you think I am some kind of clear and present danger. I did nothing but protest with reasonable words a monstrous war of destruction that destroys more children and old women than anything else, burns them up with stuff made by our best corporations."

I think I heard the collective sigh of patience. De Carlo was the leader partly because he could still talk after such utterances as mine and even stick to a bullheaded point. "We are here to make your defense, Gerry. We will put a lawyer on your case, and you could sue the university. But we got to know if you're clean enough. And if not, we'll get you a good job back here, so don't worry. This is your family."

We talked more, a good part of the waking night. They were alternately with me and against me. Some of it they called my wild youth, some of it the uncontrolled red views of the times I caught, much like measles. And some they met with silence because they agreed or wanted to. I went back to my room (which was now called the guest room) and sat holding my head. Something had ended. And gone forever were the years of sweating out articles to publish to beef up the vita so as to get a job closer to Columbia than Indiana. But even with a stash of articles, I would still get nothing—now.

A week later the day dawned clear and cold, the day of the big game. A letter from the midwest telling me I had been made an official martyr with the Gerry Defense Fund now set up and collecting funds to pay lawyers and sign-painters and press reps. I went upstairs with the important missive and wondered, sitting on the bed, if anybody ever stopped history and made it turn around.

I wrote back to Bernstein: "Do it. Do anything you want. I am hiding out in my father's house for the duration of my headache and am not capable of much more than pain and fear. If they can club me down and then fire me, the Gauleiters are here ready to gas me and have a celebration. And down here my champions have become people I laughed at, after two degrees, describing them with disparaging ethnic names. So I was wrong on both ends. I am one big defeat."

Bernstein wrote back: "Keep trying, buddy," and added a copy of Spinoza (Jews are so shifty) and Kierkegaard (and so comprehending and understanding of what a pain in the kishkas really means). I put the books down on the bookcase, which held two other books on its top shelf: Renan's *Life of Christ,* and *The Divine Comedy,* by an old Italian guy. None of it was much help in healing the muscle and bones. For that, God came along as I was walking along the street in Eastchester one day and was stopped by a woman. "Gerry? Is that you behind the beard?"

She was about five ten or so, with large, round shoulders, freckles all over her face (I love them), tits so large they hung near her rib cage and below that, too. And a blank face that was somehow full of passion.

"Rose Anne Delaney," she enunciated, and high school came back.

Yes, I swear it. She was my high school girlfriend, the only one who meant anything to me because she did not traffic in false poetry, romance, love words, arguments about being hurt because you don't love me as much as I love you, and the rest of the gift-wrapped crap from the gilded age of queens before we were born to our own truth.

Rose Anne, once she squeaked her fear about committing a mortal sin, let her body shake and bake and become one with my body, take it into every orifice we could find together: and since she was chubby, we had a long time to work.

She was now working at the Grand Union, was married, had one baby daughter she deposited at her mother's in the morning and one Irish husband who worked in the train yards and deposited much of his pay at the bar after work.

Rose Anne did check out with the new computer register but still retained that burning red flame of hers. We embarked on such a spree of thought-free fucking that I shall never forget her, nor be happy in the state of marriage (with or without licenses) because I know that passion is the stuff of humankind while marriage is the stuff of stuffy moralists who love greeting cards as their bible and haven't fucked very much themselves.

So fucking saved me until about 1972 when Poppa bought me a new suit and kicked me out. I told Rose Anne I was leaving town for a job on the Coast, and she kissed my right hand there in the street before going into her supermarket and said, "It was the best time. Send me a nice present from out there."

I borrowed the money from my father—I really was hunting for a job—and an extra thousand dollars with which I went to Lord & Taylor in Eastchester and brought the perfume she liked—about three hundred bucks worth of it—and bras and dresses and earrings and rings and silk kerchiefs and nightgowns until I hit a thousand, paid and left, having them deliver it all to her at the store, which they said they would do.

I left Rose Anne to explain it to the Irishman, but as I pondered her problems on my way out to San Diego, I thought they couldn't be too bad—and if she had memories of the fucking as I had, memories that are in your bones and muscles, she would be smiling, whatever anyone might yell or complain about or be suspicious of—at least for a year or so. Then what? Who knows or cares? I was myself ready for the seventies and eighties, which I was fairly sure was a time that would be characterized by the famous mot, WHY BOTHER?

(Here the prisoner's notebook terminates. Ed.)

# The Word to Go

"This here belonged to Momma. She had it made right after she was married. By Mr. Nardone, who had the store on White Plains Road. Across from the precinct. You remember the old man. Some of you. He was a wonderful carver. Look at the claws on the table legs. That's his work; I can't believe none of you want it."

Millie was talking too fast, talking to her relatives, trying to talk them into what they should be grabbing for—the special furniture pieces of their mother and father, from the house in the Bronx where they had gone to live forever in '31, but all of it shipped to Westchester after the death of Mr. Di Marco when the change started in the neighborhood. It was as if the death of the fathers, one by one, allowed the small corner lots to be sold to apartment-house builders and then city projects, and permitted what was called "the new element" to come move in. These were the people who went to Immediato's pork store, his window flashing with fresh, just-made sausage, and asked for ham hocks and chitlins he never heard of.

No one wanted the double bed with headboard and footboard in shining inlaid wood or the chifforobe with carved doors or the two long tables with ivory in the tops. It was stuff that didn't go in White Plains.

Millie understood this, but she could not leave the country knowing the pieces would be thrown out. "I just can't give it to the Salvation Army," she said again and again. "And you can't even *find* handmade stuff like this today. They're getting big prices for it."

Millie was continually seeing the pieces exposed somewhere on a street, in a store window covered with filth, or destroyed, just as she thought of her parents' graves in Good Shepherd, unattended because she was leaving for good.

And most of them kept saying she shouldn't go. Which made it all the harder. And her friends said, "Oh don't worry, you'll be back in a year." But how, if they sold the house? Mario would have social security and what they had saved, plus the cost of the house. They were signed up for a place outside Padova, but Millie had nightly dreams of floating in the air and calling and nobody around on the ground to help her down. As long as she floated, she swelled up, and once she got too big, she would explode and die. At sixty-five, the dream of dying was worse than ever.

That's why she was talking like a salesman. "None of this is Ludwig Baumann stuff," she said, as if angry. "All that 149th Street crap we got sold and threw away when we moved up here. This is handmade stuff, and even the Protestants know how expensive it is. I bet Larry could tell you. God rest his soul."

The memory stopped Millie, of her oldest brother, gone before his time at fifty-three from a heart attack, his wife living out in Huntington with two sisters, only heard from at Christmas with a card and a few snapshots. What could she use the furniture for, three old widows in a little house packed to the walls with their own stuff? When Millie visited them she saw that they had almost everything in triplicate: couches and tables—and three TVs, three toasters, broilers, electric fans—like a store.

Jack's wife Emma felt the mention of Larry connected to her own feelings of loss for Jack, her husband, and the second brother to go. Emma knew that Jack would have taken some of the pieces: he had so loved them and everything about the old Bronx house, always remembering those sweet, peaceful days, summers when he stained and waxed that furniture. But Emma had sold her house, too, and was living with her daughter Noreen and family, in an upstairs apartment with hills of stuff trucked from her own house, furniture and lamps that nobody wanted to buy; she understood Millie now.

"Throw it all away. The hell with it." It was Billy. Billy was really disgusting. Emma looked across at him as if he were somebody's waste.

"Why?" Emma said to him. "Don't you think they're worth it? Your mother's stuff?"

Billy looked at her, in shock for a moment because she did not speak this way. But she was a widow now and had to speak for herself. "Emma," he said. "I know it's good stuff. But if it's an anchor, if it's going to stop them from leaving, then Millie won't go just because of some damn wood."

"So maybe something is saying she shouldn't go?" Emma said. "Did you ever think of that? That maybe she doesn't want to leave her own people. Did your crazy head ever tell you that?" Emma's face was in her hands, trying to handle the tears and the breathing.

They all knew she had become very nervous since Jack's death because he was too young, the shock was too great, though Jack had weighed two eighty-five and smoked three packs of Camels a day.

But Billy always got her. Jack had told her years ago that Billy was a socialist, the one brother who went to CCNY where they come back Commies.

"It's up to her," Billy said. "I agree with you. But I'm only talking about not making these things stop her life."

"Her life, her life. A couple more visits you could make up here and see her life and how it is." Emma had surfaced again, spoken, and then lowered her head.

Millie watched her brother carefully: Billy had been born when she was fifteen and had been like her own child. She had kept him in her room when Momma was shopping or cooking. And now he stood in the center of the room, with no hair on his head, with wrinkles around his eyes. She could not take it; his was the one aging face that shocked her, as if what time did to others was understandable. But not in Billy, who had become an old man in a week.

His baldness had happened like the rest, a short time after coming back from the war. Momma had blamed the hair loss on the steel helmets pressing on the hair muscles, but Millie had heard the stories of the islands where they burned out Japs from caves and sat smelling burning flesh for weeks and then even found their own men chopped up like pigs. She could never think of bamboo without getting sick, as if knives were going through her.

"I'm not going to change my mind now," she said as quietly, to avoid hurting Emma by seeming to side with Billy. "But me and Mario, we talked about this for over a year. Over and over. It wasn't no easy thing."

Emma had stopped crying but was reacting to Millie's tone by feeling the slow depression that came over her these days. She couldn't shop when it happened, couldn't watch TV, couldn't talk to people for more than a few minutes without feeling like throwing up. She was living on Donnatal and Stelazine. It was coming on, and she was turning pale, feeling the expectations of something, as if she would begin to shrink.

Her daughter Noreen moved close to her, recognizing the mood, and held her hand. Late afternoon light began to hit the room, and the furniture turned red. It was the rich, steady light of dusk, so transient but looking like it could stay forever. Noreen loved Millie, who had no children because of a late marriage and had named her first daughter for Millie. Noreen had asked her husband about the furniture, but he had explained it was perfect stuff for a country house, if they could only afford one.

Noreen looked up at Millie, sensing that she was going to speak, and Millie caught her attention, smiling before she started. "Look, we all know what it is here now. I mean, why not get out of here? We don't breathe anymore. We live inside chimneys. The streets of Manhattan, the East Side, no less. You can't walk without getting attacked. Dope addicts own the sidewalks. Mario calls it the city of dogs. The streets are just filth, people with dogs doing their duty all over the whole place. When he makes a delivery of plants, you can't believe it. Did you know they can't grow lichens down there anymore? That's right. In those penthouse gardens. Lichens can't exist anymore in that city."

Noreen was nodding. "Maybe you and Mario should buy a country place. Like New Hampshire. We could all chip in and maybe run a hotel up there."

"Oh we saw it up there," Millie said. "And how about the food all frozen, and cotton bread, one TV channel, and cheese inside paper. Winter maybe nine months a year. People who don't talk to each other. And you think they want us?" Millie looked at the room again. "Mario wants to rest. And with his own people around. The family is so nice there. We don't feel strange there. Remember, I got a pretty dark complexion."

Billy laughed, but not the others, who did not like such comparisons and never thought of them. "Get out," Billy said. "I don't blame anybody for getting out right now: we are a country of bomb throwers. Jailers. We're going to start putting everybody away. Because everybody you don't like is a Chinese Commie."

Millie did not like this kind of talk, even in joking. Billy was always knocking the country, but he had never lived anywhere else, not even traveled to see what she had seen last summer, the police department making everybody register. Mario's people had to keep identity cards.

But she had to admit that they were always seeing each other, always making little trips, picnics up in the mountains and fresh fish from the rivers. There had never been the loneliness of White Plains, people too busy to see each other, the cold weather locking them all in, and hopeless for anyone who had never learned to drive, like herself.

"Don't look at me like that," Billy was saying. "You all see the head-breaking in the streets. Kids getting shot. The big shots letting us die in our poisoned air. Some say twenty years and New York will have only poison air. We'll all be dead."

Millie believed some of this. Mario, who had spent most of his life in Italy, saw it too but accepted without comment. He did not attack America; it was only a dirty factory to him, where one came to earn money. And now his head was full of the days they would have, the geese and eels and river fish, good cornmeal for his polenta, and wine as fresh as running brook water, Valpolicella, and animals that had grown up eating food and whose meat was not a chemical factory. And market days, the inviting mountains ready in all seasons, and Venice nearby, and Cortina, the white paradise. Because of this, America was never an evil vision to Mario (as it was to Billy). It was only the land of locked-in people nibbling bad food and unaware that loneliness was not a perpetual state.

"Well, we just can't take it anymore," she said to take away the rage the others were feeling toward Billy. "Mario has worked day and night here, and we can't keep money in the bank. You have to buy something even when you don't have to buy. If you know what I mean. Shopping here is like day and night; there's just two of us, but I'm shopping all the time. Most of my mail is a list of specials all over. And last week Mario's truck was robbed again. That makes three times. Oh, you all know about all this. We just want a place we can go in peace."

Noreen wanted to prevent arguments, too. She saw her mother and Billy both near a blow-up state, and wanted to make it calm. "I hope you find it nice. With the relatives and all that. Anyway, you can always come back if it got bad."

"That's what I told Mario. And he laughed."

"Sure," Billy said. "Come back to Bond bread and muggings and gas poison." He was going again. "And a new war every day. And your tax going for more boom boom. Let me tell you, if Millie gets even *one* year of happiness over there, it's worth it."

"Oh yeah," Emma said. "We'll all be dead. Where did you hear that one, big expert? I suppose they're going to let us die of poison—the President will watch his daughter choke. Yeah sure, I can almost believe it."

"He's not going to stop the cars, the planes, the factories. The President is there to protect all the profits. He's not going to stop anything. And the cops get sent out to chase bookies while the gas company is our hero. The airplane makers add a few billion to their bill. The oil company doesn't even pay a tax. They got laws from payoffs to the men in Washington. And do you read how nice those cars we buy are—like they forget to tie the brakes on."

"Oh, he knows everything." Emma turned to the others, but they were not excited enough, and she sensed it. "What is this man? Our God? That he knows everything. And how long before I'm going to choke him to death? Oh, come on."

"I don't make it up," Billy said. "I read it in the papers. The same paper you can buy for a dime. You don't even know that they're yelling, that people get silenced. Thank God we're Italians. We don't yell about nothing. We swallow all the bullshit they hand out from upstairs. Love it or leave it. We wave the flag. We stick it on our cars. And that means, if you don't shut up, we'll kill you."

Millie could see that the afternoon was breaking up. The others were beginning to move about. Fidgeting with their coats and purses. Noreen got up to straighten her dress and went into the kitchen for water. Emma began to put on lipstick, and her son, Marty, who had been quiet on the couch, sat forward with the wish to punch his uncle, who disturbed everyone with his screams.

Billy saw them turning away from him and became more excited. "They all came over here to find something good." He turned to them one by one, like a man being spun in confusion. "And now it's gone bad. Don't you see it? Don't tell me you don't sit in your chairs expecting the end. You're just as scared as me, even if you don't know why. Maybe you sit too long in front of Johnny Carson. You spend more time with Johnny than going to Sunday Mass. Two hours a day for Johnny, an hour a week for Jesus. Your eyes are full of shit. You never walk anymore. You go for vacation and lock yourself in a hotel in the mountains that's your own bedroom on a mountain."

"Please, Uncle, there's women here." Marty had stood up straight, to remind his uncle of the language.

Billy looked at him, trying to understand. He would not willingly insult women. "What is it?"

"What you're saying."

"What did I do?" Billy's face was almost wild, a confusing series of old shocks fusing inside him. Were they leaving him alone? Were they trying to silence him?

"I'm not crazy, Marty," he said. "Your generation knows what's happening. What kind of future have they left you?"

Marty did not answer; he had been working for nine months with a computer company, and they had already told him about benefits he had not dreamed about. The company had just offered him two weeks at their own country club.

Billy turned to his wife and stared at her; she understood the shocked face, the despair of being hated when he spoke with love for people and hate for the cruelty inflicted upon them. And when he sensed that people were moving away from him, he began to feel the weight of blame, as if he had done something wrong.

He no longer could speak and stared at his wife. The others began to leave, went to the hall closet or the kitchen, moved through Millie's rug-covered rooms getting prepared and saying good-bye. Billy's wife Joan stood up and went and held his hand. "Let's go," she said, and Billy began again. "Wait. Just let me tell Millie. Millie?" He walked after his sister and found her in the kitchen. "Millie. I'll take all the pieces. Whatever you want to leave."

She looked at his sad face and almost turned away. "All right, Billy. Thanks. Thanks a lot. We'll talk about it. Talk it over with Joan."

"Joan understands. We'll find a good place for it. I got stuff I wanted to throw away. And I'll pay you. You can use the money over there. And get things for your new place."

"This is not for money. It's all our property. I just want it safe. In a place it can stay."

Joan came in with Billy's coat and together they said good-bye and went to the car on the quiet street. Billy changed after he had driven a block, the concentration of the driving chasing off his hysteria.

On the expressway he started talking again, out of his thoughts. "I wish I could just turn the car around and drive someplace. Way far away."

"It's the winters that get you," Joan said.

"The winters. Joan. It is the end, you know. When I think of Millie going back, it's like the end of the whole thing. No one would dream of going back. Italy was only like a playland in the heads of our mothers and fathers."

"But he's a special case." Joan turned to face him. "Mario has family over there, as you know. And that's a different thing."

"The best way is don't consider it at all. Sure. Just like the rest of them. But I'm telling you something. We moved into emptiness, and it's inside us now. I just want to get away from that."

"How? Just say how. You can't get a job there. And nobody I heard of ever ran back there."

"But Millie's going back."

"Yes, I know she's going back. And I know she's got no kids. And she gets social security. And they got relatives waiting. Mario's father has a business."

Billy nodded and was silent. Then he said, "A business? I got people come into my store who left Hungary with nothing. They made it. They're okay right now."

"People are coming here," Joan said. "There's all that Communism

215

over there. You have to admit that. People run away all the time. Cuba. Every place."

"Don't give me that Commie crap. That's what they give me when I say anything. If I say we got more generals than garbage men. What do I care about Communism? They aren't killing me. It all reminds me of a man who gets handed a glass of poison by a priest, and you tell him, don't drink that, it's poison. And he says to you, you don't want me to insult the Church, do you?"

Joan grappled with the illustration; there was something wrong with it, but her mind was obscured by her irritation at Billy's insults. "How could you ever live in Italy if you talk like that. They'd arrest you in a day."

"Arrest me?" Billy was getting an echo of the heavy feelings, as if he had done bad things.

"Yes, Billy. It's a Catholic country over there." Joan paused. "There's only one country like this where you can speak what you want."

"I speak all the time and nobody even stays in the same room." Billy felt he might cry; then the mood turned to anger. "Anything you tell people that cuts into profit is bad bad bad. If they should lose a buck? Their balls would fall off. Take my kid, but don't touch my car. Oh, I don't care. I just don't give a shit!" Joan turned quickly to his cracking voice. "So the end comes, Joan. The road goes one way, and then the road goes back."

"And *you* are telling *me* you want to go there, too. You really want us to go?"

"If I had something left inside. Maybe I could get out. But that store has a lock on me. A forty-five-year-old man is a pail full of payments. And that's the way it is." He was silent for a while as he drove along. Then he put his right hand in Joan's lap and drove with one hand. "Maybe I could swing it," he said. "If I didn't get so mixed up. My head's got furniture inside."

Joan did not answer and held his hand and let his mind rest as they drove the rest of the way home. The Yonkers' streets were wet and empty in night. The lights of the Cafe Puglie were lit, and two men on the sidewalk were looking up at the sky while they talked.

Billy parked the car and locked it while Joan waited. The lights in the front rooms were lit as they walked to the porch. Billy turned around to look at the sky. "Joan. Look. There's a moon coming up over the church."

She stepped back and looked up as the moonlight grew strong and the clouds separated. After a few minutes, the cold drove them inside. Joan went upstairs while Billy paced through the house, unable to do anything or find his thoughts. Finally, he phoned Millie. "Mario came in a minute ago," she said. "And he thanks you. He couldn't see shipping all that stuff over there."

"Then you're set," Billy said. "You can go."

"There's so much to do. How can I do it all while Mario goes on working? We'll have to wait till he sells the business, and he can make some decisions with me."

"Just take one day at a time—"

"And suppose I want to come back, Billy. And what if we couldn't. And they took our citizenship."

"Stop talking like that. You're not going into the jungles."

"Why does it have to fall apart here, now?" Millie was talking to herself. "It didn't used to be like this. What happened?"

"Maybe it was always falling apart?" Billy said.

"I never heard of a time when the world could end in two days. Really, you have to be a monster to exist here today. Mario says, in private, he isn't strong enough to live here. He's got to have some peace. And he's the only husband I got."

"That's right," Billy said.

"So we got to keep going, pack up what we can. If I can just keep remembering how nice it was over there. I take out the pictures we took last summer every night now. And remember the times we had. And that keeps me going a while. I just have to believe it's real over there. And not forget how good it was. Then I'll make it."

# Leaving Vermont

The snow is in your mind before it comes, unlike Manhattan where you fall asleep on a warm night and find five inches on the ground in the morning. Here the cold makes you excited for the coming snow, as if you needed it. When it falls, it fills up too much, making you want to get away before it buries you.

But he hadn't left it, even to see the lawyers in New York. Let them keep getting postponements: let them get him time to run up the new business and get out of the old one. The new was health food. The natural food freaks could go for it and did: they are getting orders from Idaho, Nebraska, hamburger home-fried country. It was shooting up all over, like nice green weeds.

And if the Feds went after this, he would sell out all of it and put his money overseas, at least buy his father a villa on the Calabrian coast and let the old man act like a Signore and eat the old specialties in the sun, what he had not had a chance to do racing away as a kid to work his ass off to pay rent on Bleecker Street. He and the old man could complete the circle together over there on a terrace.

Which was more crap. He was never going to be a Calabrian, even though the old man had told the kids every day that's just what they were, while they sat on White Plains Avenue under the Lexington tracks eating kosher hot dogs and watching the Irish ass as if they were visits from Heaven, but never had a dream of the Other Side. And once, one time in eight years, a teacher mentioned Italy, the second largest producer of silk in the world. The geography book had a picture of silkworms but not Italians. So much for Italy in P.S. 103.

But his sister Angie was the closest thing to success for Pop and Mom: she spoke American with a slight accent, she knew only the Italian word for certain things, wore black and print housedresses and seemed squat— a form of imitation Italian Momma.

Up here he had stopped feeling blame about the books and magazines. What had he done? Sold what people wanted: it was no more days of Jiggs and Maggie cartoons, the old jackoff pictures. It was better stuff, and the money came from the gibbonies on Canal Street, who wanted to clean up some bookie money or loan money, little mountain ranges of Vig to invest, all nice cash.

And Tony went, for them, to America uptown, to candy stores and beauty parlors and bookshops with dildoes in the window and bars and restaurants and nice video stores and all over. They sent Tony to Chicago and Kansas City and Peoria and Tulsa and Dallas and Santa Fe and Phoenix and St. Louis and Tallahassee and even Waterloo and Oxford and Pasadena and San Diego, right up to L.A. The gibbonies could see the whole country as well as Tony taking orders that multiplied beyond any expectations.

Tony's friends had stopped laughing at the job: a few called his work filth and smut, suggesting he forced the writers to come in with the erotic books they wrote. He never read the shit. He had an M.A. in Sociology, though he often thought like a wide hat about money. He was also a *gumba,* yes. He was practically his grandfather Annunzio, a recreation of the old man but talking American and wearing suits from Chipp.

He was also none of these when he bought a co-op on Eighty Ninth and East End and then this cabin in Vermont. He was also unlike them when he lived with Joanne Little from Little Rock, who wanted to act (but when) and who shared five easy years and then amicably parted, leaving him like a widower looking for kids he never had. Or was his grief over the silence, which turned him into Annunzio again because there was no hand on Joanne to lead him through doors and pubs and Zagat-approved places off the river with classy lights.

The doctor said his Joanne-grief was connected to his mother's dying when he was eight. Plus the hidden hatred of himself because of his dirty business. After three years of shrinkage, the man had only morality in his bag of tricks: a nice, kindly Jewish priest. But he had also made some good hits, explaining to Tony how he blamed himself for not preventing his mother's death while he hated her for leaving him alone on the planet. It was a nice double hook; it was a brick wall to hit on the highway. He was sure of one thing from all the sessions: in some way he made it up again and again and acted as if the dead were alive and betraying him all over again. He made it up where he was. He knew that, but he could not yet say fuck it to all of it and make it disappear.

The law had been the latest hook: he had prepared himself for punishment, stiff fines, loss of business, but not embarrassment, pictures of him in the papers with accompanying story about the handsome, young filth merchant, whose name proved his pockets were lined with Mafia gold, not to mention his soul entire. But not his printing press in Pennsylvania, a big Wasp corporation they never mentioned. The papers had made him and unmade him in ten days. Even his phone had stopped ringing. He had left the apartment for Vermont, a message on the machine: Hello, this is Tony. I'm away from the phone a moment; please leave a message and your number, and if you're the cops or the reporters; please also go fuck yourself—

No, he had not done that. But right now he could hear the phone bell right here in Vermont, in the next room, an old black curvy phone with curled wire attached to speaker.

It was Angie: "Tony, I'm so sorry to bother you long distance, and I heard you were having personal trouble, but it's Poppa. They say he may not last the week."

"It's another stroke, isn't it?" he said.

"I think you better come home," Angie said softly.

"All right, thanks, Angie. Thanks for calling."

"Tony, you're not coming down?"

"I'm leaving here in about fifteen minutes. Pack a few clothes and driving right down."

"Please don't speed."

"Is he in the hospital?"

"The doctor brought the oxygen over here. So he's here."

"Is he in a coma?"

"He can hear you, but he can't talk back to you. The breathing gets very hard all of a sudden. You can see it. His face turns blue."

Tony put the phone down and looked at his long brown room, logs and panels and beyond it the glass porch with wicker chairs (where he and Joanne had spent good hours together.) The old maple furniture crowded the small rooms but looked right because the family that had owned the house had lived with it (and sold it in a package to him ready-made-homemade.)

He went to his bedroom and packed, then walked the rooms, leaving a few small lamps lit, windows closed, then the last walk, out, suitcase in trunk of car, and on the road.

The parkways were clear of snow as far as White Plains, but the New York highways were smacking with slush that sprayed up and covered the silver of the Mercedes and made him incognito when he finally drove into the old neighborhood Bronx streets.

The ride down had also been a pile of thoughts, like garbage collecting, but at last ending with thoughts of Karen Gaines, who worked for him in the office (but did not know about some of the products) and who seemed ready and maybe also dumb enough to make him act dumb again at thirty-nine and a half. Her face took years off him, and her voice filled rooms and invited itself into his Manhattan condo but also echoed with eyes of amicable partings: he would perhaps die from these thoughtful, civilized women with their priorities written out and spelled out and sticking out.

The lights of the northeast Bronx had come up as he passed the junkyards on Boston Road and then hit the discount gas and beer places and started thinking, beer and gas, beer and gas, this is the real working man: he puts gas in his car and beer in his mouth.

The interior streets were dim, a lone man standing at the curb staring across the street while his dog relieved himself.

The house he grew up in embarrassed him as he stood there at the bottom of the stoop steps and did not want to go inside. The shabbiness of it was what he allowed Poppa, though the whole neighborhood looked the same. Angie called from the porch. She had been keeping her usual vigil but had missed him. "Tony, anything wrong? You're out there. You want to come inside?"

He came up the steps to the porch. "I was so tired from driving in snow." he said.

"Oh, Tony, I am so scared."

He embraced her and felt her shoulders, soft, grown heavy in the house. "How is Pop right now?"

"The doctor's in there. They brought more oxygen and the tent."

"That's not good," he said.

"See, now they say he could go tonight. If the lungs clog up. Tony. Now Poppa's going. We're alone. That's all we're here for, isn't it, to die?"

"Where's Ed?" Tony asked.

Angie was embarrassed. "I called him a few times," she said. "He just can't leave the yards up there. He's in charge of the whole thing. He runs it."

"He runs all right. Does he ever come home at all?"

"Sure he comes home at all. Now don't start with that again. This is my husband you're talking about."

"He should be here now, that's all I'm saying. In times like this— forget it."

They walked to the kitchen and sat at the porcelain table. Angie felt hurt and got up again. She went to the stove to heat coffee. "You want some eggs or leftover macs?" she asked her brother.

He asked for eggs and looked at the kitchen while she prepared, the white table he had sat at weathering twenty-five years or more, the sacred heart pictures on the wall, fading but reluctant to go, like the memory of their mother. And Eddie's bowling cup golden and white on the fridge.

He liked Eddie but felt forced to complain about his drifting off for periods of time without telling Angie. And she put up with it, bringing an ancillary disrespect to the family. Still, Angie kept reminding him that Eddie was her problem and that was it.

But Eddie had been convincing when he told Tony that man was a wanderer and always alone no matter where he was. It had impressed Tony at fourteen. "I like Eddie," he said aloud.

"I know you do," Angie said.

"Then why do you get so hurt if I defend you?"

"Because." She came to the table and served the eggs, then poured his coffee, looking into his eyes. "Because you think what kind of stupid I am that I stay married to the hobo, the tramp. But I'm the one that knows him, what kind of man he is. He's a good man."

They heard fast steps growing louder at the staircase and went to the front hall to meet the doctor, whose eyes were wide open, the forcing of a tired man. "Look, folks, he should by all rights be moved to the hospital. And maybe we'll do it. Right now it could be worse to move him. So let's look at the problem as we go along. You the son, Antonio?"

"Yes," Tony said. "I thank you, doctor."

"I think he said your name. You could go up a minute, but no visit, you know. I'm going to make a few house calls; then I'll check with you again."

Tony walked upstairs while Angie went to escort the doctor out. His father looked decayed, hidden in the tent. Tony backed out of the room as his temples felt the swelling; he stood near the open door trying to press out the pain.

His father moaned, and he stepped back, out of the room into the hall. He thought he heard the sound of something falling; his face was burning. His father had been at the end of a passageway.

Angie's hand was on his back. She embraced him and led him along the hall. He could not tell her his wish to run.

"I'll go see if he woke up," she said.

He kept his eyes on her and saw her lean into the doorway; she came back and led him downstairs. They waited together in the kitchen and went up after an hour, but the old man did not respond to calls. "You go get some sleep first," Angie said to her brother.

"I can't sleep now," he said.

"Then I'll go catch a few winks," she said. "I've been up about eighteen hours. Wake me up in a few hours."

After Angie shut her door, he began pacing the hall, looking in at his father now and then. He hated this upstairs hallway because his mother's closet was here, and they had never removed her clothes from inside. None of them could ever decide. And some kind of stupid minor fears came through the redwood door.

The walking brought him back to tomorrow, the thing waiting for him at the courts. He had not listened to Poppa saying, I FORBID YOU TO WORK WITH THESE PEOPLE. But the old man shut up year after year getting steady checks from Tony, leaving them only the holiday seasons for conversation. Blame rode him now like the darkness of this damn hallway full of what was not here.

Angie relieved him some time in the night; he had been sitting near his father's bed. He went to the guest room and was awakened by her in daylight but did not see the message in her face right away: their father had died during the night.

She led him through the next three days, held his hand at the funeral parlor and when they walked behind the casket after Mass and at graveside and then led him back to the limo. He watched her praying and then on her knees and stepping out to throw a flower on the sinking casket the men let down: he stayed hunched over his stomach as if he had been beaten.

At the house the cousins had come to talk and bring food and eat. By four he sat alone with Angie as she read the Mass cards to him and said, "Did you even think there were so many left that knew him?"

Tony suddenly wanted to leave. The white porcelain table was too much an announcement to Manhattan that dumb guineas resided here. "Angie, do you need any money?" he said.

"Poppa had some put away, you know. I didn't check the book. And he had a policy, about five thousand. I don't know how much it covers."

"Well, look, why don't you tell Marteri to send me the whole bill. All the cars, too. Right to my office. You got the address?"

Angie nodded. "All right, Tony, if you're sure you can do it?"

"Angie, what the fuck else do I have but money?"

"I just thought, right now, maybe it's no time for you to do this." She looked away from him as she had done when he was a bad boy many years ago.

Tony felt the heat inside his chest with heartbeats like a little drum as Eddie walked in, still silent as he had been the last two days, his pleasantly grim smile stuck on. He leaned against the sink, a visitor waiting to leave, looking much younger than Angie, his round face without a line in it. Tony watched him and wanted to call him a miserable fuck.

Angie cleaned up and then went to lie down. As she left the room, Eddie came and sat in her chair. He watched her go and then leaned close to Tony: "You OK? I seen pictures in the papers. You're passing through a lot of trouble. What are they trying to do to you? What are you up on?"

"Pornography. And bad connections."

"The mob? You mean? You with the mob?" Eddie smiled.

"Why not? I'm a *gumba*. Right? My name ends with the vowel. I must be with the mob. We all have cousins in the mob, and we all stick together— in one big mob, you know what I mean?"

Eddie said, "Then you're saying that's all you really do is you print the stag books?"

"Books and magazines, that's right. I distribute them all over the world, which is what they don't like. I'm getting too greedy for them. A wop is only allowed so much money he can make."

"So what's the problem? We got the Laconia Theatre right here on the Avenue showing all the hardcore you want. It's on TV already. You can get a tape and the machine."

"A VCR?"

"The machine that plays the thing into the TV."

"But Eddie, they still want me downtown, and downtown, when they want you, they get you. No matter what. Unless you want to live in Brazil."

"Brazil?" Eddie's eyes were alight. "So what's your next move?"

"I don't know. Run. Sit. Fly. I don't know what the fuck to do. If I knew it was just a big fine, I'd pay it and get out. And take off. I am trying a food business in St. Louis."

Eddie was nodding. "I had ideas like that, taking off to another place in the world. Another business. But then you need the base, the money, so I thought, how much could I raise. And some said Florida was the best, but still I ended up here, and I don't know what the hell to do or where the hell I am. Now you take Angie—she always knows where it's at."

"I know what you mean," Tony said. "From the last three days. The only one of us who could get around and do everything that had to be done."

"Sure. That's because she's got The Beliefs. And that's it."

Tony stopped a moment at Eddie's quiet craziness, then asked him, "And what does that do?"

"The Beliefs?" Eddie's flat face was always the same; his nickname was the Chink. "The Beliefs is that Angie never has to look for a place to go. If I only had that—"

"I thought your wish was money."

"Yes, but if I had The Beliefs, I could live here satisfied. I could live in a box." Eddie looked down at the table for a long while, then spoke again. "They say you make a lot of money with dirty stuff. In the papers."

Tony looked down, too. "I make some, but not enough to get off the world and relax in the south Pacific. The papers make it sound so big that people can hate and dream. Look at that lucky bastard, retired with all that money, at thirty."

"You sure?" Eddie said.

"That the papers are bullshit or how much I got?"

Eddie said, "The money. You have it yet? Like half a mill? Even a quarter could do a lot, with the right investment. Like eight percent bonds and some good stocks. You could live six months here, six months on a Greek Island; you could go down and get that high Mexican interest, you could change money and make dollars. You could buy property and sell—"

Eddie was rushing with excitement, but Tony interrupted: "Is there any aspirin? I got a headache like an axe."

Eddie was up. "I'll ask Angie. We got to have some around the house."

Tony watched him leave and looked at the tablecloth as he waited. He saw the casket on rollers. He wanted to get going. He had to stop at the office and get some papers and then check his condo.

Eddie came in with the aspirin bottle and Angie. Tony took two pills as they watched. Eddie said, "If you ever need advice on management— I mean, call me. I studied this twenty years. I could show you every parlay there is."

Tony stood up and shook hands with Eddie, then embraced and kissed his sister. "You will definitely hear from me," he said to Eddie, whose fool face was believing. Angie said as they stepped on to the front porch, "You sure you're all right to go?"

Tony leaned to kiss her again and looked out at his car covered with soot after four days. He drove to Sunoco for a car wash and then filled the tank and started downtown. But at Seventy-ninth he went off the exit and under the bridge to the uptown side and right out of the city.

He reached Vermont by midnight; he had not stopped to eat and enjoyed the hollowness. The lamp was still going in the house, and he went in. The house was warm, the room welcome. He made a fire to look at the flames and brought a bottle of Sambuca to the armchair.

He wanted to call Karen Gaines but could not cross that line yet. Something about his father's death made it pressing: the wish was the fear as well. Only Angie had removed some of it today by reading the Mass cards and talking about Poppa taking his seat next to Momma in Heaven.

And if he died up here, alone? Then what? He would leave a bottle of Sambuca unfinished—only a venial sin. He kept sipping. Two more days, and he would fly to Ibiza and join a monastery where the Danish nuns prayed topless in the sun.

When the bottle was finished, he fell asleep. He preferred the couch to the beds because it gave the best sleep and had protection in it.

He awoke just before dawn and tried to drain some of the liqueur from the bottle and started to cough from the sting. He sat there fifteen, twenty minutes and then dialed his sister.

"Tony? You all right? You didn't call."

"I thought you got up early so I would call you after some sleep. I'm sorry if it's too early."

"I was up already. It's just I'm not used to you calling in the morning."

"Listen, Angie, did Eddie explain the trouble I'm in right now?"

"He explained a little bit. If you don't have enough money, I can use Poppa's."

"The money's no problem. I just wanted to talk to you. Ask you something."

"Ask me what?"

"Your opinions. Advice. What I should do now."

"You mean, like what do I think about it?"

"Yes. Like should I move away fast? Like go to the Spanish islands to live?"

"Did you ever think of marriage?"

"Angie? Now? In the midst of troubles. Get married?"

"I was only asking. Like asking you different things and see what touches you."

"I'm very mixed up, Angie. This wouldn't be a time for things like that, even if I had a person in mind."

"Well, what is it, then? Are they going to take your money away? Then next time, don't get involved with bad people."

"I told Poppa I was not involved with them. Year after year I told him." She would not answer. "Angie, listen to me. I am asking you because you know me, you took care of me, you brought me up. And we're brother and sister. That's an important bond."

"I don't know what I should tell you, Tony. If you want to come down and stay here, I'll be very happy. You could stay as long as you like. It's better for us to be close now we're both alone."

"All right, Angie, all right. I'll try to make it. I'll call you when I get back. But then I'll also be with lawyers night and day. I don't know what I'll be doing, what kind of time I'll have."

"Anything you say. Just call when you get the chance." There was a long pause before she spoke again. "Tony, I wanted to tell you I'm sorry."

"Sorry for what?"

"That you're not feeling good. It's going to pass, though. Try not to worry too much. You're still young."

"Thanks, thanks a lot." Tony said good-bye and put the phone down, then walked to the bedroom door, taking his suitcase off the bed to lie down. Light of day was coming off the snow now. The sun stripes falling on his body had already made the silk of the comforter warm to the touch. It was a good time to sleep for a week, get it together, get over the funeral, get ready to go down into Manhattan. And he had to go down there now before they ate it all up. Down into their mouths. And with his lawyers behind him, shut them all up for good.

# Part Three:
# Blendings and Losses

# The Last Sabbatical

I walk along hallways, thinking, *It must be time to look at my life's work.*
A little static in my head, then a voice saying *What do you mean, your life?*
"What do *you* mean?" I ask aloud. But I catch on. I had a whole bunch
of years of Life before my life's work began. Starting with my baby goopy
years plodding through the unknown planet with the help of my big sisters Ida, Eva, and Lola—Momma being occupied by the shopping, cooking, and midlife hormonal mini-explosions.

Followed by my school years, with an interruption of four more of big
war in big bomber. Then nine years more of school, getting diplomas to
hide behind before we went into a dive and crashed at Post-Traumatic
Syndrome Airport.

Where are we, then? I need looking back at more than the hallways
behind me where the ghosts of war are much more quiet and have become
existent shadows.

Let me see. My oldest brother, Londo, still drives a truck for
Brunkhorst: he's now the boss of all the drivers. But I don't see him as
much since I've lived up here at Sunnycliff Manor College where I came
to rest a goodly time ago like a whale following smaller fish into the sand.
Londo? I am not sure how he measures out his life these days—probably
with the inexorable slave-master alarm clock in the morning and the
melodies and commercials of the late nite TV shows for sleep orders.

I was the last of that nice brood of loving people I loved from the start of life. But I was chosen to go to many schools so that I might gain wisdom—and (who knew?) alienation from most of the folks who people the world. In the good old USA, after Pop made it, it was supposed to be one son a dentist, one in politics (which meant law), one in construction, one to the FBI or the police (state trooper preferred), one for Wall Street or the banks.

The last one was often a sacrifice to success, to selling out, and this one usually sensed his role and tried to become a dropout, a bohemian, a radical, a hippie—the name is changed every twenty to fifty years or so. He—or She these days—is supposed to carry the expanded pride of cleansing revolutions in him or her. But it's always the same story: that final droplet of genes is the one who is supposed to show by his life-actions that the others may be living an absurd, life-defying lie.

I was one of those a while. Michael Joseph Spinelli. I left the old streets of the lesser parts of Scarsdale where Poppa's stylishly designed raincoats had season after season earned him more cash heft to exit the Bronx and eat away at the mighty mortgage he paid for fourteen rooms and trees.

Yes, I was the one who wandered, meandered, by ship and plane, to all the places the others never saw. Travel can also be a duty, I found out (that is, anything more than a Perillo package).

It's also too erotic (often) for the success-guys, whose *coglioni* are just not ready to be wandering after ten years at the brokerage. It was OK for me because the family assumed that I already had indulged in all the sins success forbade them, a kind of turn around, you know, because we are brought up to believe that once you get the big bucks (like Hollywood stars and pro football players) then you commit the fun sins everywhere.

Good old Poppa: how he loved his freak (while castigating him verbally as uncontrollable). But I think he knew he had also created me out of his own Unconscious.

He used to embrace me when I came in from California or Ibiza with a lot of hair and all brown of skin. "Save one for me, Mikey," he would say (and my brothers got to copying him with that fun slogan). They could visualize the line of beauties I had had on beaches everywhere.

"Mikey, Mikey," Poppa would call; my name was a cookie on his tongue. "Watch out; don't catch anything; don't touch needles; carry the rubber—" He went on through the cautions told him by the blue light networks where the truth came from.

He finally would remind me of that great playboy, Tennessee, who built a vast audience for his fantasies of castrated and purified sin, all for the bored of Westchester where Poppa was becoming a new, hip American of the living room.

But I am not here to describe the wreckage, Boys and Girls. This is a life that has been going by our eyes. The aforementioned was like a list for all conglomerations, be they wops or the sweet slaves of any color or ethnic schtick, whose religion, no matter what they profess in words, has become the House and the Caddy, the House and the Mercedes, the House and even the Lexus and Infinity.

We all convert to it easily; it is our legacy AND our freedom; we marry it: money. And if we don't, we are the scabs of society. Like me, although there were scab levels, starting with the lowest, which the Italians called the disgraced (*I disgraziati*), the perpetual underclass, who have no money and do not even seem real to us. Politicians often use them in speeches to promise helpful laws that prove how much they love the *disgraziati* without cash in their pockets. Oh yeah!

My niche is up a few drawers: like the Sunnycliff teacher with lots of great scenery around him when he works, wonderful people to work with and talk with every day—but no endowment, which means "no-dough." (Only private colleges can have this category because the public ones get along on taxes, all folks with cash in their pocket pay.)

I digress like that old master, Jerome the first and best. Let me say that I did do something after the Big War that got rid of the Nazis in Berlin (but planted some of their ideas in Idaho and the Dakotas on grumpy farmland). When I was discharged, taxes were ready to pay my tuition. I found top schools ready to welcome me (didn't they know what my vowel-suffused name meant I was? Or had Pop's portfolio and bank accounts and ownership of a small raincoat corporation made us totally new post-war Americans real fast?)

I wasn't sure how it went, but I stayed and stayed, got three Latin badges with ribbons. Then I taught in schools. Then I quit, lived in New Haven, a city of lotsa Italo-Americans (I had learned how to hyphenate like a good boy) and studious strangers. Then I left for Vermont, where I tapped sugar trees, baked black bread, and saw the best of all dreams ridiculed (again), laughed at, and finally jailed. Many of my old friends called me adolescent, noting my long hair as if I had grown horns instead of hair.

Very cold one night, the ice seeping through the cracks of the door, I heard a silent voice screaming inside me. I hugged my best girl close and suggested marriage. We rushed down to Cambridge, Mass., where she began to teach nursery school and try a little makeup at night. I looked at her and repeated to her, "Please don't leave me"—until our marriage was consummated.

And we lived six years after that with totally rational behavior patterns (we believed), expressing the necessary anarchistic minority thoughts in our heads (like organizing peace marches while the war factories were expanding daily). Our only sin was mocking the bourgeois outbursts of my family, though Pam was always asking Momma for more of her recipes.

Then one day Pam returned on the MTA from teaching young girls music and thinking on the ride back. She described a chimera haunting her: her eyes were being forced to follow babies in carriages. Her clocks were moving too fast; she must become the mother of her earthly dreams as she approached, only a few years away, the pinnacle of thirty.

"Mother?" I said. "What is a mother? And you, Pam, with those great tits—*you* are talking about mothering?"

Pam nodded, unaware that I had forgotten where the milk comes from and goes to.

I went on. "Pam, we have balled in every nook and cranny of all our flats and houses. And this was to be our Cambridge shack made exclusively for shacking up. I am a man—and only balling will do for me. And you, too, the new woman, the new freedom rider, the new freedom-of-choice-chick."

"You're only worried about money," she said. "But babies cost no more than ten cents a day. And what do they eat? Less than a dog."

"All right, then," I said through a haze of sudden guilt and idealism. "Since I am the natural boy Poppa pressed out of the mold, I accept."

Any refusal, I thought, would brand me a moral fraud and dump me right back into the Bronx where the message engraved on the neighbor-hood walls says, WOPS NEVER MAKE IT UNLESS THEY SHOOT YOU AND TAKE IT.

And babies came. To ourselves and to our friends. We held babies and fed babies and dressed babies and later walked them to school and traded in our MGs for vans and wagons and bought a house a little farther out and a second car (small) and another TV (large).

Then I tried to run from these mountains of things but soon found, indeed, that everybody was doing it, and the movies were singing, "oh how we love death and money, money and death." I was in the real world again. But it made me run away again.

Now the mists are covering years which had no labels or identity. See me falling into Sunnycliff Manor, sanctuary for the odd, the defeated, the smart, the hypersensitive who are too ashamed to try opiates. Oh, what a group we collected there: gays with high morality, who had to stuff it into pillows; women who still loved their fathers too much; couples who both taught, he Bio, she History, and drank together all night, with long pauses of silence.

And me, the alienated clown who couldn't find his way back to the Bronx, yet if he could have, would now have called it pukey, tacky, too much.

Are you discouraged now? Would you prefer to hear that Pam and I got together again?

All right, then. We met by chance at a concert in New Hampshire on a languorous summer night and fell in love again and made love in the grass while the orchestra played Vivaldi. And had twins nine months later, one who looked like me, a girl, and the other a spitting image of Pam, a boy, and both normal, healthy, brilliant—graduating from prep schools with full scholarships, four years at Harvard, he's now doing his residency in pediatrics, she running an engineering project in the slums, as head environmental engineer.

Or would you hear some of our history? Of the parties where some listened to the Four Seasons, Mick and then some rockabilly and countrywest. Or the new tube-churchmen warning us about the atheistic Commie pornographers and send them a holy check, all on the channels, where it's Mickey Mouse and Father Feelgood.

But no more. There are just couches and apartments. Note this interior. The apartment is spacious. The furniture more attractive. This large leather couch is from Milan. One in corduroy from Knoll. Sheets are all Marimekko. A real Tiffany lamp in greens. Soft overhead lights from Lighting Associates.

The friends are seated together counting the years on their fingers.

Jack: I am forty-two years of age. I work every day for my wife and family. And that is my job and my purpose. I provide charge accounts and plastic cards, and they provide the shopping energy. At night before falling asleep, I wish I could live alone for a long while in the Maine woods. With antibiotics, of course. And if things went well—well, forever.

Jill: My husband's family business has become a success. He sold out to a conglomerate for multimillions. We bought a Colonial on the Cape near Wellfleet, a condo in Boca, and part of a new group condo in Phoenix. The summer place on the Cape has become my refuge: I go down whenever I can. That beach keeps me alive, those walks when all you meet is the gulls. And the kids love it, too. Mary, who left college and is trying to make up her mind, wants to live on the Cape the entire year. Alone. I'd rather she had a boyfriend with her. I ask her what she wants to be. She doesn't know yet. She needs to think. "My husband and I have slept together ten times in the past ten years, usually following New Year's parties. Everyone tells me I have hardly aged."

Dick: When I go on business trips, I often dream of meeting a girl I can fall in love with. I am not out of love with Martha. We are like friendly roommates; marriage has been like a hall of good friends in a dorm. And when I travel, I see it and regret what it does to me, namely, remove my passion. I sometimes want to go with a tart and curse at her while we make angry love. I'm ashamed to say this, but I must because I am a man, and we are phallic, and you have to face that fact. Though I have had some experiences on business trips, in hotel rooms, with paid women, after which I felt a massive emptiness that is enough punishment for all my sins of thought.

Jane: I had a scholarship to Julliard when I was eleven. My mother and father both worked to pay for everything else, and by the time I was eighteen got me an apartment on Claremont near the conservatory. At my concerts I saw that I was good, only good. No one tells you what to do if you're just good. I should have gone into teaching. The man who became my husband was not the one I loved. Not even one of the two I loved. But he had money. Today we have three homes, with a Steinway in each one. When my husband told me he was going to leave me for a younger woman, I got my large bottle of sleeping pills and showed them to him. "This is my decision," I told him. "You go ahead and do what you want." Two months later he broke his back making a new fireplace for a cabin we bought in the Adirondacks.

We simply never get to the movies anymore. I can't explain where the time goes. Supper ends, and we watch the nightly news, then a sitcom. Then somebody starts to doze; somebody else has to get some tax forms ready; somebody has the flu; somebody has the curse; somebody gets a long distance call and talks while the others are silent. And it's too late.

THE LAST SCENE

It's me again, your spinning Spinelli. I can't decide what to do. I am here at the threshold of looking at my thirty-five years at Sunnycliff Manor. Was this my life's work? What do I look at now that I have reached my last free year paid to improve my mind; write a tome, study something, recharge my verbal brain batteries?

It's probably too late for a tome on the power in the wisdom of the past to help the present (at least, from me). Nothing has stopped the nuclear boys, and it must have probably started with the Romans: when a lower boy gets his time on the throne, he starts making more delivery vehicles than before. To nuke the bad guys (which includes the planet).

But as I say this, I hardly believe it. *You* don't believe it. Should I just sublet and go to Europe, imitate English and German travelers looking for Virgil along the Amalfi coast? Or should I bank the sabbatical money and work another job, praying I may live long enough to collect the interest with my pension so that I can sit on my ass like a cop or a postman in retirement (though not as rich, of course)?

Or should I put my money where my mouth is and rejoin a peace action group or a Nuke moratorium band or a concerned-about-the-death-of-air-and-trees committee? Or go teach in the slums of Rwanda and keep the secret hope that those starving darlings will not be nuked because they are worthless (no cash in pocket) but then again maybe the survivors of a nuclear exchange amongst the smart-guy countries with the delivery vehicle factories?

Or just read Rilke and Shakespeare again and make believe art will rebut the new death because it is immortal?

Or maybe I should work in a graveyard and get ready quietly? Plant good, strong grass and flowers that can bloom in the shade. Get used to life as it is lived now. Order an original headstone, with Teflon finish— and some quality poetry on it by a great death specialist—Mark Strand, for example.

I must do something because I have told different faculty colleagues different stories. I told one I was doing a book on Wallace Stevens because everyone has had one planned; another that I am teaching in the Congo for the year; another that I am traveling to Brazil to research a book on native literary influences on Brazilian writers. And more—too many to burden you with.

But perhaps I should just sit down as my father did and write my own book of life rules? I happened to visit him one July afternoon when he was eighty something, bringing with me handmade lemon ice from our pastry maker friend D'Alessio.

Pop was writing in a large notebook and said he was putting down rules for men to live by. I asked to see it, but he closed the book and went for the tart lemon ice before I could see anything.

At the time, I thought his statement about his book quaint and vaguely impossible. I thought perhaps his mind was going into the childhood of dementia. All because I was not sure how well he could write in his first or second language. (Why do I still believe that he and I are illiterate? Who did that to me in this land of freedom and opportunity?)

I went down to the Scarsdale house a week after he died, looking for that book. The wake was affecting everybody because the center of us all was gone. But I did ask Ida if she had seen it around.

She remembered that it was in a box with other papers of his, all of which she had thrown out. Ida threw everything out. If I left a book or a sweater at the house when I came down to visit, the Sanitation men got it in a week. I had the feeling the garbage men thought our pile was a little free consigment shop.

Everything went. Suits and dresses. Shoes. Smudgy sneakers. Anything old put in the cellar marked SAVE. Trousers too tight or too large; worn rugs that might be useable one day in a spare room. Valuable old 78 rpm records and then tapes (after the introduction of CDs). Rusted bikes and sleds. Strong cardboard boxes holding old handmade baskets. Blenders and toasters with frayed wires or cracked plastic mixing bowls. The first microwaves, now become too small and too slow.

The piles near our garbage cans were well-known. Neighbors scouted by very slowly at night, snatching what they liked. Ida dumped with determination and never wavered.

Perhaps best to dedicate this memory to her, for her victory over shit, under which I and modern humankind reside, pulling the mass over us like a blanket as we lie on our backs, looking up, watching the President on all channels, hoping for complete cover before the brain can activate the heart.

# Hits of the Past

Gerry and Jane have just met at the river bank in Cambridge, that mini-city in the belly of Boston. In the background, from a band shell, music. People sit on the embankment, perhaps in sadness. Not far away, Harvard Square, ice cream, eateries. About 1975.

Gerry has driven up from New York, and Jane is down from Brattleboro. Soon Gerry will leave for Hartford to meet Eileen. Jane will sleep over in Cambridge on Bond street near the observatory, with Todd Heming, an astronomer.

Gerry and Jane meet each June to discuss summer plans for their son, Paul, now ten. He never comes along on this trip.

Jane and Gerry were married for seven years and then divorced. For the first six years of their marriage they tried to have a baby with no luck. Then, after they had separated, when Jane was settled in Vermont again, she found out she was pregnant with Paul.

Gerry still tells people he loves Jane but that it was impossible for the two of them to live together. Simple as that, he says.

Jane, on the other hand, says he was selfish and brooding; that he fooled around with a woman economist less than six months after they were married.

Jane uses *fooled around*. With her close friends, who enjoy her quips, she also said Gerry had sought academic, spiritual, economic as well as erotic nurturing with Gretta Cohen, who had tenure.

Jane has two academic degrees but has committed herself to being a painter. Her white landscapes look like New England fields after a wind-swept snow. She is a painter of bleak inner moods. Gerry tells his friends that her pictures are as bland and scary as she often was.

Gerry has three degrees. Together he and Jane have a combined schooling of thirty-eight years, and both were members of the first American generation to give up smoking and alcohol for non-religious reasons.

For a while, both worked for institutions. Now neither has any affiliation, though last year Jane collected welfare for six months. She refused alimony in the divorce. She stays home most of the time, painting. Her devotion to painting is fierce. She will neglect Paul or anything for it.

Gerry was an assistant prof when the Vietnam War became the main feature on our screens at home. He had been hired by Indiana to teach history; it was only three years after his doctorate at Columbia, but he had published ten articles already.

Gerry was drawn into the protests against the war, admiring first the students. They in turn followed him, the first faculty member to join them.

One day Gerry led a group to the campus gates to lie on the ground and forbid the army trucks from entering. The police were angry. They plucked Gerry from the ground and the crowd and beat him until he bled and was photographed.

His picture in the papers made him a hero while he sat in jail. He was also fired by his dean for unprofessional conduct. He also saw his friends organize a defense committee. A fund was begun and court fights were fought.

Gerry won back pay and lost his job and never was hired again by an academic institution. Prospective employers called him controversial and not sufficiently objective and too narrow in point of view.

Then one of his articles grew into a book, a text in American history. It was called the first revisionist view of history. Gerry was attacked in reviews for being a revisionist. But a hundred twenty colleges bought the book for classes.

Gerry was able to support himself on the royalties of the book and updated editions; he became distinguished and unknown, energetic and depressed, all at the same time.

Visiting his father in New York, driving from Washington where he works at what is called a left-wing-think-tank, still finds the shaking right hand of Italo-admonition as his worried widower, ex-baker father tries to lead Gerry to safety before the arthritis takes him away from earth and the chance to save Gerry from the doom given to those who talk too loud.

He says to Gerry, "If you could just keep out of it sometimes. Tell me why you have to bother with things like that? If they have wars in some little country, the big shots, then they got reasons. And you should keep out of it. Because *you* can't be the big shot. Do I make myself clear?"

These words, with love, follow Gerry along Pelham Parkway and on to the turnpike in Connecticut and begin to drift out of the inner space of the Datsun 210 at New Haven.

Look for a moment at Gerry. Gerry is dark; his hair is black, but at least half the curls are grey. His brown eyes, their glint, their open-lidded staring, come genetically from the docks of Naples. But Gerry is dressed in furnishings from Chipp.

He turns to Jane now for personal matters; there is an intermission in the music. He has been looking around and realizing he is in another academic community, and they make him nervous. He asks Jane, "Do you want to have Paul in July or August? I *could* take him all summer this year. Even starting late June: Eileen and I are going to New Hampshire in June."

"At his age I think he needs a camp. *This* year," Jane says.

"But perhaps not all summer?" Gerry says.

Jane pauses. She is respecting the money problems Gerry might have. But if he can provide a summer vacation for his new girl, then he can't be *that* broke. Gerry says, "Eileen is renting the cottage. Near Franconia. Friends of her family. It has three bedrooms."

Jane says, "The experience of camp has meaning when a child has enough time to integrate himself, to know all the rhythms of the place, and time to know his counsellors and make good friends—"

"And create a family substitute he needs and does not have." Gerry stops his parody to avoid a fight with Jane.

Jane is composing herself even more than usual. She has said that she admires Gerry's honest Latin outbursts of emotion, but frankly she would gladly have lived without them.

And today she has things to do.

Gerry has been made defensive by the silence. "Oh, come on, Janey," he says. "I barely get a chance to see Paul during the year."

Jane speaks inside herself: *then why didn't you get on a train a few more times.*

She stops, begins word-eating until she reaches something that can be said aloud: "Gerry, is that your criterion of what's best for Paul?"

Gerry looks closely at the spring grass; it is yellow-gold, getting darker as it nears the river. "Janey," he says softly. "I am his father. *I* am what's best for Paul."

"Can we just leave it that that is still a moot question in your case?"

Gerry sees four sculls coming by on the river and keeps his teeth shut tight as he watches the quiet young men row by. He watches their gliding. Jane is silent as well. Gerry feels sweat on his neck and wipes it with the back of his right hand.

He tries to clear the dryness from his throat and coughs. Then he says, "Are you going to say something else?"

"Why?" Her voice becomes animated, which means anger in her. "Haven't you seemed to have said it all?" she says.

Her voice is shallow. It makes him guilty, but he says to himself, what's the use, and looks up at her face. It is closed. Her beauty is held behind the perpetual good taste of keeping control.

They pause; then slowly they make plans, and as in previous years, they compromise. Paul will go to camp in July, then stay with his father and Eileen in New Hampshire for August.

\*

Gerry is racing the Datsun along the Mass Pike under sweeping white clouds that touch the sliced highway hills, leaving the Boston rain behind him. He keeps going until he arrives in Hartford, a bar there where Eileen sits.

She sees his agitation as he comes in: he hates to be late; it is like a prelude to punishment inside him. She will try to drive it out quickly. "I just got here myself, a second ago."

He laughs at her transparency and exchanges a glance only those in love give. He is nodding. "You're a real buddy, you know that," he says.

She is smiling; she loves his gratitude; she still thinks like a mistress. Eileen is tall, with long legs, thirteen years younger than Gerry, who at forty-two looks solid, healthy, younger than thirty-five.

"Was it rough?" Eileen says, and passes her beer to him. He looks at it, picks up the bottle and drinks.

Then he says, "It's always the same. We're like two people created to disagree with each other. *I* used to call it cultural, and Jane called it psychological. That took us from psychoanalysis to advanced feminism. And here we are today; all those fads are over—and we just fight. That's awful. To be that way with *any*body."

He pauses and Eileen asks, "How long were you married?" then realizes that the question has struck Gerry like an accusation. It is as if she has said that he is culpable forever. "I am sorry, Gerry. I am really sorry," she says.

He takes up the bottle: the label reads *Samuel Smith. Tadcaster.* He looks at the other words, enjoys the newness, drinks, puts the bottle down on the redwood bar. "We're at the crossroads of two belief systems, as regards morals—"

He looks at Eileen and smiles. "I was about to punish you with a lecture. Insights as sharp as tacks in your butt. Yes, I messed it up. But the only really bad thing now is Paul's going to camp all July."

Eileen takes Gerry's left hand. "Well, now how bad can that be on a scale of one to ten?"

Gerry smiles, relieved, the pleasure of Eileen's changing favorite expressions. For a long time she used to say *at this point in time.*

She kisses his right cheek softly. It has been his salvation that she can show sensuality in delicate ways, in a bar, at a theatre, on a plane.

Eileen knows that their hours together are the best in his life now. And she knows that he must immerse himself in play with his son to show he is a good father. She knows that absent men confuse dogma with guilt.

Yet Eileen is irritated and tired of speaking with sympathy about Gerry's disappointments. She wants to say something about her position. Instead, she lights a cigarette and listens to Gerry warn her again about the dangers of smoking.

Then she says in conciliation with what she is not sure of: "Just remember, darling, we'll be in New Hampshire, and we can drive up to visit him on weekends and bring him toys and food. Games, too. Games above all. I loved it when my mother came. Didn't you always want your mother to be a cookie sender?"

Gerry looks at her with seriousness: "I delivered bread in the Bronx from the time I was nine."

There is no way for Eileen to picture this. She can only give compassion, a form of love that contains no greater vision than other forms.

Eileen also resents deeply, so deep she can barely sense it, the more fashionable poor childhood Gerry had.

Gerry is smiling: "Paul loves those giant chocolate cookies. And raisin faces. Does the shack have an oven?"

In the pause, Eileen has felt the mistress-hurt that comes from his forgetting her function, her wishes in that cottage. "It does," she says, seeing the cottage without Paul. "And we can make cookies every day."

Her generous hypocrisy is painful now; still, Gerry picks up no nuance. Eileen is pleased that Gerry now leans to touch her and moves his hand across her shoulders, then along her neck. She kisses his chin. "We can snorkle in the lake, Betty Gomes told me. She owns the place. Is Paul old enough?"

Gerry smiles, still close to her. "The kid's pretty good in the water." Gerry watches the sweet shine of her light face and the glow of what *he* loves about her, but what she thinks is ugly.

"The freckle," he says, "is mankind's truly unrecognized beauty mark."

"Are we going to start that now?"

Gerry stands erect a moment, backing off from his stool. "And the science of which parts freckle up and which do not is an exploration I am planning this summer in my New Hampshire laboratory."

Eileen cannot enjoy it; she tries a smile that Gerry knows is politeness. Gerry says, "You know what I'd like to do this summer? Build a raft. And put it on that lake."

"That's funny. I've been thinking of night fires. I used to love them so much at camp. I thought, well, why can't we make our own night fires and just sit around?"

"He'll go crazy for that. He'll freak."

Eileen looks at the excited face. "Who?"

"Paul. What kid doesn't love night fires?"

Eileen orders another beer. Gerry calls for a gin and tonic. She speaks, looking across the bar to the bottles and mirror behind them. "Oh, he'll have a terrific time," she says. "I've been there—once. It's a kid's paradise."

She turns to Gerry; he sees the shine of light on her lip coating, the lipstick. Eileen says, "Let's get going before it gets too late. Some of those roads up there are hard at night."

*

Paul is looking at the babysitter and says, "Gretchen, I want to sit in your lap."

She is from Putney and is wearing a jean skirt with green sweater. She is a busty sixteen-year-old. "Don't be silly, Paul," she says.

Paul sits on the floor to see up her skirt. "Take me to the Dairy Queen," he says to her. "Jane left five dollars for fun money in the Super Yeast can."

Gretchen follows him out to the Chevette. He hates her, but as they sit and drive, he looks and wants to get on top of her and hold her down. "I could hold you down all night," he says aloud, and she shakes her head slowly. He is one of the kids from the city people who came here to act poor.

Paul eats the largest cone, with sprinkles and dip, and looks at Gretchen sucking hard because William at the window made her frappe too thick.

When they get home, Gretchen says, "Now be quiet while I call your mother. If she's not coming back, I'm sleeping over."

"We have to sleep in the big bed in her room."

"Don't be silly." Gretchen is holding the phone and waiting for Paul to stop.

"No, you have to sleep in the same room as me."

"Come on, Paul, don't be an ass." Her finality makes him move away from the phone table. He watches her dial, looking at her finger. If he got on her now, he would hold her down all night. And that's it.

Some of her hair rests on her shoulders and trails down the front. It is

*246*

blond. Jane is grey. "I can hold you down," he says aloud, and she says, "Now stop the fooling around. I mean it. And I can't hear Cambridge."

\*

Jane is speaking to Gretchen on the phone. "If you think you can do it, Gretch, I'd be eternally grateful."

Gretchen is agreeable, but Jane goes on. "Trying to drive back in this kind of rain alone panics me. Can you dig it? "

Gretchen assures her she will stay over. No sweat.

Jane pauses after hanging up. Paul does not like to be alone. He will get her for it. Paul also likes Todd and would have enjoyed seeing him and getting rides in the green MG. But she is never alone and never alone enough with Todd.

She comes to the table in the kitchen that overlooks Bond and the Radcliffe courts across the way. It is dim, but she can see the white lines. It looks like the rain is ending. She wants to go to the North End tonight for a meal.

She sees Todd come from inside. He is tall, almost gaunt, and still keeps the scraggly beard of the walking days in Vermont when they were all there. Or thought so.

Todd gets two beers from the fridge, a new brand the place down on Huron carries: *Harp*. They go to the terrace with the beers. Todd says, "Did you get it all haggled out?"

"As much as one ever can with Gerry," Jane says.

She examines her label. Todd drinks and then asks about Gerry again. "What is he really doing these days?"

"Well, he is still the same stiff pain these days," Jane says. "But no one will give him a teaching job. And he's one of the best men in his field. You saw his text—"

Todd is nodding and holding up his hand. "I am not surprised. We will just *never* be forgiven."

"For what? For not going to med school quick enough?"

"Look, here's my déjà vu." He sits back a little and looks down the street before speaking. "I am sitting with my Dad at our house in Westbury,

247

and he is pissed at my coming home with the beard. He keeps asking me just what have I *become*. So I try to tell him, and no matter what I say, he says the same thing: 'Then, as I understand it, Todd, you are now a Communist?' And he looks around the big room, and that's when I see it. They gave us all this—money, possessions, more junk than any kids ever had. And we grew beards. In rags—"

"*Some* of us grew beards," Jane says. "Look, all we really had was different ideas, and they couldn't stand that with their liberal bellywash. And that's all we did." Jane looks at Todd's face. "And what does he say these days?"

"These days he's eclectic." They both laugh. Then Todd says, "Sometimes he says, 'Why don't you marry Jane? She's a nice girl.' "

"That means she's from a good family, good blood, no bad strains in the litters—"

Jane breaks off. Todd sits straight in his chair, nods, smiles at Jane, then lifts his bottle to his lips after waiting for Jane to say something more. He drinks, then puts his bottle down softly. "It's going to clear," he says. "You can probably drive up now."

"Sit on it," Jane says, and he tries to laugh.

Then he says, "You were talking about Gerry."

Jane shakes her head. "You were talking about Gerry. Well, Gerry has still another chippie, of course. And I didn't ask him much."

"Is he still at the Institute?"

"Todd, I don't care."

*

Eileen looks up. "Gerry, that sky is something we never see anymore. New York doesn't have a night sky."

"It's there, though," Gerry says. "Behind the commercials. The sky has sponsors in Manhattan."

They are seated on the front porch of the cottage. "I wish this night could stay. Suppose, if you wanted a night to go on, you could turn a dial and make a night last three weeks?"

Gerry puts an arm across her shoulder. "And no more phones," Eileen says, his face close to hers. "Why do we have to go back at all? Let's just stay here. Anything we need we can buy in town. I'll call my sister to go by and lock up. Then we drive down in mid-July."

Gerry is enjoying it. Then he remembers he must phone Jane for dates. He holds back. But he must say it. "You know, the only problem with this is I always go up in June to take Paul on his big shopping trip for clothes. It's a thing we do before summer every year—we get his whole year's stuff. I told you Jane never took alimony. So I do this. And if he's also going to camp, that means extra—"

"And of course this would be the only time you could get that stuff before he leaves."

Gerry kisses her face. Eileen keeps talking about what they can do in the remaining three days they have now. Gerry smiles and slowly pushes her down while she speaks. They are on the worn porch couch.

As Eileen goes slowly back, looking up at Gerry's face, she tries to accept the pleasure within herself; she sees the moon sway and move in the sky. She holds Gerry tightly.

This story is over.

# Twenty-Nine Steps towards Re-adhesion

1. Florence. 1982. The broom (Ezio calls it *ginestra*) is brilliant yellow against the green hills of Chianti. Leaves of the wine grapes overhead. We are going to Greve for lunch. Ezio swears he will take me to a different town in Chianti every day: we will have a *pranzo,* taste the local wine all afternoon. By the time I leave, we will have tried all the Chiantis. This is also to distract me gastronomically and aesthetically, he says. Yesterday I found a book in Via Tornaboni, the shop just up from Piazza Trinità. A history of all the Chianti wine farms. One hundred sixty-four pages, and each page a different label with a minihistory of the farm. My liver will go before we drink them all.

2. Ginny liked broom. She went to sit in the fields of it the first day she saw it. And cried. We had rented a car in Florence and were on the way to Siena. We never made it. We sat drinking Chianti we had bought on the road, and she remembered her mother. Something about the two of them and the fields of broom on the Cape: the only year she was ever happy.

3. I was saying nothing when Ezio stopped for the broom. Atypical for him to ever stop. And the way he turned to look at me. With what? A compassionate stare? A pitying grin? Did he know Ginny liked it, the broom? I thought he was about to mention her, but he looked at me with that look. He catches my emanations perhaps. He often says that Ginny was blind. "On her magic carpet ride, like those women of Henry James. What does she do? She falls in love with her picture of an Italian, and he

isn't even an authentic one." I nod at his certainty, the dogma that haunts Italian men. He says, "You must know by now that the woman falls in love with her construction of love." My silence gets him eventually, and his voice goes up. "Let it go, let it go. It happened only inside her head. You had yours. Now let it end."

4. He is a Florentine. They have been business men since God knows when. They hold the scales of trade always in hand. Everything can be weighed out. Proper measuring makes logic, makes conclusions. For instance, he sees me tainted with bad blood from my father's side, Naples, the South. We see love as a candy heart. We want only to suck on the sugar—then we get sick. He attacks me for that when he gets a bit drunk (something he learned living in the states): "You don't know what is over is over. You want to feast on your wound. *Senti?* If you can say to yourself, *Over,* then it is gone." I stand up and salute him: "*Sì, Commandante.*" "Sit down, *stronzo,*" he shouts, and laughs at his word.

5. Lillies, red poppies, blue wildflowers I can't name in Italian. Did I know them as a child? I am fluent but for the fishes and the flowers. Ezio was looking up at the broom and said the yellow makes the green greener this time of year. Like Ireland. He tells me Ireland has the greenest grass in the world.

6. As we drove through the Tuscan hills, the cypresses going brown in clumps along the way, I thought of what a great place this would be for Paul to come and paint. But his last letter said it was getting too hard: getting a one man show, making it in that world of cliques; if you didn't toady up, you faced a century of hunger. So he was thinking of med school again, without illusion, as he put it, that there are doctors who paint on weekends. I mentioned it to Ezio, who said that paintings were no longer necessary—nor books—except for old dogs like us. The young have the Tee Voo, which does everything for them. It provides for their aesthetic needs. I said to him, "Do you really believe that?" And he paused, pursing his lips to show the heavy thought, adding slow slight nods. "Michael, I think we are dead," he said. "*You,* especially. Because at least I can keep the past here a little. You threw out the Victorian furniture of your mother when you moved out of the Village. What did you get? You inherited Yonkers. And now you live like a man on the back of a truck. Downtown

the young gays buy and sell your living room as antiques and make a new world." I said to him, "This must be your new cyclical theory of history." And he shot off one more tight Medici mini-smile: DENY IT AS I WISH, IT WAS STILL TRUE, his face said. Like Galileo.

7. "Good friends and friendship, *caro mio,*" I said, "means being pissed off and eating it all the time." And Galileo spoke again: "I can only tell you the truth," he said. "A friend is to speak the truth you can't see."

8. I am silent, sullen—whether from his lectures or the returning, I don't know. I can't remember anything Ginny and I did or said. I can't remember *her*. I experience brief bites—like a toothache—of memory, feel something and then am very quiet and down. It happens fast. And just as I have tried to probe it, Ezio begins again as Galileo: "Michael, *senti*. Everything comes round again. People change hands. The haughty German countess who was caught by the Russian army and raped by a platoon of peasants is in power again—did you read it—and shot one of the Russians thirty years later. Did you see it? He was on business in Berlin." I looked up at his disturbing story, and he was nodding, "Yes, only books and paintings do not change."

9. He must think I'm drunk most of the time. Each morning he leaves for work as I am getting up to go to the john. He returns at one thirty, and I'm just shaving. I tell him I've been revising my book, and he looks down at the pages which look exactly as yesterday and nods. "Is it on Caravaggio?" he says. "Caravaggio and a few others," I say. Then we go out to Chianti for another lunch.

10. Yesterday we had lunch in San Casciano: first a restaurant and then, after, a walk to a *pizzicheria* that made coffee. Ezio and the proprietor started talking. Ezio told him I was an American. The man explained he had four hundred different types of prosciutto. I said that that was difficult to believe. Ezio said, "How about the French and four hundred cheeses?" I nodded to Galileo, then watched the owner, who wanted me to do a tasting. The best was thinly sliced *finocchioncino*. I watched an old man squeezing lemons into his wine. Ezio said the farmers believe it cools them off in the heat. Like the Chinese putting warm rags on their faces. Ezio says, "The lemons really work." Galilean truths abound. I offer no questions.

11. Ezio's apartment is his monument in the making. Two great rooms and a kitchen, a foyer larger than a Manhattan studio apartment. It faces the piazza the Medicis built for a fish market. Now it's a flea market for imitation furniture and imitation armor and what tourists seem to like. Ezio found old craftsmen who knew the ancient techniques of stucco and the waxing of beams with beeswax. The men chopped out the modern ceiling that was built in the sixteen hundreds, found the beams from the eleven hundreds, and restored them. You look up at incredibly long hand-cut wooden beams. And Ezio has filled the rooms with his objects bought on business trips. In Yugoslavia he found an old man who made church wall hangings in plaster and wood, painted in bright tempera. Stations of the Cross. Christ being soothed by Mary. Treasures. Ezio found a tile man who redid the floors with old red tiles he found in a barn out in Chianti. He has a carved wooden table, bits of the ivory inlays fallen out, on which he places the Etruscan stuff he bought from grave robbers he knows in the hills. Gold pins, the Etruscans knew how to work pure gold—and vases and dancing figures. In the corner is his pride, an old wood carving made from a tree trunk. A monk in habit, Cappuccino, I think. It reminds Ezio of his first employer, Brother Clementino, the miracle monk who lived in Fiesole and received thousands of letters a day from all over the world (Ezio delivered them up the hill). "I can't believe you never heard of him," Ezio says to me with irritation. "Even people in Russia used to write to him for a miracle."

12. Ezio gets excited about a little *gita* up to Fiesole. He wants to show me the monastery where Clementino worked, built over the Etruscan ruins, and where Ezio played as a boy. He is the most eager tourist. Anywhere we go, he searches down all the narrow streets, more curious than any foreigners he has shown the town. He calls me inauthentic but not yet a foreigner. He says of me, "Born of Italians and away from Italy by mistake, an accident of history." This historical accident has come to Florence to commune with fragments that might be left. He wishes to complete his puzzle. I told Ezio I really had no Italian persona—unless I make it up. Ezio says I am obscured from myself running from the wounds of Ginny. I tell him a broken love affair has nothing to do with

remembering my first two years in Italy here. And he says, ending it, "But you were born here."

13. One day after lunch—always after a meal—Ezio said, "Why don't you just try living here permanently?" I said to him, "I would miss bagels and Katz's deli too much." His face turned into a false smiling, nodding at me. He doesn't believe what I say. He says, "It's time you found out where your home is. I was ten years in Chicago; they offered me a vice presidency. But then I knew I had to come back here. Because this is home inside me. When I thought, vice president means Chicago forever, I left." I said, "But New York has made me Jewish." "Bullshit on toast," he said quickly. "You're about as Jewish as I am. Listen. Home is the place that stays inside you wherever you go. Now what *is* that, for you? Find it."

14. Maybe I could do it here with somebody who loved it with me. Ginny used to say she wanted to live here. And I believed her. And started to consider it. But she was back here by herself in May. Maybe she was thinking of it. I mention this to Ezio.

15. He nods and seems about to answer, then stops himself. He does not speak about her anymore. If I bring her up, he will be about to say something, then think better of it.

16. Now and then he busts out, usually late at night after we have sat for some hours drinking and talking. (His own drinking seems desperate to me.) He has not mentioned Marianna, his ex-wife, who lives nearby, somewhere in town. She told me his screaming frightened her when they argued. One night Ezio started on me: "You must stop moping around. Ginny was a woman trying to escape. She met you, she used you a while to get out of prison. Then she wanted to go back inside." He wanted a rise out of me, but I was silent. "The woman didn't like you!" He had begun to scream. "She could not even see you! Her eyes were on the locks of her door, and that's all she could see. Be thankful she came out a while for you. And stop thinking she needed you. She told me she didn't even like you. Now don't get hot. It was in May. She said you were spoiled, always stuck in yourself—"

17. I walked out of the room to my bedroom on the second floor and heard him shouting up the steps. "Don't get mad at the truth. Come down.

Listen, I'm worse than you; ask Marianna. Nobody can bear to live with me, either. *Stronzo!* Come down again."

18. Last days. I wanted to go to Greve again. We ate at a restaurant in the main piazza. There were geranium flowers in pots blooming along the cement wall. The statue in the center of the piazza was Verrazzano. I asked Ezio what the ocean navigators were doing deep inside Chianti. "A mystery I often think about," Ezio said. "How did these inland towns produce all those amazing explorers who opened up the world for Europe? They never even *saw* the water. You know about Verrazzano?" "Yes," I said. "He's a bridge, and he comes from Staten Island."

19. The restaurant was a long, shallow room, high-back chairs in dark brown, simple Tuscan decor. The melon and *prosciutti*—we have at least three or four each time now—were optimum, the veal chop like a T-bone steak before the invention of muscles, the stuffed zucchini beefy in the Tuscan style, the artichokes tender enough to eat raw. And the local wine better than other days. I tell Ezio I can't remember which wine was best after all these months. "Then we'll have to start again," he says, and shakes my hand.

20. We drove to an eighth-century town above Greve—Monteferallo—and walked the very narrow streets to get the feel of the past. Ezio wanted a *digestivo,* and we found the town bar. It had three rows of Scotches, and Ezio had one. He reminded me of the day ten years before in Milano when he ordered me a large glass of Fernet Bianca for my birthday. "I thought it was rat poison," I said. Ezio slaps my back and laughs, invites me to have a Fernet now. He has another scotch. Then we drive to the Enoteca shop in Greve where the growers keep a small museum at the site of ancient wine cellars. The two men in charge looked like Amherst profs in their tweed and leather patches, both pipe-smoking, lean. But then again, Tuscany looks like Vermont.

21. Ezio worries about my inaction. "Why don't you get out and go around Florence when I'm working? We are so near the Bargello. You always liked Santa Croce. It's just down the street." He believes that true therapy is getting off the butt, never sitting down, doing something fast.

22. In the mornings here I have remembered my mother. The voices and the silences here are different and let me daydream. There is no hum

of surrounding thruways that make you feel as if the phone is about to ring and you're due somewhere soon. I walked the street where my mother lived as a girl and tried to imagine something I didn't remember or know. I could only see her in exile, a New York kitchen. Three young women went by, and I followed them, listening. But nothing happened. I walked downtown and stopped for coffee in Piazza Duomo and began to feel guilty for making the trip alone. But everyone had said, go, go, you need it. I responded like their favorite patient. But something has changed. I enjoyed Greve the second time. To the depths of me. I can't recall a place that sank deeper than Greve. Leaving me feeling a lightness I thought I could never have again.

23. Ezio is snoring. He has had seven Scotches since we came back to the apartment, each in a small liqueur glass. The Florentines have really fallen for Scotch, but they drink it in little glasses, warm, with their after-dinner espresso. Ezio goes for the Scotch every night when he gets home. He says it comes from living alone. I asked him if it takes the place of a fight with your woman. He didn't want to talk and said tomorrow we would visit old Fantini in the morning and then drive to Pisa for my plane.

24. We saw Fantini in the Siena hospital. Seven hundred or so friends in his room. Hospital rooms and halls full of families all day. Nobody stops them. All the sick with squads holding their hands and milling around the bed. Like worship. Italians think affection can actually cure. At least, it is the medicine of choice for them. A great argument now begins. Workers, unions. You cannot fire even the worst *stronzo* of a worker anymore. In fact, you must keep money in escrow to pay him for a few years should you go bankrupt. Imagine! Ezio is screaming. Horrible! Fantini had to start fixing his own trucks at night because the workers walked off at four. And that's how the big back door crushed his right hip. Sabotage! Ezio began shouting on the disappearance of craftsmen, what I call his whatever-happened-to-the-Renaissance speech. Final conclusion as we are kissing good-bye and tears of regret for me, the fool who is leaving Florence: salaries of the workers are too high. Italy will collapse. Then Ezio drove me to Pisa.

25. I checked my baggage and then went outside to the gate where Ezio was looking at the plane on the apron. "What is it?" I said. I thought

he had been crying, but there was more in his look. "Don't you think I'm ever coming back?" I said, and even as I did I caught on. I don't know how things come together, expressions, tones, the eyes. I said, "It's all right. We were totally split when she came here in May. Whatever you did between you and her was your business. I have no connection to her anymore." He kept crying softly and turned his head away from me, striking his cheek on the fence. I put down my plastic carry-on and embraced him. "Stop it now," I said, but he could not speak.

26. In Milano the 747 was not crowded. People walk out to the plane. Alitalia and its blessed vagueness. All right to board? *Sì, signore*, why not? I am leaving a country where the size of things does not shrink me. The 747 is my first reminder of grandeur in three months. I am reluctant to be at the leading edge of the hi-tech future.

27. The movie begins quickly: shut curtains: no sky watching here. The film is an English actor sweating out a silly love story that ends in joy and confusion. He is one of a group today I call the pooches. They appeal like small terriers or poodles—brisk, light, huggable, shallow. Americans love to watch those pooch men in the movies today. They tell us we are gentle and would never press the button.

28. I think I see snow along the runway, but it is summer in Washington and Virginia. Eddie and my sister Blanche pick me up and invite me to stay at their house in Falls Church a few days. They want to check me out before releasing me. I am OK, I tell Blanche, but she sulks. I tell them to take me to my apartment. As we ride I say, "Did you know there's a blight that's killing the cypresses in Tuscany?" Blanche nods and comes back at me. Did I know that Momma has more friends in Florida than she ever had up here? And she is waiting for my call.

29. I am left off. I watch them drive away, and I go up to my rooms on the third floor. Inside, I feel the eight hours in my muscles. I want to sleep. But as I take my clothes off, I smell the airplane stinks, and I must shower. I come out with my robe on and tour the apartment. I feel as if I've landed in a pleasant new country. I want to call somebody to say I'm back. I shall stop myself from calling anybody. I will admit to jet lag. I will try to sleep Florence away. Work starts tomorrow.

# Memories Reflected in Palm Springs

"And what did you ever do that I asked you?"

You are listening to the call of the wild (on the long-distance phone line), a shout that is also rolling down 233$^{rd}$ Street where it is shaking the Bronx to its very rusty hinges. And even though I'm way out West, I can picture *it* and *him* and the force that made me escape.

The shout is rolling out of Misericordia Hospital today and over the heads of the latest immigrants who think those stuffy, stuck-together red brick houses where I was weaned are their reward for making it out of Bangladesh and Pakistan and Lebanon.

The telephone speaks into my ear: "I ask you, Frankie, as my son, to make me one promise on my dying bed. I gave you advice all your life, and what did you ever do I asked you? This time, do it!"

That voice, which has just topped all the Jewish mothers in history, is actually Lord Nelson of the Calabresi (in North America ), my own esteemed paternal *padrone,* still sticking his two cents into my life, even though he reclines right at the entrance to the jaws of death, is actually leaning into the jaw, is resting on one tooth—I can't believe it. That happy Hitler of my home, still inhabiting the crunchy leather face, still unable to believe I reached puberty, even though I'm fifty-five and myself exploring arthritis out here in Palm Springs at the pool of Jack Freed, who merely has one Jewish mother in the closet of his past days and places.

You Malibu mentalities, you fully assimilated, you who will never have to speak into this phone in one language while thinking the following in another—listen: *But Poppa, you seem to forget I have become Jack Robinson the All-American Ragazzo and am now immune to your ghostly persona of yesteryear, your spiky rules, your salty locks, your fucking fist like a ballpeen hammer that played tunes on my soft brain of childhood, I, I who believed you, no matter how stupid your instructions, no matter how brainsick the motivation— I who said this is my father and thus I obey.*

That's what we call tradition, you Lebanese surfers who have changed your name to Todd and Bruce.

But tradition can be cured, and I will tell you what cures tradition. Money cures tradition. Money and California. California has no tradition nor fathers nor families—merely freedom.

I am not bitter. I am the sweet son, the baby, as a matter of fact. That's why Poppa called me with the following instructions: *Come see me before I die and while you're here, make up with your wife* (by which he means ex-wife, from whom I have been divorced ten years—but then I married again, albeit to the will-o'-the-wisp).

Bad enough I'm trying to get her, that juvenile delinquent, down here into the sun while she insists upon working. (And in the tradition of Poppa, I now offer some advice; the problem with June-September marriages is that the young one wants to work and start new businesses while the old one wants to sell out and sit in the sun. I hear Jack call his son every morning and ask *how're things going:* his work of the day.)

Pop is still talking to me, talking in a wilderness where I am eighteen awaiting his daily word transfusion, as if I were a new man on his drywall crew congregating on a cold morning in a ditch called the building site to listen to the Pontiff of Calabria give the orders of the day (in broken American) through a toothpick stuck to bits of Entenmann donut and stained with luncheonette coffee.

"Frankie," he says again to me. "Estelle came here to the hospital to visit me, and this woman, I'm telling you, she made me sit up in bed, I thought I was going to jump out. She didn't age, she's a lovely woman, and she still didn't get married. Make me one promise. Fix it up between you."

He translates my silence: "I know what you're saying to yourself right now. You say this old man, one foot in the grave, he must be crazy by now. No blood to the brain. But I also told you this, when was it, five years? I said, look, so you had luck with the movies, but look at your life, look at three divorces, look at the women you brought in here to meet us: look how they looked on us. I wooden give you two cents for the lot of them. And listen, I didn't expect you to stick around here and grab yourself one of these Bronx dream girls in their Spanish pants and beauty parlor hair that looks like clay. I didn't want that. I knew you had to go out; you was the child to do it. I'm proud you became something better than here. But I am only telling you I seen Estelle, who is still your real wife, and if she was a dumb lasagna maker, I would keep my mouth shut. I wooden talk. But here is a woman that looks better right now than when you married her."

We are hearing the ancient philosophy which says that one must never drop the first wife because she is the Madonna of the Sorrows who would never buy you a cheap casket and put the rest of the money in a Mercedes and a younger boyfriend after you've gone.

I swallow many lines before saying, "And what do you suggest I do about my present wife?"

"You know so much, you figure it out. But this woman has a better face and a better body than all the *puttanas* you ever brought to my house. What else do you need to know?"

After the phone goes down, I sit back in my plastic strap chair, the phone on my lap. I watch the pool, then call Anne in L.A.

The busy signal goes on and on: a memory shakes out of the sound. It is a view of the mind's eye. Six-story brick apartment houses on a Bronx hill (before lotsa wars) going down to the New York Central tracks. The houses tight together, holding each other up. The rooms inside are little boxes. Hallways that hold smells forever and lightbulbs behind glass covers that collect oily dust.

Once my brother Lou, back from the Navy on leave, was standing in the hall with me and said, "We make rockets that can do everything but talk, but we still live in little shitboxes the way they did ten thousand years ago."

Inside our apartment, a small square foyer unusable for anything but a standing wood coatrack: but it is also crammed with the glass door oak case of Aunt Netty, given to us upon her God knows when demise. It holds gray, faded wispy plates with flower borders Granma had made somewhere where they lived I have never yet traveled to. And a ceramic, hand painted, is it ashtray, is it candy dish: yellow streaked by Uncle Larry when he had the hobby for his hypertension. And a red cheek boy in loden shorts and a Dutch girl in a bonnet. And still another candy dish in silver (fake) and glass (real), so it can be valueless and also breakable. And one more cuplike, bowl-like blue thing that is used for tie pins, paper clips, fallen rosary beads, a saint's medal, a wooden nickel from a joke store, a single earring, a coin that reads Saint Frankie in embossed letters.

The living room belongs to the children only when it rains: TV and monopoly sets and records and then tapes. The couch covering is so pinchy it makes skin red after only a half hour. On the wall, a print of *The Last Supper* as framed by Woolworth.

The kitchen is the homework room after dishes are done. Here we also see playing cards, comics, football jerseys needing numbers sewn on them.

The new Hollywood princess has at last answered the phone present in reality land: "Frankie, is that you, darling? I was out. Where you calling from?"

"Where am I calling from? Annie, I told you I was going down to Jack Freed's in Palm Springs, and you said they wouldn't have a call on the weekend so you were coming down."

"Frankie, this part means a lot to me. I worked for it, and it's just right— I won't jeopardize it by chance. I'm not going to miss it by a phone call."

The brilliant female mind, trained by movies and old Stanislovsky tales, expects me to believe those lines. "Annie," I say very slowly. "Put the answering machine on forward, and they will direct the calls here. And I will charter you a plane if a call comes."

The significant pause of 37 million microseconds. "Frankie, please don't let me tell you again. This is something I do for myself, by myself. I told you marriage was another thing. I do my work my own way—and I never asked anyone—"

"All right, all right." I hear my voice imitating Peter Falk in one of his parts. I stop.

"Frankie, listen to me. I think there's a man been following me."

"See, they're following you around to offer you parts all over—"

"It looks like a private dick. I swear, Frankie, if you're doing a thing like that. If you think because I'm young I can't know anything about monogamy, then you better just call your lawyer. I will sign any paper right now that says I want nothing of yours, not a nickel. And you will sign that paper agreeing you want nothing of mine, including my phone number—"

"Don't get nasty, don't get hot. If there is some mistake in what I am asking you, I am trying to seduce you into coming down here. If that's not possible, what's important to you comes first. I thought that was agreed."

"I know, I know. You're trying to be nice. You want me to meet some people."

"Now wait, these are *my* friends and *their* friends. Nice, simple people. Intelligent people, and also people in the industry. One learns simply by talking with them—you know what I mean. But in a sense, in this industry, we're all on the edge of the outs. You got the most brilliant people, if they had no record lately, I mean no recent track record, then they're nonpersons. But the same nonpersons, if they're over fifty-five, say, they still have great knowledge of the industry and can help any of us—"

The silence. She had hung up, and I heard myself talking to myself. She doesn't want to admit I learned something. How many kids you know who have to do it alone? If they don't say it, they still do it that way. And part of it is that what we tell them, what anybody fifty-five tells anybody twenty-five, is inapplicable, not wrong, but a foreign language already. Take the Martian advice of my father—please.

How can I tell Annie that the only courtesy we have left is the enjoyment of each other just by being together (a thought she shuts phones down on). I hear her saying, *I'm sorry, Frankie, that's not good enough.*

She's a Mormon. She's from Salt Lake. Is that the reason? Isn't that Mars, too?

Before I surrendered the instrument, my sister Samantha called from NYC saying *Poppa is in a coma.* Delivered in the ancient Egyptian style. Big days at the undertakers coming up, casket that will knock their eyes out, limousines a block long in file. Good old death. It will make him a saint. Maybe Samantha will try to jump into the hole when they lower the coffin. Or Grace will come from Scranton with her husband and try to lift him out of the casket on the second night of the viewing. Are you ready, Mouseketeers?

I land at Kennedy thinking I will go up to the Bronx and stay with Samantha and her family—perhaps even stay at Pop's new apartment, which I have not seen but can picture: the widower's retreat of two and a half rooms. I can smell the oilcloth tablecloth (still sold on Arthur Avenue), see the glasses and cups on the table, the can of Medaglia D'Oro coffee on the stove, old folded copies of the *Daily News* on the kitchen chairs.

I book a room instead in Manhattan near Grand Central, the new Hyatt—glitz in glass to cheer me when I come back downtown from the funeral parlor and get off the subway.

In the hospital I see his familiar grizzled face, his eyes shut, no, *closed,* like sleep and dream together, a form of magic done on him—inside, the emperor of roast peppers beginning the trip to his pyramid.

Outside, they hand me a letter. *They* is actually a nurse of about fifteen years of age, with shapely skinny legs covered in those provocative white stockings. The note was left by Estelle.

*Dear Frankie, Poppa keeps telling me we have to get together. If you have the time to call me, my work number is 372-4566, and I'm usually home at night by eight. This year, with Jean away for the first time, I am not holding to much of any schedule, but this number and the home number which you have will get me most of the time. E.*

I go downtown after an hour of silent witness at Pop's side. I think of Estelle on the train ride. She who puts up with the lean times and gets dropped when the going is good. She is, then, a reminder of what rotten bastards men are after they get married. The first wife is the undying reminder. That is the function.

What I did, as bastard, was announce to Estelle that the energy of the marriage had ended after seven and a half years. All she wanted was things like drapes and other signs of perpetual nesting. We had no emotions left. No energies like the old days.

Estelle was stunned and confused. Of course the youthful ardor had gone, she agreed. What was so bad about that? Look at our mothers and fathers and everybody else who is real. (Not the movies.) Real meant we had a child and a nest. It was the goal of centuries, achieved. Estelle tried to explain to me. Just fifty years ago. All our lives would have been spent trying to get a nest.

What did I want? Go west and fool around? Do it. Do anything silly that men like to do. Do it, but don't break up the nest. I went west on the wings of pragmatism and paid a lawyer for the rest: he broke up the nest.

Three days later Poppa died while I watched the doctors and nurses hang over him with instruments. I then made phone calls for a day, setting up an ancient funeral for my family's necrophiliac joy.

At the funeral Mass, Estelle looked beautiful in black, stirring up in me some lost sensual excitement, something that came from her face without makeup. It was an excitement shaken out by death, a fight against the usual lack of facts about death. Pop died, and I felt weak and aching, as if I had fought the messenger of death and lost him. All by sitting in a chair.

I am shaking hands with women wearing black gloves. They smile, pleased that I am weeping. A man in tears is always refreshing. It makes the thing more authentic.

Some of the women embrace me, and their bodies press against mine and change my crying. The last one is Estelle, and I stop as she touches me and smiles. In fact, I get a hard-on as she hugs me good-bye and her massive breasts against her black dress drive into my chest.

People are walking out of the cemetery holding each other by the elbow. My father's cigarette cough is heard on the lawn. Cars are racing to the exits. Cars are speeding to motels to fuck. Everyone will fuck today in Pop's honor and to forget their own death.

The next morning I pack and call Estelle from the hotel. We meet in midtown for lunch. The erotic aura is gone. The excitement had been the light from another sun. The hard-on had been for somebody else. We talk about money and the price of four years of college at Smith for Jeannie. Estelle says she wants to explore government loans and for that she would need to know my approximate salary for this year. "I think your income's been going down a little," she says. "And I could pay half now."

I reply: "Since I can do art director stuff as well as sets, I think I could go up again." I barely believe this because I have said it aloud. It may be true. It is enough to end the lunch.

At 8 P.M. I sit in the airport and know nothing about women again. I fly off to be picked up by Annie. She is very sad about Poppa's death, very solicitous when we get home in a way I never saw in her. She seems older, almost a family member the way she can feel for me. She hugs me often, and I start to feel that cemetery excitement. We drive instead, on her suggestion, up to Mulholland and stop to look down at the valley. I begin to cry as I watch it. I don't know why? The vastness? The lines of light go as far as Bakersfield. But it is vastness from here, and I think of my father whirled out of his easy Bronx bed into space where the other millions are all on a trip, not knowing which way to go.

Annie is behind me, and she has been talking: "So you'll have to get a look into those emotions right now. So promise you'll see your therapist."

I don't have a therapist, yet I smile at her and want to say, "I am actually Hieronymous Bosch the set designer, and I would like to suffer so that I can paint grotesque pictures of suffering and thereby transcend fifty minute hours."

"You don't have to talk about it right now," Annie says. "But sit back and let it roll through your head and your memory for tomorrow."

We sit in silence after this. I know she will be on me to call tomorrow. A half hour or so goes by smoking cigarettes and looking down at the lights.

Annie says, "I never got the chance to tell you. I got the part. It looks like a good little movie, and I play almost a second lead. I worked my ass off for this one."

I turn in the car seat and look at her. The face is firm yet still innocent. I begin to cry again. "Why do I keep doing this?" I say.

"I'm not ever going anywhere on you," Annie says with the woman's prescience.

We talk about her movie, and it sounds nice. Then Annie says to me, "Who all did you see back there?"

I tell her, leaving out Estelle. I become aware of leaving out Estelle as I talk more. Then I add it. "Oh yes, I also met my ex-wife at the funeral, and she looked great. She's got a terrific job with a real estate company."

"That's nice. Maybe she won't need so much dough from now on," Annie says on my behalf.

"Don't count on it yet," I say.

"OK, Santa," she says.

I look at her and smile. She catches the smile. "You know," she says, "now I can go to Palm Springs for a week. Is the invite still on?"

"The invite is always on," I say.

She starts the engine and taps the gas pedal a few times to make the motor get smooth. Just as she is about to put the car in gear—her right hand is already on the gearshift—she turns to me. Our eyes meet, and she smiles. For that moment we are the closest people in the world. We live for what we think that smile means from the other person. But Pop's eyes have been shut for three days.

# Shrinks

"Let me just tell you what happened yesterday." His sister Grace was angry.

"We took the car out to go to the doctor's. And he went and disappeared. We had to go looking all over the streets for him. You know where we found him?"

"I think it means he doesn't want to see this kind of doctor. What can a man like that talk about with a psychiatrist?"

"John, he told us he ran away because we were taking him to the doctor for his infected toes. And they would make him cry. Does that sound like your father?"

"Gianni?" Their father's voice came from downstairs. He had reached the front porch after going for cigars and seen the big car. Grace looked frightened. She stopped still at his footsteps on the stairs coming up.

John was staring at her. "What's the matter? You scared of him?" Grace nodded but did not speak.

The door opened. The old craggy face was smiling out of control. "Ey? When you came?" He used loudness to hide feelings but walked quickly to his son, embraced him, and held on too long.

"I'm here no more than five minutes," John said, and held him until he was solid on his feet again. "Pop, I came to ask you why you're trying to escape this doctor."

The old man sat down slowly in a kitchen chair and, seeing Grace, waved a hand that meant he wanted coffee. Grace went for the pot. He looked at his son: "This doctor has money. He don't need me."

As his daughter poured the coffee before him, he stood up, waiting silently for the completion. Then he took his cup and led John towards the parlor, saying nothing to Grace, who called after him, "Momma got the car out again, you know. You going this time?"

"Let me speak to my son first," the old man said.

John could see something different, but it was only a rearrangement of the old irritations. His father was still being *padrone* of the mind.

Grace walked to her room after the slight by her father. The old man entered the parlor and sat in the green armchair, looking up. "Johnny, I didn't know you was coming. I took a walk."

John stood watching him and the doilies on the chairs, now like the color of the old white walls. John remembered that the doilies had been crocheted when the porch was enclosed to make another room, and his mother bought new furniture.

As he sat on the couch across from his father, John said, "Where did we ever get this fabric that pricks the skin?"

"From the Americans. Ask your mother."

"You never liked this stuff, did you, Pop?"

The old man coughed deep in his throat, then made a sound as if to spit but did not. "This is fake junk. Is white pine they cover with stain and nails. They tell her good enough for the *contessa*. The *contessa di merda*. You understand that?"

"Yes, Maestro, I understand that much. Listen, where's the old Atwater Kent?"

The old man leaned forward and looked at the corner of the room as John added, "The big radio."

"Look in the cellar," the old man answered, and looked around the room. "They put it all down the cellar."

"They're back in style again," John said. "Put a new finish on them— even the old radio shows—"

He saw that his father was following him—but perhaps not listening. John asked, "Remember when I used to sit under the radio and listen?"

"And your mother telling me, get him to eat. Get him to eat!"

The old man was smiling in recognition. John said, "Do you remember a lot these days?"

The old man smiled a different way. "That you asked me every question. You was the special son. I said, this one will *be* something."

"I checked it out, Pop. They said *no,* Consoli is not a famous name."

"You shouldn't talk like that. You with the senator now. You go with the Washington people. Don't bury yourself because the Americans invite you into the grave."

John shook his head. The old man always had his one or two Brechtian lines. John should have taken the old man for coffee every week. Fridays at the *cafe.* They would have smoked a Tuscan cigar and talked their lines. "Pop, when exactly are you moving?"

"A few weeks. We go live with the millionaire. And eat American bread. And get full with cotton. But I save you money. When I go, you don't call the undertaker. You just drop me in the hole, and I am nice soft cotton."

"I can't understand *why* don't you want to leave here? The burning houses are a block away. Nobody's cleaning it up. And the senator even tried. They just don't want to do it yet."

"Your sister tells me. So I go now to the world of the priests, the shower. I take a shower every day and put butter on my bread and spray under my arms to smell like a *puttana.*"

John began pacing the room in front of his father, trying to turn the tone to joking. "Then I take it you are really very excited about making the big move to Florida."

"Yes, I will make a party and give cigars and then I go into the ground, six feet down, fric frac, cover the hole. This man is over. Forget this *chidrool.*"

"I hope they get you a Jewish one," John said softly.

"What's that?"

"That doctor, the doctor you will go talk to."

"You mean *psicologo*—"

"Therapist, psychiatrist, whatever you want to call him—*shrink.*"

"Shrink. What? Shrinks the head?"

"You got it, Pop. Now *why* do you think they made up that word?"

His father looked at him intently for a moment, then folded his right leg over his left to bring his toes closer for examination. Then he looked for a cigar in his shirt pockets as he spoke, "It means—it means the head gets full. From living in this house, all what happened. Your life."

"And what is your head full of?" John asked. "Is it Calabria when you were a kid?"

The old man stopped smiling. "My head is full of things you don't know." His thoughts were passing too fast. He would lose them if he had to talk.

John interrupted him, "Which is why I'm asking you."

"Which is why I don't tell you. You can't understand. The shrink can't understand. And nobody in here can understand."

"You mean nobody who wasn't a stonecutter and then sold produce at Bronx Terminal market."

The old man nodded.

"You remember in high school when I tried to work in the early morning with you and couldn't stay awake?"

The old man nodded but did not remember more than irritation. John could not forget the shame of it when his father had said at the table that each of his children got weaker and without energy or stamina and that eventually the ideal American child would not be able to walk and would only watch things with its eyes but would be able to watch TV forever, even in its sleep.

The old man asked, "Why wasn't you a doctor?"

"I hated the sight of blood," John said.

"You loved the blood. You cried for me to take you to the poultry market in Ely Avenue. And you loved to watch the chicken heads come off. You love it."

"I thought you told me I was a sweet, gentle kid," John said.

"But what kid don't like to see the chicken head chop off?"

"The guilty ones," John said, and saw his father's smile of confusion. John added, "The ones who want to chop somebody else off?" John felt his face flush. It was not a joke. It was not a thought he intended. His face got hotter.

His father was lost in his own thoughts. "They don't kill a father anymore," he said. "Now they send him to Florida. Give his money to Merrill Lynch." The old man stood up suddenly to exercise his toes. "You like these shoes? This is your mother's shoes."

"They look all right."

"They look all right? You, too, crazy, *Giowan?* They are making me into a woman around here, and you say all right. You should help me. Let me come live with you, and then your mother and sister can go have a nice time together."

The old man sat down and lit his cigar. Mrs. Consoli came in with a tray of coffee and pine nuts and sat after pouring around. Then she explained that John would stay over and take his father to the doctor tomorrow.

Then she asked John about the new job, his trips on the plane to Washington every week. She was pleased with the names. But the old man was fighting to keep awake. His head would drop, and he would rush to bring it back up. John stopped talking and promised he would tell them the rest tomorrow. The old man got up silently and went to his room. Mrs. Consoli waited for his door to slam before talking to her son. "What do you say?"

"I don't know."

"What do you mean, you don't know? You see your father?"

John collected the coffee cups onto the tray and swept up crumbs. "Tell me something," his mother said loud. "I have to go with this man to live in Florida?"

"I see a man who wants to die," John said, and walked to the kitchen with the tray.

His mother followed him. "Tell me what I should do. He forgets my name."

"He's not that bad."

"Then *you* go live with him."

"His mind is perfectly lucid."

Mrs. Consoli looked at her son as if he were speaking in another language. "Go take him to the doctor," she said, and went to the bedroom. John saw she did not use another room.

He went in and slept after listening to the house and identifying its odors. To him, the Bronx was always smells, night and day, from stuffy rooms to bread baking on the wind.

In the morning he heard a knock; it was still dark. "You want to come walk now?" his father asked.

John got up and dressed quickly. In the kitchen he found a small cup of black coffee and drank it rather than look for anybody. Downstairs, his father was waiting on the stoop.

They walked towards Arthur Avenue as the red light of day came up. John looked at his watch when his father went in for cigars. It was later than he thought, almost eight.

The old man came out lining his cigars in his shirt pocket like pens. Then he set out fast to the edge of Bronx Park where the river was isolated beyond the thruway lanes cut through the green of the park. Between the highway and the river was an inaccessible place for walking, but car doors and innersprings and truck tires sliced in half were piled around.

They turned away from it and were quickly at the high school. John spoke as they passed the concrete yard, "I burned a lot of sneakers on that ground."

"You burned sneakers? Maybe you better come with me to see this doctor?"

It was the first time the old man had shown he knew what kind of behavior was required for this new doctor.

John stopped. "Pop. You shouldn't be afraid of this kind of doctor. I went to one myself for three years. They listen to you. They think about what you say. They take it seriously."

The old man looked at his son with what John thought was fear. Then he led John back to Arthur Avenue. "What is it?" John said. "Something I said scared you?"

The old man stopped and turned to John. Moved by his son's care, he embraced John but took his arms back quickly.

John said, gently, "Now tell me what's the matter?"

"Every morning you go to the store, you will get me a *mozzarella*, fresh, in the water, no salt, and you then go pack it up and mail to Florida."

"And how about Terranova's bread? I can send you two big loaves a day air freight."

"And don't forget *sageesh,* one pound, sweet."

His father walked again, down Arthur Avenue. As they passed the restaurant, John said, "I could even try to bottle the smell from Dominic's and send it down every week."

The old man walked to his house and stood at the car door. John let him in, then went to the driver's seat, started the engine, drove off.

After some minutes, the old man looked around. "This is the city?"

"This doctor is in Purchase. Near White Plains."

"You know him?" Consoli said.

"I heard he's a very good man."

"John, he won't put me away?"

"Pop, cut that out. Nobody does anything to you, not while I'm around."

The old man sat back in the car seat and looked for a cigar. When they arrived in front of the house, John opened the door but did not get out. The old man went up to the office, and John slowly followed, watching his father shake hands with the short, balding doctor and hand him a cigar.

When it was over and father and son were driving home, John asked, "Did it go all right?"

"All right, all right," the old man said. "This one is crazy like me."

"So you liked him, then?" John said.

The old man smiled but did not speak for the rest of the trip home. At the door to the house, John helped his father out and then got back in his car. "I have got to get the plane by noon."

The old man went to the porch alone and waved his son off. John drove downtown, put the car away, and took a cab to the airport. He had enough time for a few calls and called home. Grace answered. "Its amazing," she said. "Like a miracle happened. Let's hope this sticks. What do you think this guy did?"

"I don't know," John said. "He only said he and the doctor are crazy in the same way."

"That's got to be true," Grace said. "If he could talk to him that long. But thank God for it."

273

# Sizes

"I don't care what your girlfriend Mary told you. I don't think the Escort or the Chevette or the Cockroach, and I don't care what else you call them in Japanese, is the right size, any of them."

"But I want a small car, Pop. You understand, I want a small car and not a big bazoom—though if you wanted to buy me a Jag, I wouldn't fight you."

"You, my dear, you think everything is the style and the color. Even the size to you is style. But I am not talking style. I am talking a strong chassis, a protection in the car you drive that's not just the pieces pasted together. *Gabeesh?*"

"Yes, I *gabeesh,*" Denise said, her voice going down.

Her father did not pick up the appeasement in his daughter's tone and kept on. "A small car is like a paper tiger, if you know what I mean? Looks strong outside, but tissue paper if you collide with a dog."

Her father assumed a stance. She knew it was his way of making the mood lighter. Denise examined him. She looked away from the wrinkles around his chin, like small knife cuts. She turned to the driveway outside the house lined with cars, her mother's large Cadillac, Johnny's Camaro, and at the end, her father's big Mercedes. Her father had begun pacing before her like the dog when it wanted to go out.

She turned back and noticed his tuxedo jacket, pulling at the sides, as if he were wearing two hip guards. Still, he was handsome. He had that look. And he loved to go out formal.

"Where is it you went out today?" she asked.

"Today was the first Cotillion at the club." The words were uncomfortable for him. "Your mother's vice president this year, so I had to look dressy. I didn't have a choice. It was daylight on the lawn."

"Don't kid me, you love it," Denise said.

He walked across the kitchen to his daughter and leaned down, almost touching her face: "And how come you know everything, you little peanut?"

She put her right finger on his nose. "Because I'm smarter than you, that's why. Didn't you know women are the superior breed?"

"That's what they tell me. Except with cars. How long before you all become automotive engineers?"

He walked to the refrigerator and opened the brown door. "Will you tell me if your mother still does any shopping around here? I can't find a glass of mineral water in here."

She saw his face light up, left her chair and pushed him away from the door. "I knew it would be right in front of your nose. What is this green bottle?"

"The San Pellegrino."

"The San Pellegrino." Her repetition made her father smile like a boy, and she continued. "Listen, you are damn lucky I didn't ask you for a Mazda RX or a 280Z."

Her father sat where she had been sitting and watched her pour a glass full of the water. "You bet your sweet life," he said. "And you would get a Jap car over my dead body. This much I'll tell you right now. Nobody will take me on *that* trip again." He had the glass in the air and was shaking it for emphasis. "There's one mechanic who fixes it, he's in South Jersey, and the parts—they're in Poughkeepsie. For ten times the price of what we got here."

"But I still don't want a big load. I haven't starting smoking cigars yet, you know." She moved back by instinct and let her weight fall back on the sink.

Mr. Polero drank his water slowly and made her sweat. Then he said, "And now I got another comedian in the family. Listen to me, Joan Rivers. A medium car is not a big load, you know. Take a two door. Go

275

out and see some Chevies. Take a look inside. GM is a sensible car."

Denise walked to the white archway that led to the dining room and the hallway. "And some little ones are sensible, too. Didn't Johnny have a Fiat Brava a long time?"

"Him? Him you don't look at. And the Fiat Brava, they don't even dare import anymore. But your brother and his friends, they can handle a breakdown on the road, they can tune a car, they can change points on the spot. For you, you want a dependable, solid thing in your hands."

"All right. But I read up on the Escort and the Lynx, which is the Mercury version. They have heft."

Her father assumed the pose again: she called him Mussolini many times when he was like this. "Heft?" he said. "And where did you learn that one?"

"Wouldn't you like to know?" Denise said.

"Look, Denise, do me a favor, will you? Don't get me too excited for once? And listen to me once in a while, at least about men things. Like maybe I had more experience in cars than your friend Mary has. And that I buy ten trucks at a time for my stores and maybe through the years I learned a little about cars you don't have to read up on?"

"I showed you the *Consumer's Guide,* Pa. And I asked you to discuss it. They have testers, engineers or whatever. Remember what they said first about the Honda, and then everybody who bought one said the same thing."

"And I'm telling you years of experience is worth more than some little magazine you buy. Don't you think those magazines take a little payoff from a company now and then to help the sales?"

"You said that about Ralph Nader, also without any facts. These organizations get letters every day from car owners—about what the cars do—and then they test and test—"

"Denise, I swear to you." Mr. Polero stood up and placed his glass neatly on the cloth and looked at it. He said, slowly looking up, "Denise, let me tell you I do not shoot my mouth off. I have talked many years with mechanics, friends of mine. I have thirty years of retailing under my belt. I talk when I know about something. The question I ask of *you* is why don't you trust me?"

She had begun to pace as he had earlier. "Because this is not a trust thing, Pop. You haven't yet said one bad factual thing about a small car. Not one thing. Give me a list of things that show they are worse than mid-size, for example. That's all I ask, give me a list. But your mind was made up in 1971. Nothing good could come out after then. So you don't even look at the little cars of today; you just condemn them."

"So is that what you think I am? He who condemns without looking?"

"No, I don't *think* that. I been your daughter twenty-three years. And just go ask Momma."

"Ask your mother *what*? Ask the lasagna expert about compact and mid-size cars? Sometimes you make me sick, you know that? You all make me sick. No spit."

"Don't bring everybody into this. This is a simple thing between me and you."

"Me and you?" He looked at her, trying to feel his feelings. They all said she was his image in every way, but he did not see it. "You are a twenty-year-old snotnose—"

"Twenty-three and a half," she interrupted.

"Who talks to your father like he was an illiterate ditchdigger too stupid to know the Consumer's Union which I knew before you was born."

"There he goes. Every time we have a disagreement, you pull out the wop stuff—"

"Don't use that word in my house."

"You taught me that word."

"Denise, I taught you nothing. No words to say to me like spit in my face."

"Thank God you taught me nothing, then."

"What did you just say?"

"I'm sorry, but that word came into my ears in this house, and I did not invent it. I never even knew I *was* something else."

"And what does that mean, *something else?*"

"Italian."

"You damn right you never knew. Because you never made one move for us."

"Who's us? Come on, what is this *us*? Don't put that one on me. There is no *us,* and you know it."

"I know it, but you don't believe it. Because it's not in Ralph Nader's book; they didn't review it in the *Consumer's;* it wasn't on sale this week in Caldor."

Denise stepped closer to the kitchen table and to her father. "Pop, sometimes I wish I could get you a good kick in the ass."

"Oh, very nice."

Denise turned on his words and went for the staircase, her steps becoming silent as she hit the rugs.

Her father followed; she stopped at the landing as he pointed a finger at her: "To a father, a girl says that right to his face. What should I say? I should say at least she's honest. I wonder, is there one thing left that I might know better about from experience than you? Like maybe how to flatten you on the floor with one punch? And the big mistake is that we stopped slapping your little fannies when you were growing up. You wouldn't of had those words inside your head to say to me."

"And maybe you just don't like it that I *have* the words to tell you that what you tell me about cars is unproved, undocumented—"

He held up both arms, hands out to her: "Stop with those words. Please? You are going too far. I feel my hands moving without me. I'm choking. I swear to God. I will lose my control. I will break your head open if you can't talk right to me."

"*Right?* What's *right* to you? You know what you mean by *right?* Forget it, I'm not saying it. I don't want you to get a stroke. Just forget the new car, all right, will you? Just forget the whole thing. I wanted to get the best buy. It's my money this time. I just wanted something that could take me to the hospital. Transportation. With no repair trouble. Which they all said was Toyota. And then the war started."

"Transportation. And that's what I want, too. That's all I always wanted." Mr. Polero was feeling dizzy. "Denise, that's why I went with you."

"But you wouldn't let me *buy* it. You didn't let me *sign.* You put your hand over the contract—"

"Because. Because I am trying to tell you that you was buying a little piece of junk. With paper dashboard and plastic grille."

"You do not buy a dashboard and grille for getting there."

Mr. Polero had reached the steps; now he smiled and stepped back, letting her go up a few steps. "You see, my dear, I did not want to buy it and feel humiliated in that showroom where I knew that man was giving you the business."

"And how did you think I felt?" She leaned over the banister. "'How nice,' the salesmen must have said. 'This little bird is his slave. This parrot. She buys whatever he wants.' But I am paying this one off myself."

Denise continued up the steps. "It's better. If I need a little more, I'll take a loan."

"You know what?" His voice was calm as he looked upwards: the raising of his head calmed him somewhat. "They once told me, no matter what you do for them, they'll knife you in the end. They'll pick a stranger over you. And listen to him."

"And don't think I don't know what you think of *me*. You disapprove of everything I do. You're on my back as if I'm training to be a hooker. You spy on me like I'm in a drug ring. You look at Billy when he comes into this house—when he used to come because now I meet him outside this house. You treat him like he's some form of puke."

"There is no answer, my daughter. You just said you hate me, too. Listen to your own words. And you used to accuse me of causing all the troubles of the Black man in this country because I never hired enough of them. I only tried to tell you what I learned from my mother and father. Either you live by a few things that are supposed to last or you go down the drain."

Denise stood on one carpeted step and looked ahead, taking her hands off the banister. "I just don't understand what you're talking about so what's the use. Why bother? All we do is fight. We fight even when we're not fighting. I have to go to work tonight so I'm going up to do my hair and get dressed for work."

"Go right ahead, I'm not touching you," Mr. Polero said.

He watched her go silently to the top landing and down the white hall. He turned and walked back to the kitchen. Then, still festering from the words, he walked out to the back garden and looked at the late afternoon light, a new redness that meant summer was on its way.

From the corner of his eye he picked up the spot of glisten from the medallion of his Mercedes and walked to it at the back of the line of cars. He looked at it and the others and shook his head and walked back to the door and around the house to the front lawn. Up through the window above the entrance he could see Denise in her room: he turned away quickly when he saw she was in her underwear with no top. He felt his face red and flushed. He went to the side of the house for the hose. He found it in the grass coiled near the spigot. He began spraying the lawn and put his head down when he came round front again.

When the water would not sink through the grass anymore, he shut off the hose and came inside and stood at the head of the staircase a few minutes before calling his daughter.

She came out; she was dressed and made-up and looked like Blanche at that age. He spoke with as much calm as he could find: "I'll go with you for a car whenever you want. And keep my mouth shut all the time."

"What could we do, then, Pop? I don't want a big load, and you don't want a little dink."

He was smiling at her tone. "All right, why don't we take a look at the new mid-size Pontiac and the Olds they call Omega. They're supposed to be solid and also trimmed down small."

"You want to go *again*? Now?"

"I could drop you off at the hospital after we shop around, and you could take a cab tonight. Or I'll come get you."

Denise went for her purse in the kitchen and came back to the front thinking plans. "Actually, you don't have to pick me up. I'll get Billy to do it. He's working late."

"Working? Late?"

"He's bartending at Mario's."

Mr. Polero turned his face away as soon as he was aware of his expression, but Denise caught it. She smiled and shook her head slowly. He mimicked her by nodding just as slowly. They both laughed. Then Denise put out her hand. "Peace? Shake," she said, and her father began to shake hands.

But as he took her right hand, she yanked him to her and kissed his right cheek. "I'm going to wait," she said, "as long as it takes, for you to grow up."

He began his guilty boy's laugh again as he led her to his Mercedes at the end of the driveway.

# Friday Supper

Sarfatti's telephone voice ran through his head like a memory itself, the way memory brings back bits of conversation silently inside the mind and the same way he had been hearing voices most of the year, phrases in Neopolitan dialect as he was about to reach for a second pastry or even jaywalk into a street.

Sarfatti's voice echoed a mellow mood—philosophical, speaking out of reflection, saying to him, "Anthony, listen to me, please. I am saying *yes,* it is all right to change your name legally. It is not an insult to the people of your personal past, of the people who produced you and so forth—all those grandmothers and fathers from Naples—you know what I am trying to say?"

"Not from Naples. Most of my people come from Calabria, as a matter of fact," Anthony said, and wrote on his desk pad.

"All right, then, they're from Calabria or Sicilia or Upper Swabia—it's all the same, don't you see what I'm telling you? It's a nice heritage we saw for a moment in time. And it got buried under another one, a new one, a hip one. And that's the train we happen to be on. You know what I'm trying to explain? I am saying it is only history. History. And I am saying this is America's age. Right now. Rome had its day and then the English were the lords of it all and the Germans had their days and the rest of them; they all had their day. So now it's America, and we happen to be Americans. A happy accident of history. And everybody in the world is trying to get on the bandwagon. My cousins in Italy ask me to send them the L. L. Bean catalogue and Timberland shoes. They know trout streams in the Catskills I never heard of—"

Anthony stopped Jack's flow with his own enjoyment, "All right, Jack. Now listen to my question. I want to ask you this. How come you're still Jack Sarfatti? Why aren't you Jack Sarfield?"

Anthony was smiling.

"Come on, Anthony, will you not make issues where none exist?" Jack's voice was losing the thin edge of respect he usually kept for his boss, as he went on talking, "So nobody in my family got around to it. That's all it was. But one more thing—nobody in my family ever got to be a vice president of a big corporation. You'll be giving seminars and speeches in Phoenix, and they will introduce you from the platform. A name change becomes simply a very practical thing. Like making a ledger that people can read very clear. You simply become Anthony Collins, and you get straight to the point. You don't ever have to give them diction lessons and spelling help. No more explaining to people that the *ci* in Cöllucci is pronounced like the *ch* in choo-choo. You know what I'm saying here? And the first minute you have to spell it out, you lose half the audience— or somebody mispronounces it—right away people think, a weirdo from someplace foreign. And your own people who can't pronounce your name right—they get pissed off at you for having that unpronounceable name— that makes them seem stupid. They don't forgive that."

"All right, all right, you win." Anthony's hand was raised, but he was alone in his office. Jack, of course, could not see him. It was not even ten o'clock in the morning. "Jack, I love you," Anthony said. "I pray that I can be sure of everything in the world like you are. But right now I can't even identify the feelings I have. Is it embarrassment? Betrayal, the way you say? Why do I feel so uneasy?"

Anthony heard only silence in the wires and spoke again, "But listen, Jack, don't think for a minute I don't appreciate your input. I really like what you say. Thanks for being a real *paesan*. Why the hell is this thing giving me so much trouble?"

Jack laughed. "Trouble. All right, don't worry, be happy. And I want you to know right now that even after you change your name, you still get permission to use ten dialect words a day. Like *Gavoṇe* and *maron* and *strunz* and *fongool.* Do you *gabeesh* me?"

"That's enough. I *gabeesh* that I got work to do. I have to leave the office early. Tonight's my supper with the family."

"But you said you would have a drink with me and listen to my presentation I'm going to make out there."

"Jack, right after supper—about nine—I will be hitting you for free drinks. You can read it to me. I'm never long down in the Bronx. I couldn't survive it."

Anthony put the speaker down and went back to his desk. The rest of the day passed without meetings, and by five he was deep in his papers, having lost track of time. Denise came in to remind him—time to go to the Bronx.

To his secretary, Denise, a Westchester man of Anthony's position still eating with his folks in the Bronx was erotic. It made her think of the big weddings in the olden days and Anthony as the vanguard of a new man, a new hope, a man-fan of white lace and bridal shops and gift-filled showers. She watched him get his jacket, pack his case, and leave, with a sense of awe.

Fifteen minutes later he was stuck in a line of stopped cars on the Bronx River Parkway. He knew it was like this every Friday night, but he always raced out of the garage under the offices and went straight for the nearby parkway entrance that took him to this same spot where he always waited bumper-to-bumper.

He saw, the edges of his eyes saw, the park paths along the river and a small waterfall that came through white birches and paths that led nowhere into green foliage—a place he had always intended to come to and explore on a Sunday.

The look of stillness at this spot always attracted him and held him back at the same time. He could not explain it, but he felt the double pull every time. It was the place where he first began remembering his dream, first like pictures, like snapshots that appeared and got bright only a moment before going dark.

It was the same dream: inner pieces of his rear molars were sloughing off, falling down like a shore of soil after heavy rains. Like silver fillings that had lost their molecular strength, they fell in pasty chunks between his thumb and index finger, and as he probed his mouth, they turned into gray, silvery sand. Then he awoke, startled.

It was such a vivid dream that he would always check his teeth right away and be surprised that there were no spaces.

Ironically, his actual teeth had been getting bad; Steinfeld, the dentist he trusted his mouth to every six months, sent him to a periodontist, who was young and super-confident and who wove a story of decaying gums reabsorbing themselves into nothingness. But he nodded for Anthony, one of the lucky ones, because many come in with gums that are impossible to save.

*Impossible to save* held inside his head like an echo. Last night he had called his internist about waking in the middle of the night in a sweat and finally thinking it might not be the dream. "Yes," the doctor's voice said, "it could have been something to do with the heart. But you had no pain, no numbness, none of the symptoms to worry about. And it also could have been your hypertension, but nobody will ever know how to diagnose that as long as you are obese. I've told you that for a long time now. But why not try some Tenormin at night. Another fifty milligrams before you turn in."

Anthony came out of the reverie, shaking his head while he watched a man who had appeared near the waterfall with a black-and-white dog. The man and the dog walked under the birches, caught in patterns of light and shade. Then Anthony lost the two of them as the cars in front of him moved, and he had to join the speeding line.

But as the car accelerated, he felt another dream, something more recent, closer than the teeth—June, the air seemed just like June—he was a child—he looked eight or nine. He was also his present self walking at the side of this child.

He knew without words the child-fears inside the child, looking now for its home street, lost in its own neighborhood.

He was going up the steps of the old house near Arthur Avenue; he had just arrived to find the family already seated for dinner—Sunday. He announced to them all that he was *going on a diet:* he had heard the phrase somewhere.

They were laughing at him, and his mother was talking to him in

Italian. She was saying *let's see, let's see if you can do it.*

And one other glimpse: he was sitting in a chair in a bedroom, and the voices of the family downstairs could be heard having a holiday party. He faced the sunlight slanting in through the windows and was about to weep, lost again in the upstairs.

Now he saw that this was part of even more dreams, of many. The traffic moved and drew him away from reflection; he began passing cars through the narrow lanes along Bronxville, and by Mount Vernon and the city line was ahead of the pack and coming too fast to make the Gun Hill Road exit.

But he made it, with great brake squeals, bouncing up the exit ramp and almost into an old couple in a vintage light blue Honda. He watched their lips move silently a short stopped time before passing them and accelerating along Gun Hill Road eastward, very far east, to the new house, which he called *the great compromise*—not exactly total escape from the Bronx and the new Jamaicans, but far enough east to see only a few of them.

The neighborhood was essentially Jamaican now. And Anthony's father liked them: they were neat about their houses and their clothes. They were always fixing things. It was this aura of industry about them that made his immigrant mind happy and calm: they must have virtue.

Still, the old man would look down the streets and say, "But it all happens too fast. I don't deny any man his house, but where is my world?"

"Yonkers," Anthony would reply, but his father would ignore the son for interrupting his poetry.

His mother was concerned with magic stories, wherever they might be, underneath the surface. The new immigrants, the ones they hear about from the ancient islands and forgotten hills, now housed illegally in Queens—they brought new magic.

Anthony stopped his thought train; he was actually listing the agenda for tonight's supper conversation and starting to do all the voices. It was Friday, all right—linguini and clams and mussels and shrimp (if you can get them real fresh) and sometimes squid, if not frozen, and a vegetable, a salad, followed by a large argument for dessert.

And during the meal someone would surely say, "You know what I got the woollies for these days? Some nice, old fashioned squid with the raisins and the anchovies and pine nut sauce. Remember that dish from the olden days?"

And then another, as the fish plates were being put down, would mention again that you really didn't have to eat fish on Fridays anymore if you didn't want to, though a lot of people still stick to it out of respect.

He could actually make tapes and send them by messenger on those Fridays when he was out of town on business.

The house now appeared, and he parked in front and walked up the path between the small grass lawns on either side. A new pink flamingo, a steel rod in its middle, stuck up from the grass on the right lawn.

He found his father waiting at the open front door. Anthony pointed back to the flamingo and shook his head.

"What do you want me to do?" his father said. "Last week the new neighbor, Mr. Kelley, he brought it to me. I think you met him, too, the day you was here he was looking."

The old man watched his son's face: it always held his wife's knotted, light fury in it. He spoke to mollify it. "So what I'm supposed to tell him? I'm sorry, Kelley, but I can't take no flamingo because my son Anthony, he's with the big corporation now, they put his picture in the paper last month, and he thinks pink birds is tacky. So I can't accept. Anthony, this man had it gift-wrapped special for me; he carried it from Florida just for me—by hand. Come on."

Anthony walked through the door toward the kitchen, his father in pursuit. At the kitchen door, Anthony said to him, "I just got a great idea. Now you give *him* a black jockey holding the brass ring—for *his* lawn."

His father smiled but did not answer. His mother looked up from the stove, "I just heard the both of you. Anthony, don't tell me you don't know what is *mala figura*. It's looking bad in front of others. You have to accept a thing like that or it makes a bad impression. But where you been so late?"

"It's the Bronx River Parkway. They won't change it, and the traffic is ten times more—"

"How long could it take from White Plains, I'm saying to myself. And then I'm saying 'God forbid anything happened to him.' "

286

"Mom, they haven't changed that parkway in sixty years—so five o'clock comes, and it's a parking lot."

"Well, I say thank God there's something in this country they don't change every five years." His mother held up her right hand.

Anthony turned to his father and nodded; the first salvo had been fired. His father sank into his kitchen chair (with pillow only for him) and said nothing. Retirement had shrunk him to the size of the kitchen.

Anthony was overcome by it often; he did not like his father becoming miniaturized because his mother had so much energy left while his father contemplated retirement, which he regarded as a prelude to burial. "Pop," he said, "you been thinking about my offer? Take a fast trip down to Florida. Stay a while, look around. Feel out the rhythms. Give it a try. Then buy what you want, and I'll assume the mortgage. Or just rent something, and I'll take care of the rent—and you can come back up here whenever you want. And when you want some company, I'll fly down a weekend."

His father's tone became whiney, "You know, my dear son, in *my* time, in *my* years, I made my moves in the world. I even came here from the old country with five cents in my pocket, and I worked from the day I got off the boat. Then I lived in Brooklyn, Grand Street, Arthur Avenue, and out here. Don't tell me you forgot my journey?"

Parts of it, in some way, sounded false to Anthony, a story much too old to be true, much too familiar not to be constructed from the typical, like a movie that starts as if new and then gets stale without anybody knowing how.

All right, the new movie was still Florida, where Fusco had gone to thrive in Orlando (before they built Disney) with a big Sunoco station even larger than anything he had on Southern Boulevard.

Anthony now brought up Fusco, and then Zambetti the contractor, re-energized in Hallendale, and the Colosimo's, with two stores going strong in Naples, and even little Di Nome, the Allstate agent with a bad heart doing great down there.

But the old man said, "All right, *I* will move down when *you* move down. All right?"

Anthony answered quickly, "But you can go right now, and I wish I could. I need to stay at corporate headquarters a few more years. There's more to come."

He saw his father's head nodding, sinking a little, the miniaturized look. "But Pop, I'll be down—I'll come most weekends, I'll talk to you every day. We'll have lots of time together."

Mrs. Collucci had begun putting food on the long table: artichokes stuffed with bread crumbs and parsley and garlic chips, peppers in oil, linguini with shellfish, and two pans of fish fillets with a tomato and caper sauce on them.

"Where's Ralph and the kids?" Anthony said.

His mother shook her head while she studied the table, "Your older brother, for a change, is late. The only man who gets lost in Massapequa when it's time to come over here. You didn't hear that—he needs a radar for Christmas. He called and said start without them. Call you sister upstairs."

Anthony went to the bottom of the staircase and called his sister's name and came back to sit next to his father. "Pop, I just can't help feeling that you would like Florida. Even more than escaping the winters. Your whole gang's down there. You should give it a try, too. See just what it is."

His mother's head leaned close to him as she lowered a basket of sliced bread to the tablecloth, "Anthony, listen to me a minute." Her voice was low and tight. "I am hearing many things about down there, you know what I'm saying. Like the water. And *things* in the water. Some say one day all the water down there will be bad. Then you can't cook, you can't wash without bottles. To make a cup of coffee you go buy a bottle of water first. You want that? And the new people down there who come off the mountains from Cuba, from Peru, from San Salvador—they have germs inside them from when they was born that don't kill *them*. But once it touches *us*, it kills. We have no resistance. Like what they brought in, the AIDS. They brought that, you know. That came in from Florida."

Anthony held back and began to eat very fast, using his fork to go after food in the serving plates. His mother straightened up and kept her stare on him for response.

He nodded to her as he filled his mouth. "All right," he said. "And what makes you think we don't have people like that up here, too?"

"Yes, but up here I know how to handle them. I got ways to ward them off. I can keep them away from here. Though I heard in the hospitals downtown where they have their babies—born with diseases they don't even know what they are yet. Babies who look like monsters. Germ babies who are green when they give birth. Babies with two tongues. And do they bury these babies? No. They hand them to the mothers and let them go down to the streets like the rats in the tunnels and the subways."

It was the alligators-in-the-sewers story again, a new variant. Anthony was losing control and put his fork down on the tablecloth, about to speak when his mother turned back to the pots still on the stove. A voice came into the pause, "And don't think that's so crazy, my brother."

It was Catherine, come from her room, knowing she was older and always speaking to Anthony as if she were wiser. She knew he was about to explode and tried to stop him. "Anthony, this is real stuff," she said. "These people come from the primitive countries with germs our science never heard of—and have lived with these germs thousands of years. Like the Bangladesh."

She said the name like an incantation and then shook her head for her brother's stolid face. "Just read the magazines," she said to him. "These germs are killing us off like flies. Because we don't live in *that* particular dirt and squalor."

"All right," Anthony said with mock calm. "Please tell me how does dirt and squalor protect people from disease?"

"Because, my little brother—" Catherine came round the table and sat across from him, "because *this*." She pointed a finger at him over the food. "The filth they live in is their salvation. It kills off a lot of them when they have babies. The ones that survive are immune, and they can come here and kill us just by sneezing in our face."

"Is this out of the New England Journal of Medicine or the *National Enquirer?* Which medical journal do you read? Tell me, do these people also walk the night? And do they glow in the dark?"

His sister turned her face away from him and took an artichoke, eating it leaf by leaf, biting and scraping to expel anger, and finally said, "Once upon a time you used to believe us."

"I know," Anthony said. "And I'll be sorry when one morning I wake up and find my teeth falling out."

Anthony stopped; he was suddenly in collision with memory. He tried to make connections. But his sister's voice kept talking to him, "You know when you'll finally be satisfied? When the crazies come and get you, and you're full of blisters and too weak to move—"

Anthony remained silent, his face losing expression. His mother noticed quickly, "You feel all right? Catey, look at that white face on him. I could tell something was wrong with him the minute he walked in here tonight. Go get the thermometer."

Mr. Collucci, who always strove for continuance, stood up and leaned over the steaming bowl of linguini, "Come on, let's eat first," he called out. "*Bon appetito* now and talk later."

He began serving with the big steel spoon and fork, Anthony first, then the others. "Come on, it's Prince Spaghetti day; you got to dig in."

Catherine smiled at her father's reference to the old commercial and his incongruous, new, slangy phrases. Anthony looked down at his plate, and Catherine asked him, "Did I say something to offend you? I didn't intend it, you know."

Anthony looked up from his food, "No, Catey, not at all. I just made some kind of connection—which stuck in my head when you just said something. Some word? I don't remember what it is. I couldn't remember—"

His sister said, "Oh, that happens to me—I'll hear a word, and it will lodge in my head like a rock, and I can't see around it, like—"

Anthony was nodding at the picture; their father smiled at the amity. Mrs. Collucci was leaning over her final pot, and they watched her flourish as she poured its steaming water into the sink, then came up with the asparagus, which she slid quickly onto a serving plate.

Catherine had been chopping garlic buds, holding the slices in a small dish while her mother covered the asparagus with olive oil from the copper pouring can made in Naples seventy years ago. Then Catherine sprinkled the garlic slices over the plate, and her mother squeezed a lemon over it all. "This is the spring," Mr. Collucci said. "God says, see, I am still magic for you. I make this again out of nothing."

"God. Just *him,* God," his wife said. "Who can't find his way to Mass even on Easter."

Anthony accepted the first plate again but waited for his mother to sit. She seemed happy to see them all and pleased with the fresh asparagus, yet began talking instead about dope addicts who were pregnant and shooting cops in Queens and giving birth in jails, making a Bronx Brueghel of this potential army of babies and drugged mothers about to rush upon the full-grown Italians.

Then she went into rough sex, a new and more mysterious horror: boyfriends strangled their dates during this seizure, though Mrs. Collucci knew the TV didn't tell about a lot more that was worse. "It must be too kinky," she said, using another of her new words learned from the children, this one for describing not only slum monsters but also mayors and ministers and congressmen and all the others we used to think were people to look up to—better people.

She was interrupted by the arrival of her first son and his family. The attention turned to little Mark and Marie. Anthony now made his regrets, citing night business meetings, knowing his mother would now lecture on overwork and its dangers as described on the six o'clock news. The sin called STRESS.

He watched her get up and start for the kitchen, but Catherine had anticipated her and already had the large weekly brown bag for Anthony.

Mrs. Collucci took the bag and said, "It's only a few chops, some left-over pasta and fish, you better eat this right away for the fish, and a little prosciutto we had twice already and it's almost a pound left. You could put it in a light sauce with a little tomato, you could have with a little mozzarella—I put some provolone in, too, because it goes good with that."

It helped him ease out of the house on smiles, and his own smile was still stuck on his face when he reached the parkway entrance alone with the brown bag on the passenger seat next to him. His last picture of the house held—his father turning away as Anthony said the final good-bye, as if his father were trapped in there and now abandoned.

But now they would all sit and say things about his excessive work, his neglect of family, and eventually settle down while Catey read the astrology page aloud. By TV watching time they would have forgotten his rudeness.

When he reached his apartment, the White Plains streets were quiet, enough to make a nice slowdown inside him. He walked up the steps to his apartment house instead of taking the elevator. Once inside his door he went to make coffee, after dropping the brown bag on the bottom shelf of the fridge; it took up the entire shelf and pushed up the wire rack above it.

He gained back his own rhythm by watching the coffee drip down, then took a cup with him to the living room as he took off his jacket.

This cup of hot coffee and the couch and the TV remote box were his expurgation. He pressed buttons and went through all the stations: fights, chases, stabbings, blood spurting from rolling eyes, creatures spewing forth sticky goo from holes inside them, human faces melting into molten puddles, a knife with its own brain chasing a woman down a dark street in green shadows, and finally an advertisement for the eleven o'clock news and the real-life horrors coming up.

He tapped off the sound and picked up the evening paper as the phone rang. Jack's voice was talking to him. "So I am still waiting for you down at Oliver's."

"All right," Anthony said. "I am just recuperating from supper. I just realized my mother and sister get all their facts on what is going in the world from the TV news."

"So we all have hallucinations. Tony, believe me, I know what you feel right now. I know how it works on the head. I call my father's house the echo chamber. I hear the same words every time I go there, the same words, do you understand me? Followed later by the Greek chorus—so you forgot your mother's birthday, your father's name day, your sister's anniversary, your niece's christening, your brother's saint's day. And whatsa matter you stay away; you must love your job more than you love your mother, your father, your brother, your sister, your grandfather's memory, your niece, just fill in the blanks. Want me to go on?"

"Only if you want to hear a man puke over the phone."

"Then come on down here, Tony. I got a little surprise for you that popped into Oliver's and is looking for an active evening, eyes tight, under the sheets. So don't start pining again for that woman."

Anthony was smiling. "No pining. I'm in a new stage. Patching. I'm patching."

"Good. Then come and get your Band-Aids. Come and meet Miss Reality. Come on."

"Great, and start the same thing over again? I got to take it easy."

"Nobody in this place wants to get married tonight, Tony. I swear it. Just a little doobie doobie do. Don't you *gabeesh*? Come on, don't be an asshole. You broke up eight months ago. I got two nice people down here. I'm buying the drinks—"

"I'll try. But if I don't show in an hour, you'll know I fell apart." He put the phone down fast, before Jack could answer, and walked to the bedroom where something made him turn down the bedspread neatly before washing up and putting on his jeans and corduroy jacket.

He looked at the bed; the woman cleaned on Friday, and the bed always looked especially neat, composed, inviting. He began to think of Beth in that bed; she had ordained the going into it and the going out of it from irrational reasoning he still could not fathom.

He was ready to leave but went to the bathroom to brush his teeth and then put some holding fizz on his hair. As he put the can in the cabinet he saw the box of condoms and stared at it a few seconds before taking a packet for his wallet; he was embarrassed.

He went to the outer door and switched off the lights and stood in the darkness a minute or two. He was sweating again. It came from bad planning. He must rearrange Friday nights and always have some people he liked to see after the supper with the folks, some quick icy minds like Jack's.

He closed the outer door and walked to the elevator. The trip down was quick and his walk less than a block. Jack was talking with two women when he walked in. Both had black hair and the one on his left a shapely thin body, while the other was shapely but heavy.

Their hands moved in familiar ways as they spoke. "Here's my buddy coming right now," he heard Jack say, and both women turned to him as he came up to the bar.

He put out his hand; the woman nearest him, the thin one, nodded at his hand and then looked into his eyes. "I'm Denise," she said. "We were just about to give you up. I thought he was making believe."

"Well, Jack sometimes thinks I *am* invisible in this world," Anthony said, and watched the women smile.

The heavier woman let out a brief laugh, and Jack said, "This is Merlene." She smiled at Anthony and said, "And that's not Marlene."

Merlene was warning Anthony of something. They began talking, exchanging the information of bars, who-do-you-knows in Westchester and Manhattan, though neither had many Manhattan contacts anymore.

Anthony watched Denise behind Merlene, her hands and arms; he followed her huge, squared-off fingernails in shining cherry red and her eyes with the blue paint underneath.

She was like the girl a few years ago, before Beth, who looked like Liza Minnelli, had that same joyous manic energy, and was wearing Frederic's underwear. But as he touched her, the voice that came out of her was like tears, like grief; please don't please don't please don't—over and over, something pathological in the poor girl, but it got inside him with its fear. And when he confided in Jack, the old Sarfatti dismissed her as one of the Catholic girls who dress like trollops and think like nuns.

Anthony moved to the right of Merlene as they all turned now to the bar. "Tell me what it is you do," she was saying.

"I manage part of a large corporation—an engineering section."

"Jack said you'd be too modest. That you're one of the big bosses."

"Well, let's say that right now my job lets me push Jack and the other engineers around. The rights of a boss is to *skootch* others."

She smiled at a familiar word and said, "You must be Italian, using that word."

"Doesn't everybody know that word by now?"

Merlene was smiling. "They don't even know we're not all in the Mafia—yet."

"I have a librarian friend, looks like a mouse—a mouse who's been beaten down—with the same name as a big gangster. They give him special tables soon as they hear the name in a restaurant or other places—"

"If they really wanted to catch crooks, let them catch the Colombians— killing people on the streets of Queens. They kill cops, they'd kill anything on the streets, and I mean senators, ministers. They sell nuclear bomb stuff that goes inside the bomb. They inject people with AIDS. They change people's brains."

Anthony reacted abruptly, and the woman noticed it. "Something go wrong?" she said. "Anything I said?"

"No, no, not at all. I just remembered I have to brief Jack before he flies out to Denver tomorrow. And I didn't bring my briefcase with my notes. Hey Jack!" He had leaned over the bar to get Jack's attention. "Let me run up and get my briefcase, and we'll do a little briefing."

"Want me to walk with you?" Merlene said.

"No, I'll just jog it and be right back."

Her face showed that she was caught in the midst of response. Anthony left on that hesitation, catching Jack's uncomprehending eyes— he knew there was no need for the case.

Anthony did not know what to tell him—only that he had to get away. In the street he jogged and on the elevator heard his breathing like radio static. Once inside his apartment he double-locked the door and placed a kitchen chair against it. He did not know what he would say when the phone rang or if he would answer. But he knew he would not go back.

# LANNAN SELECTIONS

The Lannan Foundation, located in Santa Fe, New Mexico, is a family foundation whose funding focuses on special cultural projects and ideas which promote and protect cultural freedom, diversity, and creativity.

The literary aspect of Lannan's cultural program supports the creation and presentation of exceptional English-language literature and develops a wider audience for poetry, fiction, and nonfiction.

Since 1990, the Lannan Foundation has supported Dalkey Archive Press projects in a variety of ways, including monetary support for authors, audience development programs, and direct funding for the publication of the Press's books.

In the year 2000, the Lannan Selections Series was established to promote both organizations' commitment to the highest expressions of literary creativity. The Foundation supports the publication of this series of books each year, and works closely with the Press to ensure that these books will reach as many readers as possible and achieve a permanent place in literature. Authors whose works have been published as Lannan Selections include: Ishmael Reed, Stanley Elkin, Ann Quin, Nicholas Mosley, William Eastlake, and David Antin, among others.

# SELECTED DALKEY ARCHIVE PAPERBACKS

FOR A FULL LIST OF PUBLICATIONS, VISIT:
## www.dalkeyarchive.com

# SELECTED DALKEY ARCHIVE PAPERBACKS

## FOR A FULL LIST OF PUBLICATIONS, VISIT:
## www.dalkeyarchive.com